KNIGHT TRIALS

KNIGHT TRIALS

A JORJA KNIGHT MYSTERY

ALICE BIENIA

Issued in print and electronic formats.
ISBN 978-1-7771779-6-6 (Paperback)
ISBN 978-1-7771779-7-3 (EPUB)
ISBN 978-1-7771779-9-7 (MOBI)

Editing by: Adrienne Kerr Freelance Editing
T. Morgan Editing Services
Cover and Interior Design by: Damonza.com
Published by: Alice Bienia | Calgary, Alberta, Canada

For Kevin

ONE

GRABBED A FISTFUL of hair and yanked my wig back until I could see past the blond, polyester fringe. My scalp itched from the cheap fibres and sweat trickled down my back under my fleece jacket. I pivoted away, feigning interest in this month's Healthy Meals magazine as Dave approached the exit. A large bag of Doritos wobbled over the top of the bag he carried. I didn't need Sherlockian deduction skills to know he was headed for another night of junk food and video games.

This was my fifth day of surveillance on Dave Morgan and it was about as exciting as watching poker on TV. Then again, it was my only active case. Dave Morgan seemed like a decent enough guy. As an independent IT consultant, Dave worked all hours, including evenings and weekends. His girlfriend, Lydia, wanted my assurance it wasn't on pleasing some other woman. So far, all I had seen was a guy who was working and eating himself to death.

My cell phone vibrated against my hip. I pulled it out of my jacket pocket and smiled at the name on the screen. Gab Rizzo is my best friend. More than that, she's like my sister—except we never fight.

"Hey Gab, what's up?"

"Jorja, thank gawd you answered. I'm in so much doo-doo.

My sous-chef is stranded in Kelowna. He can't get a flight out until later tonight."

"And that's a problem...because?"

"Don't you remember? Tonight's the night I'm catering that dinner in Pump Hill. If I don't get someone in to help, I'm seriously going down in flames."

I'd been hearing about this dinner for weeks. Gab had launched her own private catering company, right before I opened shop as a private investigator. A year in, we were both struggling to find solid footing. Tonight, her food would be tasted by some of Calgary's movers and shakers.

"Is there any way you can come and give me a hand? Please, Jorja. Please."

I stared at Dave's well-padded frame as he lumbered away. He exhibited none of the usual signs of a man trying to impress a new woman. He wasn't exercising or dieting. He hadn't shaved in days. His hair was shaggy and unkempt, and he couldn't even be bothered to iron his wrinkled polo shirts or khakis. I couldn't imagine two women wanting him. I'm not saying IT guys can't be smoking hot, just Dave wasn't. I had followed him to several residences and three small businesses over the course of the week and reassured myself all was kosher.

I glanced at my watch and sighed. A night watching Dave play video games suddenly seemed decidedly more appealing than spending an evening with strangers. Then again, Gab wasn't inviting me to attend, she needed help chopping and slicing.

"Okay. Where and when do you want me?"

And just like that, those few simple words turned my boring surveillance case into a perplexing and dodgy tangle.

TWO

I SPOTTED THE PRESTIGIOUS Pump Hill address Gab had rattled off and wedged my battered Ford F-150 in between a silver BMW and a black Ferrari. I checked my hair in the rear-view mirror, grabbed my bag and got out. A brute of a man, straining the threads of his grey suit, stood at the foot of the driveway eyeing me. Security.

"I'm with the catering company, Thyme to Dine?" I said.

"Up the drive and to your right."

I nodded my thanks and moved up the brick driveway, quashing the urge to pull at the lush green lawn to check if it was real. A four-car garage flanked one side of the massive two-storey structure, a portico with white columns worthy of a Marriott, welcomed guests in the middle. I passed the front courtyard and veered right. Irrational thoughts about how they made their money filled my brain.

A woman wearing a name tag that said Jeannine opened the side door. I followed the squeak of her rubber-soled shoes down a narrow black-and-white tiled hall, into the kitchen.

"Jorja." Gab rushed forward and threw her arms around me. "Thank you, thank you, thank you! I can't tell you how happy I am to see you!"

Despite the wide smile, the beads of sweat on her forehead gave her away. Gab never sweats, even when we work out.

"You may regret calling me. You know what I'm like in the kitchen."

"You'll be fine. Gawd, I'm so far behind. Can you set the tables? Everything you'll need is already in the dining room." She turned, pushed some papers around on the counter behind her and held one up triumphantly. "Here. This is a sketch I made of the table layout."

I took the paper, stepped out into the hallway, and glanced back at Gab. She pointed left. The back hall was narrow, dark, made darker by mahogany panelling and obviously part of the original house. Well-worn floorboards creaked under my feet and the faint scent of lemon wax muddled the stale air. The haunting weight of past lives settled on my shoulders. Don't know why but old houses had that effect on me. I reached a stairwell and froze. A figure, cloaked in black, turned on the landing and disappeared. Hand over pounding heart, I reminded myself: real people live here.

I found the dining room, googled place settings to figure out what went where and got to work. Flowers were delivered. Several people drifted in and out. Finished, I ducked into a washroom I found in an alcove off the hallway and changed into the white shirt and black pencil skirt Gab had asked me to bring. By the time I returned to the kitchen, Gab had already donned a pristine chef jacket.

"You realize I've never worked as a server in my entire life."

"I don't know how you managed to escape such a monumental rite of passage," said Gab. "Remember, serve from the left and remove from the right. Stay near the dining room entrance and keep your eyes open for anything they need. Keep their water and wine glasses filled. If we pull this off it's going to be a miracle."

"Hey. You're the one always telling me to be positive," I said.

"You're right." Gab laughed. "We're going to serve a fabulous meal and receive copious accolades."

"That's more like it."

Gab turned as a woman strutted into the room on four-inch heels. Razor-sharp hipbones jutted through her skinny-fit emerald-green dress.

"Big smiles, Gabriella," the woman called out, clapping her hands. "The guests are about to arrive, and I need everything to be perfect."

"Oh, Dee Dee. Good evening."

I turned and busied myself checking hors d'oeuvres plates for nonexistent spots. I recognized the woman's affliction. Cheerleader syndrome. It's a real thing. I had a sinking sensation she was going to be difficult to please and I wasn't good at pleasing anyone. Even myself.

After she left, I turned to Gab. "Who was that?"

"Mrs. Deirdre Boussard, the hostess, but she goes by Dee Dee."

"What are they celebrating?"

"The Boussards own a company called Riteweight. They've developed a weight-loss pill that melts off fat."

"No shit. I want some of that."

"Right? It's going to be big, real big. I'm not sure what tonight's all about. A new partnership or merger, I think. Dee Dee referred to some of her guests as investors." Gab wiped her forehead with her sleeve. "Let's go have a final look."

The tables were dressed in white linens and set with silver-trimmed white china. The centre of each table held tall, silver, tapered candles and bouquets of cream-coloured hydrangeas, tangerine and coral dahlias, red viburnum berries, eucalyptus and white roses. Linen napkins were rolled and held in place with monogrammed silver napkin holders and the silverware and crystal sparkled. The room still retained the warmth of the afternoon sun, but Dee Dee wanted the fireplace lit.

Gab tinkered with the fireplace while I ambled over to the patio doors at the far side of the room and cracked one open. As the fire caught, we went over the seating plan. Three of the guests needed special plates. Two were vegetarians, and a third was allergic to a list of items that read like the back of a meatless sausage package.

The front doorbell chimed. Our eyes met. "Show time," we murmured simultaneously.

First to arrive were a couple in their forties. The man was dressed flawlessly, from bowtie down to patent leather shoes. Average in build, with brown hair tinged grey at the sides, he reminded me of Perry Como, a crooner from the fifties and sixties my mother had adored. His companion trailed behind.

Dee Dee hurried toward them. "Carl, there you are," she called out.

I recalled the name from the seating plan. Gab had circled Carl Johnson's name at least three times and written allergies below it with red pen.

Dee Dee linked her arm with Carl's and pulled him into the room, leaving the woman to trail behind. Her soft baby face, framed with mousy-brown poodle hair, remained expressionless. The loose ankle-length black skirt and black sequined top made her look matronly and a lot larger than she probably intended.

A large muscular man with a Texas accent arrived next with his dark-haired, Stepford-looking wife. The woman swept a glass of champagne off my tray and turned to air-kiss her hostess' cheeks. The man sidestepped me and made a beeline to the sideboard along the far wall and poured himself a drink from one of the decanters.

A surly but not unattractive man, with dark wavy hair and

droopy eyes, arrived next. His upright carriage in direct contrast with his swarthy Roma resemblance.

"Daryl, ol' buddy," the Texan called out. "Just poured myself a drink. What'll you have? Bourbon?"

As Daryl passed, his eyes met mine so piercingly, I stepped back. The small sardonic smile on his lips angered me. I squared my shoulders and nodded at him as he slipped past. I turned away as he reached the Texan, who already held out a drink.

A stocky, broad-chested man with thick lips, thinning hair and a strong accent entered the room, shepherding an older couple ahead of him. Dee Dee rushed forward, her energy level frenetic.

"Dimitri," she cried out. "How lovely to see you. And our most honoured guests." She grasped the older woman's hand in both of hers, making some comment that brought smiles from both her and the older man and a laugh from the one she called Dimitri. I moved toward them and Dee Dee scooped two champagne flutes off my tray and handed them to the older couple, the stocky man, Dimitri, declined.

After a few minutes of chit chat, Dimitri excused himself and crossed the floor to the sidebar. He and the Texan fist bumped. Daryl continued to survey the room with eyes that gave away nothing.

"And how's Professor Frink tonight?" Dimitri laughed, slapping Daryl on the shoulder. Daryl stiffened, and glanced coldly at the hand on his arm.

After that, I lost track of who came when. I made the rounds with champagne, picked up a tray of whatever Gab plated, ran it out and repeated the process several times.

Dee Dee was a toucher, laying a hand on a shoulder here, patting an arm there. She tipped back her head at something the Texan said and laughed. The dowdy-looking woman who arrived with Carl stood alone, off to one side. Her thickened fingers slowly turned the champagne glass in her hands. A large ruby on her right hand caught the warm glow of the fire, sparked momentarily, then fizzled. For the hundredth time that night, I straightened my shoulders and reminded myself to smile.

With the hors d'oeuvres served, Dee Dee prompted her guests to sit. Place cards at each table quickly sorted the group out. I poured wine and hustled back to the kitchen to help Gab ready the appetizer. Every few minutes a boisterous laugh filtered into the kitchen.

We finally caught a moment once the main dish had been served.

"Jorja, I don't know what I would have done if you hadn't been here." The tightness around Gab's mouth loosened and she no longer looked like the first person to arrive at a bad accident.

"You know I'd do anything for you. Okay, except Karaoke."

Gab raised her eyebrow and smiled as another round of laughter erupted from the dining room. "Sounds like they're having a good time. Who's the guy with the contagious laugh?"

"His name's Dimitri. I think he might be one of the investors. He came with an older couple who speak limited English. He's been translating for them. Russian or Ukrainian maybe."

I returned to the dining room and cleared plates while Gab prepped desserts. I glanced up at a burst of laughter from Dee Dee's table. Dee Dee lifted her napkin to dab at the corner of her eye. "I can still see the look on her face. The poor dear."

The older woman at the table leaned forward and said something to Dee Dee, which elicited another piercing laugh.

I noticed Rose, the dowdy woman who arrived with Carl Johnson, didn't join in the laughter. She hadn't eaten much of her meal either. Just following orders. I overheard Carl admonish her not to eat everything on her plate as I served them. Had I been her, he'd be wearing my wine, but she sat docile with a half-smile plastered on her doughy face.

The fire still crackled and snapped in the fireplace and the room had become unpleasantly warm. I moved to the patio doors and pushed one open wider. Cool air grazed my flushed face. I took a deep breath. Another hour and this would be over.

After dessert was served, JP, the host, rose and tapped his water glass. Tall and fit with dark hair combed back from his forehead, he was an obvious match to Dee Dee's purchased perfection. Conversation dwindled as faces turned toward JP. Dee Dee gazed up at her husband, the adoring expression on her face straight from a scene in a high school musical.

JP's voice was smooth and strong, his stance confident. "I promise I won't spoil this delightful evening by launching into a long, drawn-out speech, but then again as the highly prolific British author, G.B. Stern, once said, 'Silent gratitude isn't of much use to anyone.'"

Laughter rippled through the room. I noticed Daryl scowling at something on his phone. JP resumed and I turned back to the kitchen.

Seconds later a tearing sound rolled through the room. JP stopped mid-sentence. I turned. The European man at Dimitri's table stood, fist pressed against lips. Red faced, he rushed toward me. I stepped aside and pointed down a short alcove to a washroom. *Gab's first accolade.*

JP made some comment and a small titter flared up and quickly faded. The blond woman next to Daryl shot up and rushed toward me, beads of sweat visible on her upper lip. I sent her down the hall to the back washroom. A less-than-pleasant odour permeated the room. Amid embarrassed giggles and murmurs I made my way to the patio doors and pushed one open wider. Dee Dee was now standing, her back to the room, hand on her husband's shoulder, whispering in his ear.

I headed back to the kitchen, hoping my smile hid my concern. As I passed the alcove, I heard loud retching. My stomach flip-flopped.

A high-pitched scream pierced the air. The hairs on the back of my neck prickled. I spun around.

"A bee, oh no, a bee," Rose screeched, hopping from one foot to the other, arms flapping uselessly. "Carl! Oh Carl! Someone help!"

Carl slumped sideways in his chair. Dimitri jumped up, knocking over his chair, and he and JP rushed to Carl's side. Chaos erupted. A strangled sound came from Carl's opened mouth, his lips already blue. Desperate to draw air into his heaving chest, his fingers clawed at his throat. JP tore through Carl's jacket pockets. "Where's the damn EpiPen?"

Rose sank to the floor, wailing. JP shot a glance over his shoulder as he and Dimitri lowered Carl to the floor. His eyes bore into mine.

"Call 911."

THREE

GAB AND I watched in stunned silence as they loaded Carl onto a stretcher. Dimitri's face was an alarming purple, JP's deadly white but controlled. The remaining guests huddled to one side, speculating. Had he been stung by a bee? Or was it a heart attack? I caught murmurs about food poisoning. Several guests covertly stole glances our way. Dee Dee and JP didn't appear sick nor had Carl's wife when she left with the paramedics. The European woman whose husband had been the first to flee the room looked fine. Oddly, a few appeared ill, yet others seemed all right. The first few guests who rushed for washrooms now emerged but wasted no time getting themselves out the front door.

Gab and I returned to the kitchen. Gab collapsed across the counter, head on her arms. "What the hell? Tell me that didn't just happen."

"Gab, I'm sure he'll be okay. I heard JP tell the paramedics they gave him two shots of epinephrine before the ambulance arrived." I made my way to her side and gave her shoulders a hug.

"But Jorja, everyone's sick."

"No…not everyone. I'm sure it will be all right."

"Oh god, Jorja, why tonight? I'm toast. When word gets out, I'll never work again."

"Don't say that. Sounds like he got stung by a bee. Let's clean up and get out of here."

We were wrapping up when Dee Dee stormed in, eyes wild.

"Dee Dee. We're nearly done here," said Gab.

"You're definitely done here," she hissed. "I need you to pack up and leave. Now."

"I…I'm sorry," Gab stammered. "I hope everyone's okay. I don't understand what happened."

"I'll tell you what happened. You poisoned my guests. I want both of you out, pronto."

Gab's chest curved inward as she sank back against the counter. I slid to her side. With lips pressed tightly, Dee Dee flung us a squinty-eyed look filled with hatred and marched out of the kitchen.

"Jorja, what am I going to do?" Gab wiped away tears as she packed up her knives and the supplies she had brought while I gathered up our personal belongings. We slunk out the back door and loaded everything into the back of her Mustang. Shutting the trunk lid, we stared at each other in silent shock.

"Bit of a shit show wasn't it," I said.

Gab burst into tears.

⌁

It had been well after midnight by the time I crawled into bed. Now, I struggled to hang on to a fragment of an eclectic but soothing dream. As hard as I tried, it slipped away. An annoying buzz intruded my peace and replaced it with mild annoyance.

Prying open one eye I fumbled for the phone, peered at the screen and tapped the accept call icon.

"Hi, Gab," I rasped. "How're you doing?"

"Did you see the news this morning?"

"No. What time is it?"

"Carl died."

"What?"

"Carl Johnson. He died."

I sat up. "How awful."

"It's on the morning news."

"Did they say why?" I pushed my hair back behind my ears, finally alert.

"No. They said he'd been at a dinner party, got sick, and was rushed to hospital where he died a short time later."

"They didn't name your company, did they?"

"No—but I'm sure it's just a matter of time."

"Let's not jump to any conclusions. There could be a dozen reasons why he died."

"I know...still... What about the others? What the hell happened? I need to figure out why people got sick."

"What are you going to do?"

"I don't know. Maybe check with my suppliers, see if anyone's reported any food-related illnesses."

"That's a good idea. Let me know if I can do anything."

"Thanks. I will. I just need a minute to think. We still on for brunch tomorrow?"

"You bet. Same time, same place."

Carl's death was disconcerting. Several people seemed quite ill, although they all managed to eventually get themselves out the door. Well, except Carl. Maybe he died from a heart attack or a bee sting. With all his allergies, bees must be on the list. I pulled on running gear, grabbed my cell phone and keys and made my way downstairs.

I exited the elevator, crossed the lobby and stepped outside.

The air was cool, even though the sun was already high in the pale, cornflower-blue sky. I stretched for several minutes. Dry curled leaves skittered on the paved pathway in front of me and whispered winter is coming. I plunked in my ear buds, tapped the music icon and began my shuffle.

It was almost noon by the time I headed out to my real job. I thought the run would clear my head, but instead it made me antsy. Last night's events reminded me I wasn't as in control of things as I liked to imagine.

I hadn't grown up wanting to become a PI, but as my fortieth birthday approached, the sense I was watching life rather than living it grew so big it became intolerable. I needed to take charge of my destiny, take some risks, before I became *that* woman. The one who socialized with colleagues at work then went home to her cats, takeout food and television. Let's face it, I had been that woman, minus the cats. So last year, I walked away from my steady but staid career as a forensic lab analyst and hung out my shingle as a private investigator. I smiled ruefully. Of course, it took being attacked and stabbed by a fellow employee who lost his shit to be the impetus for the change. The universe does work in strange ways.

I didn't exactly have a bold, hairy, audacious plan, but some days I felt the real me was about to burst through the protective layers I had bound around myself. Until that happened, I'd take one day at a time and see where it led. Right now, it led me to a neighbourhood west of Calgary's downtown core.

Turning left off Seventeenth Avenue I made my way into Dave's neighbourhood, a mixture of apartment buildings, 1950s bungalows and the occasional remodel. I was growing convinced Dave wasn't cheating on Lydia. At least not with a woman. I had followed him to several clients over the course of the week. He spent one night at Lydia's. The rest of the time he stayed home, catering to his love affair with junk food and video games. A few more days of mind-numbing surveillance and I'd have enough to convince Lydia and myself all was kosher.

I turned down Dave's street and slowed. Several emergency vehicles blocked the road ahead. Something was happening at Dave's house. Well, technically not his house. Dave rented the basement suite in an older, blue-trimmed bungalow. I parked and made my way over to a small group huddled on the sidewalk. An ambulance rolled up the street, lights flashing.

"What's happening?"

A woman wearing a down-filled jacket and plaid pyjama pants turned to me. She dragged deeply on her cigarette, pursed her lips, tilted her head and blew out a stream of grey. She probably meant to miss me, but the smoke hit my right eye, making it water.

"Someone got shot," she rasped out of the corner of her mouth. "The ambulance is hauling 'em off."

"Do you know who it was?"

"Naw. Some guy from the basement of the white stucco. The one with blue trim."

My heart sank. *No freaking way.*

FOUR

THE ONLOOKERS WERE starting to disperse. I tapped Lydia's name in my contacts list.

"Hey, Lydia, have you talked to Dave today?"

"No. Why? I sent him a couple of texts, but he hasn't answered."

"I'm at Dave's place. His Jetta is parked in front of the house. I don't want you to panic, but an ambulance just left. It might be someone from upstairs. The police are here. I'm going to see if I can get some info from them. You might want to sit tight. Hello… Lydia?" I stared down at the blackened screen.

A police officer stood on the sidewalk talking to an older man. I waited until they finished, then walked over.

"Hi. I'm a friend of Dave Morgan's. I've been trying to get a hold of him. Can you tell me if…" A red Toyota barrelled down the street, car horn blaring. It screeched to a stop in the middle of the road. A woman bolted from the car. Hair askew, navy sweater ends flapping over white T-shirt and grey sweatpants, she ran toward us. She clearly hadn't stopped to put on a bra. *Crap. Lydia.*

"Oh, my god, where's Dave! Where is he? I need to see him."

The police officer and I both moved toward her. He gently but deliberately blocked her path.

"Lydia, calm down," I said.

The officer turned to me. "You know her?"

I nodded. "This is Lydia Bietz. Her boyfriend's name is Dave Morgan," I said. "Is he the one who was taken to the hospital?"

"I'm afraid so. He's headed to the Foothills Hospital with a non-life-threatening gunshot wound."

Lydia sank to her knees. Her hysterics made it hard to make out anything she was saying.

I squatted next to her. "Lydia. Calm down. I'll take you to the hospital, but you need to get yourself together. For Dave's sake." *And Mine.* The police officer shot me a grateful glance and advised her to take me up on my offer, as she was in no condition to drive. I moved Lydia's car off the street and helped her into my truck.

Somewhere between Seventeenth Avenue and Memorial Drive, Lydia turned on me.

"How could you let this happen? You're supposed to make sure he's okay. Now look."

Technically, I was supposed to find out if he was the cheating scumbag she thought he was, but she was in no mood to be corrected. I was having trouble myself accepting Dave had been shot.

As soon as I parked, Lydia was out the door. Fuzzy pink mules slapped against her heels as she ran full tilt to the emergency entrance. I locked up and followed.

Inside, I had no trouble locating Lydia. Several medical staff were gathered around her, Lydia's hysterics now in 'the whole village has been attacked' mode. I explained the situation. We were led to a smaller waiting room and told to wait while they went to find out where Dave was and assess his condition. Lydia insisted she be taken to him, but an intern, who probably competed as a mixed martial arts fighter on his days off, assured her it wasn't going to happen until she calmed down.

The next hour crawled by. Lydia alternatingly wailed, sobbed quietly and shot hateful glances my way. Where was the woman who threatened to disembowel her boyfriend if she found out he was cheating? When I was certain I couldn't stand it a minute longer, a doctor arrived to speak to Lydia. Dave had suffered a flesh wound to his thigh. The police wanted to take his statement and he'd be free to go. They reassured Lydia he'd be out as soon as the police finished with him.

"I'm glad he's okay. See, it's nothing. A minor flesh wound," I said.

Lydia glared at me.

How the hell had Dave managed to get shot? Perhaps he *was* cheating on Lydia and a disenchanted husband, brother, lover or friend of his mistress paid him a visit. I should have been there this morning. I shook off the thought. There was no way I could follow him twenty-four seven and I had told Lydia that. "Look, I'm sorry about Dave, but we don't know what happened. Probably a B&E gone bad. Sounds like he's going to be okay though."

Now done crying and cursing, I could see the worry in Lydia's blue eyes. I watched as she sat, repeatedly pulling a strand of light brown hair across her lips while her knee jiggled a hundred miles a minute.

An hour went by and Lydia resumed her demands to see Dave. Even I was beginning to think something was wrong. Lydia rocked back and forth in her chair, a tissue pressed to her lips. I stood up, desperate to stretch my legs.

"Ms. Bietz?" a nurse called out from the doorway.

Lydia stood up and we followed the nurse into a small, curtained cubicle. We were told a doctor would be in to speak with us shortly. I tried to ignore my own growing sense of dread. Finally, I couldn't take it any longer.

"They're probably going to go over post-hospital care instructions with you," I said. "I'm sure he's going to be fine."

Lydia sent me an eye roll.

Finally, a young man in scrubs arrived. "I'm Dr. Roe. I was the attending physician when, your...boyfriend, is it"—he checked his tablet—"was brought in. The good news is the wound to his thigh is superficial. We've given him a prescription for pain medication should he need it. Unfortunately, we uhm...aah, can't locate him. It appears he may have already left the hospital."

Lydia jumped up, startling both of us. "My god can't anyone do anything right! You mean I've been sitting here, cooling my jets for hours, and he isn't even here?"

Dr. Roe caught my eye, desperate for support. I gave him a weak smile and shrugged.

On the way out of the hospital, Lydia shrugged off any help. Once in the truck she continued to glare at me. "Where the hell were you this morning? Why didn't you stop this?"

"Stop what? Dave getting shot?" How could she possibly think I could have predicted or prevented it? "I'll take you back to Dave's place and you can pick up your car."

Lydia pulled out her cell and started punching in numbers.

"He's not answering. Shit, shit, shit! Why hasn't he called me?"

"Could be he didn't get a chance to grab his phone, or maybe it's broken."

I turned onto Dave's street and let out a sigh of relief. The Jetta was parked where he'd left it. Lydia's car remained across the street. We parked, got out and walked up to the side entrance to the basement suite. Yellow tape had been strung over the door, but now flapped in the breeze. An older man worked on securing the entrance.

He removed several nails from between pursed lips. "If you're looking for Dave, he's not here." He shook his head. "I'm going to have to replace the frame. See here, it's splintered right through."

"Are you his landlord?"

He grunted his reply.

"Dave left the hospital a while ago. We thought he might be back."

"Nope. He's not here. He can't stay here tonight...place isn't secure like this. I'll get a new door installed tomorrow."

Lydia and I made our way back to the street.

"I'm sure he's okay," I said, regretting it as soon as the words were out of my mouth.

"Yeah sure, if you say so."

"Are you going to be okay? Do you want me to drive you home? I could come get you tomorrow and bring you back here to pick up your car."

Lydia turned and gave me the one-finger salute as she marched across the street to her car.

FIVE

I DRAGGED MY YOGA mat from behind the couch, took a deep breath and tried to clear my mind. I hadn't yet mastered the art of meditation but some days achieved a Zen-like frame of mind that lasted several minutes. Today my mind kept returning to the Boussards' dinner. Several people had gotten ill. Sick to their stomach. Clearly something they consumed disagreed with them. Gab and I could really use news of a listeria breakout or some such thing in the city. Carl's death was disconcerting. He probably died from a heart attack or a bee sting, something not related to food. Had I let a bee in? *Stop it.* It's not like I saw a bee and deliberately let it in. Besides, aren't bees supposed to be dead or comatose by mid-October?

I put my yoga mat away, checked email, journaled for half an hour and jumped into the shower. An hour later I was heading out the door.

Gab was already at Mollie's Café, by the time I arrived. She waved to get my attention.

"Sorry I'm late." I slid into a chair across from her. "Traffic was murder."

Gab smiled but her eyes were troubled. She had taken the time to pile her thick hair into a messy but attractive up-do and her bright-green nail polish matched the colour of her finely knit sweater. I had on my usual jeans and black shirt left untucked. Hoping commiseration would ease her worries I launched into my saga.

"I had quite the day yesterday. The guy I've been doing surveillance on got shot."

"What? Killed?"

"No, no. Just wounded and taken to hospital by ambulance. But he's left there, and no one has seen him since. I hung around his place until midnight, but he didn't show. My client isn't overly pleased. Actually, I'm pretty sure she fired me."

"Aren't we the pair. I swear, Jorja, I don't think I can take one more thing going wrong. Did you catch the news this morning? They're doing an autopsy on Carl."

"That doesn't mean anything. There are certain situations when an autopsy is mandatory no matter what. Dying in a hospital within twenty-four hours of admission is one of those."

"But they brought up the fact he attended a catered dinner at the Boussards', and several guests became ill the same night."

I didn't like where this was going. "Don't panic. Let's figure out what we need to do, if anything, after we eat."

"Sounds good. We have to stay positive."

"That's the spirit. Anything new on the home front?"

Gab gave me a weak smile. "I have a date tonight with a guy I met on Natural Selection. I might cancel. I'm in such a funk I'll probably make a bad impression. What's new with you? Seeing much of Adan these days?"

Adan was a street minister I met a few months back while working another case. Something in his blue-grey eyes made me melt and sucked me in. His solid, muscular physique sealed the deal. There's no denying my attraction to him. He either had a will of steel or my girl pheromones had stopped working.

"We've gone on four dates. We always have a good time, but he hasn't really shown any romantic interest in me."

"Maybe he's taking his time to get to know you."

"Maybe." I took a forkful of egg and chewed thoughtfully. "Or he might be saving himself for God. I sure as hell can't compete with that."

Gab laughed but I could tell her mind was somewhere else. We were halfway through our omelettes when Gab blurted, "What if I killed Carl?"

I glanced around nervously and leaned forward. "Gab, you didn't. We didn't. We went through this. How could you possibly have caused his death?"

"Why did everyone get sick? It looked like food poisoning to me."

"I admit, it does sound like food poisoning. But how, and from what?"

"I picked up the meat from the butcher and put it straight away into the cooler I brought with me. The meat went right into the fridge as soon as I got to the Boussards'. The whole trip took less than twenty minutes. Then I went back out to get the rest of the supplies."

"See. It couldn't be you. You bought fresh ingredients and the dry goods aren't likely going to be the issue."

"That's what most people think. But some of the worst cases of salmonella have come from imported herbs and spices."

"Really?"

"Sure. They have checks and balances in place, but it's impossible to filter out every contaminant from hundreds of different spices and herbs. I got to see the raw product arrive when I visited some of the spice markets in Asia. I totally get it."

"Okay. But it could be something completely unrelated to the food."

She pursed her lips. "Yeah? Like what?"

"A bee might have stung Carl and sent him into anaphylactic shock. Maybe he had a heart condition or something. I heard that guy, Dimitri, tell the paramedics they gave him two shots of epinephrine. Why two shots? Maybe it was too much. Maybe his heart went into cardiac arrest."

"This is terrible, Jorja. I can't stop obsessing. It's not just Carl. Other people got sick too, but not all of them. It can't be a coincidence."

"I admit that part's weird. You said you used the same ingredients in both dishes, except the vegetarians didn't get the lamb and got the quinoa and extra vegetables instead."

"That's right. The people who got the lamb dish got sweet potatoes instead of the quinoa. Both dishes had kidney beans, except it was made into a puree for the lamb dish, instead of the sweet potato and bean terrine I made to go with the quinoa. The spices were different though…"

"Maybe it wasn't the dinner. Maybe the few people who got sick ate or drank something before getting to the Boussards'. Doesn't food poisoning usually take a few hours to show symptoms?"

"I guess." Gab put her head in her hands. When she finally looked up, tears spilled down her cheeks. "Jorja, it may have been the beans."

A spasm rolled through my gut. "What do you mean?" I held my breath.

"Raw kidney beans are toxic. A lot of people don't know since they typically use ones already cooked. Unless properly prepared, kidney beans can make you very sick."

"But you knew, right?"

"Of course. I soaked them overnight. The day of the dinner, I drained them then cooked them in fresh water at a high temperature like you're supposed to. By the time you arrived, all I had left to do was put them into the terrine or the mash and heat it all back up."

"Then it wasn't the beans."

"I've gone over this in my head a hundred times, but it's the one thing that keeps coming up."

"What are you saying here?" Normally, I'd be the one second guessing myself. Now the woman, who often declared we had nothing to fear but fear itself, was afraid.

"I don't know, Jorja. I know I cooked them properly. I must have."

"You did. I know you. You take such pride in what you do, there's no way you would have made a mistake like that."

Gab chewed her bottom lip. "It's a cinch the media isn't going to let this story go until they find out what happened. Did you know Carl Johnson wasn't only the CFO but a partner in Riteweight? And an Order of Canada recipient?"

"Oh. No wonder his death is top of the news. Why the Order of Canada medal?"

"Besides being a respected businessman and entrepreneur, he was a philanthropist. He founded Ella's Trust, for children with special needs."

After breakfast, we sat over coffee and devised a plan. Gab wasn't going to rest until she knew what made her client's guests sick. If Carl's death ended up attributed to something he ate, an investigation would be launched by the medical examiner's office in conjunction with Health Canada. Either way she wasn't taking this lightly.

Gab had reconstructed a full list of the ingredients she had used in the Boussards' dinner. The fresh ingredients, the lamb, the sweet potatoes, the beans, tomatoes, olives and onions had all been used up. Leftovers had been discarded and plates washed. Gab still had some of the spices she used, packed up in the cooking bin she hauled around with her to various venues. She used cumin and coriander from Dee Dee's pantry.

Gab tapped her teeth with her pencil as she went over the list and divvied up the work.

"I've already picked up some vials from the lab. I'll take samples of the spices I used in for analysis later today. Do you think there's any way to get a sample of the leftovers from dinner?"

"I suppose, if the garbage hasn't been picked up."

"Would you mind?" She cocked her head to one side and grimaced.

"Hey, what are friends for?"

"I know this is asking a lot, but can you try to get a sample of the cumin and coriander I used, from Dee Dee's pantry? I don't dare show my face at her place."

"I'll see what I can do."

"That's it then. I've already contacted all my suppliers to see if there have been any reports of illness from any of the ingredients I purchased. Now we wait and see."

"So, what's the protocol here? Will you be sending Dee Dee an apology or just the invoice?"

"Very funny, Jorja. When word gets out, I'm never going to work again."

"Oh, come on. You're a great chef. You *will* work again and get all the clients you need and more." It sounded awkward coming from me. Gab was always the one urging me to reframe thoughts positively.

"I suppose I can always go back to pickling veggies to sell at the Farmers' Market or writing articles," she said.

"There you go. You could write an article on how to do away with someone at a dinner."

"Ha, ha, don't even joke. I love cooking, I'm not giving up."

After leaving Gab, I drove across town to Dave's place. I was glad to hear the determination back in Gab's voice by the time we finished brunch. I hummed a line from some song I had forgotten the lines to. The sky was a perfect pale autumn blue and the sun shone unabated, fuelling the illusion of a warm summer day. Several stands of trees still held their golden foliage, although most had dropped their leaves, now carpeting the ground. I had a sudden urge to point my truck west and drive until I was in the mountains. Or further.

The Jetta was still parked out in front of Dave's place. I parked, got out and jogged around to the side of the house. The door had been replaced, but no one answered when I rang the bell. Had Dave answered, I had my story ready: I was searching for my missing cat.

I walked back to my truck and called his cell. His voice mail was full, probably thanks to Lydia. I hadn't heard from her either. No surprise there. Maybe Dave had shown up at her place. Either way, I was pretty sure she wanted me off the case, which was fine by me. Something didn't sit right about this whole thing. I'd miss the money but if someone was gunning for Dave I'd rather move on. As to protocol, I wasn't going to send an apology, just the invoice.

On the way home, I swung into the Boussards' ritzy neighbourhood. The wrought-iron gates were secured across the Boussards' driveway, not a soul in sight. I circled the block, noticing each house stood on an oversized lot, back to back with the adjacent house. Most yards were enclosed with six-foot-high wrought-iron fencing. Garbage bins were tucked away in garages or locked up in sheds.

I pulled over and googled the waste-disposal collection schedule on my phone. Pick-up was on Monday. Rummaging through garbage in this neck of the woods wasn't likely to go unnoticed and I'd probably have no more than a few minutes to try. I put the truck into gear and wove a meandering route out of the neighbourhood, gawking at the houses. Part of me was chomping at the bit to get a sample of leftovers and prove the food to be a non-issue—the other part was nervous about what we might find.

SIX

I HEAVED THE SHOPPING cart into the bed of my truck and paused to breathe. I wasn't stealing, merely borrowing it for a while. And 'my truck' was a leased vehicle from JumpIn Jalopies. After my car was totalled in an unfortunate incident I dubbed The Wrecking Ball, I found leasing to be more convenient. Maybe even cheaper in the long run, as the PI business is a tad hard on vehicles. JumpIn Jalopies' vehicles were older models with something expensive to fix, which given the age of the vehicle, didn't justify fixing. But they were all mechanically sound and came with insurance and free maintenance should issues arise. The ventilation system in the 2004 Ford F-150 I was currently driving was stuck in air-conditioning mode. Not a problem in summer but with winter approaching I might need to trade it in.

With the shopping cart securely tied down, I drove the short distance to Pump Hill and parked alongside a green space a block west of the Boussards'. Pulling a woollen toque over my hair, I rubbed some dirt on my cheek, blackened my front tooth with waterproof eyeliner and got out. Sweat rolled down my back as I wrangled the cart out of the truck. The three coats and the ski pants I wore did a good job of disguising my shape but might be overkill. I threw in a half-filled bag of garbage brought from home, pulled on a pair of gloves, put my head down and pushed off. It was already after eight, but I was positive the city wouldn't send noisy trash collectors into the neighbourhood before its well-heeled citizens were up and well into their day.

I turned the corner and focused in on the Boussards' house. A green compost bin stood at the edge of the driveway, the blue bin for recyclables next to it. I kept my head down, swinging it slightly from side to side and hummed to myself as I continued down the street.

I stopped at the neighbour's trash, lifted the recyclable bin lid, and pulled out two empty liquor bottles and a plastic pop container. Tossing them into the cart, I pushed on to the Boussards'. I opened the green bin and swore. Loose yard clippings and branches filled it to the top. I frantically tore through the debris as the garage door slowly rolled upward, and the driveway gates began to swing open. My fingers closed in on a compostable bag and I yanked, pulling grass and dead leaves out with it. A man across the street opened his front door and yelled something. He shook his fist and started down the front sidewalk. I threw the compost bag into the cart and pushed away.

The damn left front wheel wouldn't roll. The man's voice now drowned out by a dog, barking and snarling at his side.

I ran to the front of the cart and dragged it behind me. Sweat rolled down my forehead and burned into my eye as I ran. The uncooperative wheel left a long black skid mark. Rivulets of sweat trickled into my gluteal cleft. Vaulting into the back of the truck, I reached down and yanked the cart up until it contacted the floor, then heaved the cart inside. I didn't stop to tie it down and drove off seconds before a police cruiser turned onto Pump Hill Drive. Grateful for the air conditioning, I tore off my toque and drove my stash of goodies down to Fish Creek Park.

Once parked, I stripped off a layer of clothing, pulled an empty trash bag and a pair of latex gloves from the glove compartment and climbed into the back of the truck. Cursing silently, I transferred the putrid contents, item by item into the trash bag. None of the remnants from Gab's dinner were in the mix of used paper towels, coffee grounds, leftover Chinese food and limp vegetables.

A van pulled into the parking space next to me. A woman climbed out and shot me a dirty look, before heading down one of the trails with two black Labs. Suddenly I remembered my dirt-stained face and blackened tooth. I climbed out of the truck, slid into the cab and put the truck in gear. I dropped the garbage off in an industrial waste bin at a construction site and returned the cart to the mall parking lot. If the food was somehow contaminated, it would soon be in the landfill, buried for good.

∽

Hair still slightly damp from my shower, I climbed out of the truck and made my way to the Boussards' front door. I pressed the doorbell and waited as the notes to Westminster Chimes faded. One of the enormous wooden doors swung open slowly and a young girl, around twelve years of age, stared up at me. She wore a burgundy jacket and burgundy-and-grey plaid skirt. The jacket had Oak Hill Academy stitched on the breast pocket and below it, the school logo.

"Hi. I'm here to see Mrs. Boussard."

"Mother, someone's here to see you," she called over her shoulder.

I wiped my hands down the front of my jeans and swallowed, trying to separate my tongue from the roof of my mouth. The rapid clicking of heels warned of her approach. Today Dee Dee wore skinny jeans, open-toed suede booties with a three-inch stacked heel, an off-shoulder grey sweater and large gold hoop earrings. Suddenly, I had a flashback to Mary-Lou Fisher, standing in front of me in a white baby-doll dress and heavy-duty combat boots, informing me everyone was so over pink converse sneakers and jeans.

"What are you doing here?"

"I'm Jorja Knight. We have an appointment at three." She ignored my outstretched hand.

"I agreed to see a detective. Why are you here?"

"I am a private detective," I said, digging my licence out of my purse to show her. "I also happen to be a friend of Ms. Rizzo's and was helping her out the other night, as her regular sous-chef was indisposed." My nerves were getting to me; I was starting to use my fancy words.

"I have nothing to say to you. You can tell your friend I'm going to make sure she never works in this town again."

"Mrs. Boussard, Ms. Rizzo hired me to help her find out what caused the gastrointestinal upset at your party. She knows her reputation is on the line, but more importantly the health and wellbeing of her clients. She wants to find out why some of your guests became ill and to make sure it had nothing to do with the food she used in preparing the meal."

"I'll tell you what happened. My guests arrived happy and healthy, ate food prepared by you and your friend and became gravely ill. Carl died. He had allergies. He was supposed to get an allergen-free plate. You two killed him."

"Mrs. Boussard, I know how distressing this is. I'm sorry to hear Mr. Johnson died. I'm sure the autopsy will shed light as to why. At this point, I'm more interested in what made your other guests ill. It's entirely possible whatever made them sick has nothing to do with Mr. Johnson's death. My client wants to know how and why your guests got ill. I have a few questions if you just have a minute."

She crossed her arms and moved aside so I could enter but didn't invite me in any further.

"You'll have to be quick. I have to take my daughter somewhere."

"Ms. Rizzo has gone over the menu extensively. None of the items Mr. Johnson was allergic to were used in any of the recipes. Everyone got the same main ingredients; except quinoa was substituted for the lamb in the vegetarian dishes and of course the ingredients were prepared differently with different spices and herbs. A few guests became ill, but others were fine. Did you get ill yourself, or your husband?"

"No."

"Do you know anyone other than yourself who did not get sick?"

"How do you expect me to know? I didn't do anything requiring an apology, yet I called each of my guests and apologized for the hideous evening we hosted. It would be rather crass to ask them if they spent the night vomiting or having diarrhea."

"Can you tell me when the kitchen was last used before Thursday?"

"The previous weekend. We had my mother-in-law and JP's brother and his family over."

"Was the dinner catered?"

"No. My mother-in-law made dinner. And no one got ill."

"Who restocks the pantry?"

"My assistant Jeannine looks after supplies."

"Do you use one supplier?"

"No. We have accounts with our preferred suppliers like the Herb and Spice store, Natural Goodness and Chef Mate. It keeps invoicing simple. But in a pinch Jeannine might go to a local grocery store."

I remembered the vegetables in their trash bin. "And the fresh ingredients?"

"We don't store much more than the basics. Whoever is cooking will put together a list and Jeannine will pick up what's required. Everything's fresh. If we have dinner catered the caterer brings the ingredients for the menu. Why? What's this got to do with Carl's death?"

"Ms. Rizzo used ingredients from both her own supplies and your pantry. She is having all the staples she used tested and is checking with her suppliers to see if anyone's reported food issues. Unfortunately, we can't test the fresh ingredients since they've been used up or discarded. Ms. Rizzo used two ingredients from your pantry. Would you be willing to provide a sample of those ingredients for us to have tested as well?"

"This meeting is over."

"If someone tampered with those products or they are contaminated, it would likely have occurred on the seller or producer side."

She turned on her heel and clicked her way across the dark walnut floors. "Jeannine! Please see Ms. Knight leaves."

The encounter went pretty much like I expected. I didn't need Jeannine to see me out, as the front door was still open. I walked back to my truck and pointed it toward home. It was hard enough to make a living as a PI, without being implicated in a food poisoning. Or a death. Not to mention it wasn't exactly a productive day.

I pulled into the underground parking lot, parked in my designated stall and took the elevator up to the eighth floor. Opening the door to my condo, I stepped inside and threw my purse and keys on the table. I liked the way the whole place was one big open room except for the bedroom and a washroom to the right. And I loved its location, right across the street from the park and a pathway system ringing Glenmore Reservoir. A small outdoor mall at the east end of the reservoir served my need for food, alcohol and occasional desire to be with people.

I kicked off my shoes and padded silently across the dark laminate floor to the bedroom. After changing into yoga pants and an old Bon Jovi T-shirt, I made a grilled cheese sandwich and watched four episodes of Mad Men, back to back. Afterwards I sat cross-legged on the couch, checked email and kept one eye open on the news.

As the day wore on, a sense of impending doom solidified. Lydia's parting wave told me she was done with me. I'd confirm tomorrow and start scrounging for more work. I had an email from someone looking to do a background check on five potential new hires at one of the accounting firms I had provided services for last year. Probably less than a day's work. Nothing from Adan. I was tempted to open a bottle of wine, but afraid to in my present mood.

The eleven o'clock news came on and Carl's death was the first item up. The newswoman read out, "Police have not yet released the cause of death but are calling it suspicious. The homicide unit is investigating." My phone rang, and I didn't even have to look at the screen to know it was Gab.

SEVEN

I ROLLED OVER AND pulled the pillow over my head to block out the intruding sunshine. Gab and I had talked for over an hour last night. Well, Gab talked, I listened. I had never heard Gab so distraught, not even when her last boyfriend ran her credit cards up to the hilt, then departed for greener pastures. I didn't know what to say to make her feel less miserable. I had found myself repeating everything would be okay to the point it sounded meaningless even to my ears. I rolled out of bed, resigned to face whatever the day brought. It couldn't get any worse, could it? I executed my morning routine mindlessly and headed for the office.

Cursing, I circled the baby-blue cinderblock monstrosity housing our office, for the third time. The building's proximity to the downtown core meant parking was at a premium. I was sorely tempted to leave my truck parked in a reserved parking lot, but it came with a hundred-and twenty-dollar ticket, if caught. More if I got towed.

A Hummer pulled away from the curb on Tenth Street, opening a spot for me and a Smart Car, which pulled in inches from my back bumper. Minutes later, I was in front of the rundown eye-sore Gab and I called headquarters. I stepped through the glass doors, crossed the small lobby with its single ancient, incredibly slow elevator and into the stairwell. I pounded up the stairs to the second floor. Most people were taken aback to hear I shared offices with a private chef. Although slightly unconventional, it was a cost-effective arrangement and made sense to us, especially as the work we did didn't happen there and neither of us had much in the way of drop-in clientele. Besides, Gab's ex-boyfriend had stiffed her with huge credit card debt and an iron-clad lease on office space taken out in her name which she couldn't get out of.

My eyes adjusted to the gloom as I made my way down the narrow hall to the last door on the left. The door was partially open. Our laminated sign hung by one corner.

Thyme to Dine – Personal Catering G. Rizzo
Knight Investigations – J. Knight

Gab was already sitting at the front reception desk, her head bent over the morning paper. She lifted red-rimmed eyes up to mine. "Hey, girlfriend."

"Hey."

"It's in the morning paper."

I squeezed around to her side of the desk and peered over her shoulder. The page was open to a picture of Carl Johnson and several paragraphs of text. My eyes scanned the article.

Carl Johnson, rushed to hospital from a privately catered dinner at the home of financier and venture capitalist Jean Pierre Boussard, has died... Several guests became ill... Catered by personal chef Gabriella Rizzo of Thyme to Dine... An autopsy has been conducted to determine the cause of death...results indicate Carl Johnson died from anaphylaxis or respiratory failure, the cause yet undetermined... blood tests revealed toxins...further tests are being conducted.

"Crap."

"I've already had two cancellations this morning. You have to help me prove I didn't do this. Jorja, you know I didn't do this."

"I'll do whatever I can, you know I will." Secretly I was afraid for her, and for me. I pushed down the panic tying my intestines into a knot.

"Thank you," she said, wavering. "I sent off the samples to the lab yesterday."

"Good. Unfortunately, Dee Dee wouldn't even entertain the idea of providing samples from her pantry. I guess she'll have no choice if homicide or Health Canada wants to have a look."

"Did you get a chance to look through the garbage?"

"I retrieved the top bag…nada. Didn't get the bottom bag. Any luck with the suppliers?"

Two miserable green eyes stared into mine. "I talked to all of them. No one has caught even a whisper of an issue." Tears spilled down her cheeks. "Jorja, it had to have been the beans."

"We've been through this. No way you improperly prepared the beans." A sick queasy feeling materialized in my gut.

"I've gone over this in my head a hundred times, but it's the one thing that keeps coming up."

"Okay. For one *insane* second, let's entertain the idea the beans were the cause. Why did some people get sick and not others?" I answered my own question. "Unless body weight comes into play, or they became ill later. Do you still have a copy of the seating plan?"

Gab opened her laptop and pulled up the seating plan Dee Dee had sent her the day before dinner. Table one held spots for JP and Dee Dee as well as Carl and Rose Johnson. The Texan and his wife, Mr. and Mrs. Walker, sat on JP's right, and an elegant middle-aged couple, a Mr. and Mrs. Perez to JP and Dee Dee's left. Google search revealed Mr. Walker owned FWS Corporation, the fourth largest retail pharmacy chain in North America, headquartered in Texas. The Perezes were investors who made their original money in the US tree-nut market. JP and Carl were partners in Riteweight, JP the CEO and Carl the Chief Financial Officer.

"Whoa, some pretty well-heeled people at that table," I said. And most of them were about to get richer. The newscasters reporting on Carl's death were calling the product Riteweight was getting ready to launch a miracle weight-loss pill the world has been waiting for. It was creating more buzz than Carl's death.

The second table held spots for the surly, bourbon-drinking Daryl, who we now knew was Daryl Henshaw, Riteweight's head of operations. He had occupied himself with his cell phone during most of dinner. A woman with shoulder-length bleach-blond hair, a firm thirtyish body and a chest rivalling Dee Dee's sat adjacent to him, but they didn't act like a couple. The seating chart identified her as Kristen Lee. Dimitri Asentanko, the stocky man with the boisterous laugh, sat next to Kristen and the European couple, Mr. and Mrs. Gruba, he had arrived with on his left. Rounding out the table were Dan Hyde, the lawyer who had penned whatever deal they were celebrating, and his wife Judy. The last spot at the table was merely labelled accountant on the seating chart. I remembered a man sat there, thinning hair, brown goatee. Either Dee Dee didn't know his name or didn't think his position in the company warranted one.

"We know Mr. Gruba got sick. He was the first to leave the room." I waited while Gab put the number one next to his name. "The blond woman at his table, Kristen, left right after him. Interesting."

"What?" asked Gab.

"Mr. Gruba had the lamb, but Kristen had one of the vegetarian plates. They both got ill. They also have dramatically different body size. And Daryl, the guy next to Kristen, also got a vegetarian plate but he seemed fine."

"There goes that theory. Was it only the people at that table that got ill?"

I shook my head. "A few minutes after they left the room, Mr. Perez, who was seated at Dee Dee's table got up and left the room. He didn't look so hot."

"He had the lamb," said Gab. "Okay, we have people sick at both tables, one a vegetarian, the others not. Wouldn't that kind of eliminate the lamb and the quinoa?"

I could see how Gab had managed to convince herself it was the beans. The lamb had been served with a bean and sweet potato puree and the vegetarian dish a Mediterranean quinoa, bean and sweet potato terrine.

"On the other hand," Gab mused, "some people are psychosomatic. When people around them feel ill, they believe they're ill too."

"Good point. Other than Mr. Gruba and Kristen Lee, we really don't know who else got sick."

"Except for Carl," Gab added.

"Yeah, Carl. His wife, Rose, didn't seem sick when she left with the ambulance. I asked Dee Dee if she or JP got sick, but she said no."

"Do you really expect she'd admit to something as human as diarrhea or vomiting?" said Gab.

The ringtones on our respective cell phones chimed simultaneously. I stepped into the back office to take my call and give Gab space. I heard her say she was sorry to hear of Carl Johnson's death, her thoughts were with his wife, family, friends and co-workers. She had no other comment at this time. *Must be a reporter.*

I was somewhat surprised to see my call was from Lydia. She had left me with the distinct impression she no longer cared to engage my services. I forced a degree of cheerfulness into my voice.

"Hi, Lydia."

"You have to find Dave," she ordered.

"You haven't heard from him?"

"Would I be calling you if I had?"

I tried again. "He probably went to a friend's house to recover."

"Someone tried to kill him."

"You can't jump to that conclusion. All we know is someone tried shooting their way into his apartment, injuring him in the process. We don't know why. Could be a botched robbery. Maybe whomever it was didn't expect anyone to be inside."

"I need you to find him."

"Your best bet is to let the police handle this."

"No."

Her reaction the night Dave was shot didn't sit right with me. And Dave's behaviour after being shot didn't either. Why had he run off? If someone was gunning for Dave, did I want to put myself in the middle? I waited. Thirty more seconds of my life went by.

"There's something I haven't told you," she said.

There it was. This is what I was afraid of.

"I'll be at Doodlebug's in an hour. Don't disappoint me... again."

I stared at the blank screen on my phone. *Of all the nerve.*

EIGHT

DOODLEBUG'S IS THE kind of place you go to when you're desperate for a drink, but all the good bars are full. Dark wood floors, scarred wooden tables, mismatched grubby velvet chairs, and exposed brick walls covered in graffiti. Definitely on the slummy side, but the toilets worked most of the time and the booze was cheap. A group of twenty-somethings sat at a table near the front throwing drink straws at one another. Three other tables were occupied by lone, grizzled-looking men.

I arrived late, my way of playing tit for tat. Lydia sat at a small table by the back wall, ramming a drink straw up and down in her drink. I pulled out the chair across from her and sank into its grimy softness.

"Hey, Lydia. How are you doing?"

"How the fuck do you think I'm doing?"

I didn't need this. I could always get a part-time job packing groceries. I got up.

"Hey, don't leave. Come on…please?"

I turned and studied her for a second.

"I'm sorry. I'm not a bitch, honest. I'm just…stressed."

I sighed and sat down. The waitress arrived. I ordered coffee. Lydia held the straw against one side of her glass and took a swig, lowering the volume by half. Eyeing the waitress, she pointed at her glass and gave a small nod. Lydia tapped the table nervously while we waited for the waitress to return. Two fingernails were painted blue, the rest bare and chewed to the nub.

Our drinks arrived. Lydia stared out the window and continued to play with her drink straw.

"You said on the phone you had something to tell me."

"I need you to find Dave."

"Why?"

"I'm worried about him."

"You told me you thought he was cheating on you. You said if he was so much as looking at someone you were going to dump his ass. Now you're worried?"

"I didn't exactly tell you the truth."

"He isn't cheating on you?"

She rolled her eyes, picked up her glass and drained it. She set the empty aside and pulled the second one over.

"Look, if you want me to help, you'd better tell me what's going on. I can get off this chair and leave anytime. I don't have to keep you on as a client, I can terminate our contract whenever I want."

On the one hand, I needed the money. On the other hand, I had to keep vigilant. There were lots of weirdos out there eager to have an unsuspecting PI ferret out information to help them in their nefarious ways. And Lydia was definitely a weirdo.

"Dave said something funny was going on at work. He was scared."

"So why tell me he's cheating?"

"I thought, you know, you could keep an eye out for him. Follow him around—make sure he got home all right. I thought you'd be able to tell if someone was following him or if you saw anything suspicious."

"I still don't understand why you didn't just tell me the truth."

"I should have. It's just all so bizarre, I wasn't sure you'd believe me."

My gut was telling me to run from this one, but my curiosity took over.

"Well, here's your last chance, so you better start talking."

Lydia scrunched up her face, her eyes on her drink. "A couple of months ago he got a call from some company. They wanted him to check all their computer systems."

"You mean like an audit?"

"I guess." She shrugged. "Anyway, Dave said their systems were a joke. The head honcho wanted Dave to beef up security on their systems and put in all the right doodads. While he was doing that, Dave discovered their data was hacked and all messed up."

"Oops—not good."

"Ya think?"

"Do you remember the name of the company?"

"I've been trying to, but nothing comes to mind."

I tried to meet her eyes, but she wasn't having any of it.

"Seriously, Lydia?"

"Look, whenever Dave starts yakking about all his IT shit I tune out." She shook her head, guzzled back more of her drink, and wiped her mouth with the back of her hand. "I know Dave never worked for these guys before because he was all excited to get another client."

Great. "Go on."

"Dave was spending a lot of time at this client's place working late most nights. Then a few weeks ago he started acting weird."

"Weird how?"

"He'd shut his laptop whenever I came within five feet of him and he always took his cell phone with him. He even started taking it to the john." Lydia paused to slurp up half of her second drink. "A few times he made some lame excuse to run out, late at night. At first, I did think it was another woman. I called him out on it. He told me no way. That's when he told me there was some bad shit going down at this place."

"What kind of bad shit?"

"I don't know. He said if he didn't come home one night it would likely be them. You know"—she switched to her version of a gangster accent—"now dat you know, ve vill have to kill you." She teared up. "He's always saying stupid nerdy shit like that."

I waited while she swiped at her eyes and took another swig.

"Are you saying he was worried someone would come after him because of what he found out at work? If that's the case, you need to tell the police."

"Quit with the police, will ya. When have they ever done any good? They don't seem to be able to do anything until someone's dead."

I pondered this for a minute. "Let me get this. You hired me on a pretense, so I could follow Dave around to make sure no one else was? And someone tried to break into his place, and he got shot. What do you want me to do?"

"Find Dave and keep me from getting killed."

"Why would you imagine anyone's coming after you?"

"'Cuz I got this." She pulled out a folded paper from her purse and set it down between us. I held down one corner gingerly with my finger and used a fork to open the folds.

Forget Dave. Forget what you know. The words were scrawled in pencil.

"How'd you get this?"

"It was left under the wiper blade on my car. I'm next. I know I am. But I don't know anything. Neither does Dave."

"Convince me."

Lydia scowled and sighed. "A few weeks ago, Dave started getting threatening messages."

"Was he still working for these guys?"

"I guess so."

Holy mother Teresa. She was testing what little patience I had.

"What kind of threats?"

"They warned him to keep quiet. They sent him a copy of the contract he signed and highlighted the confidentially agreement section, like he didn't know."

"So? A tad blunt, but it doesn't sound particularly threatening," I said.

Lydia took a deep breath, sat back and slid down in her seat. She slowly rotated her glass. "He got other threatening messages."

"Do you have copies of any of these threats?"

"No. I didn't ask to see them. Why would I? Besides, Dave clammed up whenever I asked anything. But I could tell he was nervous."

"Do you know if the messages were paper or electronic?"

"He said they were in his mailbox. I assume he meant email. No one sends stuff by snail mail anymore."

I didn't point out someone hand delivered her note. "I still think you should tell the police. At least they'd know it might have been a targeted attack on Dave and not a random event."

She drew her lips into a tight line. "I'll answer questions if they ask, but I don't even want to be seen talking to the cops. These people know about me and where I live."

"I can't watch you twenty-four seven. The police can protect you, I can't."

"Yeah, like I'm going to believe that. Remember that girl who was getting death threats from her ex-boyfriend? She went to the police and they had a nice chat with him. Three days later he broke into her parents' house, where she'd gone to stay, and killed her and her mother."

"Right. I was going to ask you if you had anywhere safe to go, like a friend or relative's place."

"Yeah, not gonna happen. I'll go to the police once I have something concrete to tell them. That's what I need you to do. Find me something concrete."

"The note's concrete."

"Sure, but what does it prove? It could have been left there by anyone."

She was right. She could have even written it herself for whatever sick game she was playing. How was I supposed to tell if she was telling the truth this time?

"What do you have in the way of home security?"

"The apartment has an intercom and there's a peep hole in my door and a chain in addition to the lock."

"Are the windows secured?"

"The patio doors open to a balcony and the bedroom window slides open. But I'm in a corner unit six floors up. There's nothing below or above the bedroom window. Someone would have to use a rope."

I didn't tell her it had been done before. "Do you have a key to Dave's apartment?"

"I did, but it won't work now, remember? The landlord had the lock changed."

"Dave's landlord doesn't know you?"

"No. Never saw him till the night you and I went there."

"You don't know where Dave was working? Never saw an invoice or a bank statement that would show who was paying him?"

"No. Like I said, Dave was acting weird, secretive. Besides, if I wanted to see his bank statements, and I don't, I'd have to know his password."

"Are you sure you've told me everything?"

"Yes." She stared at me defiantly.

"If I find out you're lying or conveniently forgot to tell me something, I'll be off the case so fast you'll spin in my wind."

"Okay."

"I'm going to rewrite the contract I have with you. There's no way I can agree to keep you safe. I know a guy who knows a guy who could beef up security at your place if you want. All I can agree to is to try and locate Dave for you. Then I'm done. End of story. Take it or leave it."

"Deal."

Why was my gut telling me I just made the biggest mistake of my life?

NINE

ONCE HOME, I altered Lydia's contract and emailed it requesting her approval. Lydia had already been in touch with Dave's closest friend, Colby. He hadn't seen Dave since the weekend before the attempted break-in. Dave's parents lived in Airdrie, a small town, twenty kilometres north of Calgary. Lydia hadn't tried contacting them. She didn't want to explain why she didn't know where Dave was.

Lydia hadn't been able to get a hold of Dave's other friend, Akar. I found his Facebook page and sent him a message, asking him to meet me. Then I called my guy.

"Hi, Mike, it's Jorja."

"Hey, gorgeous, what are you up to?"

I met Mike five years ago when I transferred to Calgary from Vancouver to work at Global Analytix' new Calgary office, where I had worked as a forensic lab analyst. Global's clients included private, public and government departments, including police services. My job required testing stuff largely from industrial accidents, but I'd also been assigned overflow work from the police department when their own labs were backed up. Mike had arrived in Calgary at roughly the same time, newly retired from the Toronto Police force and bored. Luckily a contract position in

Global's Investigative Practice division had opened up and Mike snagged it. He still worked for Global Analytix, on contract. He also provided training to the city of Calgary's police recruits. As newbies to the city, Mike and I had become fast friends. There wasn't anything romantic going on between us. The twenty-year age difference wasn't the reason. We had this comfortable solid friendship going and neither of us saw any need to mess with it. At least not yet.

"Just got home from a meeting with my client. What about you? Still at work?"

"Just wrapping up."

Mike launched into a brief rundown of his day. I walked over to the fridge and opened the door. A slightly withered apple occupied the fruit and veggie drawer. The orange juice had expired. A quick search through the cupboards revealed half a box of Captain Crunch, a handful of unsalted almonds and a box of whole-wheat crackers.

"Do you have time for a quick beer?" Mike asked as he finished his story. "I can't stay long; I'm working on a risk-management presentation I have to deliver tomorrow."

"Sure, sounds great. Give me twenty minutes."

I hung up and ate several handfuls of Captain Crunch. I could kill two birds with one stone. Get something to eat and the name of one of Mike's retired ex-police-force buddies, who now ran a security company. I put the cereal box down and walked into the bedroom.

I had come close to losing the place a few times this past year. The mortgage was a reasonable nine hundred and fifty dollars a month for my five hundred and eighty-six square feet of living space, but some months it had been several hundred dollars more than I had on hand. Thankfully, the initial ups and downs in my business had levelled to its current but steady poverty-line level.

I opened the closet, pulled off my sweater and surveyed the contents. I pulled out a black blouse with sheer lace sleeves, slipped it on and checked the mirror. I fluffed my hair with my fingertips and unbuttoned another button on the shirt. I did up the button again, then took the blouse off. I pulled out a burgundy sleeveless halter top with a wide-ruched hem and slipped it on. The silky fabric had more of a going-out look than a have-a-beer-with-a-pal look. I checked my watch. What the hell was I doing? I grabbed my old UBC rowing sweatshirt off the floor of the closet, shook it out and slipped it over my head. I gathered up my jacket and laptop and headed downstairs.

Mike was already nursing a beer by the time I got to Sixteen Hundred. A Holy Grail waited for me on the table.

I sat down, picked up the beer and held it up. "Aren't you a sweetheart. Cheers!"

"Can't help it," said Mike. "It's in my DNA. How's your week going?"

"I've had better."

"That bad?"

"Very funny." I should have worn something other than a ratty sweatshirt. Mike looked nice in grey dress pants and a black long-sleeve Henley sweater. "You're looking good. Been working out or something?"

Mike raised an eyebrow. "How much is that going to cost me?"

"No really…you look…professional. Although now you mention it, I could use a favour."

Mike chuckled, shook his head, and took a swig of beer.

I told Mike what I needed. He pulled out his phone and made a couple calls. By the time Mike was ready to leave, it was all arranged. A guy named Lennie would meet me at Lydia's in the morning to see what could be done to secure her abode. It was all

I could do for her tonight. "Sorry, I can't stay longer," said Mike. "Maybe we can take in a game next week."

"Sounds good. I'm going to hang out here for a bit. Good luck with your presentation." I watched Mike walk away. Inside that solid physique, lived a genuinely nice guy. After two failed marriages, Mike swore he was done with relationships. I could relate. But someday, some woman would notice what a great catch he was and worm her way into his heart.

I pulled out my laptop and while it booted up opened the menu the waitress had left. My eye glanced over the salads, but nothing called my name. The mozza mushroom burger looked good. I looked down at my sweatshirt. We were all going to die anyway. Would anyone really care if I ended up needing to be cremated in a stretchy sweatshirt and yoga pants. Besides, a miracle weight-loss pill would be available soon. I ordered the burger, another beer and typed Jean Pierre Boussard into the search bar.

Besides being president at Riteweight, JP sat on the board of several other companies. After graduating from Laval University with a business degree, he went to work for Boussard, Thorton and Smeltz. I checked them out and discovered it was run by Jean Ricard Boussard, JP's daddy. Must be nice to have the old man give you a job and introduce you to his rich associates and wealthy clients. After five years there, he went to work for several other prestigious financial institutions and eventually began investing in start-ups.

JP and Dee Dee were media whores. I churned through pages of news releases, articles and photos of the Boussards at school openings and charity events. Riteweight was prevalent in the last few years. I read news release after news release announcing Riteweight's progress as they moved closer and closer to the December launch date of their weight-loss product. A product touted as a revolutionary miracle weight-loss supplement. I felt better about my dinner choice.

Carl's LinkedIn page was still up, and I wondered if his wife, Rose, would eventually take it down. Carl acquired a business degree from Queen's and seven years later obtained an MBA from Harvard. He and JP formed Riteweight five years ago. Carl was on the board of the Alberta Diabetes Foundation and the United Way. His entrepreneurial spirt and his philanthropic work earned him an Order of Canada medal. There wasn't much of an internet presence for Rose, other than mention of her name in recent news articles referencing Carl's death, and several family obituaries including her brother-in-law's, two years earlier.

Daryl Henshaw, the surly-looking guy at JP's dinner and VP of Operations at Riteweight had a chemistry degree from the University of Toronto and a Doctorate in biochemistry from McGill. His LinkedIn page showed a headshot of him wearing a bowtie below lips firmly pressed in a straight line. If he had entered "dare to contact me" below the photo it would have been perfect. He listed three pharmaceutical companies in the work history section, names and dates only. His page listed no interests. The skill section was blank.

Daryl was neither photogenic nor prone to being quoted. The few pictures I found of him on the internet showed a man clearly unhappy to be attending a public function. In addition to the usual bio and meagre data on several who's-who sites there wasn't much else. Except for the personal bankruptcy notice Daryl filed six years back. It didn't say what led to his financial downfall. If I could believe even half of the marketing hype surrounding Riteweight's new product, he'd soon be redeeming himself.

I looked up Riteweight's headquarter address. I was familiar with the building. Most of the tenants were small companies leasing space and shared administrative services from the main tenant, a company called Common4ce.

I read until the place emptied and one of the staff started mopping floors. A lone customer sat at the bar chatting with the bartender who washed up glasses. A foursome in one corner were having an animated discussion about which band could be considered grunge and which fell into the post-grunge category. I packed up and headed back to my condo.

Kicking off my boots and dropping my jacket on the kitchen table, I poured myself a glass of Pinot and curled up on my grey sectional with my laptop. Two hours later I'd learned the following:

The weight-loss supplement business generated a hefty twenty-three billion dollars in revenue annually, in North America alone.

Obesity was cited as the most prevalent cause of disease. Thirty-six percent of the population in the US and twenty-five percent in Canada were obese and the number was growing with each passing year.

Weight-loss supplements aren't subject to FDA approval. In Canada testing is required to ensure the quality of the product. In other words, the ingredients listed on the package had to match what was in the product.

And most interesting of all, products with poor results, or those not living up to their marketing promises of rapid weight loss, still survived and raked in millions. JP and Carl's company was a potential gold mine.

Too bad Carl died six weeks before the big launch. His luck was worse than mine. I wondered who would inherit his share of the company. Someone had wanted him out of the way. Suddenly the image of his wife, Rose, sitting meekly at his side, eyes downcast but with a small, satisfied smile on her face, floated into view.

TEN

I EVENTUALLY CRAWLED INTO bed around one a.m. and now regretted it. I told Lennie I'd meet him at Lydia's place at eight and with rush hour being what it was, needed to leave soon. I got up and staggered into the washroom.

I studied the face in the mirror and mentally debated if I'd ever fix the small gap between my upper front teeth. Assuming I had the money. I'd hated the imperfection as a child but was slowly growing to appreciate that my smile was distinguishable from the perfect, over-bleached smiles prevalent everywhere.

I clapped my hands together rapidly, flashed myself a smile in the mirror and announced, "It's going to be a great day. I'm excited. Wealth and happiness are coming my way." I repeated the mantra three times while clapping.

Call it crazy but it did raise my energy. As a card-carrying member of the world's unofficial introvert club, I found it a good way to get out of my head and ready myself for the day. In addition to changing career paths a year ago, part of my promise to myself was to stretch the boundaries of who I was as a person. I needed to take more risk, put myself out there, be vulnerable, not always take the scientific, rational or logical path. Maybe do something crazy once in a while, wear red underwear, eat sushi.

Lennie was waiting at the entrance as I pulled up to Lydia's apartment. After introducing ourselves, I buzzed Lydia and she let us in. Like Dave, Lydia was self-employed. Unlike Dave she went the artistic route and was eking out a living as an illustrator, mostly children's books. She met us at the door in a fuzzy white housecoat and pink slippers.

Lennie installed a strike plate and deadbolt to supplement the flimsy chain on her door and drilled screws into the upper track of the windows and patio door to prevent them from being lifted out. Lydia and I worked out a code word we could insert into an email, text or phone conversation in case of trouble. She insisted on Cydnee Bristle, the name of one of her illustrations, a female hedgehog secret spy. I would have preferred something shorter, but I could live with it.

Lennie made plans to install a camera in Lydia's underground car stall with a feed to her cell phone. If someone left her another note, we might get to see who. I armed her with pepper spray and warned her to stay upwind and cover her face if she had to use it since the back spray hurt like hell. She agreed to send me a text letting me know where she was going and when she expected to be back and confirm her safe return. Not exactly round-the-clock support but the best she could afford.

After leaving Lydia's, I pushed the speed limit and got to Koko's right at nine-fifteen. A man waited nervously by the muffin bar.

"Hi. Are you Akar?"

He brightened. "Jorja? Yes. I am Akar."

I bought tea, coffee and muffins and we sat at a small table by the front window.

"Thanks for meeting with me," I said as we settled in. "Did you hear someone attempted to break into Dave's place last week?"

"Yes. How odd. And frightening."

"Like I said on the phone, Lydia hired me to find Dave. She hasn't seen him since the night of the break-in. How long have you and Dave been friends?"

"We met at Petro-Canada about fifteen years ago. I had just arrived from London, after finishing up my degree there."

"You both work in IT?"

"Yes. I'm propagating the stereotype. You know, Indian guys all work in IT and talk funny. I don't know what Dave's excuse is. You probably know Petro-Can was bought out by Suncor. Once they began right-sizing I left and joined Reclink. Dave went into business for himself. Better to take one's own fate in hand than wait to be punted to the curb."

"When's the last time you saw or talked to Dave?"

"Two weeks ago. We planned to go to the new Unplugged Expo this weekend at the Convention Centre. Of course, we met in Zarwar several times."

"Zarwar?"

"Oh yes." He squirmed excitedly. "It is a most remarkable game. The goal is to find and hoard food and weapons in preparation for the final battle between earth and Zargon. It's great. It's got ogres and zombies and aliens all rolled into one."

"You play this online?"

"Oh yes. Unquestionably, I was fighting Hiary, Dave's avatar, the day he got shot. One moment Hiary is standing over my avatar Indikar with his sword raised…and then nothing." He giggled. "I got away with his whole arsenal."

"And you haven't seen or talked to Dave since?"

"No. Not even online. Hiary remains silent."

"Did Dave ever discuss work?"

"Yes and no. Mostly we bitched to each other what a pain in the arse clients can be. Occasionally he would text me a question or I him. Like how to disable a particularly nasty virus, or some such thing."

"Nothing specific about the client or the work itself?"

"No, nothing specific."

"Do you know who Dave's clients were?"

"Let me see." He stared at the ceiling long enough that I had a glance myself. Embossed tin. *Nice.*

"Oh, oh," said Akar, sitting up. "How could I forget? One of his clients is the sign shop. They make those large posters for big events. Like the Comic-Con posters and the big cut-outs of Star War characters you see at the movie theatres. They even make cut-outs of the storm troopers and the wonderfully lavish Ronin Boba Fett." He shook his head. "Forgive me. The company is in the south, somewhere on Macleod Trail. Dave also worked for a doctor in Kensington. Dr. Lam, I believe. They were moving their patient records online. Personal information has to have utmost security."

"Any new clients? Say in the last couple of months?"

"There was one, yes. I don't remember the name or perhaps Dave never said. I know they are in the downtown area because we thought we might get a chance to meet for lunch from time to time."

"Did you?"

"No. This client ate up all of Dave's time. He put in an entire network for them. They had nothing, just a bunch of guys with laptops running around, losing their data."

"They were losing data?"

"Pardon my figure of speech. I gather they ran the company off standalone computers. I know they gave Dave a tight deadline and he was putting in a great amount of overtime. Which is good, of course. More money. Hiary and Indikar lay low for weeks. But he must have finished because Hiary came looking for Indikar two weeks ago."

"Do you have any idea where Dave would go to lay low?"

"If Lydia has not seen him then I do not know. I wasn't aware he was missing until our friend, Colby, phoned to ask if I had been in contact with Dave. That is when I discovered what happened and realized Indikar's fortune had come at the expense of Dave's misfortune."

"And you don't know what kind of work his new client was in?"

"No. Dave said he was putting in a new system and procedures for them. He must have finished. He wouldn't disappear and leave his client like that unless he had."

After Akar left, I got a refill and revisited what he'd told me. I called Dave's friend Colby and left him a message. Maybe Lydia wasn't completely off her rocker. Had Dave inadvertently stumbled onto something while putting in a new system for his client? Or had he taken advantage of the situation and taken something. Something they didn't want anyone to know about.

ELEVEN

I HAD TAKEN TWO anti-acids before leaving home, but my stomach still churned. Talking to the police always unnerved me. Or for that matter, anyone in authority. The thought of being grilled by a tough, unblinking, tobacco-smelling man with scars on his face made my palms clammy.

Gab was settled in at the front desk leaving me the back office, which suited me better. Dark, gloomy and cramped, Phillip Marlow would have loved the place, except the building was smoke-free. I plugged in my laptop and sank into the chair, aware my shoulders were hunched up around my ears. I knew why.

Homicide was run by Inspector Luis Azagora. No one died in this town without Azagora hearing about it. I already had several run-ins with him, and he wasn't my biggest fan. I, on the other hand, had a completely juvenile crush on him. I didn't know why I was so nervous; it wasn't like he'd be coming to interview me himself.

They arrived at nine on the dot. Short brown hair, average builds, tan trench coats, clones except one was older by a decade or so. Pleasantries were exchanged. Gab got the younger one. The older one, a Detective Birdie, joined me in the back office.

Detective Birdie removed his coat and we sat across from each other at the small round table a previous tenant had crammed in between the desk and the row of file cabinets along the back wall. I didn't detect any scars or cigarette odour.

He opened a black portfolio and slid out a pen.

"We're talking to everyone who was present at the Boussards' the night Carl Johnson took ill. I'm here to take a preliminary statement. We'll contact you if we need a more detailed one later."

"Okay."

"You work for Ms. Rizzo?"

"No. We're good friends and we share this office space. I'm a private investigator. Gab's sous-chef didn't show up for work that night and I agreed to help out."

"You help out often?"

"No. It was my first time." *And hopefully the last.*

"Do you have a professional interest in this case?"

I swallowed. "Gab's reputation is on the line. She asked me to help her clear her name."

"She thinks she'll be implicated in Mr. Johnson's death?"

"Oh god, no." I took a deep breath. "A few of the guests suffered gastrointestinal upsets. Gab's taking steps to assure the source of the problem didn't start with her. She has been checking with her food suppliers for any reported issues and has sent the leftover herbs and dry goods for testing."

"There were leftovers from dinner?"

"Not exactly. The dinner leftovers were discarded and the dishes and such cleaned up before we left. Nothing remained other than a smattering of raw uncooked ingredients used in the recipes."

"What were the results?"

"The lab results aren't back yet. You can check with Gab, but she told me none of the suppliers have heard of any issue with any of the supplies she obtained from them."

"Can you describe what you did and saw the night Mr. Johnson was rushed to hospital?"

I didn't hold anything back, now that homicide was investigating. On the other hand, I had already learned the hard way not to hurl accusations or make innuendoes without solid proof. I stuck to the mundane facts as best I could.

"Did anyone else have access to the kitchen or were you or the chef in the kitchen the whole time?" he asked when I finished.

"We were in and out of the kitchen dozens of times. We were running full tilt, setting tables, chopping and stirring, and of course once the guests arrived, serving."

"So, the kitchen was unoccupied at times. For how long?"

"I don't know." I wiped the palms of my hands against my jeans.

"If you had to guess?"

"A few minutes, maybe five or six." My face grew hotter. *It couldn't have been more, could it?* My mind flashed back to the time we were both in the dining room, opening patio doors, starting the fire in the fireplace, checking the table settings. I looked up. Detective Birdie stared unblinking, eyes on my face.

"I can't imagine it being more than ten," I said.

"Did you see anyone in or by the kitchen who shouldn't have been there?"

"No. I didn't see anyone suspicious. Mrs. Boussard came into the kitchen at one point to check on progress, as did her assistant, Jeannine. Flowers and wine were delivered but the deliveries directed to the storage or dining room not the kitchen. The other people I saw, apart from the guests, were the security guard at the front gate and Rose Johnson stopped by at one point. I saw her talking to Mrs. Boussard's assistant in the back hall, although at the time I didn't know who she was."

"No one else?"

"No. I mean yes. Well, not really. I saw someone going up the back stairs, thin, black hair, black clothes. I assumed it was one of the Boussards' kids."

"Did he or she come into the kitchen?"

"Not to my knowledge."

"How long has Ms. Rizzo been a chef?"

"She set up her business last year. She's been cooking all her life though."

"What about formal training?"

I tried swallowing without moving my throat muscles. "She's self-taught."

I watched him scribble something in his notebook.

"What is your experience with food preparation?"

I swiped the palms of my hands on my thighs for the second time in as many minutes. "I'm really good at opening Styrofoam containers and I'm very familiar with the microwave."

Detective Birdie looked up. "A man died, Ms. Knight. Several people became ill. Why don't you tell me what you think happened?"

I swallowed several times, hoping Birdie wouldn't notice. "I don't know. Maybe some of the guests met somewhere for drinks before the dinner and ate or drank something there that made them ill. Maybe there was something wrong with one of the ingredients Gab used. It wouldn't be the first time that's happened. Remember the spinach thing last year? Maybe Carl's death is unrelated to the gastronomical upset some of the guests felt. Maybe Carl was stung by a bee and had an allergic reaction."

"Did you see a bee?"

"No. I heard Mrs. Johnson screaming something about a bee. Did he get stung by a bee?"

"There seems to be confusion on that point."

I waited while Detective Birdie sat tapping his pen on his

notebook. "That's a lot of maybes, Ms. Knight." He leaned forward. "Here's what I know. Your friend, Ms. Rizzo, is in a lot of debt. *Maybe* someone approached her to be just a tad careless. *Maybe* something got into Carl Johnson's food that shouldn't have been there."

My heart shifted into overdrive; blood rushed to my face. "No way. You don't know Gab like I do. She'd rather die herself than harm anyone."

"That's what everybody says, until they find themselves in a desperate situation."

Birdie continued to stare at me. I shook my head and looked away.

"Tell me again what happened, when Mrs. Johnson called for help."

I reiterated my story about how I had rushed back into the room in time to see Carl struggling to breathe. "He was slumped over and Mr. Boussard and Mr. Asentanko caught him and laid him on the floor. His face was purple, and he was struggling to breathe. Someone yelled for his EpiPen. I couldn't really see him after that. Mr. Boussard and Mr. Asentanko were kneeling next to him, and a few other people were standing around them. Then Mr. Boussard yelled out to call 911."

"You made the call?"

"Yes."

"What did you do after making the call?"

"Ms. Rizzo and I went back down the hall and waited at the doorway of the dining room. Mrs. Johnson was quite distraught, and one of the guests, Mrs. Hyde, was trying to comfort her. Someone said they gave him two shots of epinephrine. That sounds like a lot, doesn't it? The ambulance arrived within minutes. After EMS arrived, Gab and I went back to the kitchen to clean up."

"Did you see who administered the EpiPen?"

"No. Mr. Boussard was going through Carl Johnson's jacket pockets trying to find it. I left before it was found."

"Were you aware the Boussards stored an extra EpiPen in the supply room next to the kitchen?"

"No."

"You and Ms. Rizzo weren't made aware of that fact, even though you had been told one of the guests you were preparing food for had numerous food allergies."

"I don't know if anyone mentioned it to Gab. I wasn't aware of it."

"Then what happened?"

"We were almost finished cleaning up when Mrs. Boussard came in. She told us to finish up and leave." I left off mentioning the ugly threat she had issued. I didn't see how it would help.

"And you did?"

"Yes. We were out of there by eleven fifteen."

"Anything else you want to tell me?"

"No." I looked down at my hands while the little voice in my head taunted. *You mean like, that your boss already thinks I'm incompetent? Or that I'm scared shitless for me and Gab.* "No that's all."

"Okay, that's it," he said, snapping his portfolio shut. "Appreciate your time. Please call me if anything else comes to mind." He slid his card across the table.

After the detectives departed, Gab and I compared notes.

"He kept talking about toxins. I told them I used raw beans which can be toxic if not prepared properly," said Gab, her worried green eyes on mine.

"You did the right thing. If they're not already aware of their toxicity, they'll find out."

"I gave them a copy of the list of ingredients I used and made note of which ones we had sent off for testing."

I nodded. I didn't share Birdie's line of questioning regarding her and my qualifications in food preparation. Or that Birdie mentioned Gab had a lot of debt.

"Jorja, what am I going to do? If I don't get this cleared up, I'm going to be ruined." She looked up with tortured eyes. "What if I did cause his death?"

"How can you think that?"

Gab sank to the chair and covered her face with her hands. When she finally looked up, the fear on her face was real. She whispered, "Oh god, Jorja. I didn't say anything to the cops, but I know they're going to find out. I had sex with JP."

TWELVE

I PEERED THROUGH THE mostly bare elm trees lining the boulevard for number thirty-four. Little remained of the original neighbourhood, except for the trees. Most of the houses had been replaced with sleek, contemporary two-storey infills. Stucco siding, straight lines, flat roofs, and an abundance of floor-to-ceiling windows. Nothing in this area sold for less than two million.

Number thirty-four had a more traditional aesthetic than its neighbours, marrying modern with heritage styling. The front of the two-storey house faced southward and was sheathed in stone. A small main-floor balcony overlooked a sunny bricked courtyard complete with fountain, now turned off for winter. I pulled over, killed the engine, and sat thinking.

I wish Gab hadn't shared that little tidbit about her and JP with me. She had rushed on to say it was a onetime thing and it was all her, she had initiated it. She first met JP when she went to the Boussards' to meet with Dee Dee to discuss a potential menu and her guests' dietary requirements. The meeting ran long, and Dee Dee found herself running late to pick up her daughter. JP emerged from his home office as they were packing up. Quick introductions were made, and Dee Dee ran off leaving JP to see Gab to the door. Gab said, she found herself flirting with him.

He returned the banter. He rang her the next day. They met for drinks a few days later and well—sex. It was just sex, Gab said. Nothing more.

I made my way up the front walk. Maybe I didn't know Gab as well as I thought I did. We always vowed married men were off the table, well unless they lied and told you they weren't. Gab insisted it was all her, but it obviously wasn't. I was having a hard time not being all judgy.

Gab having sex with JP couldn't possibly have anything to do with Carl's death. It wouldn't do her any good though if word got out. It might allow unfounded insinuations to form. Insinuations that maybe other favours were exchanged, like JP offering her some much-needed money to fix Carl a special plate. I knew Gab had nothing to do with Carl's death. It just gave me more to worry about. I reached the front door, set aside my worries and tapped the lionhead knocker against the strike plate.

The door was opened by a svelte, well-dressed woman in her fifties. Her platinum-blond hair was streaked with threads of grey and tastefully arranged in soft waves around her face. Two muzzled Dobermans stood watchful behind her.

"Hi, I'm Jorja Knight. I'm here to see Mrs. Johnson."

"Please come in. Rose told me you were coming by. I'm Nadine, her sister."

"Thank you," I said, stepping warily inside. The dogs remained motionless. "Please accept my sympathies on the loss of your brother in-law."

"Thank you. I can't believe Carl is gone. Jake, Lucy, come," she called to the dogs. She led us through the foyer to a small sitting room on the right. "Please make yourself comfortable. I'll go tell Rose you're here." She turned and left, the dogs pattering silently after her.

Two wingback chairs covered in rich gold-and-mocha brocade

were carefully arranged on either side of the patio doors. The back of each chair was draped with a multicoloured, striped afghan. Crocheted doilies adorned the chair arms. Maybe to keep off the dog hair.

I took several steps forward and looked around. This was the room I had seen from the outside, the one with the Juliette balcony. A large stone fireplace anchored the far wall, and the adjacent shelves held a collection of carefully arranged leather-bound books, family photos, and art objects. I was looking at the items on the shelf when Nadine came back, this time dog-less.

"She'll be down in a few minutes. This has been terribly hard on her."

"Do they have children?" I nodded at a picture of a teen-age girl in a silver frame, but the clothing was reminiscent of times past.

"No. Rose always wanted to have children."

"Her husband didn't?"

"When they first got married, I imagine he did. But Rose had a couple of miscarriages and afterwards...I guess they stopped trying."

We chatted for a few minutes and Nadine turned at a noise by the door.

"Oh, here she is. I'll leave the two of you to talk."

Rose stood in the doorway clutching a wad of Kleenex. Her eyes were red and swollen, but dry. She wore pastel-pink polyester pants and a black knitted cardigan, with penguins or fat crows running in a horizontal band across the chest. Two buttons below the bust strained to keep the cardigan closed over a dark-grey turtleneck. If she had been standing on the street instead of the sitting room of her multi-million-dollar home, I would have pegged her for a bag lady.

"I'm sorry for your loss, Mrs. Johnson. I can't even imagine what you are going through. Thank you for seeing me."

She shuffled over to one of the chairs and motioned at the other.

"My poor, poor Carl. He didn't deserve to die," she murmured, staring at her hands now folded in her lap.

I waited until she gazed back up and made eye contact.

"I'm not sure if you remember me," I said. "I was there the night your husband fell ill. Ms. Rizzo is a friend of mine. She catered the Boussard dinner. When Ms. Rizzo found herself short-staffed that night, she asked me to help out."

Recognition slowly fill her eyes.

"I'm a private investigator." I handed her my card. "Several people became ill at the Boussards' dinner. It likely has nothing to do with what happened to your husband, but Ms. Rizzo asked me to help her get to the bottom of it. Not merely for the sake of her reputation. Food-generated illnesses need to be reported in order to prevent others from getting sick. Please let me assure you. Ms. Rizzo never met your husband before the night of the dinner and it's inconceivable she'd want to harm him."

"He was a good man. Everybody loved him."

"You don't know of anyone who might want to cause him harm?"

"No, of course not."

"And the purpose of the dinner?"

"Carl's company recently reached an agreement with FWS Corporation. They were going to sell Luzit through their stores right across North America."

"Luzit?"

"Yes. It's the weight-loss supplement my husband's company developed."

"Are there new recent partners in Riteweight?"

"Yes." She seemed flustered by the question.

"Were the new partners at dinner that night?"

"Yes. Dimitri Asentanko and one of his investors, Mr. Gruba."

"How did Carl feel about the new partners?"

"Carl was the one who arranged it. He said it would help the company expand. Go international. Otherwise it wouldn't happen."

"Your husband wasn't upset or anything?"

"No."

"I remember seeing you at the Boussards' in the afternoon, the day of the dinner. Of course, I didn't know who you were at the time. Do you mind telling me why you dropped by?"

"I wanted to see if there was anything I could do to lend a hand."

"Did you talk to anyone?"

"I talked to Dee Dee's assistant, Jeannine, to remind her of Carl's allergies. She said the chef had already been advised. Then the flowers arrived. I was admiring them when Dee Dee came into the room. I asked if there was anything I could help with but she said no."

"So you left?"

"Yes, I went home…to get ready."

"Do you remember what time you got home?"

"I'm not sure. I had to stop at the cleaners to pick up Carl's shirt. It might have been around four-thirty."

"Did you or Carl eat anything at home, right before leaving, or stop anywhere on your way to the Boussards' for dinner?"

"No. Carl took an antacid is all. He always did before we went out to eat."

"And when you arrived at the Boussards'. Did you see anyone near or in the kitchen when you were there? It's important if someone tampered with the food."

Her eyes dropped to her lap and she pulled at the Kleenex in her hand.

"I don't understand. I gave them a list of the things he couldn't have."

"Ms. Rizzo was given a list of items to avoid and she didn't use any ingredients your husband was allergic to. But multiple people suffered stomach upset after dinner. I understand your husband died of respiratory failure and they found a number of toxins in his system."

I sensed a shift in mood. Rose remained quiet, her eyes on the ball of tissue in her hand.

"Did you get sick the night of the party?"

"I don't remember. It was so upsetting—to see Carl like that."

"Do you know kidney beans contain toxins called lectins? If the raw bean isn't prepared properly, as few as five or six undercooked beans can cause severe stomach upset, vomiting and diarrhea."

Her fingers shredded the Kleenex. Her eyes refused to meet mine.

"Ms. Rizzo swears she prepared the beans properly. She has done so hundreds of times. We know of two people who became ill. It's hard to imagine it being the beans, since all the guests were given red beans in some form or fashion."

"Well they couldn't have killed Carl. He isn't allergic to beans, but they don't agree with him. He wouldn't eat them."

But he did eat them. I remembered his plate had been clean when I cleared.

"You didn't eat your sweet potato and bean puree either," I said. "May I ask why?"

"I don't care for them either. Maybe whatever happened to the other guests had nothing to do with dinner. Like the stomach flu."

"It's certainly possible. We haven't talked to all the guests yet."

"A bee must have stung Carl. He was allergic to bees. I don't understand why the EpiPen didn't work."

"The EpiPen didn't work?"

"I mean, they gave him an injection. Why didn't it help?"

"And you think a bee stung him, Mrs. Johnson?"

"I don't recall, but what else could it be?"

"The official autopsy results haven't been released. I heard they are running toxicology tests. I suspect they may be looking at the possibility someone deliberately poisoned Carl."

"Poisoned?" Her voice rose. "No. He couldn't have. Why would someone poison him?" She emitted a jagged cry, barely muffled by the soggy ball of tissue.

"I'm sorry, Mrs. Johnson. I didn't mean to upset you. I've not personally heard what they found during the autopsy, only that further tests are being run."

Rose struggled to stand. I stood, relieved to see Nadine in the doorway.

"I'm sorry. I didn't mean to upset her."

She nodded and wrapped her arm around her sister. "I expect she's exhausted."

I let myself out as Nadine helped her sister up the stairs to the second level, the dogs' nails clicking on the tile behind them.

I sat in the truck for a minute before starting it. Why had she insisted Carl wouldn't eat kidney beans, when he had? How could this naïve and helpless woman have been married to someone like Carl Johnson? Then I remembered her smile at dinner as I cleared plates and a chill ran through me.

THIRTEEN

I SWUNG BY MY favourite Italian market and picked up a few groceries. Nothing perishable. With the bags tucked safely away on the floor of the cab I unwrapped and ate my hot porchetta on ciabatta. Whenever I imagined the people who lived in these beautiful big homes, they always appeared healthy, vibrant, happy in my mind. The last few days were messing with the visual. Was nothing as I imagined true? What about my fabulously exciting life as a globe-hopping private investigator, and my torrid love affair with a gorgeous minister who adored me yet respected my daring and sometimes dangerous life. I threw my empty wrapper on the floor and turned the key in the ignition.

I drove past Dave's on the way home. The Jetta remained parked in the same spot. Dave must still be on foot, although he could have rented something by now or high-tailed it out of town on an airplane. With my luck, Dave was holed up with the mistress whom I saw no signs of. I had tried his cell phone several times, but his voice mail was still full.

I parked, got out, marched up the front sidewalk and around to the side door. I rang the doorbell not expecting Dave to answer but I was here anyway. Dave's mailbox was stuffed with flyers. I removed a few and poked through the rest but there was nothing of interest, only a utility bill and the usual pleas from several charities. I rang the doorbell again. When no one answered, I went around to the back of the house. Kneeling at the basement window, I shielded my eyes from the glare and peered into a tiny kitchen. The table and counters were littered with pizza boxes, soft drink containers and Doritos bags, the sink piled high with dirty pots and dishes. I got up, dusted off my knees and walked back to the truck.

Extracting the extra sweater tucked behind the seat, I pulled it over my head and climbed into the cab. I didn't know how much longer I could keep the truck. I had already duct-taped the air vents to prevent the constant ice-cold air from hitting me, but now the cold seeped into the cab through various other nooks and cracks. Bundled against the cold, I headed back out onto Seventeenth Avenue. I had one more stop to make.

My phone call with Colby hadn't yielded anything of use. The last time he saw Dave they met at Flames Central to watch a game and have a few drinks. They didn't talk about work.

Colby told me Dave was a good guy and really knew his stuff, but he wasn't always appreciated in corporate circles. I was all too familiar with what Colby meant. Too much focus on problem solving, not enough time schmoozing and making people feel like they were instrumental to the solution. Dave's social circle was small, a few close friends and a handful of online pals he'd never met. Colby couldn't imagine anyone wanting to hurt him. He promised he'd let me know if Dave contacted him.

I had also run down the companies Akar mentioned, calling each of them on the pretense of hiring Dave. All three had nothing but good things to report. Dave was prompt when called, fixed everything correctly, and offered helpful suggestions. I asked if anyone had used him to do a data audit or put in a new network or improved security procedures. I got a no from all of them, but the woman in Dr. Lam's office thought it might be something they should consider. I guess Dave owed me one. If he ever showed up.

I made a quick stop at my condo, put groceries away and continued to Pump Hill. The street the Boussards lived on was one continuous loop with two exits onto the main drag out of the neighbourhood. I parked near the closest exit and waited, keeping an eye on the Boussards' driveway in my rear-view mirror. It wasn't long before Dee Dee roared by in a white Escalade, probably to pick up her daughter. I pulled out my phone and called the house. A woman answered. I recollected the slight Australian accent.

"Jeannine? This is Jorja Knight." I explained who I was and that we met the night Carl Johnson collapsed at dinner. "Can I ask you a few questions?"

"Sure, but it'll have to be quick. I have to leave in a few minutes."

"Rose Johnson dropped by the house mid-afternoon on the day her husband collapsed at dinner. Did you happen to see her that afternoon?"

"Yes, I did."

"Do you know why she dropped by?"

"No. I was surprised to see her at the house."

"She wasn't in the habit of dropping by?"

"Hardly."

"Dee Dee and she aren't friends?"

"They're complete opposites. Mrs. Boussard has her kids, and she's active in the community. Mrs. Johnson stays at home. I don't know what she does with herself all day."

"Did you talk to her or know why she was there?"

"Yes. I asked if I could help her with something. She said she came by to remind us of Carl's allergies."

"Had she?"

"Several times." I could hear the annoyance in her voice. "This wasn't Mr. Johnson's first time at the house. We're all aware of his allergies. The Boussards even kept an extra EpiPen in the house as a precaution."

"Where in the house did you run into her?"

"In the back corridor, near the supply room."

"That's where the extra EpiPen was kept, isn't it?"

"That's right."

"Was it there the night of the dinner?"

"I think so. I believe one of the guests ran and got it when Mr. Johnson collapsed and used it."

"So, it wasn't there the next morning?"

"No. I imagine EMS took it away with them."

"Did you see which direction Mrs. Johnson came from when you saw her earlier that afternoon?"

"No. She was in the doorway of the supply room when I first spotted her."

"Did she leave after she spoke with you?"

"I assume so. Mrs. Boussard came down the hall to check on the recently delivered flowers, and I left."

"How did Rose get in?"

"I didn't let her in. I assume she came in the front door, which was unlocked. Security was here by three o'clock. She would have been directed to the front door, as her name was on the list of guests. The side door is for staff and deliveries."

The whole thing struck me as odd, and clearly Jeannine considered it out of character. If you didn't pal around with someone, would you invite yourself over to wander around their house unattended?

I thanked Jeannine for her time and was getting ready to pull away when a thin dark figure rounded the corner, head down, a swath of black hair falling across his face. The Boussards' man child. I watched him shuffle his way up the street, hands in pockets, shoulders curved forward. I guess he made his own way home from school, probably too old to be chauffeured by his mother. He couldn't be more than fifteen or sixteen.

I couldn't begin to imagine how the Boussards perceived his dyed, asymmetrical haircut, the charcoal-lined eyes and black fingernails. Reminiscent of Goth culture, yet different. Perhaps this was the new Goth, tight skinny, black jeans and a too-small black T-shirt. He was too cool to wear something warm like a jacket or sweater. Something about him tugged at my heart, and simultaneously warned me to stay away. I watched him in my rear-view mirror until he disappeared up the drive. Suddenly I felt exhausted...exhausted and uneasy.

FOURTEEN

MY CELL PHONE rang as I stuffed the last bite of waffle into my mouth.

"Hey, Lydia," I mumbled around it.

"The cops came by this morning."

"Yeah. What'd they want?"

"They want to talk to Dave."

"And?"

"They asked a bunch of questions. You know…who his friends are, where he worked. I told them we don't talk work. I don't get all his techie mumbo jumbo, so I don't encourage it by asking him how his day went."

"Did you get their names?"

"Yeah. A Detective Watters or Wadders. He had a woman in uniform with him. Didn't catch her name. Why?"

"In case they come see me. Did you mention you hired me to follow him because he seemed worried and was getting threats?"

"No."

"They're going to find out."

"Not from me they won't."

"Right. Okay…we'll see."

"I hope whoever's threatening me doesn't think I told them anything."

"Like what?"

"Uhm… Nothin'. I told you I don't know anything."

"That's good. Anything else?"

"Nope. Just that the cops came by. I assume you haven't found him?"

"You'll be the first to know when I do."

I sensed she wasn't telling me everything. And the minute I had actual proof, she would have to find someone else to play her game. I knew what the cops were thinking. This was no random break-and-enter attempt. Innocent victims of crime don't abandon their friends, jobs, and living quarters and go into hiding.

⤚

Calgary's lights faded in my rear-view mirror along with the daylight, while the faint glow of Airdrie's halo shimmered ahead. A community of roughly forty thousand, it was home to many who made the daily half-hour commute into Calgary for work. It was also where Dave Morgan's parents lived.

I had no trouble finding the house, an older split level, a few blocks west of the highway. The house, nothing fancy, sat in the middle of a small curve in the boulevard and was well maintained. Someone had recently raked up the leaves from the large poplar tree in the front, and the grass was trimmed, waiting for the inevitable blanket of snow.

I parked several houses down from the Morgans' and killed the lights. The front room drapes in the Morgan house were open, and I could see through the darkened front window to the lit kitchen. A woman moved in and out of view. Her tightly pin-curled hair and matronly figure reminded me of Rose. I assumed it was Dave's mother.

Soon the activity in the kitchen settled down and the woman disappeared. I slid out of the truck and made my way past the Morgans', down the block and around the corner. I crept down the back alley until I was directly behind the Morgans' house. A grey-haired man and the woman I'd seen earlier were at the kitchen table, eating. The rest of the house remained dark.

I strolled back around to the street, sauntered up the neighbours' driveway and hopped the two-foot-high hedge separating their property from the Morgans'. Kneeling, I cupped my hands around my eyes and peered into the basement window, first at the front of the house and then the one on the side. Both were covered tightly, leaving me with nothing for my efforts.

I moseyed back to my truck and got in. The temperature in the cab felt colder than outside. I pulled out my phone and punched in the Morgans' phone number. A woman answered.

"Oh, good evening. May I speak to Dave please?"

"I'm sorry, he's not here at the moment."

"Do you know when he'll be back?"

"Oh...no...I-I mean he doesn't live here anymore."

"Do you know how I can reach him?"

"No, sorry. I mean...you must have the wrong number. There's no one here named Dave."

If Dave was holed up in the basement, he should have spent more time coaching his mom on what to say. I watched the house for another hour, but nothing changed. The lights in the neighbour's house came on and several children ran in and out of the front room. It grew colder and darker. The silence crackled in my ears.

Suddenly I was aware of myself sitting alone on a dark street, while families gathered inside their homes to eat or settle down in front of the TV. Something dark and foreboding awakened in my soul and continued to grow. Maybe Carl's death reminded me how uncertain life really was. Reminded me of how close I had come to death myself when a distraught fellow employee at Global Analytix picked me as his hostage. How truly alone I was with both parents dead, any remaining family estranged. And I couldn't shut down my worry for Gab. I couldn't let anything happen to her. She was the closest thing to family I had.

My feet were like ice and my breath came out in white slivers and faded into nothingness. I couldn't—wouldn't let this feeling eat away at me. Again. All the books I read, all the therapy sessions I attended said the same thing. We create our own experiences on earth. All the shit that hurts…we create it. And because we're the creators of our own misery, we can theoretically change course, move on and find our happiness. We all possessed the ability. It was somewhere inside us. *Likely behind the liver or tucked in behind the thalamus.*

I took one last look at the warm glow of the Morgans' front room, fought back the emptiness filling my chest, and pointed the truck home.

FIFTEEN

THE FOLLOWING DAY it was in all the news. Carl Johnson's autopsy revealed various toxins in his body. But the toxins weren't what killed him. Carl died from a lethal dose of cyanide. The newscaster called it a bizarre twist to a death which had originally been attributed to anaphylactic shock. Carl Johnson's death was officially a homicide.

It was still early by the time I arrived at the office, but Gab was already there, hunched over the morning paper.

"Don't believe everything you read," I said, handing her a coffee I had picked up on the way.

"Listen to this." Gab read, "Guests were sickened at the party. One attendee speculated the food may have been tainted." She sat back. "Even though they found evidence of cyanide poisoning, they're still bringing up the dinner I served and toxins. I bet the attendee they refer to is Dee Dee."

"You have to admit, from a newspaper's perspective, it certainly makes for a more intriguing story. Did you manage to contact all the guests?"

"All except Mr. and Mrs. Gruba. They've already gone back to South Africa."

"What did you find out?"

I pulled up a chair as Gab pushed the paper aside and opened her laptop.

"A few but not all of the people seated at table two got sick. Kristen Lee got sick. By the way, I found out who she is. She works for the marketing firm hired to manage Riteweight's launch campaign. Kristen had the vegetarian dish, but Daryl Henshaw had the other vegetarian plate and said he felt fine."

"What about Dimitri Asentanko? He was at their table."

"He reported being queasy and shaky, but the effects wore off after a few hours."

"He's a pretty big guy, bigger than the others at the table. Or he might just have been feeling the aftermath of adrenaline considering he and JP fought hard to keep Carl alive until EMS arrived."

"We know Mr. Gruba became ill. You heard the retching noises emanating from the bathroom yourself."

"Right. And we know at table one, Rose didn't get sick, nor did Dee Dee or JP. Or at least none of them will admit to it."

"Mr. and Mrs. Walker reported a few hours of queasiness. Mr. Perez became ill, but his wife did not. And of course, there's Carl."

"When I cleared plates, I remember most of the guests at table two ate everything on their plates. At table one, Dee Dee left all her bean puree. JP ate everything. Rose left her puree, but Carl ate his. Mrs. and Mr. Walker's plates were licked clean. I don't remember the Perezes'."

"Well if the beans were the culprit, it might explain why Rose and Dee Dee didn't get sick. But not the others."

"What about the others?"

"Mrs. Hyde ended up going to the hospital, dehydrated. Her husband felt a little off but otherwise was fine. The accountant hasn't returned my calls."

"So, the same pattern. Random."

Gab had already checked websites and spoken with her suppliers. The last E. coli outbreak involved fresh spinach last summer. None of the suppliers reported any problems with any of the fresh produce, the meat or any dried spices. The meat had been stored cold, cooked through, and sent out to the dining room promptly. Underprepared beans, which could cause the type of gastrointestinal upset we saw people experiencing, remained the most likely source.

"Then there's the cyanide," said Gab. "Cyanide is found in a number of foods. Apricot seeds, apple seeds, almonds, lima beans and cassava root all contain cyanide. Thank god I didn't use any of those ingredients."

Our bodies could deal with small amounts of cyanide. Larger amounts were another issue. And larger didn't necessarily mean large. There were reports of children dying after consuming three or four cherry pits.

We studied the dinner guest list again.

"Maybe the guests who didn't get sick had strong constitutions," I said. "The least ill didn't eat the sweet potato and bean puree or not much of it or had a larger body weight."

Gab puzzled out loud. "Could the same thing apply if someone slipped cyanide into the food or their drinks?"

"I'm not sure tiny amounts of cyanide would create the type of reactions we saw."

"Dee Dee is so toxic she probably wouldn't even notice a tad more poison running through her veins," said Gab.

We couldn't eliminate much, but the undercooked beans remained first on the list of likely culprits for the gastrointestinal symptoms.

"Let's pray there's no cyanide in any of the samples I sent off. It would put me squarely in the limelight," said Gab.

"Not necessarily. If you tampered with the food, why send the tainted product to the lab?"

"Right," said Gab brightening at the thought. "I know I didn't slip cyanide into anything and I'm positive you didn't either. Carl's death and the food poisoning, if that is what it was, can't be related."

"Likely not. Then again, maybe someone tampered with the food to muddle the situation, throw suspicion off whoever killed Carl. It's certainly what…I mean, with both of us running in and out of the kitchen, someone could have slipped into the kitchen without much notice." I took a deep breath. "Detective Birdie had certainly been interested in who might have had access to the kitchen that night."

"Yeah but who?"

"It comes down to motive and ability." Detective Birdie's comment about Gab having a lot of debt flashed through my mind. I firmly put the thought away. I knew Gab had debt, thanks to that mooching, no-good ex of hers, but no way would she have taken money to mess with the food. "I can't help thinking Rose will end up an extremely wealthy woman."

"Yeah, and she was at the house earlier in the afternoon," said Gab eagerly.

"I'm sure she's at the top of homicide's list." I sat quietly mulling over the other names on the list. "I wonder how Carl's death impacts JP. Maybe they had some sort of partner clause, which leaves him the majority share in the company."

"What about Dee Dee? What if she was having an affair and Carl found out about it and threatened to tell JP?"

"Stanger things have happened. And women are more likely to poison their victim than men. Men prefer to bash the guy's head in. But I'm not sure it's a strong enough motive. There's a lot at stake here. Some of these people stand to make millions overnight."

"Good point. If Carl was the only person who ingested cyanide, someone could have slipped it into his food or drink anytime," said Gab.

"True, although it's pretty fast acting." I vaguely recalled Carl popping something into his mouth right after the main meal. It was so vague, I couldn't tell if it was a memory or an idea that had just popped into my mind. Probably just an after-dinner mint.

"I think we need to keep what happened to Carl separate from what happened to the other guests. If I were homicide, I'd be laying bets one of the guests poisoned Carl, not the catering staff."

"Let's hope they're as smart as you. But they keep mentioning toxins. It's the beans, I just know it."

I was comforted by Gab's continued insistence that the beans were what sickened the guests, even though it meant she would be front and centre if Health Canada investigated.

"Then we have to prove someone tampered with the beans," I said.

"How do we do that?"

"I saw a teenager in the back hall, shortly after I arrived. I think it might have been Dee Dee's son. I want to talk to him. Maybe he saw something."

"How are you going to do that? Dee Dee's not going to let you talk to him."

"Already on it. The kid's name is Malcolm. I followed him to the private school he attends, this morning. I'll be waiting for him when school lets out."

SIXTEEN

A BUZZING SOUND CUT the air, startling me. The front doors opened and a steady stream of young men with saggy jeans and backpacks and girls with cleavage poured out. I had no trouble spotting Malcolm and his friend. Both were dressed in skinny tight black jeans and T-shirts at least a size too small. A large crucifix hung from Malcolm's neck. Eyes downcast at separate cell phones, Malcolm and his friend made their way toward me, heads down, speaking to no one.

"Malcolm?"

An eye peered out from under a swatch of pitch-black hair hanging over his face.

"My name is Jorja Knight. I'm a private investigator. I was at your parents' dinner party, the night Carl Johnson died."

"You're the one who was digging through our garbage."

"A girl's gotta do what a girl's gotta do. My friend catered the dinner that night. She hired me to try and find out why a bunch of people became ill that evening. Mind if I ask you a few questions?"

Malcolm shrugged. His friend lifted a hand and continued down the sidewalk, turning right at the corner.

I walked alongside Malcolm. "Is that a yes?"

"Sure—if you walk with me to the bus. If I'm not home right after school, Dee Dee has a meltdown."

"Dee Dee's your mother?" His use of her first name threw me.

"She says she is." He snickered.

"I see. I saw you the day of the party," I said.

"The day old Carl died. Yeah. I got home around four, right after chess club."

"Did you see anyone when you got home?"

"Sure. Lots of people."

"Can you tell me what you did after you got home?"

"I came in through the side door, then went upstairs and dropped off my backpack. Then I came back down to find Dee Dee or Jeannine. I have to let one of them know I'm home."

"Grounded?"

"Thirty lousy days."

"So, you checked in?"

"I tried Jeannine. She wasn't in her office, so I went looking for her or the Deed in the dining room."

"And?"

"I found Jeannine, said hi and went upstairs."

"Did you see anyone else?"

"Rose was in the kitchen when I went by."

"Wait a minute. You saw Rose go into the kitchen?"

My mind raced over the timeline. After I arrived, Gab had sent me to the dining room to set tables. The flowers had arrived around then, and Gab had come into the dining room with the delivery guy to show him where to put them. Jeannine arrived and Gab had stopped to speak with her. They chatted for several minutes and left the dining room together.

"I didn't see her go into the kitchen. She was in the kitchen when I went down the hall to Jeannine's office and she was coming out of the kitchen when I came back down the hall."

"Rose Johnson?"

"Yup. That Rose."

The bus came, and he and I crowded on, along with fifty or sixty students. We ended up standing in the aisle hanging on to the bar overhead. I dwarfed him. The doors closed with a hiss and the bus lurched forward, throwing those of us standing back and then forward.

"What else do you remember," I asked, as the bus lumbered on.

"Not much."

"Where exactly in the kitchen was Rose when you saw her?"

"She was at the side counter. Her back was to me."

"The side counter. The one with the double sink?"

"Yup."

"What else did you see?"

He shrugged. "Nothing much. I was on my way back when I saw her come out of the kitchen. I turned at the stairwell and went upstairs."

It must have been around that time Gab had stepped into the back-hall washroom to change into her chef jacket.

"What did you do during dinner?"

"Played video games, Warcraft and other stuff."

"Did you eat?"

"Not what they ate. I have my own supply of food upstairs."

It must be a meagre supply. Each bone and joint in his neck and arms was visible. The tight-fitting clothes didn't help.

"Was your sister home?"

"No. She was at a friend's sleepover."

"Can you tell me what you heard or saw during dinner?"

"I didn't hear anything until the ambulance. When it pulled into the driveway, I came downstairs. I saw them loading Carl onto the stretcher. I figured he had a heart attack or something."

"You didn't want to know what happened?"

He shrugged again. "Not really."

I waited.

"In the morning, Jeannine told me Carl had an allergic reaction to something and had been taken to hospital."

"Anything else?"

"She said my mother was upset."

"That's all?"

He shrugged. "I found out later Carl didn't make it. Then I saw you rummaging in our garbage."

"You have good powers of observation. I figured dressing like a homeless person would be a decent disguise."

"Normally it'd be legit. But it's why I noticed you. There aren't many homeless hanging around Pump Hill. It doesn't appeal to our sensibilities, or so I'm told. The security guards run them off."

"Good to know. What was he like?"

"Who? Old Carl?" He swallowed hard, then shrugged. "He was okay. He didn't bother me none."

Carl had been barely a few years older than me. I was certain he'd refer to me as old Jorja after I left.

"What do you think of Rose?"

"She's okay. She's more like his mom than his wife."

"How so?"

"She was always warning him, fetching him stuff he didn't want. *Here's your glasses, Carl; Carl, you better not eat that; I brought you water, Carl.*" He shook his head.

"She and your mom didn't get along?"

"Nope. Here's my stop."

"Oh, okay." I peered past heads out the window. "Thanks for talking with me. I'm going to stay on and loop back to my truck."

He nodded and pushed his way toward the back door.

I don't know what I expected, but Malcolm seemed like a

decent kid. His choice of clothing might not be serving him well, but what did I know.

"Hey, emo," a pimply-faced kid called out. "That your girlfriend?" A few others snickered. Malcolm ducked his head and swung through the back doors. He brushed the swatch of hair from his eyes and stuffed his hands into the front pockets of his black jeans. The group sitting with the pimply-faced kid broke out laughing. Good thing I wasn't carrying a gun, or I would have pulled it and ordered them all on their knees.

The loop back was longer, taking most of an hour. Halfway back I managed to snag a seat. I sent Gab a text. *Rose was in the damn kitchen!*

Rose made no mention of it when I asked her why she dropped in at Dee Dee's during the afternoon. She hadn't poked her head in for a quick gander either. She had been standing at the far counter. The one with the double sinks. The counter where the kidney beans had stood waiting to be pureed. Now why did she feel she needed to keep that little tidbit a secret?

SEVENTEEN

AFTER RETRIEVING MY truck, I drove to a fast-food place and picked up a chicken salad and a bottle of water. Too wired to go home and veg out in front of the TV, I parked and contemplated my next move. I picked up the last shred of lettuce and stared at the bottom of the Styrofoam container. Turning the key in the ignition, the truck roared to life. I turned and looped through the drive thru, emerging with a strawberry milkshake and chocolate chip cookie in hand. I pulled out onto the main drag and turned in the direction of Rose's place.

The night Carl died had been a big deal. Riteweight acquired some new partners, which meant an influx of money. They had signed a deal with FWS Corporation for distribution and were ready to launch their product. Weight-loss supplements were cash-generating machines. Who wouldn't risk a mere nineteen ninety-five for a chance to lose weight fast—by doing nothing. Nothing but pop a small white pill each morning. A tiny investment for a potentially life-altering result. Of course, if it sounded too good to be true, it probably was.

I wondered if Rose would inherit Carl's share of the company. Would she also become JP's new partner? What would he think of that? Maybe I wasn't giving Rose enough credit. Perhaps the

Mrs. Doubtfire-like appearance masked a smart, clever and astute businesswoman inside. I thought back to our last conversation. She had said Carl wasn't allergic to beans, but he wouldn't eat them because they disagreed with him. But he had eaten them. And she seemed upset that he had. And then there was the whole bee thing. Had it been a ruse of sorts? Why did she say "No, he couldn't have" when I mentioned Carl may have been poisoned? Who couldn't have? Or did I mishear what she said. I parked across the street from Rose's house, pulled my sleeping bag out from behind the seat, unrolled and draped it over me. I settled in to watch.

Bolting upright, I shot a glance through the semicircle in front of me. *Where the hell was I?* Still disoriented from my abrupt awakening, my eyes focused on a growing square of yellow light. I pushed the sleeping bag off to one side and rubbed my arms. I was freezing. Using a corner of the sleeping bag, I wiped the condensation off the windshield and watched a car back out of the garage. Rose sat behind the wheel. I checked the clock on the dashboard. Nine-twenty. As soon as she drove by, I put the truck into gear and followed.

Rose pulled into one of the parking lots at the north end of Glenmore Park and turned the engine off. It was dark here, the reservoir a black void circled by glowing dots from the surrounding houses. Large snowflakes drifted silently to the ground, a nasty reminder longer nights and colder days were upon us. I killed my lights, pulled in at the opposite end of the parking lot and turned off the engine. Two lone cars remained in the parking lot, besides ours.

A few minutes later, a Cadillac Seville turned in and parked next to Rose's Subaru. Rose emerged from her vehicle and climbed into the Cadillac. I rooted around in the glove compartment until my hand landed on the cool exterior of my binoculars. Bringing the binoculars up to my eyes, I adjusted the focus. Rose and Dimitri came into view. They sat facing each other, talking. Rose swiped at her face with the back of her hand several times.

They talked for over an hour, an intense conversation. My feet were like ice cubes, the sleeping bag tucked in around me. I switched out the binoculars, pulled out my digital Sony and waited. Dimitri leaned across Rose and opened her door, flooding the interior with light. I zoomed in as he gave Rose a hug. Rose got out and climbed back into the Subaru. I watched Rose back out and pull away. Dimitri sat in his idling car for another ten minutes and then drove out of the parking lot. I waited a minute and followed him to a high-rise condo building in the downtown. I watched his car enter the underground parkade, then pointed my car south.

For the first time in days a shaft of light pierced the heaviness weighing on me. Rose had an evening rendezvous with Dimitri in a deserted parking lot merely days after her husband died. And she may have inherited her husband's interest in the company right before an expected windfall. Who would have imagined? Freakin' Dimitri and innocent bumbling Rose.

Had Rose tampered with the beans, hoping it would be enough to cause some sort of ill effect in Carl? Rose insisted kidney beans didn't agree with Carl, so why tamper with them? Unless she lied about Carl not liking beans to throw me off. Then again, the beans didn't kill him, even if they had been tampered with. The cyanide did. Had two separate people tried to kill Carl?

Rose and Dimitri both seemed upset minutes ago when I saw them conferring in Glenmore Park. What were they up to? Perhaps some plan wasn't working out like intended. Maybe someone else had been the intended target at dinner and Carl an accidental victim. Either way, I couldn't help feeling ridiculously pleased with myself. We had an eyewitness who saw Rose in the kitchen. It would go a long way to taking the focus off Gab. I started humming snippets of a song that was stuck in my head and arrived back at home invigorated and wide awake.

Firing up my laptop, I poured myself a scotch, sat down at the kitchen counter, and entered my query for anything on Dimitri. At first, I was puzzled by the bits of disjointed data I found on him. I dug through various databases then hit pay dirt. Dimitri Asentanko, formerly known as Azjientankovich, was a former Russian Olympian boxer. As best I could gather, Dimitri defected in 1984 sometime during the Olympic Summer games in Los Angeles. He lived in the United States for a while and eventually moved to Canada. While in the US, he sold his story, which may have been one way he bankrolled his career as an investor. Fascinated, I read excerpts from a news article on his rise to the top of his profession and his twice-botched attempts to defect.

I found his LinkedIn page which in turn pointed me to an Angel Investor site. I found his name associated with two start-ups in addition to be being listed on the Angel site as an investor. The Angel site contained information about investors seeking investment opportunities and entrepreneurs describing projects or ventures seeking capital, like a dating site but for business tycoons. I also found his name associated with two start-ups he funded in the last five years; both were reportedly doing well.

Still pumped from my recent discovery, I glanced at my watch. As good as the news was, it didn't warrant calling Gab at one in the morning. I marvelled at how my current investigation mirrored my experience in the lab. Any event can appear random or accidental if its context or purpose remains undiscovered. But if we take an event and start examining larger events around it, we gain greater perspective until the whole picture comes to view. Business guru Peter Senge called it systemic thinking; a process critical to solving business problems. But equally applicable to solving any problem. It's why all the great detectives started with the most minuscule of events and examined it in the context of when and where it occurred until the larger picture revealed the why. All I had to do was find out why Rose was in the kitchen the day Carl died and why she and Dimitri met in a deserted parking lot late at night.

EIGHTEEN

THE LOBBY SMELLED of wet carpet and dirt, no doubt brought on by last night's precipitation. Bypassing the elevator, I entered the stairwell and took the stairs, two at a time. I rushed down the hallway, not surprised to see our office door ajar.

"Hi, Gab. How are you holding out?"

"Fine."

"Just fine?" I grinned.

"I'm checking out what courses I need to become a sommelier," she said, nodding at her laptop screen.

"Good idea! Supplement your chef credentials."

"Or replace them."

"Aren't you the one always telling me negativity is wasted energy?"

"I'm not being negative. A good sommelier can make a ton of money. They get to taste the best wine, judge competitions, write articles and reviews. I'm already writing articles and blogging, but I don't make anywhere near the money they do. Some make a hundred and fifty thousand dollars a year."

"Wow."

I had spent a lifetime watching Gab flit from one venture to another. It wouldn't surprise me if this was going to be the next shiny object she chased. She was like a cat though, always landing on her feet. In a way, I envied her ability to live life with what I perceived to be carefree, unmapped direction.

"I might start today. Want to come over tonight and help me hone my tasting skills?"

"Sure. But I have to run out to Airdrie first. It would be late—say, around ten o'clock?"

"Works for me. My last booking just cancelled. Not like I have to get up early tomorrow or anything."

"Want to hear some good news?"

"Gawd yes."

"You know how I texted you that Dee Dee's kid saw Rose in the kitchen? Right by the beans?"

"Yeah."

"Rose might be playing footsies with the new investor, Dimitri."

"Noooooo!"

"Yes!"

"Maybe Rose killed Carl to get him out of the way for Dimitri!"

"They say love is one of the prime reasons for murder. And greed. In this case, both may be at play. And if Dimitri's recent investment in the company included voting shares, Dimitri and Rose might have controlling vote of the company."

"Oooh, even better. What do we do now?"

"First we need proof she tampered with the food," I said. "Malcolm saw Rose in the kitchen. Obviously, we weren't in the kitchen at the time. Seeing no one around, Rose didn't turn around and leave. She went all the way in, to the far counter. Why?"

"What if someone was in the kitchen when she first arrived, like Dee Dee or Jeannine?"

"A good premise. When Malcolm got home, he went in search

of Dee Dee or Jeannine. He saw Rose in the kitchen, alone. He continued down the hall to the dining room where he heard voices. He found Jeannine already in there. She could have been in the kitchen when Rose arrived, but that's not what she told me. Jeannine said she first spotted Rose in the back hallway, after the flowers were delivered."

"Okay, good. What about Dee Dee?"

"Malcolm said after he announced his arrival home to Jeannine, Dee Dee came into the dining room from the reception area. There are two ways in and out of the kitchen, both doors exiting onto the hallway. The shortest route from the kitchen to the dining room is the hallway. If Dee Dee had been in the kitchen a minute earlier, it wouldn't have made much sense for her to leave the kitchen, cut through the storage room, then the cloak room, and walk through the reception area, just to reach the dining room."

Gab considered it for a minute and nodded. "Makes sense. I remember right after the flowers arrived, you were still setting the tables, I checked with Jeannine as to which serving trays I should use, then stepped into the washroom and changed. I was out of the room for maybe five or six minutes."

"Okay, so Rose goes into the kitchen and no one's there. Why hang around? Better yet why go right across the entire kitchen over to the side counter?"

"She might have checked out what was being prepared."

"Possible," I replied.

"She might have even sampled something. Or added something!"

"It's the option I'm favouring. She seemed awfully upset when she met with Dimitri last night, though. I can't help wondering if she did something to the food to make people sick, but something went horribly wrong and Carl died."

"Maybe her target was someone else in the room? Like Dee Dee? From what I hear, they aren't exactly bosom buddies," said Gab.

"She'd have to be pretty angry to go after Dee Dee, but we can't discount the possibility someone other than Carl was supposed to die. First, we need to prove she did tamper with the beans. Then we can focus on why."

"How are we going to figure out if she did?"

"Let's assume she tampered with the food. The only food over at the side counter were the beans, right?"

"That's right. What? You think she added cyanide to the beans?"

"Ummm, maybe, but I'm thinking not. The guests who got ill seemed to have digestive issues, not respiratory issues like one might expect with cyanide. What if she added undercooked beans to yours? I mean, what with Carl's allergies, she already knew what was on the menu for the night."

"Oh, my gawd, that's it! You're brilliant. How are we going to prove it?" asked Gab.

"You told me most people purchase cooked beans. I know I do. Most of the stores I shop at don't even carry raw beans." I pulled up a map showing all the organic stores near the Boussards' and Johnsons' neighbourhoods. "Let's start with these."

I called each store representing myself as Mrs. Johnson's caterer. I said I was trying to track down the same variety of beans she had previously purchased, but she couldn't remember which store she purchased them from or the variety name. I asked if they had any way of telling if Mrs. Johnson purchased beans from their store in the last two or three weeks. The first store I called didn't carry raw kidney beans. The second store had sold to one customer, a caterer. It was the store Gab had used. Raw kidney beans weren't a hot-selling item. The fifth store I tried sold a pound and a half, three days before Carl's death and a half a pound yesterday. I was interested in the first order. It had been paid for by a credit card. A minute later I had confirmation the credit card belonged to Rose Johnson.

"Jorja," Gab squealed after I disconnected. "You did it. She must have substituted or added raw or undercooked kidney beans to the ones I prepared."

"Whoa. We still haven't proved the beans she bought made it into your dish, but this is a great start."

"So how do we find out if she did?'

"I have an idea that just might work."

NINETEEN

THE RESULTS FROM the samples Gab shipped off to the lab arrived. No cyanide, no heavy metals, no toxins. If anyone suspected Gab or I of tampering with the food, these results wouldn't do us much good since we were the ones to select the samples and send them in for testing. It did, however, tell us which items did not cause the illness suffered by Dee Dee's guests. We kept coming up with the same item: the kidney beans. It was time to extract the truth from Rose. All I needed to do was clear Gab's name with respect to the gastronomical upset. Homicide could deal with Carl's death.

At four o'clock I was standing on the Johnsons' doorstep. Today, Rose answered the door. She appeared more with it today, but tired. Someone should tell her the colour black is rarely flattering to those pushing fifty. And that murder is exhausting.

"Mrs. Johnson. Thank you for seeing me."

"Please, call me Rose." This time, she led me down the hall to a small lounge off the kitchen. She shuffled from side to side like an out-of-shape eighty-year-old woman, her long black skirt sweeping the floor behind her. I kept an eye out for the dogs, but they didn't appear.

"Would you like some coffee? Or tea? I just made a fresh pot."

"No thank you, Rose. I've been drinking coffee all morning and I've reached my limit."

She perched on the edge of a stiff, winged Queen Anne chair and motioned me to the other.

"I have some tough questions, but I think the answers will help both of us. I need to clear Ms. Rizzo's name. She is being vilified in the media. No one wants to hire a chef careless enough to sicken her clients. If we can expose what in fact did happen, it will clear her name and help you and the police find out what happened to Carl."

What little colour Rose had in her cheeks faded.

"What were you doing in the kitchen the afternoon Carl died?"

"I…I went there to talk to the chef. I wanted to make double sure she knew about Carl's allergies."

"Did you talk to her?"

"No. She wasn't there."

"But when you saw no one in the kitchen why didn't you leave?"

"I thought I'd wait a minute or two to see if she showed up."

"Did you notice the red kidney beans on the side counter?"

She tilted her head back, averting her eyes. Her chin quivered. After a minute, she lowered her head and glanced at me with moist eyes.

"I didn't notice anything. I waited a few minutes and left."

"It doesn't take many raw beans to make someone sick."

"I don't know why you're telling me this."

"Do you usually prepare meals using raw kidney beans?"

"No, not often."

"Why not?"

"They're too much trouble since you have to soak them for hours before cooking. And even though Carl wasn't allergic to beans, they didn't agree with him."

"So, you do know they're toxic if not properly prepared."

"Yes, of course."

"If they're so much trouble to prepare and they disagreed with Carl, and you yourself don't care for them, why did you purchase one and a half pounds of raw beans three days before Carl died?"

"I...I...I didn't." Her eyes searched the room wildly for a better answer. When they didn't find one, her gaze fell to her lap.

"Yes, you did. I have a store clerk who says you purchased one and a half pounds of raw kidney beans at their store. The police can easily get access to your credit cards or the receipts to confirm the date and the purchase."

"I didn't kill Carl. Oh please. I...I didn't kill Carl. Why would I tamper with the beans when I knew he wouldn't eat them?"

"I don't know. All I know is he did eat them, and he died. Other guests got sick. And my client's business is suffering. Her reputation and livelihood are at stake."

"He had so many allergies. I always worried about him. Why would I check to make sure the food didn't include anything he was allergic to and then try to kill him?"

"Perhaps you didn't mean to kill Carl. Maybe you intended to make one or more of the other guests sick. After all, you said yourself, you didn't think Carl would eat them. But he did. Maybe with all his allergies it affected him more than others."

She covered her mouth with the back of her hand to stifle the sobs bubbling up. She stood, her angst clear through teary eyes, turned and fled. Her skirt caught the vase on the side table and brought it crashing to the ground. I heard her sister call out to her. A minute later Nadine stood at the doorway.

"Sorry, I seem to have upset her yet again," I said, standing up to leave. "Her skirt caught the vase on her way out. It doesn't look salvageable."

Nadine sighed, shaking her head. "I've never seen her like

this. I know Carl's death has been a big shock, but I never imagined she'd fall apart like this. She can't sleep at night and cries all day. She's getting more depressed."

I knew from experience it was impossible to predict how someone would react to the death of a loved one. Those who were rock solid could dissolve into quaking sand, and the sensitive and meek find strength beyond measure. On the other hand, most murderers didn't fall apart so easily, especially ones who planned their murders. I made my way back to the truck while pondering if Rose was always this emotional or only when confronted with her actions the night Carl died. Maybe she carried out a plan concocted by Dimitri but was now breaking under the guilt that it had been her hand administering the final blow.

TWENTY

WEARING MY BEST dark-grey pencil skirt and black patent heels, I slid out of my truck and up the sidewalk to the House of Peace. The wind cut through my shawl and pulled and tugged at my hair, throwing strands across my face. The smell of dry leaves and barren soil barely discernible. The last few days hadn't yielded anything exciting except news of Carl's funeral. I pulled the plum pashmina tighter around my shoulders and stepped past several dark-suited men having their last hit of nicotine. I traipsed through the propped-open glass doors and smoothed down my hair.

The chapel was already filled to near capacity. I slid into an aisle seat at the back and peered over the heads in front of me. The coffin was classic, shiny mahogany with pewter hardware. A large photo of Carl Johnson stood to its right and a massive arrangement of white roses beneath it. Rose Johnson and her sister, Nadine, sat in the front pew. JP, Dee Dee, their two children sat behind them. The front pew on the other side of the chapel was occupied by an elderly couple along with a middle-aged man, a woman and two young men.

I spotted Daryl sitting about halfway back. The lawyer and his wife, who had also been at dinner the night Carl died, sat next to him. As the chapel filled, I kept an eye open for other guests who had been at the Boussards' dinner but couldn't spot them without making a spectacle of myself.

I glanced back and noticed Detective Birdie standing by the back door. They say murderers often attend their victim's funeral. Was he hoping to spot the wretched soul who did away with Carl? What would he make of my attendance? Or Gab's absence. The minister arrived, cutting short my musings, and the proceedings got underway.

Carl's life marched by on a large screen in front of us, the song *Blackbird* played in the background. Images of a chubby blond-haired boy changed to one of an impish teen, a proud university graduate, happy groom kissing his much thinner bride, Carl at various black-tie fundraisers, to the final picture of a dignified Carl proudly accepting his Order of Canada medal. JP took the pulpit and spoke of their escapades as young men, their long friendship and his respect for Carl as a business partner.

The middle-aged man in the front row turned out to be Carl's cousin. He mentioned the hardships Carl had endured as a child when his father died leaving his mother to raise Carl and his handicapped sister by herself. The sister had succumbed to her illness several years earlier and his mother last year. Carl had been an honest, upstanding, intelligent human being who could be counted on to do what he said he would and always helped those in need. No different than anyone else who died.

I'd choose cremation for myself. Nothing fancy afterward. Perhaps food and drink at my favourite bar, where my few friends could be spared the awkwardness of mingling with strangers while trying to come up with something nice to say.

Carl's casket was carried out to a waiting hearse. Dimitri was one of the pallbearers. I wondered how Carl would feel about that. Rose, her sister and a few family members and close friends, including the Boussards, climbed into waiting cars and drove off to execute the final interment. Lay him to rest. Odd phraseology considering his body had been drained, cut open, organs lifted out and studied in minute detail.

I joined the people who remained behind, laughing, chatting, eating cookies and drinking tea in the courtyard. The tall cotoneaster hedge buffered the wind, and the sun broke through the clouds. Life went on.

Detective Birdie was nowhere to be seen. Maybe he was keen to see who showed up at the gravesite. I noticed Daryl didn't accompany the family and close friends to the gravesite. I spotted him crossing the road and getting into an older-looking four-door sedan the colour of mud. I turned to find a tall man with a goatee standing in front of me.

"Hi. I'm Todd Cooper. I met Carl at Harvard. How did you know Carl?"

"Oh, you knew Carl for a long while. I met him quite recently at a business dinner. My name is Jorja." No need to mention I was the server at the dinner that did him in.

"What a waste. Carl was such a good man. I'm going to miss him. We're all going to miss him. I still can't believe he might have been murdered."

"Shocking, isn't it. And on the eve of his company going live, big time. Makes you wonder, doesn't it. I heard there's some big money involved. Somebody might have gotten greedy."

"I wonder if someone might have a more personal reason for wanting Carl dead."

"Really? Like what?"

"Carl's sister was born with several birth defects, the result of an anti-morning sickness drug his mother had been prescribed. Not Thalidomide. There were several drugs used after the Thalidomide disaster. Drugs to treat nausea after chemotherapy, prescribed 'off label' to treat morning sickness in pregnant women."

"Meaning there was no hard proof the drug was safe for expectant mothers."

"That's how it is, unfortunately. Human beings always end up being guinea pigs for anything new on the market."

"So how do you see the two connected?"

"Maybe someone has a beef with these quasi-pharmaceutical health-product companies. Had a bad experience with one of the other weight-loss products on the market. Decided they're all bad."

"An interesting thought. You think Carl may have been the token fall guy for the industry's mistakes?"

"Wouldn't surprise me."

I didn't buy into it. I might, if Carl had been run down in the street or pushed off a C-Train platform in front of an oncoming train. But he was killed at his long-time business partner's home, at dinner. More than likely by his wife, or his wife's lover, or a business partner or a disgruntled co-worker. Someone who was there that night. People well known to Carl and instrumental in Riteweight's imminent success or failure.

"Let's hope they catch whoever is responsible."

I was relieved Todd's theory didn't include accidental poisoning by the chef who prepared Carl's last meal. I mingled with the guests, hoping to pick up what little tidbit I could about Carl's life. Everyone claimed he was in the running for sainthood, but obviously at least one person didn't agree. Several people made comments about poor Rose, how devastated she was.

Finally, I slipped out of the courtyard, walked back to my truck and climbed into the cab. Glad to be out of the wind, I checked my hair in the rear-view mirror just as a black sedan drove by, followed by another. Those who went to Queen's Park Cemetery, for Carl's interment had returned.

I watched as Dimitri climbed out of the first sedan and turned to help Rose, who exited the vehicle headfirst. He waited and held out a hand to Nadine as she placed a patent leather heel onto the road and slid gracefully out. Nadine reached out to take her sister's arm, but Rose stepped back and leaned her head on Dimitri's arm. Dimitri placed his hand on her back as they crossed the street, leaving Nadine to follow. Her tight-lipped smile made it clear she disapproved of how chummy Rose and Dimitri looked.

Dee Dee and JP extracted themselves from the second car. The car drove off, maybe to take the kids home. Dee Dee held down a black pillbox hat with one hand and carried her Louis Vuitton bag with the other. She stopped several times during their short walk to speak sharply to JP, who followed behind. At the entrance to the courtyard, JP stopped and pulled a cell phone out of his jacket, looked at the screen and answered. Dee Dee marched on with one final directive issued over her shoulder. A man exiting the courtyard stood aside and bowed slightly as she passed. Dee Dee flashed him a blazing smile and stepped into the courtyard.

JP paced outside, phone to his ear. Whoever was on the other end was doing most of the talking. JP futilely smoothed back a lock of hair the wind repeatedly flung over his forehead, a scowl on his face. After he hung up, he looked around, then rushed across the street to one of several waiting taxis. Jaw set, he climbed into a taxi and seconds later the taxi drove off. Storm clouds were forming in paradise.

TWENTY-ONE

ARRIVED IN AIRDRIE with the last fingers of daylight. At first, I worried Lydia would be hounding me hourly, but other than one quick phone call, I hadn't heard from her in days. I had all sorts of theories as to why. Today, the Morgan residence remained dark. I parked a few doors down from the house and pulled my binoculars out of the glove compartment. Nothing moved inside.

I got out and walked briskly to the end of the block, crossed the street and ambled back on the other side. The Morgans' house remained dark. I made my way up the sidewalk, past the attached garage and to the front door. A quick glance through the garage window told me the Morgans were out. Both cars were gone. I had two choices, head home or freeze my ass off watching an empty house. I compromised. I'd wait an hour or until someone came home, whichever came first.

Back in the truck cab, I manoeuvred my leg around the gear shift, pulled up one leg of the ski pants I had brought with me, then the other. I took off my coat, added a sweater and zipped my coat back on. I wasn't comfortably warm, but my teeth stopped chattering.

An hour went by, then another twenty minutes. I glanced at

the house and sat up. The faint glow of light must be coming from the refrigerator, the rest of the room remained dark. I picked up my binoculars and focused. A shadow cut across the light and the kitchen went dark. I put down the binoculars, opened the door and slid out. I hurried across the street to the garage.

I couldn't see any movement in the kitchen through the darkened front room window. Crouching, I ran past the front window and around to the side of the house. It was even darker here. I slowly picked my way along the side of the house to the back. I crept around the corner. A large dark figure hurried toward the back fence.

"Hey, Dave. Dave? Is that you?"

He glanced over his shoulder, hitched up his pants and broke into a run.

"Dave, wait! I'm a friend of Lydia's," I yelled as I jogged across the back lawn to the gate. The gate slammed against the fence and bounced back open from the impact. I barrelled through the gate and into the back alley. A beefy guy sprinted down the gravel alley, already twenty feet ahead of me. This was either Dave, or someone who had just robbed the Morgans. Either way, I was going to find out.

I ran. The distance between us grew.

I couldn't let an out-of-shape, heavy-set guy wearing Chewbacca pyjama pants and carrying a backpack outrun me. I turned it on, pouring out everything I had. My legs and arms pumped furiously. My face jiggled. I was keeping pace, but he was at least thirty feet ahead of me. How long could I keep this up?

Forget the pain. You've got this.

Sweat trickled down the middle of my back. I swiped at the droplets on my forehead before they rolled into my eyes. *Damn ski pants.*

He was at the end of the alley now, paused momentarily,

looking both ways. He hitched up his pyjama pants, turned right and disappeared.

Pulling the night air deeply into my lungs, I picked it up a tiny bit more. Turning the corner, I spotted him running across the street toward a playground.

Head down, I ran full tilt. I was gaining on him. I could hear his ragged breathing. *Or is that me?*

Suddenly I was airborne.

Everything fell away, and I lost sight of Dave. I saw the grass coming up toward me in slow motion.

My hands scraped along dirt and gravel. I rolled several times and came to a stop on my back. The dark sky above me continued to swirl.

I raised myself on one elbow and gazed around.

A playground elephant mounted on a spring grinned down at me. A foot further and I could have impaled myself on his upturned trunk. Someone should report it as a safety issue.

I peered over my shoulder. The playground was encircled by a wire cable strung two feet off the ground between three-foot-high posts. *Shit.*

I pulled myself into a kneeling position and staggered to my feet. My chest hurt and it was hard to breathe. I moved my arms and legs. Nothing broken. *Thank goodness for the ski pants.* I crawled back over the wire, holding onto the wooden post for balance, and hobbled up the street. For some peculiar reason, my teeth hurt.

It was painful getting back into the truck cab. My hands shook as I slipped the key out of my jacket pocket and fit it into the ignition. I pulled down the sun visor and flipped open the mirror. Reaching up I flicked off the piece of gravel imbedded in my forehead. A quick check revealed the small space between my front teeth remained the same size. *Freaking hell*. I couldn't believe he got away.

⟨⟨⟩

I woke up stiff and sore. And mad. I swung my legs over the side of the bed, confirming it wasn't going to be a fun day. I shuffled into the bathroom, popped two Advil and turned on the shower. I was out of shampoo. *Screw it*. Grabbing the soap off my counter, I climbed into the shower and stood with my back to the spray until the water went cool. Now I was hungry. I towelled off and returned to the bedroom. A quick look outside and I pulled on a sweater to go with my jeans. Summer breeze. It looked blue to me, but nothing was named a normal colour anymore.

I made my way into the kitchen and pulled open the fridge door. My anger returned. I couldn't believe Dave escaped. And not by leaping off a cliff into a raging river or jumping onto the roof of a fast-moving train. He outran me wearing *Chewbacca* pyjama pants and left me eating dust in a playground.

I opened a yogurt, three days past its expiry date, picked up my cell phone and punched in Lydia's number.

"I saw Dave last night," I said as soon as she answered.

"Oh, my god. Is he all right?"

"He seemed in pretty good shape."

"Where was he?"

"At his parents' house…raiding their refrigerator."

The pause was deafening. "Lydia? Are you okay?"

"Yeah. Fabulous."

"What's wrong?"

"Just pissed he didn't call me."

I could relate. "Well, I guess you can go ahead and call his mom now."

"Thanks. I'm going to wring his freaking neck."

Aww, the love between those two. I hung up. My job was done. I found Dave and now I could move on. The fact he was hiding out days after someone tried shooting him was reason enough to feel relieved to have Lydia off my roster of clients. I wondered if he stole or *borrowed* something from his client and then tried bargaining with them for his silence. If the cops came asking me about him, I'd tell them what I knew, but with Lydia reassured Dave was alive and hiding out in Airdrie, my life could return to normal. Normal meant scrounging for more work. Gab was in the same boat, which made me feel better momentarily, then ashamed for thinking that way.

The phone interrupted my thoughts. Rose Johnson's name popped up on the screen.

"Hello?"

"Jorja? Ms. Knight? Oh please. I don't know what to do. You have to help me."

TWENTY-TWO

ROSE OPENED THE door before I reached the top step. The navy-blue yoga pants she wore today highlighted each bump and ripple on her thighs. An old stretched-out grey sweater clung unflatteringly to her chest, the uneven neckline and irregular stitches smacked of homemade. She clutched the now familiar wad of tissue in her hand and had several more tucked into her sleeve.

"Thank you for coming. I didn't know who else to call. Please come in."

I followed her back to the lounge off the kitchen where we had sat before, keeping one eye open for the Dobermans. I selected the same stiff Queen Anne chair as before, Rose the other. She ran her hand through her short grey curls, pulling the ends out straight and letting them spring back into a medusa-like shape. She crossed her leg, the ballet flat dangling off the end of her toes. I watched it dance as her foot jiggled. Her expression was frozen, vacant, the makeup, if any, long wiped away by Kleenex.

"The police came by this morning."

I waited.

"Why did you tell them about the beans?" Her tear ducts sprang into action.

I sighed. "I didn't. Is this why you asked me here? To accuse me of doing something I haven't done. You might have more in common with Mrs. Boussard than you think."

"The police know I purchased the dried kidney beans a few days before Carl died. If you didn't tell them then how'd they know?"

I stifled a scream and took a deep breath.

"Because they're the police? It's what they do, you know. Figure shit out. If I can find stuff out, imagine what they can do, with all their resources. I'm just a lonely team of one."

"They wanted to know what I did with the beans."

"What did you do with them?"

"I told them I made chili."

"They didn't believe you, did they?" Even I could tell it would have made a hell of a lot of chili, more than one could imagine fixing for one or two people.

Her voice wavered, rising four octaves. "No. They demanded to know who ate it, why I made such a large quantity, what I did with the leftovers. They think I killed Carl."

"Now why would they think that?"

Rose missed the sarcasm. "I don't know. It couldn't have been the beans. Carl didn't even like beans. I don't know why he ate them."

"Why did you buy them? You didn't make chili, did you?"

"Nooooo," she wailed.

I waited. Was she always like this? Maybe Carl killed himself by wolfing down the beans and any other allergens he could find. I would have been sorely tempted had I been in his shoes.

"I...I...I did buy the beans." She hiccupped. "I saw the menu for the dinner a few days before...you know 'cause of Carl's allergies. I soaked the beans for an hour or two and cooked them just enough for them to soften. Then on the day of the dinner party

I went over to Dee Dee's. I poured out some of the cooked beans sitting on the counter into a freezer bag and replaced them with the ones I had prepared."

"What? You did this knowing undercooked beans can cause people to get sick, genuinely sick?"

Her face flamed red. "Yes," she whispered. "But I didn't expect Carl to eat them. He didn't like kidney beans."

"So why did you do it?"

"I only meant to get back at them."

"Get back at whom? For what?"

She studied her hands, which were shredding tissues into pieces.

"You don't know what it's like to be around that…that…bitch," she spit out. "There, I said it. The constant putdowns. And JP is just as despicable, laughing at her comments. And Carl…sticking up for them both." She shook her head and wiped her nose with the back of her hand. "I see how they look at me. I wanted to ruin their posh little celebration. I didn't want anyone to die…I wanted them to feel ashamed and embarrassed…just once."

An image of Rose, standing alone, looking miserable at the Boussards' dinner floated through my mind. I waited.

"Then it all went all wrong." She wavered. "Carl ate the bean puree and you opened the window and a bee flew in and stung Carl and your friend is losing business and Dee Dee is going around making snide comments and now the police think I killed Carl."

"What makes them think it was you? What did they say?"

"They don't think the beans killed him. They think the beans were meant to muddle the situation and take attention off how Carl was actually killed."

"Ah yes, the news reports said it was cyanide."

"I'm so confused. They found a lot of adrenaline in his body. More than they expected from the epinephrine injections JP and the paramedics gave him. They said his heart went into cardiac arrest. If it did, it would increase the adrenaline even more. But he also had mercury and cyanide in his system. It's all so confusing. Kidney beans don't contain cyanide. And they kept pushing me for answers, what Carl and my relationship was like, how we got to the Boussards', what we talked about enroute."

"Was Detective Birdie one of the officers who came?"

"Yes. He kept asking questions about our finances. He thinks I did it for the money! I told him I didn't have anything to do with Carl's death. I loved Carl. Why would I want him dead?"

Beads of sweat stood out on her forehead, her face now a bright red.

"Because of this." I reached down and pulled a photo from my purse. A photo of her and Dimitri at Glenmore Park.

TWENTY-THREE

I JUMPED, THINKING A steam kettle had gone off, until I realized the sound was coming from Rose. I glanced at the door, certain the high pitch would summon the Dobermans. Instead her sister came at a run. She shot me an annoyed look and rushed over to Rose, who lay slumped over the arm of her chair. Nadine put her arm around Rose and urged her to stand up. But Rose arched back, dug her heels into the Persian carpet and waved her off. Nadine left to make a pot of tea.

I didn't know if I should go over and pat Rose's shoulder, wait or leave. I sat silently feeding her a steady supply of Kleenex from the box on the coffee table. A lot of snot came out of that woman over the next twenty minutes. Slowly mucus production diminished, and her puffy red eyes refused to produce any more tears.

"Are you going to tell me what's going on?"

"I miss Carl." She hiccupped. "I do. I truly did love him…he was my first and true love."

"But…?"

Rose blew her nose loudly and sat up straighter. "After seventeen years of marriage I know where I stood. Carl loved me, but I wasn't *his* first love." She dabbed at her eyes. "Carl loved his work. He loved playing golf, then came watching football…and his charities. I was way down on the list. I was married and yet the loneliest person I knew. At least single people occasionally go out on a date. I mean, sure there were parties and events I went to with Carl, but they were all work or charity related. Over the years, I grew to resent each one more and more."

She wasn't painting the kind of picture her defence lawyer would be wanting.

"I didn't always look like this." Her arms flew dismissively across her plump body, spread over the cushions. "The more miserable I became the bigger I grew. I hated it when Carl began chiding me. Warning me to not eat certain foods...right in front of people." She dabbed her eyes again. "I didn't make jokes about the size of his...his...penis. How dare he demean me like that!"

The show of backbone tweaked my attention and a tiny bit of admiration.

She leaned forward, her face contorted in pain. "I had enough. Even after the company became successful, it would by no means be the end of it. Not for Carl. I'd never have the children and family life I wanted." She dabbed at her eyes. "And to think...I knit my ass off for that man!"

"So, you had an affair with Dimitri?"

"No! Well, not technically."

Oh please, not the Clinton defence. "Okay. Then what?"

"We're just friends. I met Dimitri this past spring, through Carl. We had him over to dinner a few times. He's the only man who paid attention to me since Carl and I met. He's interested in me, what I do, my opinion, what I like or don't like. I started to imagine what it would be like to leave Carl and live a different life. But it was a fantasy. I'd never be brave enough to leave Carl. Now...he's gone," she wailed. Her shoulders shook and after a minute or two she emptied more mucus.

I handed her several new tissues. "So, you and Dimitri became friends."

"Yes. Dimitri and I enjoyed going for walks or chatting over coffee. I never slept with him. I'd never do that to Carl. I don't feel like I was cheating on our marriage by spending time with Dimitri. Besides,"—her chin tilted upward—"if that's the definition of cheating, then Carl's been cheating on me his whole life."

She had a point. Empathy was creeping in. I had once spent three years of my life with a narcissist, investing my emotions, time and affection and getting little back in return. It was like flirting with a black hole. It sucked all the energy out of me, until I had nothing left. Once you reach emotional bankruptcy you start to self-destruct. There're lots of ways—food, alcohol, out-of-control shopping, risky sex with strangers. Desperate attempts to restore a hint of emotional equilibrium.

"What I was doing wasn't on the up and up, but I wasn't planning to leave Carl, let alone kill him. I couldn't ever kill anybody. I can't even watch the abandoned animals on the humane society commercials without crying."

I could totally relate. Those ads were heartbreaking.

"So, you played this stupid prank at my client's expense, in hopes of ruining dinner for the Boussards and their guests? Is that it?"

"I wasn't even thinking. I never meant anyone any harm. I just wanted Dee Dee to feel humiliated, just once."

"But the police presume you had a hand in Carl's death. Do they know about your friendship with Dimitri? Did they mention why they're focusing on you?"

"I don't know. I guess because I get Carl's share of the company. And the house. But it's mortgaged to the hilt." She sounded baffled.

"So right before the product launch and hot on the heels of a new influx of capital, from the man you claim is now your friend, you inherit Carl's shares in the company."

"Yes."

"Any idea of what the company may be worth?"

"I don't know. I guess if it goes well it could be a couple hundred million dollars. At least that's what Carl said."

I raised my eyebrows.

"But I'm innocent. I know I hurt your client. I want to make amends. I want to set it right with her. And I want you to find out who killed Carl...because I didn't."

This was a new one on me. I'd never had a primary suspect in a case ask me to work for them. It didn't seem right. Wouldn't this be a conflict of interest between my client, Gab, and her? I had a creepy visceral sensation in my gut telling me she wasn't being truthful. Then again, I wasn't in the habit of turning down much-needed work. But my gut was telling me to.

"I'm sure you realize how bad this looks. You've outlined three possible motives for Carl's murder, your unhappy marriage and growing distance from Carl, increased ownership of a multi-million-dollar company and a potential new love interest. You had opportunity, since you were the one seated closest to Carl. Once there is motive and opportunity all the police have to do is focus on finding out the means. You could have easily slipped cyanide into his food or drink."

"But I didn't! Where would I get cyanide? I know it looks bad. That's why I need your help."

"Do you have a lawyer? I mean, a criminal lawyer?"

"No, just Dan. He came over when the police were here. I asked Nadine to call. He's Riteweight's lawyer but he's always handled Carl's and my taxes, wills, all our personal filings."

"I can't take your case until I have successfully closed the current one I'm working on for Ms. Rizzo. You've admitted to switching the beans with undercooked ones. Undercooked beans cause gastrointestinal distress consistent with the symptoms being experienced by those who were at the Boussards' dinner. Unfortunately, there is still the issue of Ms. Rizzo's reputation. You might want to talk to your lawyer and discuss options. I'm sure he or she will advise you on how you might come forward with an apology without opening yourself up to a lawsuit. Otherwise, someone at the dinner may want to file charges against you for mischief and possible endangerment of human life. In the meantime, I'll inform my client of our latest conversation. I have no idea what she's going to do with the information."

I doubted Gab would launch a lawsuit. Lawsuits cost money she didn't have. But I wasn't going to let Rose off this easily. Even though her life sucked, it was no excuse for harming someone else or infringing on their opportunities.

"Please, you have to believe me. I'll make it right with your client. I promise."

"I'm sure my client will be happy when you do. I hope it includes a meeting between Ms. Rizzo, yourself and the Boussards to fess up and set the record straight. It appears Dee Dee is my client's biggest source of slanderous gossip and probably the one who mentioned my client's catering company's name to the newspapers."

"Okay," she whispered.

"Once this case is settled, we can talk."

She seemed to brighten slightly at this last comment. I still wasn't sure I wanted to be the one collecting evidence for the defence on this case in the event Rose was charged. Rose accompanied me to the front door. We stepped out into the hallway in time to catch sight of Nadine's backside disappearing around the corner. Next time, Rose should just invite Nadine to join us since she was hell-bent on hearing what was being said anyway.

I climbed into my truck and sent Gab a quick text, *Good news—the culprit confessed. Meet me later?* Gab would be relieved. In a few months, no one would connect Thyme to Dine with this unfortunate event. But a nagging thought intruded, telling me this wasn't the last of it.

TWENTY-FOUR

A FEW DAYS AFTER Rose's admission to me, Gab and I were called to a meeting with Rose and the Boussards. JP didn't show but Riteweight's lawyer, Dan Hyde, attended as did a Mr. Porter, a mediator hired by Rose on the recommendation of her lawyer. I looked over at Gab as we took our seats around the table. She looked visibly relieved to hear JP wouldn't be joining us.

Mr. Porter introduced himself, ran through some logistical matters pertaining to the meeting and began the proceedings.

"Since no one has filed a claim of injury, I'm here to help you try to reach a mutually acceptable agreement on your own, rather than drag this matter through the courts. As Mr. Hyde represents both the Johnsons' and Boussards' legal interests, at least as it pertains to their financial matters, he is here merely to observe, not to advise. If you have a question, Mr. Hyde, I will respectfully ask you direct that question to me and not the other parties present. Now, Ms. Rizzo, Mrs. Boussard, Mrs. Johnson, are you willing and capable to make a decision regarding the resolution of this matter at this meeting, without further advice or help?" After receiving three yeses, Mr. Porter outlined each party's rights and entitlements, and what to expect from the meeting.

"Now I'll ask for an uninterrupted statement from each of you, regarding your position pertaining to the matter at hand. I'd like to start with Rose Johnson."

Rose made no admission of ill will or intent. She appeared nervous but well practised in what she needed to say. Rose claimed it had all been a horrible mistake. In her desire to substitute organic kidney beans for the ones Gab prepared, she didn't realize they were improperly prepared. She had her story, and she was sticking with it. She even referenced her daily visits to the office to personally bring Carl his lunch, ensuring it was allergen free. Her good intentions had clearly gotten out of hand.

It was a good move. I had wondered how her lawyer was going to advise her to handle it. As bizarre as her behaviour had been, laying out the whole episode as a well-meaning mistake in judgment would make it hard for anyone to successfully sue her.

"I'm truly sorry, Dee Dee. My overprotective and obsessive behaviour ruined a beautiful evening." Rose began to sniffle. "And Carl paid the ultimate price for my meddling. Please forgive me, Dee Dee. Although I won't blame you if you don't."

Dee Dee gave a gruff *hmmmf* in reply and nodded her acceptance. But the glimmer in her eye and the smug curve tugging at her mouth left me no doubt she was relishing the dirt she now had on Rose.

Rose turned to Gab. "I'm so sorry, Ms. Rizzo. I had no business in the kitchen and certainly no right to mess with the food. I realize all the negative publicity that occurred as a result of what I did has impacted not only your reputation but your business. I take full responsibility for that. I want to set it right."

Gab in turn stated that in addition to her reputation, the damage to her business was tangible as three bookings were cancelled immediately following the news of her role the night Carl died and she had yet to book a client since.

"What about my reputation," said Dee Dee. "My name was splashed across the media as well."

Mr. Porter addressed his next comment to the whole group. "As far as damages go, if you are claiming damages, you will need to prove those losses, in order to recover them. Is that clear?"

Through some clever questioning, he finally got Dee Dee to admit the probability of harm to her and JP's personal finances or to their business was low. Rose readily offered to compensate Gab for the revenue she lost as a result of cancellations.

Gab walked out of the meeting jubilant. "Wow. That went way better than I expected."

"I was impressed by how Rose handled herself. I had no idea she had it in her."

"I admit, that took some guts," said Gab. "Especially as you just know Dee Dee is going to use this against her forever."

"Maybe after losing her husband, she feels it's a small price to pay for how things turned out."

"What, you think she actually meant for Carl to get sick? But he died from cyanide poisoning."

"He did. I really don't know what Rose was thinking. She told me in private she wanted to ruin the Boussards' perfect little dinner. Humiliate them. She's hurting though, that much is clear. Whether it's grief or guilt remains to be seen."

I couldn't help but think she wasn't the only one who would benefit from Carl's death. Especially if their weight-loss product was a success. Dimitri might benefit as well. But I'd need to know more about his business relationship with Riteweight and his personal relationship with Rose before jumping to conclusions.

Gab and I went to our favourite restaurant to celebrate. We had no sooner been seated when my cell rang. I rolled my eyes. "It's Rose."

"Jorja? It's Rose. I need your help. I really need your help.

I'm scared. Detective Birdie showed up again, while we were in our meeting. They had a search warrant. They started questioning Nadine about the company, about our personal finances. They went through the whole house. They took things in the medicine cabinet, my personal computer. Even went through my gardening supplies in the shed out back."

This is how the universe repaid good deeds. By helping Gab, I was now being offered an opportunity to take on a paying client. I had a quick ethical discussion with myself. Should I take on the work if I suspected she was guilty? Was she guilty? She came off completely mild mannered, naïve. It could be a clever act. On the other hand, just because someone was paying me, didn't mean I had to hide incriminating information if I came across it. But it could open up a whole lot of ugliness I didn't want to sign up for. I didn't have to accept right now.

"I'm tied up at the minute, Rose. I can come by in the morning. I'm not promising to take your case. But we can talk."

If Rose didn't throw me something that worked in her favour at the meeting, I would politely decline.

TWENTY-FIVE

I STILL WASN'T SURE what I would do by the time I pulled up to Rose's house the next morning. Nadine was loading a suitcase into a red Nissan Rogue as I climbed out of my truck, her Dobermans already in the back. Rose waited in her doorway.

"Hi, Rose."

"Jorja, come in."

"Is your sister going back home?"

"Yes. But she'll be back. She's coming to live with me." Rose didn't seem overly excited with her announcement.

"How nice." I didn't know what else to say. "She's not married?"

"She's a widow. Like me," she added with surprise. "Her husband died two years ago."

Now, I vaguely remembered coming across the obituary. "That must have been hard on her. Where's home for Nadine?"

"Lethbridge. But she's been staying with me and Carl on and off this past year. She's all alone. My niece, her daughter, lives in Melbourne with her husband. Now I'm here in this big house—all alone." Her voice trailed off.

Today we sat in the front living room. I looked around. They must have used a professional decorator. One who loved fussy fabrics, and anything curved and gilded. Maybe Carl or Rose had an interest in period furniture. But then why cover it with hand-crocheted doilies and the knit Afghans that lay everywhere? Perhaps it was evidence of compromise. Carl may have liked the décor and Rose may have put her finishing touches on it. She was clearly more comfortable in sweats and I could easily see her happily mucking around in a garden or sitting in the kitchen knitting. I chose an upholstered chair with ornately carved wood arms and back, while Rose perched on the edge of what appeared to be an extremely firm sofa.

"I want you to find who killed Carl. I promise you, I didn't."

"There are a few things we need to talk about first. You say you didn't kill Carl. Okay. Who had reason to see him gone?" I held up my hand as she opened her mouth to argue. "Look, unless you come up with a few names and reasons, you're the one left standing in the spotlight."

"But I don't know why anyone would want him dead."

"Let's start with this recent investment in capital in the company. This Dimitri Asentanko. He's a relatively new investor. And he in turn has brought in other investors?"

She blushed. "Yes, that's right. You know, it was Carl's idea. He wanted it. He said it was going to change our lives, payoff for years of hard work."

"Although I don't know any of the business details, from where I sit, it looks like you, Dimitri and JP all benefit from Carl's death."

"I don't care about things like that."

"Oh, but the jurors will, if it comes to that."

"That's ridiculous. Then I want out. I'll sell my interest in the company."

"Really? Anyone made you an offer recently?"

Rose squirmed. "Why are you asking me this? I'm not good at business. I majored in Home Economics in university. I was working as a nutritionist at the hospital when I met Carl. He was visiting his sister at the time. Poor thing. She was in and out of the hospital. Carl and I began seeing each other and we got married a few years later. Then Carl started Riteweight with JP. He was working long hours and we decided it would make more sense for me to quit working and look after the home front while he focused on business."

"So, JP was excited. Carl was excited. Dimitri was happy. The company was getting ready to hit the big times. Everything was perfect. Everyone is happy."

"Well…not exactly."

"Oh?"

"I don't know. Carl was stressed, nervous. I asked him what was worrying him a couple of times, but he said I wouldn't understand…just business." She sniffled; a tear rolled down her cheek.

I glanced around the room. If there had been scotch around, I would have poured myself one.

"I feel so guilty," said Rose softly.

"Guilty?" I leaned forward, anxious for her answer. "Why?"

"There were days I wished the whole thing would crater. Even if it meant we lost the house and had to start over."

Guilt had a long shelf life. It could reach out and play with your head relentlessly years later, unless you forgave yourself. Easier said than done. I was a master at suppressing guilt but a novice at forgiving myself. I had been so angry at my father, I cut off all contact not only with him but with my mother and my brother. Now both my parents were gone. I regretted not ever calmly letting my father know how his drunken abusive behaviour impacted me, let alone reaching forgiveness. I regretted not genuinely getting to know my mother, having lumped her in with my father for failing to intervene. And now I never would. The distance between my brother and I wasn't merely geographical.

He blamed me for the family strife since I refused not to argue with a drunk. Which always ended badly, for all of us. I know he saw me as selfish and uncaring and I suppose at sixteen I had been. And even though I told myself it was done, in the past, that I was young, naïve, there were still days when my own behaviour in fuelling a toxic family dynamic haunted me.

Rose's sniffles subsided, and I refocused my thoughts back to her.

"You thought if the whole thing blew apart, you'd have Carl back to yourself."

She nodded miserably. "Yes. And when it looked like it might come apart, I felt awful for even thinking it. But there's no way Carl would give up. He never gave up on anything. Even me."

This I understood. If Carl didn't give up on the marriage, and she was unhappy, then she'd have to be the bad guy and leave. Or put up with being number seven on his priority list.

"What made you think the deal might come apart?"

"I told you. Carl was nervous. He wanted more time before they launched."

"Why? What was making him nervous?"

"I don't know."

"Come on, Rose. Something must have happened."

"All I know is that a few months ago, Daryl and Carl had an argument. It was quite late. I had already gone upstairs and fell asleep reading. I woke up around one in the morning. I heard voices downstairs. I thought Carl had fallen asleep in front of the TV, like he sometimes did. I went out to the hall landing. But it wasn't the TV. The voices were coming from Carl's study. I couldn't make out anything but a few seconds later the door opened, and Daryl stormed out."

I waited for her to continue.

"Carl came out after him. He yelled that he didn't care

what Daryl said, they weren't going to go ahead until he got some answers."

"Do you have any idea what they were arguing about?"

"No. I went back to my bedroom. But I could hear Carl on the phone with someone after Daryl left. I don't know who. Probably JP."

"You didn't ask him what happened?"

"No. I didn't know what to do. I've never seen Carl so angry."

"Anything else?"

"Nothing really."

"So, Carl and Daryl had this big argument and then everything went on as normal?"

"I recall there were some meetings behind closed doors, more than usual."

"With whom?"

"JP, Daryl, Kristen and a couple of others I didn't know. Maybe I'm being silly. It makes sense there would be more meetings closer to the launch date, wouldn't it?"

"But not meetings with Dimitri and the other investors?"

"Oh no. They may have met at the office but not here at the house. I usually saw them at an event, like the dinner at Dee Dee's. And Carl and I had dinner with Dimitri and the Boussards at a restaurant a couple of times."

"What about you and Dimitri? You said you met with him a few times."

"Yes." Her face flushed. "I first met Dimitri at dinner with Carl. A couple of days later I bumped into him in the lobby of Carl's office building. We chatted, and he said he'd love to have coffee with me one day. We met a few days later."

"Did you talk about the company?"

"No."

She stared down at her hands which lay in her lap. I waited a few minutes.

"Never discussed Riteweight?"

"Not specifically. We would talk about what we would do if we became enormously wealthy…silly sorts of things."

"What *we* would do?"

"Yes. I mean separately, each. No…not together…not like that."

"Did you tell him about the argument between Carl and Daryl?"

"Well I couldn't, could I? I told you I have no idea what they were arguing about."

"But you did tell him they were arguing?"

"I might have mentioned it."

Pinning her down was like nailing Jello to a wall.

"Did he know you would inherit Carl's interest in the company?"

"I suppose he must have. But you'd best ask Dan."

"I will."

Her eyes widened slowly. "There's no way Dimitri had anything to do with Carl's death."

"How do you know?"

"He's not that kind of person. He'd never hurt anyone." The tone of her voice was defiant and a tad whiny. "He's a kind, understanding man."

"Let's face it, Rose. There is a high probability someone at dinner had something to do with Carl's death. Putting aside the heartache and regret, you do benefit from Carl's death or at least it would appear so at first glance. If anyone makes the connection between you and Dimitri, like I did, he'll also come under suspicion. Some might speculate the two of you planned this. With Carl out of the way, you and Dimitri can pursue your relationship, and if the company is a success the two of you, singularly or together, won't exactly have money problems."

"No. That's not what happened. Dimitri has nothing to do with this."

Insisting he didn't do it didn't make it so, but Rose wasn't open to the potential lifeline I was throwing in her direction.

"Let's say it wasn't you or Dimitri. What reason would JP have for killing Carl?"

"I don't know."

"Are you saying you don't know, or you've given it no consideration?"

She pondered for a minute. "I can't imagine why he'd want Carl dead. They've been partners and friends for years."

She was going to be a potential nightmare for JP. Each meeting would require at least two boxes of tissues. Admin expenses would go up. Then on the other hand he might be able to convince her to nod her head when it came to decisions. If she insisted on being involved in how the company was run, it could be an issue for him. Or if she and Dimitri buddied up.

"Okay, let's consider Dee Dee. How is she better off with Carl dead?"

Rose shrugged and shook her head. Her lips formed a straight tight line. She massaged one hand alternately with the other. Her voice wavered. "I know it looks bad. Now you know why I need your help."

"I don't know why I'm even considering this, Rose, but I can see you're in trouble. Given the circumstances, and especially given your little prank with the kidney beans, I'd rather my contract be with your lawyer than you directly. If he's amenable to that, we have a deal."

It didn't really buy me much, except to put me slightly at arm's length from Rose. Might come in handy if I found anything that contributed more to the case against her, than of help. That way, I could just turn over everything to her lawyer and let him deal with it.

I told her my fee was one hundred and twenty dollars per hour, which was almost double my usual rate, but I didn't share that bit with her. She didn't argue. I had a sinking feeling this was going to end quickly or badly. Or more likely, both. Before I left, I reminded her to have her lawyer set up a contract to that effect. And to call Dan Hyde and ask him to give me a rundown on the investor deal they had or were about to sign.

I left, telling myself all I needed to do was produce one or two plausible motives one or more of the other fourteen people at the party might have had to want Carl dead. Motives that didn't include Rose. I didn't need to prove anything. It would be up to a prosecutor to prove guilt, should it come to that. I had found a way to get Gab off the hot seat, I could do it for Rose, couldn't I? By evening I was struggling with a bad case of buyer's remorse.

TWENTY-SIX

A BAY WINDOW, PORCH, and tile roof had been added sometime along the way to the 1920s two-storey brick house, which held the offices of Fibb, Fibb and Hyde. The siding was bright blue, the trim yellow. I climbed the stairs and pulled open the front door. A blast of warm air hit me as I entered. A receptionist desk stood three steps in from the front door, virtually filling the small foyer.

"Jorja Knight. I have an appointment with Dan Hyde."

"Oh yes, I'll let him know you're here."

A few minutes later a chirpy woman arrived and asked me to follow her. She ushered me into a meeting room, which may have been the front parlour at one time, and offered me water or coffee which I turned down. A few minutes later Dan Hyde entered. Impeccably dressed in a dark-grey pinstriped suit with the lean physique of a runner, he reached out his hand and smiled warmly. "Ms. Knight. We meet again."

"Yes. Thank you for seeing me. I assume Rose gave you a heads-up about why I wanted to meet with you?" I stared at his pitch-black hair, attempting to discern how he kept every single strand in place.

"Yes, briefly," he said as we settled into chairs. "Would you mind elaborating? Rose isn't always clear."

"Rose hired me to help find out who killed Carl. You're aware homicide is looking into Carl's death?"

"Yes. I've already given them my statement. Hard to believe someone killed him. He was an honest and upstanding gentleman."

"It's normal for homicide to put everyone on their list of suspects and then methodically eliminate them one at a time. Spouses are always on the suspect list. At least to start with. Rose doesn't like being on the list, not that I blame her. Her criminal lawyer, Ms. Gray, has retained me to start collecting information that might help remove Rose from that list. I'm just doing some due diligence, trying to understand what the motive may have been for Carl's death. On the surface, it looks like Rose had more to gain by Carl's death than anyone else."

"I simply can't believe she would have anything to do with Carl's death."

"That may be, but then again, the fact that Rose tampered with Ms. Rizzo's meal preparations, as innocent as the intent may have been, has already raised a flag as far as homicide is concerned."

"I can see how that would pique their interest."

"Rose couldn't explain the details of the recent corporate deal. I'm trying to determine who else might benefit from Carl's death. Especially with a new investment agreement being days away or possibly already signed?"

"Sure. I can give you a rundown. Riteweight's a private company. Carl Johnson and JP Boussard were equal partners and held the voting shares in the company. The company also has a class of shares called nonvoting shares. These are owned in equal portions by their spouses, Rose and Dee Dee."

"If I remember my university business 101, the holders of the voting shares make all the decisions and the nonvoting shares have no say in the company's operations or direction?"

"Right. The holders of the voting shares decide strategy, company direction and how much of the company's revenue will be re-invested or if any of it is to be distributed to the shareholders."

"The shareholders being both the voting and nonvoting shareholders?"

"Correct."

"But recently new investors entered the picture. Can you give me a quick overview of the deal?"

"One investor. In fact, a syndicate."

I must have appeared puzzled because he hurried on to explain.

"A lead investor sets up a syndicate. In our case, Dimitri Asentanko. A syndicate allows other investors to participate in the lead investor's deals. These other investors agree to invest a certain amount in each of the lead investor's deals and to pay the lead investor an agreed-to percentage of their share of future profits."

"Like a fee?"

"Sort of, but only earned if the investment pays returns. I'll use an example. Say Mr. Asentanko offers to invest a million dollars in a company. He might personally invest two hundred thousand dollars and offer the remaining eight hundred thousand to his syndicate for a fifteen percent carry. If the company is successful, it pays back the syndicate their original million-dollar investment and after payout is reached the syndicate's profit is split eighty-five percent to the investors and fifteen percent to the lead investor, in this case Dimitri."

"What happens to the company's original investors or owners?"

"It depends on what they have or are willing to put in and the value of the company. In most cases the entity or company's shares are restructured because the lead investor makes his investment into the actual company. The syndicate investors essentially make their investment through a fund structure and do not directly hold shares in the company."

"Let me see if I understand," I said. "Through this new investment, Dimitri purchases a piece of Riteweight which his syndicate investors helped him buy with their money. But when the company starts making money, the profits will be used to pay back the investors their initial investment first and then continues to pay them a percentage of the profits after payout?"

"You got it."

"Once the deal is signed, who owns Riteweight?"

"There's a lot of complexity to the agreement but in general terms the level of investment by the syndicate will see the future profits split at forty percent to the syndicate and sixty percent to the original investors."

"Ouch. Seems steep."

"Like the old saying goes, you need money to make money. Carl and JP couldn't put enough together themselves to go big, fast. It's an extremely competitive market. If they don't move quickly, someone can appear with a bigger, better product and capture customers' dollars."

"Does this syndicate have a name?"

"Novayaera. They invest in everything from wind turbines to weight loss and herbal supplements."

"And Dimitri Asentanko is the lead syndicator."

"Right."

"Is the deal signed?"

"No. There's a signed letter of intent, but the actual agreement was to be executed the week Carl died."

"What happens now?"

"According to the Riteweight shareholder's agreement, JP inherits a third of Carl's voting shares, the rest go to Rose."

"I assume the new deal will now require JP's and Rose's agreement?"

"Yes."

"So, once Rose and JP sign the agreement Dimitri will own a piece of Riteweight and JP's and Rose's interest in the company will be reduced."

"Correct, but the new capital comes with a larger pay off than keeping a higher percentage."

"I get it. You can be a big fish in a little pond or a little fish in a big pond. Rose remembers Carl telling her the new capital would allow them to reach international markets."

Dan nodded. "Most of these start-ups have issues with marketing and distribution. All it takes is money."

"Couldn't JP and Carl have borrowed the money?"

"I can't speak to the Boussards' finances, but Carl and Rose were leveraged to the max. Money has been going into this company for years with virtually nothing coming back out. Carl maxed out bank loans and remortgaged his house. There are essentially no hard assets in the company, the office space is rented, the vehicles are leased."

"What would have happened if this new investment hadn't materialized?"

"Assuming they could get their product launched, they'd make a certain amount of money. But it's hard to keep operations going and pay back the level of debt they were carrying if restricted to a local market."

"And if the product launch was delayed?"

"If we're talking more than a month or two, Carl and Rose would probably have had to declare bankruptcy."

"So, everyone benefited if the deal went forward?"

"It's a good deal for all concerned."

"What happens now?"

"We're working on restructuring the shareholder agreement and getting it in order. Once it's updated and complete, the agreement can go forward."

If the math I was doing in my head was accurate, Rose and JP or she and Dimitri or Dimitri and JP could essentially influence the direction of the company and payout outcomes. Ideally, they'd all agree. But if they didn't see eye to eye it could turn into a doggie-eat-dog situation. Majority wins. Rose could get royally screwed. Unless her and JP's or her and Dimitri's interests aligned.

Could Dimitri have been courting Rose as a backup strategy until he and JP got to know each other and built up trust? I also had to consider the possibility Rose wasn't quite the ignoramus she appeared to be and realized she needed to get Dimitri in her corner. But neither of them would have had to be positioning themselves to get the other in their corner unless they thought Carl was about to drop out of the picture. Otherwise, all Rose held were nonvoting shares.

"What will Rose's day-to-day responsibilities be now with Carl gone?"

"She needs to familiarize herself with the company's operations, at least understand what impacts the cost and revenue streams. Daryl Henshaw looks after the day-to-day operations, but if Rose wants to protect her interests she has to get involved or give someone her voting proxy."

"Can she give her proxy to anyone?"

"Yes, anyone who's a shareholder in the company."

"In your view is the current situation better or worse for Rose?"

"It's hard to say. On the one hand and putting the emotional loss of her husband aside, she may be better off financially, at least in the long run. Instead of her and Carl splitting any dividends, whatever is agreed to will go solely to her. She also inherits the house. On the other hand, she now holds all the debt, and the house is heavily mortgaged. She also loses income brought in by Carl, so it might balance out."

"I get it. But if I got this right, Dimitri and JP could agree to expand the operation and funnel profits back into the company rather than pay out a dividend. If they did, it would leave Rose strapped financially."

"Yes, technically it could go that way."

"How will Rose pay the mortgage until the company starts to make money? Or what if the shareholders decide to withhold dividends the first few years?"

"I'm not sure if Rose has family or friends who would be able to float her for a while. She needs a revenue stream of eight thousand per month, just to cover her bills. There are a couple of small RRSPs which could be used to bridge the gap until the insurance money kicks in."

"Oh. Insurance money. What are we talking here?"

"Carl was carrying a five-million-dollar insurance policy."

This might be good news for Rose, but I considered it another nail in her coffin. No wonder she didn't want to wait passively, hoping homicide would eliminate her from the suspect list.

"And JP and Dimitri? Are they better off now or before Carl was killed?"

"From a business perspective, and other than losing a friend and a financially savvy business partner, I'd say JP might do a bit better financially, but only if the company is a success. Dimitri's position doesn't change."

I thanked him and left. I wasn't happy the way this was going. Dimitri's position wouldn't change except now he and Rose or he and JP could outvote the other. Timid Rose hadn't mentioned the insurance policy. She was going to be a wealthy woman whether Riteweight was successful or not.

TWENTY-SEVEN

CHECKED THE LOBBY registry and took the elevator up to the third floor. A receptionist with short black hair flipped up at the ends, thick bangs, and green rimmed glasses, sat snapping her gum.

"Good morning. I'm looking for Riteweight."

"Down the hall," she said, pointing to my left.

I made my way down a beige-carpeted hall, until I found Riteweight. Bright light filtered through wall-to-wall windows. The desk and side credenza in the outer office were medium walnut in colour and made of real wood. No one sat at the front desk, but a name plate informed me a Gina Mancini usually occupied the space. I slid past the desk and poked my head into the interior office. JP glanced up from behind a large desk.

"Mr. Boussard, I'm Jorja Knight. I may be a minute early."

He stood and came around the desk to shake my hand and motioned me to a circular table and four chairs in the corner. I marvelled at how smooth his forehead was. Dollars to donuts it was Botox. His wife Dee Dee certainly was a fan.

I sat as JP pulled out a chair and sat across from me. He leaned back, the fingers of both hands held together in a triangle in front of him, elbows resting on the arms of the chair.

"I only have a minute. What's this regarding?"

I could see how this was shaping up, no *how are you, want a coffee, nice day out isn't it.*

"First, let me say how sorry I am to hear your partner passed away."

JP grunted.

"My wife wasn't happy with your insinuations that something in our pantry made Carl and our other guests sick."

"I'm sorry if I left her with that impression. My client, Ms. Rizzo, was concerned when several of your guests became ill and asked me to help her identify the cause. Please rest assured we had no intention of accusing your wife or your family of any wrong-doing. The ingredients in the chef's pantry were all purchased, as were Ms. Rizzo's supplies. If something in one of the ingredients caused your guests gastrointestinal discomfort, then others should be warned of the product."

JP's eyes bored into mine and after an uncomfortable twenty seconds I looked away. My dislike of the man grew.

"I don't know if your wife had a chance to tell you, but Rose Johnson admitted to substituting the cooked beans with under-cooked beans at your dinner. Undercooked kidney beans can cause gastrointestinal distress."

"No, she didn't tell me. Why the hell would she do that?" A muscle in his jaw twitched.

"Rose says she wanted to make sure the beans being used were organic. So instead of asking the chef, she brought her own beans, and traded them out for the ones Ms. Rizzo already properly prepared. Unfortunately, the beans Rose substituted were under-cooked. Ms. Rizzo wasn't aware of any of this."

Rose had set out to embarrass her hosts. A childish act, if it had been carried out by a child. But Rose was a middle-aged woman, which made it disturbing. She had shared her real intention to me in private, and I had to go along with her more official public explanation.

"Rose will be lucky if someone doesn't sue her. This certainly isn't going to improve her social image. Is that why you're here today, you wanted to tell me that?"

"Now that we've cleared up the puzzling issue of why certain of your guests became ill the night of your dinner, Rose hired me to find out who killed Carl."

JP sat back and shook his head. "As far as I'm concerned, that's best left to the police."

"They're working on it. Rose is worried she'll be falsely accused. Her tampering with the dinner isn't helping her case. You and Carl were friends and partners for years. Is there anyone, perhaps from his past, who would want to harm him?"

"Carl is…was…the most upstanding guy I knew. He wasn't just bright and hardworking; he was a great leader. He was on the board of several charities. He took care of his mother and sister until they both passed away. He had a lot to offer the world. I never saw Carl lose his temper or make negative comments behind anyone's back. If he couldn't say it to your face, he wouldn't say it."

"Will Mr. Johnson's death impact your company's product launch?"

"Out of respect for Carl and his family, we're holding off announcing any company news for a few more days. We'll launch our product as planned. We've spent months preparing our marketing campaign and advertising as well as ramping up production. There are a lot of moving parts in motion. We can't pull back this late in the game."

"What happens to Mr. Johnson's share of the company?"

"Our partner agreement stipulates in the event of either of our deaths one third of the voting shares go to the surviving partners, and the remainder to the spouse or their estate if they are no longer living."

"So I guess Rose will become a full partner in the company."

I sensed the mood change before it happened. JP shifted his chair, leaned forward and placed his hands on the table in front of him. I caught a flash of defiance in his steel-grey eyes. His lips tightened.

"I don't see how any of this concerns you. As far as I can see, it's a police matter. Someone poisoned Carl. Who's to say you and your friend didn't have a hand in that. Under the circumstances, I'd rather not share information with you. Now if you don't mind, I need to get back to work." JP got to his feet. The meeting was over.

I thanked him for his time and made my way back through the front office. A dark-haired woman, near my age, caught my eye apologetically as I wound my way past her desk and out the door.

The meeting wasn't a total loss. JP had confirmed something for me. In the event of a partner's death one third of their voting shares went to the surviving partners. Now wasn't it lucky for JP that Carl died before the new agreement was signed and Dimitri became a partner.

TWENTY-EIGHT

THE SMALL PARK was sunny and pleasantly warm. I people-watched until noon. Like clockwork, hordes of office workers emptied the buildings and filled the streets. I was contemplating changing tactics when JP's assistant emerged from the building. I hurried across the street.

"Gina?"

She stopped and turned.

"My name's Jorja Knight. I'm a private investigator. I don't know if you remember me, but I was in to see JP earlier today. I was hoping to ask you some questions about Carl Johnson. Do you have plans for lunch or could I convince you to join me for a sandwich or salad?"

"Oh. I was going to grab something from the food truck and eat in the park."

I sensed she was a bit taken aback at the request. "Rose Johnson asked me to look into Carl's death. I'd be happy to join you in the park. My treat."

She nodded and smiled. "Okay. But you have to answer a question for me in return."

"Deal."

We bought food from the Grizzly Burger and crossed the street to the park. The benches were full, forcing us to perch on the edge of a concrete platform holding a painted cow from Calgary's Udderly Art exhibit.

Succulent juices ran down my chin with the first bite. I managed to catch most of it before it hit my blouse. I groaned. "Umm. I'm going to have to be careful. This stuff is like crack cocaine."

"I'm already hooked," said Gina. "They should set up AFTA meetings. Anonymous Food Truck Addicts."

We sat side by side, eating and moaning, until the last handful of fatty, savoury, gushy goodness was gone.

"I couldn't help overhear you telling JP what Rose did," Gina said, popping the last bit of sandwich in her mouth and crumpling the wrapper into a ball.

I had been counting on the possibility she may have overheard other conversations from her vantage point in front of JP's office. "Yeah. She's completely mortified," I said.

"It's gutsy of her to admit what she did. But it isn't what killed Carl, is it?"

"No. Even though he ate part of the underprepared beans, his symptoms were dramatically different from those of the other guests. The autopsy found lethal amounts of cyanide in his system."

"I still can't believe anyone would want to hurt that man. He was so nice to everybody."

"I understand Carl had a ton of allergies. I suppose Carl wouldn't eat anything offered to him casually?"

"Oh no. He was very careful. I kept a whole list since I'm the one who orders food in when they're working through lunch or staying late. You have to really question these restaurants and food places, especially since people don't think things through. Once I ordered Thai food and gave them the list of items to be avoided but it turned out there was tree-nut oil in one of the sauces used. Now I order from the same three or four places. I got to know them and they me and I can trust what they sent over is allergen free." The corners of her mouth dipped downward. "I guess I won't have to worry anymore."

"Sounds like a lot of people loved Carl." I cleared my throat. "Carl and Rose seem like such an unlikely pairing."

"There's no telling what attracts some people to others. I'll admit though, I was a bit surprised when I first met Rose."

"Did you see much of her?"

Gina rolled her eyes. "She stopped by pretty regularly. Popped in to see what Carl's plans for the day were. She often brought him lunch."

"She always came by?"

"Oh, at least a couple of times a week, until this summer. Then she made it her mission to know where Carl was all the time."

"Do you think she suspected Carl of something?"

"You mean like an affair?"

"Yeah."

"There's no way. If you knew Carl, you'd know how impossible it was. I've never met someone with such a strong sense of right and wrong. He and JP made a good pair. JP would go for the jugular and Carl would argue what's fair and right. They usually ended up somewhere in the middle."

"So, what do you think was going on?"

"She strikes me as a lonely person. I wondered if her insecurities grew with her weight. She probably gained thirty pounds last year. She's not a happy person."

"Any ideas why?"

"No. Rumour has it she miscarried a couple of times, a few years back. I wonder if reaching her forties made her realize her chances of becoming a mother were slipping away. She wouldn't be the first person to console herself with food. I don't know what she does all day, with no kids or hobbies or anything. I'd go crazy."

"Rose told me Carl was anxious these last few weeks. Did you notice anything?"

She considered for a minute. "I'd say yes, he seemed worried, especially with the go-live date approaching."

"Do you know why?"

"No, I don't."

"Someone told me Carl had a big argument with the head of operations, a few weeks before he was killed."

"With Daryl? I never heard anything about an argument. On the other hand, I'm not exactly surprised. There was always tension whenever JP, Daryl and Carl got into the same room."

"Why is that?"

"I really don't know, so treat this like the pure gossip it is. I think Daryl wanted a piece of the company. You know, shares, not just salary. JP and Carl weren't keen or able to offer him a partnership."

"Was it an ongoing issue?"

"Certainly, in the last year. But Daryl doesn't do himself any favours. He acted downright annoyed at the pitch party."

"Sorry. Pitch party? I'm not familiar with that."

"They get investors together and pitch the business idea or proposal to them. It's marketing really, but to investors not customers. Anyone who's interested then signs a confidentiality agreement and the business plan is shared with them. If they like what they see, they negotiate and hopefully land on something they can all agree to."

"When was this pitch party?"

"Let's see…July, I believe. Yes, July. I remember it was right before my vacation the first week of August. Daryl was downright embarrassing."

"What happened?"

"Daryl had one presentation to give. He was to go over the

results of the trials they were doing for Luzit. They were nearing the end of their last trial and the results were real promising. Most participants lost an average of three pounds per week with no change in lifestyle. Can you imagine?"

"I'd buy it."

"Me too! Anyway, Daryl had all the graphs and charts. He went through them but didn't hide the fact he was annoyed. When he finished, he stormed off without asking the investors if they had any questions."

"How did JP and Carl take it?"

"JP made a joke of it. He said although the results were astounding by anyone's standards, Daryl wouldn't be happy until his trial participants lost five to six pounds a week without trying."

"Wow. Is that possible?"

"Someone asked the very same question. JP said he didn't know any reason why it wasn't possible. Carl spoke up and said JP wasn't saying they were working on it, he meant a future possibility, like landing on Mars. Most people laughed. But that was Carl for you, realistic and factual. JP's the pie-in-the-sky guy."

"Was Rose at this pitch party?"

"Yes, she was there, although I remember she came late. She's not a fan of these events, but Carl expected her to be there at least for the social part after the formal presentations were done."

"And no affair?"

"I don't believe Rose had any reason to suspect her husband. Carl was an honest, upfront, genuinely nice guy."

"How long have you worked for JP?"

"Almost eighteen months now."

"Is your position new or did someone have your job before you?"

"No, there was a gal before me. A hot little tamale. I met her once, when Staffing Solutions first sent me over."

"Why did she leave?"

"The prevalent rumour is Dee Dee didn't like her and forced JP to let her go."

"Interesting. Didn't like her or didn't trust her around JP?"

"From what I gather, both."

"I take it you and Dee Dee get along?"

Gina laughed. "The fact I'm happily married with three kids and my hot tamale days behind me might have something to do with it."

"I wouldn't count yourself out. You look great. Well, well. I should have known Dee Dee would be the jealous type."

"Oh, for sure. She's going to make sure nothing gets between her and her man."

"Okay, your turn to ask me a question."

"Okay, don't laugh, but I've always kind of been interested in becoming a private eye. Not now when my kids are young but after they're all grown up. What's it like?"

"It's kind of like this. Trying to get information. It's pretty much all a PI does. Today there's a ton of information you can get off the internet. Everything is moving toward corporate security, fraud detection, and cybercrime. I still get the occasional cheating spouse cases but today it's easier for people to catch cheating spouses themselves. With all the technology we use, it's hard for cheaters not to leave a data trail for loved ones to find."

We chatted a bit more as to the private investigator's changing future role. There were online courses she could take to prepare for obtaining her PI licence. I told her I fancied the idea of building up my own detective agency someday but thought it best to get my own feet wet first. We agreed to stay in touch.

Back in my truck, I checked my messages then made two calls. The first was to set up a meeting with Dimitri Asentanko, the second was to Daryl Henshaw.

TWENTY-NINE

A HEAVY FOG HUNG over the city and the downtown office buildings faded eerily into its grey haze. The sidewalks were slick with drizzle. I arrived at the coffee shop and snagged the second last table in the place. With coffee ordered, I sat back and surveyed the surroundings. The dark, heavy wooden furniture wasn't my style, but some would find the place cozy and welcoming. The walls were covered with framed newspaper articles and posters of noteworthy events from Calgary's short history.

A swirl of cool air announced Daryl's arrival. I jumped as a waitress dropped an entire tray of dishes. Conversation stopped in mid-sentence. Daryl froze. I held up my hand and gave a little wave. Muted voices resumed as Daryl made his way to the table. Heart still racing, I got up and shook his hand.

"Thanks for meeting with me."

He nodded, issuing a small guttural sound, and sat down. A waitress arrived and took our order. She didn't warrant a smile from Daryl either. After she hustled away, I took a deep breath and jumped right in. Daryl didn't seem like the kind of guy who would tolerate mindless chit chat.

"I don't know if you've been told, but Rose substituted organic kidney beans for the ones the chef had prepared the night Carl died. Unfortunately, she didn't prep them properly and many of the guests became ill."

"I heard. Dee Dee called yesterday with the glorious news."

"The beans aren't the cause of Carl's death, but the police have been around to question her. She's worried her misstep has put her centre stage in their investigation. She hired me to find out who killed Carl."

"Ah, the ever-concerned Rose."

"She seems to be taking it pretty hard," I replied. *Unlike the guy sitting in front of me,* I noted mentally. "Can you tell me what you saw the night Carl died?"

"You were there."

"Yes, but I was in and out of the room and frankly not paying attention to conversation or anything else that might have been going on."

"I don't know what I can tell you. I wasn't seated at Carl and JP's table."

This guy wasn't merely brooding, he was downright bitter. I could tell this line of questioning wasn't going to warm him to me. I switched tactics.

"I understand you're the man behind the research side of this venture. I've read over thirty-three percent of North Americans are obese, twenty-five percent of Canadians. That's a lot of people looking for a solution."

Our food arrived, and Daryl busied himself unfolding his napkin. He checked the underside of his fried eggs. They must have been done to his liking because he cut in and ate a few mouthfuls. He looked older than the first time I saw him, grey skinned and dull eyed. The downturned lips and dour look didn't match my concept of what a man gearing up to launch his pride and joy would look like.

"You don't agree?" I asked after a few minutes.

He took a sip of coffee then dabbed his napkin to his lips. "I'm sure with all the marketing hype there will be a lot of interest."

Whoa. I'd never met anyone more unexcited with respect to a product or solution they'd been instrumental in developing.

"The interest isn't justified otherwise?"

"I'm just tired of JP blowing smoke up everyone's ass about how we were going to stand the weight-loss world on its head."

"This new supplement isn't the easy fix the world is waiting for?"

A bitter laugh escaped from his lips. "Without giving away any secrets, we've found a way to inhibit carbohydrate absorption. There's a fair bit of research going on out there on this topic; it's not exactly unheard of. More a question of who will be first to market."

"And you guys are ready…right?"

"Sure. Our great fame will be short lived once other companies get on the bandwagon or figure it out. It's only a matter of time."

"Forgive me for saying but you don't seem overly excited."

"Why should I be? Unlike JP and Carl and our new investors, my life's not going to change."

"You don't own shares or a piece of the company?"

"Nope, just a lowly salaried stiff."

"Isn't part ownership an option?"

"No. As Carl liked to point out, I don't have money to invest in the company." He didn't bother disguising the bitterness in his voice.

"I see." *Ouch.*

We both resumed eating quietly. There was virtually no hope of me rushing him with questions. I understood his type, better than I even cared to admit to myself. I waited until our plates were cleared and the waitress refilled our coffee.

"How did you end up working for JP and Carl, if I may ask?"

"I was doing research in a lab in Ontario. When it closed due to lack of funding, I decided to go it alone. There weren't many research labs in Canada dealing with weight loss at the time and I didn't want to leave the country to go elsewhere." He shrugged. "I went bankrupt." His eyes swept the room, and the fingers of his right hand tapped the table. "Then I met Carl. Back then, Carl was a financial adviser specializing in bankruptcy. A friend of mine introduced us. There wasn't much he could do for me financially, but he knew someone who might be interested in the concept I was pursuing."

"JP?"

"Bingo. Shortly after that, he and Carl set up Riteweight and hired me to continue my work."

"Does Riteweight have a lab?"

"I research and develop the formulas, then hire lab services to concoct the magical potion."

"And the testing?"

"Herbal supplements don't require rigorous FDA or Canada Health approval. We ran three test trials for our product. People volunteer to be part of the trial testing."

"They're not paid?"

"No. We provide the product. Each participant provides a basic health profile, height, weight, blood pressure, standard stuff. They report back regularly through a series of questions and answers, but it's up to them to report any adverse effects. At the end of the trial there's a further weigh in and questionnaire. I still don't know what makes people want to turn themselves into guinea pigs. Desperation I guess."

"The trials have gone well?"

"Better than for most products on the market. There isn't

much out there that doesn't require exercise or restriction of calories, in addition to the supplement."

"Did all your trial people lose weight? Without changing anything else?"

"A statistically significant number did. A few didn't lose anything. Others put on weight. Human beings aren't notorious for exhibiting the best impulse control."

"But gaining weight?"

He shrugged. "Some people treat the supplement like magic, a licence to eat whatever they want. It takes them a few months and ten to twenty pounds of added weight before realizing it isn't, even though we stress they shouldn't change their eating habits. It's not scientifically controlled. We can't keep people locked up in a lab like rats." He sounded disappointed. "We have a control group but it's a relatively small number of individuals."

"Are all the trials completed?"

"The third and final trial wrapped up last month."

"Why was Carl nervous about the upcoming launch?"

"Carl's a whining ninny." He stopped and ran his hand over the day's growth he hadn't bothered to scrape off his face this morning. "Sorry...*was* a whining ninny."

I nodded. "Did he have any reason to stall or prevent the product launch from moving ahead?"

"No, other than if he had his own way, we would have run more trials. But it's neither necessary, nor standard practice."

"There's no other testing, after the trials?"

"We're required to have the actual product tested to prove what we say is in the product is accurately reflected on the label and there are no extraneous substances in the product."

"Who does the testing?"

"We're using a lab in South Africa to test the quality of the product being produced. And the rich get richer." He sneered.

"One of Dimitri's investors owns an interest in a packaging plant down there."

"Is that Mr. Gruba?"

"Correct."

"Does Dimitri also own an interest in the packaging plant?"

"You tell me. All I know is all of the product will be packaged and distributed from South Africa." He sniffed, picked up his napkin and dabbed at his nose. "Look. I know it makes sense. No point testing and shipping product from multiple facilities if you don't need to."

"Who would want to see Carl dead? Or benefits from his death?"

"Your client, for one."

"She could benefit if the company does well. But what if it doesn't?"

"I understand Carl was well insured."

"Who else?"

"JP. And anyone who wants a piece or bigger piece of the pie. Assuming they can convince Rose to sell."

"Like yourself?"

"Like I said, if I miraculously came into money, I'd invest. But Carl didn't leave his money to me, he left it to his wife."

"Are there any other interested parties?"

"You'd have to ask Dimitri or JP. If there are, I'm not privy to such information."

"I sense you're not a fan of JP's."

He shrugged. "I like to focus on the product and results. JP's a schmoozer."

I could tell the intellectual side of him would withhold all respect. On the other hand, JP probably considered Daryl a socially inept geek, with no skin in the game, except for his reputation, which to Daryl would be what mattered the most.

"I'd expect there are a lot of companies knocking at your door to see if you want to jump ship. Or soon will be."

He shrugged. "I've had a few offers."

"Not enticing enough?"

"Let's just say there's the devil you know and the devil you don't. People don't understand what it takes to develop something like this. If you haven't noticed yet, I'm not the easiest guy to work with. Here I get to call the shots, at least with respect to product development. Besides, I have a contractual agreement with Riteweight."

I paid the bill and we walked out together. We parted ways at the corner, Daryl turning east to his office while I continued south. He didn't seem keen on helping Rose. Even if he remembered something odd or out of place at dinner or earlier, I couldn't imagine him ringing me up in the hopes of saving Rose from the gallows. I suddenly saw why Rose had hired me. There was absolutely no one in her corner. I was having a hard time being there myself.

THIRTY

DARYL WAS BEING guarded about something but not about the fact that there was no love lost between him and the partners. I couldn't see how he came out ahead with Carl being dead. Clearly with new investors on the horizon, he might have seen his opportunity to own a piece of the company slipping out of reach for good. Maybe that's what was behind his argument with Carl, but I got the impression it was something bigger. What did Rose say? Something about Carl saying he wasn't going to move forward until he got some answers. Answers to what?

After walking a few blocks, I changed course and headed east. I found Daryl's comment about Carl wanting more trials interesting. Carl was noticeably worried of late, worried enough for Rose and Gina to notice. Could it have been about the product itself? From what I knew of Carl, he sounded like the type of man who would have no hesitation in delaying the launch if he suspected something wrong with the product, even at the risk of his own financial ruin. If Carl had been demanding more trials, it would have delayed the product launch. But I couldn't see Daryl orchestrating his death. Or could I? Daryl wasn't going to get rich off Luzit, but as creator of the product, it would buy him recognition among his peers. But if there was something wrong with the product, he would lose that as well as a chance to profit from his work. I thought back to the night of the Boussards' dinner. The last thing I noticed before I ran back to the kitchen to call 911 was Daryl, sitting calmly, smiling. He hadn't looked surprised at all. In fact, he seemed amused.

I turned north and did an abrupt about face. JP and Kristen Lee came out of the building housing Riteweight's offices. Kristen strutted confidently in her powder-blue skirt suit and navy heels. She looked every bit the marketing exec. Riteweight's success would lie, in part, with her ability to develop and execute their launch plan. They turned west, JP's hand on the small of Kristen's back. Dee Dee had good reason to be vigilant. I followed them until they disappeared into the Cobbler Inn on Kensington, a small boutique hotel.

I pondered my next move. I had been to the hotel for brunch, several times. The front doors opened onto a small lobby with the lounge directly ahead. The dining room was to the right and the hotel desk to the left. I'd be seen if I went in regardless of whether JP and Kristen were in the lounge or the restaurant.

I crossed the street and browsed several small shops, keeping one eye on the hotel through their front windows. I had planned to go to the office and do a few hours of research before my phone call with Dimitri, but this was far too interesting. I walked to the corner and joined a group of people at a bus stop which served four bus routes, providing me a justifiable reason for not getting on any arriving bus. JP and Kristen emerged two hours later.

I followed them back to the office. The glances and smiles they threw each other were telling. At least, I never had reason to smile like that at a boss, business acquaintance or colleague. I hated JP just a bit more.

I glanced at my watch. I had less than half an hour before my appointed phone call with Dimitri.

I looped back to my truck, and using Bluetooth, called Staffing Solutions as I drove. I soon had the manager on the line and introduced myself.

"I understand your agency placed an executive assistant with a company called Riteweight, both the current executive assistant and her predecessor. I've already spoken to Mrs. Gina Mancini, but I'd like to talk to the person who held the position before her."

"We don't normally give out that information."

"Do your clients normally get murdered?"

"Umm…no."

"I'd like to speak with her regarding Mr. Carl Johnson, the former CFO of Riteweight. I assume you've heard he was murdered. I'll give you my name and number to pass along to her. That way you don't need to give me her personal information. We can meet at a coffee shop or anywhere else she likes."

She asked me to spell my name and repeated back the phone number I gave her. I was counting on hot tamale, whose name I learned was Miranda, to be curious enough to want to meet with me.

I debated grabbing a coffee at the downstairs café but parking the truck had eaten up too much time. I raced up the stairs and barely got settled into my office before the landline rang.

"Mr. Asentanko. Thank you for speaking with me. I know you're a busy man."

"Please. My given name is Dimitri."

"Thank you, Dimitri. As I mentioned in my email, I've been retained by Rose Johnson and her lawyer to investigate Carl Johnson's death."

"So tragic. Carl was a good man."

"I'm sorry I never had a chance to get to know him. I understand you not only became Carl and JP's business partner, but you've become friends with Rose."

"Rose is lovely woman. Such kind heart. Much too young to become widow."

"And yourself? Are you a family man?"

"No, no." He chuckled. "Hard to find woman who put up with me."

"I hear you're an Olympian. Silver medal in wrestling."

"Former Olympian. Silver not count in Russia. Everyone has eye on number one. Only number two if number one dies unexpectedly." He roared with laughter.

I didn't hear any bitterness in his laugh.

"Why not go back for that gold?"

"That was the plan. Win gold in Los Angeles. But opportunity came up to skip the ship—so I take it."

"You defected before your event?"

"Like I say, if you win, then all eyes on number one—including Russian counterintelligence. Before event, they look one way, I go other way." He laughed heartily.

"That's a pretty big sacrifice."

"Not so much sacrifice if you have no freedom. Now I have enough money I can make myself a gold medallion." He cracked up.

"Glad to hear it worked out for you. Can you tell me what you saw and heard the night Carl died? What happened."

"I don't know. I tell police the same thing. JP is giving dinner speech when I hear Rose scream. I looked over. Carl was blue, he could not breathe."

"How did he seem before dinner?"

"He was good."

"He was fine?"

"Ya, I talk to him. I see nothing wrong. We both joke, you know, to take off our jacket. The room was nice, but too hot. My forehead glistening like silver medal on podium."

"Was Carl sweating too?"

"Ya. Maybe more than me. I went to window, get some air."

I remembered the room had become warm through dinner.

"Was anyone else feeling hot?"

"Ladies never sweat. Men have more meat on our bones. The women, always cold."

"What about JP or Mr. Gruba and the other men?"

"I don't know."

"Rose said something about Carl getting two shots of epinephrine, before the ambulance arrived. Do you know anything about that?"

"First, we cannot find EpiPen. JP yell to bring spare from storage room. Then we find it in outside jacket pocket. JP give Carl shot in leg. But no help. Carl stop breathing. JP start the chest compression and give him air to mouth. Someone hand me another EpiPen. I give him second shot. He jerked, open his eyes for a minute."

"You gave him a second shot? Isn't that dangerous?"

"In Russia, I see guy get two, three shots. The adrenaline, it like jumpstart cable for heart."

"Who handed you the EpiPen?"

"I don't know. People standing all around. Then ambulance arrive."

Rose mentioned she'd been told Carl had more adrenaline in his system than expected. Could one of the EpiPens have been tampered with?

"Did EMS take the empty EpiPens with them?" They usually did as per protocol in these situations. Given the circumstances, they would have tested both pens by now, for foreign substances.

"I don't know."

"Someone told me Carl seemed worried in the weeks leading

up to the dinner. That he might have been wanting to delay the product launch."

"No…I not hear such thing. Everything ready to go."

"Did you get a chance to talk to Rose, after Carl's death. I mean before the funeral?"

"I call her on the phone, to give my condolences."

"When was that?"

"The next day. JP, he sent out email to tell us Carl passed."

"Did you meet with Rose?"

"No, no. Only by phone. She call me next week to ask if I will be pallbearer at Carl's funeral."

Now I wish I had been meeting with him in person, but a phone call was all his schedule allowed. Why was it important for him to hide the fact he met Rose late one evening in a deserted parking lot?

"Did she say anything to you about who might have killed Carl? Then or more recently?"

"I see her at the funeral. A sad day. Too much sadness. We didn't speak about that."

"And now? Is everything still ready to go at Riteweight?"

"We sign papers tomorrow."

"Then you'll officially become a partner. JP and Rose's partner."

"Ya."

"What do you think happened, Dimitri? Who would want to kill Carl?"

I waited for Dimitri to answer, worried he might choose not to as the silence stretched on. Finally, I heard him sigh.

"People sometime go crazy at others in better position. You know the story of Theagenes of Thasos?"

"No, I can't say I do."

"Theagenes was ancient Greek Olympian. A great boxer. No one could beat him. When Theagenes died, the people of Thasos make a big statue of him to put in centre of the city. Everyone loved and admired Theagenes. He brought great pride to Thasos. But one man was not happy. He fought Theagenes many times but could not defeat him. The statue became like a festering sliver under his skin. Every night he go to statue and whip and flog it in hatred. One night he dug out the dirt beneath the statue, hoping to push it over. The statue fell on the man and killed him."

"Interesting. Are you likening Carl to Theagenes? Someone loved by everyone except one?"

"I think maybe the killer envy Carl, like the man who hated Theagenes."

"But Carl's killer hasn't died."

"Maybe killer is flogging Carl's statue. Like the man in Thasos. One day killer may become victim of own envy, huh?"

After the call ended, I jotted notes and thought back over the conversation. Dimitri failed to mention his rendezvous with Rose at Glenmore Park, made it sound like the funeral was the first time he saw her in person. He also hadn't acknowledged that Carl had become increasingly worried as the launch date approached. In fact, he denied it.

His story about Theagenes of Thasos intrigued me. Was it his way of telling me he thought Daryl killed Carl? That Carl wasn't killed for monetary gain, but out of bitterness and envy? I remembered the cold shoulder Daryl had given Dimitri the night he arrived at dinner. And the way he rushed off after Carl's funeral service.

My phone rang, an unknown caller indicated on the screen. I hesitated a second then answered. Miranda, JP's previous assistant, was on the other end. She could meet me at a coffee shop on the north edge of the downtown core in half an hour. By the time the call ended I had one arm in the sleeve of my jacket and was heading out the door.

THIRTY-ONE

COFFEE IN HAND, I selected a table by the window. Dimitri's last comment played over and over in my head: *killer may become victim of own envy.* Did he mean it as a cautionary moral tale, or had he just predicted the killer's own death? I looked up as a gust of wind blew in and a woman, near my age but thinner and curvier, walked in the door. She stopped and surveyed the coffee shop. Our eyes made contact and she made her way over.

"Are you Jorja?"

"Yes, I am. You must be Miranda. Can I get you a coffee or something?"

"No thanks. I'm all coffeed out. I have water," she said pulling a half-finished litre bottle of Dasani from her grey, oversized slouchy purse.

"Thanks for meeting with me. I assume you heard Carl Johnson died. His wife hired me to look into his death."

"I saw it on the news. How awful. Carl was such a nice guy."

"So everyone says. I want to know more about Riteweight. How long did you work there?"

"Two years and a bit. I was with them from the beginning. They hired me about ten months after the company was formed."

"Who was all there at the time?"

"Just JP, Carl, Daryl and me. We brought in contractors to do the bookkeeping and taxes and later communications."

I wondered about the marketing company Kristen Lee worked for. "Was Flycatcher Commons looking after communications?"

"No. We used a girl on a work program from Mount Royal. Her name was Helen. I forget her last name."

"Any friction in the office?"

"Not between JP and Carl."

"And Daryl?"

"It's not in Daryl's nature to be happy. He had a big blow-up with JP and Carl right before I left."

"Do you know about what?"

"I couldn't help but hear, since I sat right outside of JP's office. Daryl wanted a piece of the company."

"Carl and JP didn't agree?"

"JP and Carl were the ones paying the invoices and taking the risk. Daryl didn't have any money to put into the company."

"What about the intellectual capital he put into it? My understanding is he's the one who discovered or concocted the formula."

"When Daryl agreed to work for JP and Carl, he knew the intellectual capital would belong to the company. He even signed a contract to that extent."

"Maybe he should have negotiated a better deal."

"I think there was bonus payment in his contract. But he had to have the product developed and ready to sell within a certain timeframe."

"Do you know what that timeframe was?"

"I can't exactly recall. I remember it was a good long while, two or three years."

"Do you remember how large a bonus?"

"No. It was complicated, based on sales after a certain time."

So, Daryl didn't only get salary, but the bonus might not be lucrative enough for him to really change his lifestyle.

"Anyone else work there, back then?"

"No. Like I said, we had a contract bookkeeper who came in a day or two each month and Helen did the press releases and built the website, mostly over the summer. After she went back to school in the fall, she continued to support the website. They used a lawyer from a firm called Fibb, Fibb and Hyde, but you probably know all that."

"Were they still using this girl Helen for computer support when you left?"

"No. She was part of a government-supported work initiative and worked there for a year and a half. Then she graduated and moved on. The last year I was there, they hired a second-year university student. He did the data entry, kept track of all the data from trials and the website admin stuff. Chris something... Adams. Chris Adams. He left before I did."

"What can you tell me about Dee Dee? Did you get to know her?"

"Dee Dee's a bitch." She unscrewed the top of her water bottle, swallowed a gulp and put it back on the table.

"How so?"

"She's a gold digger. She doesn't love JP. She loves the lifestyle he gives her."

"I take it you two didn't get along."

"No."

"Is she the reason JP let you go?"

Her eyes welled up. She picked up her water bottle and stared at it, while twirling it over and over in her hands.

"He had to. Dee Dee was making his life miserable and it was impacting his kids." She reached up and brushed back a tear, then picked at the label on her water bottle, tearing off minute slivers.

"Did Dee Dee suspect you and JP were having an affair?"

Miranda appeared to be struggling with what to say. Finally, she shrugged. "JP and I would work late from time to time and catch dinner together afterwards. She said she would get proof we were having an affair, and when the time came, he'd pay. And not just financially, she told him she'd make darn sure he didn't get the kids."

"So, she was prepared to bide her time." This didn't surprise me at all. Dee Dee didn't strike me like the kind to let chance determine her destiny.

"JP pretty much had their whole life savings in this company. It was either going to pay off or they'd be back to square one."

"I see. I guess if she filed for divorce, there wasn't much to settle except debt."

"Right."

"You don't see him anymore?"

"No." This time the tears flowed in earnest. "We met a few times after I left but JP said we had to stop seeing each other. He was worried his wife would hire a private eye to follow him." Her eyes widened and her mouth gaped open.

"Nope. You're good. Dee Dee didn't hire me. Honest. Carl's wife did. She wants me to find out who killed Carl."

"Dee Dee must be thrilled, to have JP all to herself."

The guilty look on Gab's face, as she admitted to her and JP's tryst, JP's hand resting on Kristen's back as they walked back from the hotel flashed across my mind.

"She may not be. It seems JP's found someone else to have dinner with." I hated being a shit. But I hated the idea she still romanticized her great love for a lying, cheating scumbag even more. She took the bait.

"What are you saying? He's cheating on his wife with someone else?"

"You know what they say. Once a cheater always a cheater."

"Who is she? It can't be the woman he hired to replace me," she said with disdain. The tears stopped flowing and she stared past me with narrowed eyes, her lips pursed tightly.

Why did people assume women in their forties, with waists slightly thickened from birthing multiple human beings, would be of no interest to the opposite sex? Especially other women. On the other hand, I had a hard time feeling sorry for Miranda. Why had she become involved with someone else's husband? She knew JP was a married man. I don't know what all these women saw in him. It must be the female equivalent of conquistador's syndrome. Or in Miranda's case low self-esteem…hoping she might be able to attract an unhappily married man easier than a well-adjusted, happy single one.

"Who is she?"

"Can't tell you. Just like you wouldn't want me spilling the beans about our conversation to anyone."

Miranda stared out the window, as another tear ran down her face. I waited as she fished a tissue out of her grey sack. She bunched it up and held it against her lips, occasionally using the sodden ball to soak up another tear. I was on the edge of saying something when she looked up at me.

"Their first trial didn't go so well."

That a girl! "Why? What happened?"

"Carl's wife was a trial participant."

"Oops."

"Yeah. She gained a lot of weight on the supplement. Carl wasn't happy with her. I also heard one of the trial participants died."

"What?"

"JP told me one night. I heard rumours around the office, so one day I asked him. He said the guy was obese and had a lot of health issues. High blood pressure, high cholesterol, sleep apnea, a ticking time bomb. He said it had nothing to do with the supplement. The guy just ran out of time."

"Do you know what happened? Or this guy's name?"

"No. JP said he collapsed on the street. He was dead before he reached the hospital."

"Do you know where?"

"No. I assumed in Calgary, but they don't have to be. Trial participants can be anywhere. It's not like they need to be regularly monitored. There's an initial exam by their own physician at the start of the trial, or by a doctor arranged by Riteweight if they don't have one, and a second exam at the end of six months. The participants self-report during the trial."

"Was his death linked to the supplement in any way?"

"Not according to JP. But Carl went ballistic over it."

"Why?"

"Carl wouldn't want to have anything to do with something which might possibly prove to be harmful. You know he had a sister who was born with health issues due to some drug his mother took while pregnant. He didn't like to take risks on behalf of other people. It's why he quit the financial advisory business. JP always joked that the only thing standing in the way of Carl becoming wildly successful was his extreme sense of morality. He called it moralbidity."

"Funny. What happened after the guy died?"

She shrugged. "I left shortly afterwards. They were getting ready to start a second trial."

By the time we parted, Miranda's tears had dried, but she looked totally spent. I hated bursting anyone's bubble but perhaps it would help her put an end to her JP fantasy and get on with life. I ambled back to where my car was parked.

I had a lot to mull over. Could Carl have been threatening

to not move forward until he had more information about the trial participant's death? But the timing was all wrong. According to Rose, the argument she heard between Carl and Daryl had happened recently. What if there was something wrong with the supplement?

THIRTY-TWO

I PULLED INTO MY underground parking stall, picked up my mail in the lobby and took the elevator up to the eighth floor. My phone pinged repeatedly as I unlocked the door and deposited my food on the kitchen counter. I pulled out my phone. Three missed calls from Lydia. Now what? I assumed she and I were done now that Dave had been spotted at his parents' house, raiding the refrigerator. What more did she want? Besides, I had a nasty feeling Dave was embroiled in something illegal. I had no desire to help him or Lydia extract himself.

I kicked off my shoes, wrangled my vegetarian lasagna, a salad and a chocolate chip cookie out of the bag and settled down on the couch. Halfway through the lasagna, my phone buzzed. Lydia. *What the hell?*

I sighed and swiped the accept icon. "Hi, Lydia."

"Where the hell have you been? Why haven't you answered my calls?"

I disconnected and resumed eating. Putting the empty lasagna container down, I glanced at my phone and started in on the salad. I had three new text messages from Lydia, each moving in the direction I wanted. The third one read *Sorry. Please call me. We need to talk.*

Well, I didn't need to talk to her. I just needed to send her an invoice and have her pay it. I flipped through the TV guide, but nothing of interest caught my eye. I glanced at the phone lying on the adjacent seat cushion, flipped to the recent calls screen and tapped on Lydia's name. She answered right away.

"Jorja. I need to talk to you. Please." She sounded frantic.

"We're talking."

"No, not like this. Meet me at Koko's."

"Why should I?"

"I'll tell you when you get here."

"Not until you tell me what's going on. Lydia? Lydia?" I stared at my darkened phone screen.

∽

I took my sweet time getting to Koko's, a small eatery tucked away between a Drug Mart and a liquor store on Seventeenth Avenue. No one came here for dinner. Mostly people came in after a night of drinking and ordered a plate of fries with gravy or a greasy burger, hoping to sop up the alcohol and force their liver into overtime.

It took me a minute to spot her. Not because the place was full. There were barely a handful of people scattered around the room. But it was dark. Drunks don't gravitate to brightly lit places. Lydia was in the back booth sitting with her back against the wall. A dark-brown scarf covered her head and she wore sunglasses. I slid into the booth across from her.

"Where have you been? I've been trying to get a hold of you all day."

"Hi, Lydia. I'm fine. Thanks for asking. Is that an eye infection you're hiding?"

"No." She reached up and slowly pulled off her sunglasses, her eyes searching the room frantically behind me. A pimply-faced kid appeared at our table to find out what we were having. Lydia ordered coffee, and I ordered fries with gravy. After he left, Lydia leaned toward me.

"You have to help me."

"Now what?"

"I got this last night." She pushed a folded piece of paper across the table.

I didn't want to add my fingerprints to the mix, in case it was truly relevant. "Can you unfold it for me please?"

She leaned over, unfolded the paper using her hand to smooth it down flat in front of me. *So much for fingerprints.* It was a note from Dave saying he was okay. He was going to lie low for a while. If anything were to happen to him, she was to turn over what was in the locker to the police.

"Have you seen or talked to Dave?"

"No. I called his mom, but she swears she doesn't know where he is. He won't answer his cell phone. This is all I've gotten from him. This note."

"I take it there was a key or other information included with this?"

"A locker key."

"To what locker?"

"It came with a clue, so I'd know where to look."

"And did you look?"

She shook her head.

I pushed my plate away, pulled out a five, dropped it on the table and got to my feet.

"No wait. Jorja," she hissed. "Wait."

I sat down. "You've got five minutes. I don't like people play-ing games with me or wasting my time."

"The locker is at the university. I went up there this morning.

There was this metal steel computer thingy…ummm, a hard drive. Nothing else. No note, nothing. Just a brown manila envelope with the hard drive."

I waited.

"I swear. I left it there. I locked up, went home and tried calling you." I had a dozen questions but was in no mood to ask any of them. Plus, it was kind of fun watching Lydia squirm. I ate another French fry.

Lydia shifted in her chair, peered behind me and checked outside the window. Satisfied, she leaned forward.

"You know the guy who died at a dinner party a few weeks ago? It was on the news. His company has a new weight-loss product coming out that's supposed to be fantastic."

"Carl Johnson?" I sat up.

"Yeah, that guy. I think he's the one who hired Dave."

My breath caught in my throat. My mind separated from my body. I was an observer, now hovering a foot or so above myself. I reached up and placed two fingers along my neck. My pulse was steady.

"I'm not totally sure but Dave mentioned some guy named Carl. And when I caught the company name on TV, it kinda rang a bell."

I didn't know whether to laugh or cry. Lydia couldn't have known Rose hired me to find out what happened to Carl. I didn't like having two clients related to the same case. A shiver ran through me and I swatted at invisible spiders crawling up my neck. What's the likelihood a random person shot Dave while breaking into his house the very day after Carl had been poisoned. I didn't like coincidences at the best of times, but this was no coincidence. Especially since Dave had hidden away a hard drive, I presume he didn't rightfully obtain. Possibly data belonging to a client. A murdered client. What else was I supposed to believe was on the hard drive? Dave's old university papers he wanted police to look at after he was dead. I sat dumbfounded. The universe just handed me something bigger. Not necessarily better but bigger.

"You have to turn it over to the police. It's evidence in a felony investigation. Possibly a homicide," I said firmly.

She reached over, snatched the paper off the table, crumpled it up and rammed it into her coffee. I watched, stunned, as she fished it out, popped it into her mouth and chewed. Mesmerized, I watched as she struggled to swallow, using her leftover coffee to help it down. Where the hell did she think we were, Uzbekistan?

I hated the slightly smug look on her face. "Okay we're done. I'll send you my final report and invoice."

"Jorja, no. Please. You have to help me. I don't know what to do."

"Actually, I don't have to help you and I told you what to do but you don't seem to want my advice."

Head reeling, I walked through the café and out the front door not bothering to look back. A few snowflakes started to fall. I put two fingers up to the side of my neck. My heart still beat steadily but I was light-headed and felt like throwing up.

I needed to talk to Dave. Not for Lydia's sake. She had lied to me. The news about Riteweight's CFO came out weeks ago. Something must have happened for her to call me. More than the note. As far as I was concerned, she was no longer my client, but my gut was telling me Dave was going to help me get Rose out of the spotlight.

THIRTY-THREE

KEPT ONE EYE on the clock while checking and answering emails. As soon as the little hand hit eight and the big hand twelve, I called Riteweight.

"Don't tell me private eyes keep office hours," said Gina when she answered.

I laughed. "Actually, not having fixed hours means I work all the time. I have a quick question if you have a minute."

"Sure, shoot."

"Several people told me Riteweight uses contractors to do the bookkeeping and website development. Do or did you by chance have an IT guy named David Morgan working for you?"

"Yes, we did…do. Carl ordered a complete overhaul of our systems before the company really took off. Dave beefed up security and set up a proper network for us."

"Does he still work for you guys?"

"Well we have a contract with him, but he doesn't work full time. We call him in when we need him."

"I see. When did you last see him?"

"Oh gosh, a month or so ago, I guess. Which doesn't mean he hasn't been around. He has his own security card and a lot of times he comes in at the end of the workday so as not to interfere with our work."

"Did he finish setting up your system securely?"

"He did. We had a half-day training session on the new process and rules. We don't store or take data home on our laptops anymore. People can still take a laptop home or on the road with them if they're travelling on business, but now we log into our server remotely and work on the data there."

"Had there been problems with the data?"

"Not as far as I know. I take care of letters, invoices, the usual admin stuff. Daryl is the big data guy. I'm not aware of any issues."

"Is there any way to tell when Dave was last in?"

"Common4ce runs the security system for the building tenants. They can probably tell you when he last keyed in."

"Okay. Thanks, Gina."

My mind whirled as I hung up. If the police were as smart as I knew them to be, they'd find Dave. If Dave hoped to avoid police interest, he should have diverted their interest by telling them a lot of people knew he worked in IT and had expensive equipment in his apartment. Hiding out was like putting up a billboard with the words *find me* below a big headshot of himself. It gave the police good reason to suspect Dave was holding back on what happened at his place. They probably suspected involvement in a theft ring, or a drug deal gone bad. I knew it was something bigger, scarier. Dave was afraid for his life. So much so, he and Lydia didn't trust the police to keep him safe.

I gave Mike a call.

"Hey, Jojo, what's up?"

"Hi, Mike. Got a minute?" For a brief second, I tried to imagine what it would be like to be his girlfriend. Mike was a good-looking guy, if you liked them a little rugged and not movie-star perfect. He was smart, had a good job, a sense of humour and solid values. But neither of us was willing to ruin our comfortable friendship. Besides, it was awkward moving a long-term friendship to a different level. Taboo somehow, like dating a first cousin.

"For you, always. What have you got yourself into this time?"

I would have acted indignant if not for the fact he'd already come to my aid several times since I hung out my PI shingle.

"Quick question. If I know someone who *might* have information related to a crime, and I emphasize might…at what point must I reveal it to police?"

"If I was still on the force, I'd tell you to bring anything forward, whether you believe it has something to do with the crime or not and let the police deal with it."

"Yeah, but seeing you're no longer on the police force, what would you advise?"

"Given your line of business, I know there's a fine line between helping the police and completely throwing your client under the bus. My advice? You should contact the police when you stop telling yourself it probably has nothing to do with the crime and start telling yourself it probably has something to do with it."

"I figured as much. So, what's new with you?"

"Same old, same old. Any chance you can meet me for a drink after work Friday? I have to catch a plane out Saturday afternoon."

"Sure. Where are you heading off to this time?"

"Toronto. It's Julie's birthday. I haven't seen her and the kid for a while."

Julie was Mike's oldest daughter, and the kid his grandson. Although Mike claimed his grandson was a pain, I could hear the affection in his voice whenever he mentioned him.

As soon as I hung up a gnawing guilt materialized in my stomach. I had no reason to feel guilty about spending time with Mike. For all I knew, Adan might be out having drinks with his friends Friday night too. Or more likely, attending a church concert with a woman sporting dreadlocks and unshaved legs, while everyone sang kumbaya.

Adan and I weren't exactly an item. We had dinner a few times, played Frisbee with a bunch of his churchgoers, and two weeks ago rented kayaks and paddled the length of the reservoir. I hadn't heard from him since. Adan's youth groups and street ministry took up most of his time. I told myself I didn't mind. I liked my own independence. What would I do if Adan began whining that I wasn't spending enough time with him? Besides, Adan and I never discussed our relationship. He could be seeing someone else. I could check it out, but it would put me dangerously close to stalker territory. I asked myself why I was anywhere near okay with the situation and why I hadn't pressed the matter. Maybe I didn't want a relationship.

I shook off thoughts of Adan and returned to my internal debate about Dave. Did he have evidence there was something wrong with Luzit? Is that what was on the hard drive he had squirrelled away in a university locker? What could I tell the police? Dave *might* have a hard drive hidden away in a locker. I didn't know which locker and only had Lydia's word it was at the university. Lydia wouldn't be forthcoming with answers if the police questioned her. She might deny the whole thing. Should I ignore Dave and Lydia and whatever those two were involved in?

By the time I crawled into bed I knew what I had to do.

THIRTY-FOUR

SOMETHING WAS GOING on at Riteweight and JP and Daryl weren't going to tell me what. If Rose was aware of anything, she was keeping quiet, even though her own reputation was on the line. I checked my text messages and email. Zippo from Adan. I sent Dimitri a request for a follow-up meeting and left a message for Daryl. Grabbing a jacket and my bag, I locked up and took the elevator downstairs.

Rush hour traffic had dwindled to a steady bumper-to-bumper flow by the time I hit Glenmore Trail, leaving me to contend with the usual throng of road demons. Where were all these people going and why didn't they have to account to anybody at nine-thirty in the morning? It's a cinch they didn't work for my former employer, Global Analytix, where employees were monitored like prison inmates.

I pulled up to Rose's house and wondered if her sister was back. A few minutes later I had my answer. Nadine opened the door and I made out the rapid clicking of dog nails as the Dobermans rounded the corner, falling over themselves to be at Nadine's side.

"Morning, Nadine. Is Rose in?"

"Do you have an appointment?"

"No, just dropping by. Is she in?"

"I wish you'd stop hounding her. She's already admitted to substituting the beans, not realizing they were improperly cooked. Please leave her alone."

This was a side of Nadine I hadn't seen before. Her status as permanent resident might have tricked her into believing she was her sister's gatekeeper. I glanced at the Dobermans standing vigilant at her side.

"She didn't tell you then?"

"Tell me what?"

"She and her lawyer hired me to find out who killed Carl."

Nadine stepped back. She couldn't have been more surprised if I had slapped her.

"Can you please let Rose know I'd like to speak with her?"

She moved aside, and I slithered in cautiously. Nadine made a clucking noise, turned and strode off down the hall. The Dobermans followed diligently. Since she hadn't invited me in, I remained by the door. I presumed Rose knew I'd be adding the wait time to my invoice.

"Jorja. Come in, come in." Rose huffed breathlessly as she came down the stairs. "I wasn't expecting you. Did I forget our meeting?"

"No. I was in the area and took a chance on you being available. I could come back later if it's more convenient?"

"No, no, this is fine. I was upstairs rearranging things. Clearing out a few items from the second master bedroom, to make room for Nadine."

"Ah, yes, I see Nadine has returned. This time for good?"

"Yes. She's put most of her furniture into storage and brought a few items with her. You know, her own reading chair and lamp, dresser and books and such. It's hard to move, much nicer if you can have your own things with you."

I agreed, although when I left Vancouver five years ago, I left the whole caboodle behind except for my car, clothes and a box of my favourite self-help guru's books and CDs. It wasn't a difficult choice. Most of the furniture had been purchased second hand in my university days. All I had of my childhood was my mother's watch. I preferred it, in a way. Memories were hard enough to live with without the constant reminder of physical objects. I refocused on Rose's prattling and followed her back to the kitchen.

"I'll put the kettle on for tea. Or I can make coffee if you prefer?"

"I'm fine, thank you. I downed a large coffee on my way over."

"Oh, okay." Unsure whether she should continue making tea for herself or sit down, she swayed back and forth indecisively a few times then joined me at the table. I caught a glimpse of green passing the doorway, certain Nadine had conveniently found something to busy herself with nearby.

"I've spoken to JP and most of the Riteweight staff including Daryl, Gina and JP's former assistant Miranda."

"Oh my, you have been busy."

"Were you aware of JP and Miranda's affair?"

Rose blushed and licked her lower lip. "No...not really. I mean, I suspected, but I had no means of knowing positively."

"Carl never said anything?"

"Not to me."

"Someone told me you took part in the weight-loss trial."

"Yes." Her face turned a deeper red and moisture now glistened on her forehead. "It was Carl's idea."

"You didn't want to?"

"I've gained a bit of weight over the years. Carl didn't seem to notice, or if he did, he never mentioned it. At least, not until the last year or two. Then he brought up the trial. I was humiliated by the whole thing. Having to weigh in, having my weight and measurements listed in a database. All eyes on me, watching what I did. Scrutinizing what I ate."

"Doesn't the product claim you don't have to change anything else you're doing?"

"It does, but I was part of the control group that was set up to specifically gather information on both the effects of the pill and lifestyle. The other participants self-reported their weight and only answered a brief questionnaire about how much they exercised or drank and ate in the reporting period. We had to record specifically what we ate, how much water or alcohol we drank every day. We wore a device that measured how many steps we walked during the day, how many flights of stairs we climbed. The device recorded heart rate and how much sleep we got."

"You didn't want to lose weight?"

"Of course, I did. But I didn't want each morsel I ate scrutinized or how far I walked compared with people half my size or age."

"Didn't it work as predicted?"

She ran her finger up and down the front seam of her tan, knit pants.

"The stress got to me," she said. She crossed her feet and gazed down at her hands, clenched in her lap.

It dawned on me she couldn't win. If she admitted it didn't work well, she'd be jeopardizing a potential future bonanza. If the product worked, but not for her, it would look like she lacked willpower.

"Of course, it would," I said. "I put on weight each winter. I swear I gain weight just thinking about it. Plus, I'm not a joiner. Even the thought of hiring a personal weight-loss consultant is a turn off."

She gazed up gratefully.

"How long did the trial last?"

"It was supposed to last six months, but I dropped out after four. I had gained twenty pounds by then." She shrugged. "I didn't see the point of staying on."

I nodded. "Did you meet any of the other trial participants or get to know who they were or what their results were?"

"No. I was told there were forty people in the first trial, and twenty-five of us in this so-called control group. I never met the other participants. Carl said most of them were losing three to four pounds a week."

"Did you hear one of the trial participants died?"

Something crashed. We both jumped. Nadine appeared in the doorway; her face flushed.

"Sorry. I was dusting and knocked over the big vase with the elephants on it. I'm sorry, Rose. It's smashed. I hope it wasn't a favourite of yours."

"No"—a furrow formed between her eyes—"just something the decorator thought looked good in the space. I don't really care for elephants."

"Nadine, are you okay? Did you cut yourself?" I got up and stepped forward, nodding toward her arm.

She glanced down and quickly pulled her sleeve down. "No, it's an old gardening mishap." Nadine rushed over to the walk-in pantry and re-emerged with a dustpan and garbage bag. "Sorry to interrupt," she called over her shoulder and disappeared back into the study.

Rose returned from wherever she went mentally when anything was requested of her. "Sorry, what were you saying?"

"I asked what you knew about the trial participant who died."

"Someone died?" The furrows between her eyes deepened.

"That's what I heard, but it may not have been related to the supplement. Apparently, the person was obese and had a lot of other health issues."

"No, I never heard anything." She sounded mystified. I couldn't tell if it was because of the death or because Carl had kept the information from her.

"Do you know if anyone else dropped out of the trial, other than yourself?"

"No."

"The other day you mentioned you overheard Daryl and Carl arguing. You thought Carl said something about wanting more data before going forward?"

"Oh dear. I hope there's nothing wrong with Luzit. What am I going to do?"

Nadine flew into the room, the dusting charade over.

"You'll do nothing," she snapped, glaring at me. "Do you have any proof? No, I suspect not," she continued when I didn't reply. She knelt in front of Rose and took her hands in hers. "My dear Rose. You can't believe innuendoes and gossip. Trust me, there's a lot of competition out there. Could be someone spreading rumours to make our product launch a failure, and their product come out on top. Best not to repeat any such nonsense."

Our product launch? "Nadine's right. If Carl did find something, it may have cost him his life."

"That's ridiculous," Nadine spat out.

"Pretty much everyone associated with Riteweight has a lot riding on Luzit. If Carl was dragging his feet on the launch, they'd have cause to get him out of the way."

"Why would Carl drag his feet? It'd be his and Rose's financial ruin too." Nadine leapt up, her eyes flashing.

"I think we can agree on one thing. If Carl was reluctant to move forward in launching the product, it would have to be for one hell of a reason."

"There is nothing wrong with the product."

"Then why on earth would someone kill him? A man who

would go miles out of his way to help someone in need. A man who'd rather choke than utter a spiteful word. It has to somehow be tied to Riteweight."

"Have you talked to the Boussards? Maybe JP isn't the friend Carl thought he was. Money does strange things to people. Maybe Dee Dee wanted to make sure there was enough in the pot so when she split up with JP she'd still be left with millions. And that son of theirs. It's obvious there's something wrong with that boy. Why don't you leave us alone and go dig up the real reason my sister is a widow."

Rose sat meekly while Nadine saw me out. I hadn't expected Nadine to react like that. Nadine would prefer I believe a disgruntled barista had taken revenge on Carl for leaving a meagre tip and poisoned his afternoon coffee. Or faced with yet another social obligation at the Boussards', Carl had ingested the cyanide himself. Anything but hint there was something afoul at Riteweight. But then she didn't know Riteweight's IT guy had a hard drive hidden away and someone tried shooting their way into his apartment the day after Carl was murdered.

THIRTY-FIVE

OKAY, DAVE. COME *out, come out, wherever you are.* I suspected Dave wasn't merely raiding his parents' refrigerator but was holed up in their basement. I arrived in Airdrie mid-afternoon and parked half a block from Dave's parents' place. Dave's mother sat in the front room, playing cards with another woman. I don't know why it surprised me, but it did. I'd never seen anyone play cards in the middle of the afternoon. Except on television. I found it peculiarly intriguing.

My phone pinged on the seat next to me. Hallelujah, a reply from Adan. I opened the text message. *How are you doing? Got any plans for Saturday?*

After a decent interval, hoping I wouldn't look like a desperate psycho glued to my cell waiting for his message, I sent back my reply. *Nothing planned for Saturday I can't get out of. Anything in mind?*

An hour later my phone pinged. Adan replied, *Brunch in Bragg Creek and a walk along the river? Bring hiking boots.*

I waited several minutes and replied. *You're on.*

Bragg Creek is a small community of less than a thousand, located half an hour southwest of Calgary where the Bragg Creek meets the Elbow River. A quaint little hamlet, it came complete with raised wooden sidewalks and small shops clad with rough-hewed logs. The trees along the riverbank should still have a sprinkling of leaves left on them. If nothing else it would give me an opportunity to find out where this relationship was going, or even if it was going.

Dave's mother and her guest finished playing cards and disappeared from view. I turned the engine on and drove out toward the highway, needing to find a washroom and something to eat. I exited into the Cross-Iron Mills mall, a five-minute drive down the highway from Airdrie. After meeting my immediate needs, I squandered several hours wandering aimlessly through the mall, then returned to Airdrie.

The Morgans' house was dark. I parked at the end of the street and waited. Slowly, lights came on, here and there, in neighbouring houses. The Morgans' place remained dark. I popped open the glove compartment and pulled out my Walther Compact BB pistol. I hefted it in my hand. I reached under the seat and pulled out a small box of CO_2 cartridges and slid one in, then snapped in a full magazine. My gun paranoia had forced me to this. Mike thought I could get over my fear of guns if I got used to loading one, learned how to handle it safely and adjusted to the feel of recoil when I shot it. The Walther wasn't a defence weapon, more like a bike with training wheels. I didn't plan to use it tonight but the weight of it in my hand felt good and it might serve as a deterrent, should Dave try to pull another Ben Johnson on me. I checked the safety latch for the fifth time, slipped the pistol into the pocket of my hoodie and got out.

I made my way down the block, around the corner and entered the alley. It was a lot darker here, but instead of feeling safe with a gun in my pocket it made me nervous. I should have left it in the truck. A dog lunged against the fence, barking furiously and I jumped back. Hurrying on, I arrived at Dave's back gate. The house stood in shadow, the only light coming from the neighbour's back porch. I unlatched the gate and made my way through the backyard and to the stairs. I found the key in the second place I checked, under a fake rock standing obviously out of place on the back steps. With a last glance around me, I took a deep breath, put the key into the lock, turned it and opened the door. I put the key back and entered, shutting the door behind me.

My heart hammered against the wall of my chest. I huddled on the small landing, waiting for my eyes to adjust to the darkness. My ears strained for any sound. Stairs to my left led up to the kitchen. Straight ahead of me a set of stairs led down into the basement.

Putting my hand on the wall I placed a foot on the top step. Why the hell was I doing this? And what if Dave was down there?

I made it to the bottom without mishap. It was pitch black. I pulled out my cell phone and touched the flashlight icon. I had a choice of two doors. I reached over and turned the handle of the door straight ahead.

I jumped back at the whooshing noise and stifled the scream clawing up my throat. Utility room. The sound I heard was the furnace kicking in.

Heart pounding, I closed the door and turned to the one on my right. I tried the handle. It was unlocked.

I put my phone back in my pocket and pulled out my pistol. I held it two handed, one hand below the other, like Mike had shown me, and ran my thumb over the safety lever.

I entered, gun leading, the rest of me close behind. I sidled down a short linoleum corridor, past a darkened bedroom to my right. A door on the opposite side of the hall led to a washroom. A faint light glowed at the end of the hall. My gut told me to back up and leave. What if Dave was home, working on his computer or asleep on the couch? What if Dave's Nona lived down here? This wasn't one of my best ideas.

The gun felt comfortably heavy in my hands. I checked the safety for the umpteenth time. An odour reminiscent of the boy's locker room in high school filled my nostrils. Creeping to the end of the hall I waited until I stopped shaking and peered around the corner.

A small sitting room opened in front of me. A saggy green couch and an arborite coffee table stood at the far end, both covered in Doritos bags, beer bottles and dirty plates. The wall adjacent to me held a massive flat screen TV, perched on home-made cinderblock shelves. Several takeout bags lay on the floor along with the occasional crushed Doritos chip and a lone cheese puff. I resumed breathing.

A stronger light came from the left, probably the kitchen. I was pretty sure no one was home but didn't want to back myself into a corner should someone arrive. It looked like Dave was hiding out here, the room reminiscent of the scene I'd surveyed through his apartment window. I relaxed my shoulders. Something shuffled and clicked behind me.

I whirled in time to see a dark figure emerge from the bedroom and run toward the stairs.

A beady-eyed critter slithered on the floor toward me. Three *pffts,* exploded from my hand, the blowback registering in my wrist.

Something hit my face. My hand flew to my forehead and came away moist.

I stared down at the pistol. I didn't remember releasing the safety.

Shaking, I ran down the hall toward the door. My foot brushed against something.

My hand groped the wall. *Please god, not a family pet.*

Trembling, I hit the light switch and turned.

A round plastic item and bits of its mechanical guts lay strewn in the hall in front of me. No blood. I flicked off the light and tore up the stairs.

The door slammed behind me as I ran toward the back gate. I was two doors down by the time I realized I had shot a robotic floor sweeper. Dave was nowhere in sight.

The sound of a police siren intruded my thoughts. I really didn't need to be caught in an alley with a BB pistol in my pocket.

I ducked into a darkened backyard and leaned against the garage, gulping in air, my heart hammering against my chest. If someone saw me creeping around in the dark, I could get shot, or worse yet, arrested. I peered around the garage.

The house in front of it remained dark. Crouching below the fence line I made my way up the back sidewalk and around to the front of the house. Taking a deep breath, I strolled down the front sidewalk and to the street. I turned in the direction of my truck and picked up my pace, pumping my arms up and down. Glad to be wearing sneakers, I rounded the corner.

A police car pulled up in front the Morgans' house. Two officers got out, one headed up the Morgans' sidewalk the other around to the side of the house.

I paused to stare at the police vehicle, like any good citizen out for an evening walk would, then continued down the street to my truck. I did a few stretches, resting my foot on the front bumper. My hand shook as I unlocked the door and climbed in. I pulled out the pistol and slid it under the seat. I'd remove the magazine later. I put the key into the ignition, waited a few minutes to avoid making it seem like I was in any hurry, and slowly eased out onto the road.

A mile down the highway, the scene at Dave's replayed in my head. I broke out laughing. Tears blurred my vision and spilled down my face. Fearing for my safety, I pulled off the highway into a gas station. Gasping for air I pulled down the visor and stared at the small cut on my forehead. The small red gash put me over the edge. Whenever I thought I was done laughing, another episode overtook me.

Finally, I had it under control. I looped around the gas pumps and entered the highway. Dave had a lot of explaining to do. Now that I had spooked him off, I needed to find out where he went when his parents' place no longer provided a safe hidey space. And what was on that hard drive.

THIRTY-SIX

I WOKE TO FIND the ground blanketed in snow. This didn't warm the cockles of my heart. Even though most of the snow had melted on the main arteries, the trip took longer than usual, and I arrived at Lydia's in a foul mood. Parking down the street from her condo, I pulled out my phone and tapped her name in my contacts list. She answered on the fifth ring.

"Hello."

"Hi, Lydia. Put Dave on the phone please." A minute went by. I imagined the frantic hand signals on the other end.

"What makes you think he's here?"

"For starters, that it took you a whole minute to come back with that snappy reply. But mostly because I had Lennie install a camera in your apartment with a video feed right to my iPad." A bold-faced lie, but two could play this game.

"Holy shit! You can't do that. That's invasion of privacy."

"Just put him on the line."

A few seconds later a male voice asked, "Hello?"

"Hi, Dave. We need to talk."

"What do you want?"

"You know what I want. Your girlfriend hired me to find you. Then she appeared to lose interest the minute I spotted you at your parents'. Only to call me later begging for help. But she wouldn't take my advice, so, I moved on and picked up a new client. This client of mine hired me to find out who killed her husband. Guess what? You worked for her husband. Carl Johnson. And the very next day, after Carl is poisoned, someone tries breaking into your apartment, shooting you in the process. Why do you think that is, Dave?"

"I have no idea."

"Sure, you do. You're going to tell me what's happening at Riteweight or you can tell the police. Except they're going to want to have a look at the hard drive you've got squirrelled away in a locker. Or do you have a signed work order from Riteweight allowing you to take their data?"

I heard him swear under his breath. "You shot my Roomba."

"Prove it."

"Someone tried to kill me."

I got out of the truck and made my way to the entrance. "That's why I'm outside rather than suggesting we meet somewhere more public. If Lydia buzzes me in, I can be there in a minute. If she doesn't, it'll take me five."

A minute later the door buzzed. I pulled it open and stepped inside. I scurried past the elevators, entered the stairwell and parked myself by the emergency exit. A few minutes later feet pounded down the concrete stairs. A hefty guy rounded the last flight, spotted me and stopped cold. He wore a University of Tuktoyaktuk sweatshirt above Star Wars Chewbacca pyjama pants and clutched a laptop under his arm.

"Hi, Dave. I'm Jorja. We spoke a few minutes ago."

"I need to get out of here." He gasped, looking back over his shoulder.

"Look, Dave, if I can find you, anybody can find you. I'm actually not very good."

He didn't look happy.

"Fine." He stepped down two more stairs.

"No." I motioned behind him. "Back up the stairs." I'd been outmanoeuvred, outrun one too many times. Although Dave carried noticeable excess weight, he could move like a freaking ninja when he needed to.

I followed him up six flights. Dave stopped and bent from the waist gasping. I was glad for the rest; my thighs were on fire. After a minute, Dave straightened, and I followed him out of the stairwell. Instead of turning toward Lydia's, he bolted toward the elevators.

A stocky figure, wearing jeans and a hoodie with the hood pulled over its head, waited by the elevators. It turned as Dave burst into the hallway. A ghostly white mask covered its face, the eyes open black sockets.

Dave skidded to a stop.

The figure lifted an arm, pointing a gun at Dave's chest. Dave turned and ran back toward me.

I spun around and plastered myself up against a doorway as the elevator doors slid open. I hit Lydia's phone number on redial.

Two elderly women stepped out into the hallway. Dave raced past me toward Lydia's, and I tore after him.

"Cydnee Bristle, Cydnee Bristle," I yelled into the phone, looking over my shoulder. The masked figure slid into the elevator and the elevator doors closed.

I slammed into Dave as he paused to open Lydia's door and we both fell into her hallway. Lydia screamed and flung her coffee into Dave's face. I threw the deadbolt behind me.

"Damn it. Why'd you throw scalding coffee in my face," screamed Dave.

"Don't yell at me. I got the code word. How'd I know it was you busting down my door?"

Dave looked confused. He gingerly touched the red patch on his face.

"Okay, you two. Enough with the lovey-dovey. We should focus on why a masked dude just pointed a gun in Dave's face."

"A gun?" Lydia went white.

"I need to sit," Dave huffed, staggering to the couch.

"Lydia, you might want to set your alarm."

I turned and followed Dave into the living room while Lydia punched numbers into her home security keypad.

"One or both of you start talking or I'm calling Detective Birdie."

THIRTY-SEVEN

DAVE SAT ON the couch, Lydia alongside him. I pulled out a kitchen chair from the small table nearby and set it across from them.

"I already know you were hired by Riteweight, Dave. Why don't you tell me how they became your client, and what's going on over there?"

Dave glanced around nervously, his left cheek now the colour of cherry cotton candy.

"Okay, okay. A guy I went to school with called me to tell me about the gig. His younger brother worked at Riteweight over the summer but was leaving to go to university in BC. The guys at Riteweight asked him if he could recommend anyone. He called his brother, who called me."

"When was this?"

"Mid-August."

"Go on."

"I go in to see this guy…Carl. He tells me the company is on the verge of getting a whole lot bigger and wants to make sure their computer systems are properly set up and secure."

"What did you do?" I noticed Lydia looked pained. "And keep it in layman's terms."

"I audited their current systems. They were a nightmare. I don't blame Ralph, he's a kid, still in school. The whole place essentially ran off a bunch of standalone desktop computers and laptops. A lot of data was being kept on individual computers. They had a central server, but it was up to each person to connect to it and back up their data manually."

"Not good. Then what?"

"I told Carl they had a huge risk; their systems and data weren't secure." Dave leaned forward. "He wanted me to do whatever was needed to correct the situation. I couldn't believe it, a freakin' dream job. Trouble was they needed everything in place by the end of September."

"Couldn't it be done?"

"It was going to be a real stretch, especially to transfer all the data they had. I said I'd see what I could do. I mean, they had nothing. I needed to enable remote client access using a VPN. I set up a WINS server on the LAN with proper firewalls and configured the VPN server. Although NetBIOS names can be used with network protocols other than TCP/IP, WINS was designed specifically to support NetBIOS over TCP/IP."

Lydia rolled her eyes and stood up. "Anyone want coffee?"

"I'll have a coke if you're up," said Dave.

"Come on, Dave, English," I said.

"Okay, okay. I installed a network of secure servers. Everyone know what a server is?" he asked sarcastically. Lydia and I ignored him.

"I added the software and network connections required to allow them to securely access data on those servers. This way a remote user could join the company's network without exposing the remote desktop server directly to the internet."

"Got it," I said, nodding.

"I ran a training session showing them how to login remotely and the new data file structure I set up for them. After everyone was trained, I asked them to go through their data, decide what to delete and what to keep. Then I started moving the data they wanted to keep to the new server."

Lydia returned with Dave's coke. I waited while Dave popped the tab and slammed back half the can. He belched, patted his stomach and wiped his lips with the back of his hand.

"Okay, so you moved their data to the new server," I said.

"Right. That's when the first issue cropped up."

"What issue?"

"Their head of operations, a guy named Daryl, has a snit fit. Says his data is wrong. That I messed something up. Yeah right."

"What was wrong?"

"The dumbasses had their data hacked. Too bad they hadn't hired me a few months earlier. I proved it to them. I hadn't deleted any data. I moved the data they wanted to save over to the secure server. The computer log showed it all."

"What happened to the data? What data was hacked?"

Dave looked around nervously. "Their trial data."

"Ooops. Not good."

"No shittin'. Daryl went ballistic. He and Carl had a huge blowout."

"Why? What did Carl have to do with it?"

"Daryl blamed him for being a cheap dumbass. Said they should have had proper security in place long before this, but his nickel and diming, hiring students to do work they weren't qualified to do, was going to cost them big time."

Dave licked his lips and stared at the floor. Something else was going on here. I rubbed my forehead.

"Okay, someone hacked their data. That doesn't explain why you have a hard drive hidden away, which I assume has something to do with why someone pointed a gun in your face."

Dave turned to Lydia. She lifted her shoulders, turned up the palms of her hands and shook her head.

"I don't know what's going on," said Dave. "Honest."

"Try again."

Dave shook his head and sighed. "Like I said, all I know is Daryl and Carl had a big blow-up. Daryl said someone was trying to set him up. Carl accused Daryl of changing the data himself, to hide something. Daryl lost it. He looked ready to kill someone. He told Carl he'd better be careful what came out of his mouth. He called him insane and said if he had changed his own trial numbers for some reason why would he point it out."

"Makes sense. How did he find out the data was incorrect?"

"He used to keep a copy of all the data on his laptop. He had a bunch of pivot tables and he could run graphs and analyze his data various ways. When he reran the graphs, once the data was moved over to the new server, he noticed they didn't match the graphs he made for a presentation from the pivot tables he previously stored on his laptop. But the new server I put in for them hadn't been hacked. Someone changed the data on Daryl's laptop two weeks before the new server went live."

"Someone hacked Daryl's laptop?"

"Apparently. He claimed he didn't change any of the numbers. And like he says, if he did why draw attention to it?"

"What's the big deal, couldn't they go back to the original data?" Lydia asked.

"They were supposed to be keeping their data on the main server. The data on Daryl's laptop should have only been a copy of the data. But they didn't follow their own procedures. At least not regularly. Somewhere along the way, Daryl copied the raw data he had on his laptop to the server. Unfortunately, the way they had the server set up it copied the new data over and didn't keep any of the previous data longer than ten days."

My head hurt. "Let me get this straight. So, the hacked data on Daryl's laptop got copied down to the old server and the old server replaced the previous data with the corrupt data?"

"Right, and then I moved the corrupt data to the new server. Of course, I had no idea it was corrupt. What?" Dave looked from Lydia to me. "They told me to move it."

"Now I get it. They ended up with corrupt data on both servers, and only a few old presentations—created before the data was hacked—showed the true results."

"Right."

"Couldn't they just go with the data in the presentation," said Lydia.

Dave and I both looked at Lydia, surprised to see she was still listening.

"Sure. But it's not true source data. If someone were to audit their trial results, this would be a big red flag the results might be compromised or, worse yet, not real. Not to mention the charts showing the erroneous data had been shared with their investors."

"Then what happened?"

Dave shifted and rubbed his palms on the top of his flannel-encased thighs.

"Carl accused Daryl of changing the numbers and then reporting it to make everyone think the data had been hacked. After all, the numbers had been changed on Daryl's laptop. Carl yelled, 'What are you trying to hide, Daryl' or something like that. Daryl stormed out of the office."

Dave's hands flew briskly, back and forth, across the top of his thighs. If he wasn't careful the friction would spark a fire. Lydia stopped picking nail polish off her nails and listened intently.

"Now I get it," I said. "It wasn't just that the trial data couldn't be verified if asked. Carl was worried about the product. What else did you hear?"

"I wasn't eavesdropping. I could hear Carl and JP in the office next door."

Lydia piped up. "What did you hear?"

"I couldn't make out every word, but they were discussing some woman who died. They were arguing. You could tell by the tone of their voices."

I sat up. "A woman? You're sure it was a woman?"

"Yeah I'm sure. JP was totally riled up. I had no trouble making him out, right through the wall. I just sat there. I didn't know if I should stay or leave."

"I gather you stayed. What else did they say?"

"JP said no one was going to care if the numbers were up for a few people, and a bit worse for others, the numbers weren't much different from the original results. They were on their third trial and the results were good. Oh…and the only thing that could hurt them now was Carl blithering about someone manipulating data. I heard JP say, 'Do whatever you need to do to make sure it doesn't happen again and get off your goddamn high horse.'"

"Interesting. This woman who died. One of their trial participants?"

"Yeah. That's why Daryl noticed the data. She died two months earlier, but someone entered a weight next to her name for the previous month. Well, not her name, an ID number."

"Who would have known who the ID number belonged to?"

"A few people. Daryl for sure. The ID number is there for confidentiality, but nobody really cares who is behind the ID number. There is a master data set with names, but the weekly reports are entered by the participants themselves against their ID number, using a secure password."

"We have to assume whoever hacked the data didn't know this woman died," I said. "If Daryl was messing with the data, he wouldn't have been as careless as to add data to a participant who was no longer part of the trial."

We all sat in quiet contemplation. I broke the silence. "Unless it was Daryl and he wanted everyone to think it was someone else."

"Exactly," said Dave.

"What happened after this big blowout?"

"Carl came back into the room. He wanted to know how the hackers accessed the data. I told him someone had to have accessed Daryl's laptop physically."

"That means it had to have happened at the office, Daryl's home, or wherever he had taken his laptop the days the data was changed."

"Pretty much. It's not like his laptop was stolen. It would have almost been easier to hack the server, since they had such poor security," said Dave, shaking his head. "Changing data on a laptop is risky. You have to know where it is at any given time or when it's on and in use."

"He hadn't recently gone on any trips or left it unattended at a meeting somewhere?"

"He said no. No one's broken into his house or car either, at least not to his knowledge. Based on what Daryl told me I figured the most likely places for someone to access his laptop were JP's house or the office," said Dave. "You'd think someone would have noticed someone messing with his computer at the office though."

I nodded. "Unless it was someone who works at Riteweight and had reason to be in Daryl's office. Same goes for JP's house. I can't imagine it being hacked by a stranger. I mean, sounds like they went right for the pivot tables. Someone knew what they were looking for."

Carl had been worried. If he had tried to delay the launch over this, it may have given someone cause to get him out of the way. But why go after Dave? Several other people knew about the data issue, JP for one.

"I worked day and night like a dog, putting in proper procedures. We had two weeks left to fix everything, migrate the rest of the data and train people on security procedures and proper protocols."

"I had also checked all their home computers since they were occasionally being used to access the office. You know, make sure they were up to date and configured properly to be able to log in via VPN."

"I don't need the technical details. I want to know whose hard drive you've got squirrelled away and why someone is after you."

"Geez, hold your horses, I'm getting there. It was while we were trying to sort out the data that I discovered some shit going on at the Boussards', and weird stuff started happening."

Now he had my attention.

THIRTY-EIGHT

IN ADDITION TO setting up the company network, Dave had to check personal computers since some had been used for company business. JP was notorious for bringing reports home to read on a memory stick, rather than bringing home a company laptop. The week before the data hack was discovered Dave had visited JP's home and checked all five computers in the house. He wanted to make sure the spam filters and virus protection software were up to date and that no company data remained on the hard drive.

"I noticed Malcolm's laptop had been wiped clean. No email, no browsing history. Most people don't feel a need to erase their browser history."

"Probably visiting sites he shouldn't be," I said. Maybe he was into the Goth culture deeper than just his outward appearance.

"That's what I figured," said Dave. "I asked JP if he or his wife ever worried about their kids' internet usage. It's a lot weirder than when I was a kid." Dave crushed his empty can into a flat disk. "There's a lot of creepy sites kids can get pulled into."

Lydia reached over and ripped the flattened can from his hand. "I can't believe you ratted the kid out."

"I didn't rat him out. I suggested they install spyware, which would show them when and how much time was being spent on the computer. It can also tell how much bandwidth is being used. They said to go ahead. Under normal circumstances I wouldn't have given it another thought. Except whoever hacked Daryl's laptop also wiped the browser history clean. What are the chances?"

"Okay, I see why you might have found it odd."

"Whoever altered the trial data also purged the internet activity log. I asked Daryl if he was in the habit of erasing his internet activity log," said Dave. "He said no."

"Why? Did the hacker connect to a site they wanted to keep hidden? But for what purpose?"

"Yeah. It didn't make sense."

"So?"

"So, I started wondering if it could have been the kid."

"Malcolm?" I said.

"Sure, blame the kid," piped in Lydia, from her corner of the couch.

Dave and I eyed her. For a moment, I'd forgotten she was there. Dave put his hand on her knee, and she slapped it away.

"But why?"

"You suspected something," I said. "You thought Malcolm was visiting sites he shouldn't have been. Porn?"

Lydia bristled and glared at Dave. "When did you become such an old man?"

"Look, it's not like I'm the porn police or anything. But people do expect me to be professional."

I eyed the Chewbacca pyjama pants. "So, porn?"

Dave licked his lips nervously. "Could be porn…could be other weird shit."

"Come on, spit it out. Like what?"

"Jheezzz Louise. I'm getting there."

"Hopefully before sunset," I said, barely keeping the annoyance out of my voice.

"I checked the tracking software I had installed. Not much activity. So, I checked Malcolm out online. Pulled up his Facebook and twitter accounts. It was disturbing."

"Can you be more specific?"

"He's being bullied. I know what it's like…I've been there."

I bit back a rhetorical comment…something regarding Chewbacca.

"I tried talking to him. I told him I'd been bullied. That it's not okay. I told him I could help him trace the cyberbully and have him arrested."

"Yeah right," snickered Lydia.

"He was totally salty and told me to *eff* off. I could tell he was scared. He probably didn't want his parents or anyone to know, afraid of retaliation if he reported it."

"Retaliation? Are you suggesting you helped Malcolm, and now his cyberbully is trying to kill you?" Lydia's voice dripped with sarcasm. I was glad she voiced what was going through my head.

"I've been in his shoes. And yeah, retaliation can be physical. Trust me. Whoever's bullying him is likely a so-called friend or at least an acquaintance. It usually is. I mean what's the chance of a complete stranger deciding to go out of their way to make your life miserable?"

I had no idea where Dave was going with all this, but he had my interest.

"A few weeks later, Malcolm called me. He was furious with me. I didn't do anything, so I asked him why he was so riled. He said the messages were getting weirder. Whoever was bullying him could see and hear what was going on in his house. It was like they were a fly on the wall. He was convinced someone hijacked his computer or was bugging his room."

"Okay, that's creepy," conceded Lydia.

"I went over and checked out his laptop. I even checked his friend's laptop, because the two of them hung out a lot. Replaced the hard drive, reinstalled all the original software. This, I might add, on my own time. I checked for bugs, software or apps that weren't supposed to be there. I even brought in equipment and swept the house. Nothing. When I was checking out the data on his hard drive. I... ah...saw some photos of Malcolm and some of his friends."

"I take it these aren't photos of guys playing softball or girls holding trophies at the science fair?"

"No. They were sexually explicit. There was a photo of Malcolm and his buddy kissing. Malcolm 'fessed up. He said they had just been messing around. You know."

I didn't, but what did I know. I'm old Jorja.

"Somehow, somebody got a hold of these pictures. They threatened him. If he didn't send more photos of himself in compromising positions, they'd post those online, with his name."

"I gather he did."

"Malcolm figured if he sent a few pictures the creeper would go away. But that's not how it works. It went downhill from there. Someone's extorting sex photos of Malcolm. He's terrified he'll never get his life back, not to mention being terrified about what this will do to his high-profile parents if it gets out."

"I hope you told him to go to the police."

Lydia rolled her eyes. "Here we go again with the police."

What the hell was her problem with the police? On second thought, I couldn't care less.

"He didn't want to drag his parents into it, at least not with their big launch coming up. And the police would definitely want to talk to his parents and word would leak out. I told him I'd try tracking this creep down. If we could convince him we were onto him, maybe he'd back off."

"Did you have any luck?"

Dave belched. "Luck has very little to do with it."

"Did your brilliant investigation yield anything?" I asked, making no attempt to hide my growing impatience.

"When they came after me, I figured I was getting close. At first the messages were juvenile, calling my efforts to help Malcolm an epic fail. When I didn't back off, the messages got nastier, said I was incompetent, didn't know squat and all my clients would soon know I couldn't even secure data properly. The one that totally blew me away suggested I back off Malcolm's problem and deal with his father's weight-loss scam."

"Oh shit." Lydia and I glanced at each other realizing we had uttered the expletive simultaneously.

"It got worse. The creep said it wouldn't do my career any good if the information regarding the hacked trial data were leaked to the media…from me, my email account. I've been working night and day trying to find the bastard. And I'm going to nail him, if it's the last thing I do."

"What are you saying? Someone had your place bugged as well as the Boussards'?"

Dave shook his head. "It's the damnedest thing. I can't figure out how they're doing it."

"What's any of this have to do with Carl's death?"

"I don't know. All I know is two days after I got the message threatening to leak the trial data from my account, Carl died, and I got shot."

"And the hard drive you have locked away?"

"It's Malcolm's. While all this was happening, Riteweight's lawyer was sending me reminders of my confidentiality agreement with them. If this guy leaks the data from my computer, I'll not only lose my clients, I could be sued for breaking my confidentiality agreement with Riteweight. Which by the way, I now broke, by telling you. You won't say anything, will you? Don't you have a client confidentiality agreement with Lydia?"

"Technically, I don't work for Lydia anymore."

"Come on, Jorja, there's no way you fired me," said Lydia.

I ignored her.

Lydia's tone changed. "I'll swear in court. Your word against mine."

Suddenly I understood why Lydia and I would never be friends.

I left Lydia's thoroughly miffed. The whole thing was too bizarre for words, like one of those bad jokes that go on and on, leaving you to hope the punch line will make it worth it. How did this one go? A guy dies at a dinner that a PI's friend is catering. People get sick. The PI discovers the dead guy's wife carried out a stupid prank which made people sick. But her husband didn't die because of the prank. Someone poisoned him. Turns out the guy who died was worried his company's new weight-loss product might not be as safe as his chief scientist insisted. His own wife, the prankster, gained weight while taking it, and an obese trial participant died. Someone messed with the trial data. The dead man's partner, the CEO of the company, has strayed from his marriage, likely more than once. His wife probably knows, but won't end the marriage until the big ship rolls in. His son is being cyberbullied, threatened and subjected to extortion. The weight-loss company hires an IT guy to beef up data security. The IT guy discovers the CEO's son is being cyberbullied. He starts digging, hoping to find the scumbag. Instead, he becomes a victim. Someone threatens to leak the weight-loss trial data breech to the media, and make it look like it came from him. The IT guy's girlfriend hires the PI to watch him under the pretense he might be cheating on her. Someone amps up their efforts to scare the IT guy off, or just plain kill him. Meanwhile, the dead man's wife, the prankster, hires the PI to find who killed her husband, hoping the PI won't notice she's playing footsie with her dead husband's new partner, who in turn suspects the operations manager poisoned Carl as an act of revenge. And the punch line? I hope it isn't going to be that the PI was played so well, she didn't even realize it.

THIRTY-NINE

DARYL HADN'T BOTHERED to return my message, so I paid him a visit. He wasn't happy to see me. I suggested we go to a coffee shop for a chat. This pleased him even less, but he agreed. He entertained my chit chat as we made our way to Sebastian's. We ordered coffee and snagged a table being vacated by two women and a baby.

"Are you going to tell me what's going on?" Daryl asked once we sat down.

I picked up my coffee and sipped, my eyes meeting his over the rim of my cup. "I thought you could tell me."

"I have no idea what you're talking about or what you want. And I don't care for whatever cloak-and-dagger fantasy you've got going on." His eyes bore into mine. I suddenly realized I was attracted to this man. But I was already chasing a street minister and had a crush on head of Special Crimes, Inspector Luis Azagora, who was probably a bigger dickhead than the one sitting in front of me.

I set my coffee down and leaned forward. "I know you act like you don't care and your pissy-ass persona is supposed to trumpet the message to everyone around you. But I'm not buying. You know why? 'Cause I'm real familiar with the schtick. After all, I used it myself for years."

Daryl didn't respond verbally, but I saw a flicker of acknowledgement in his eyes. Now I needed to prove to him he'd met his match.

"Look, this is the weirdest case I've encountered, and I don't mind admitting it to you. You're a bright guy, observant, hardworking. I know the only standards you're trying to meet are your own. Why wouldn't you? Your standards are a lot higher than those held by your compatriots. Their motives are different than yours. They want fame, fortune and glory. That kind of stuff doesn't matter to people like us. Sure, recognition is nice. But finding a lasting solution or solving a legitimate problem is the real prize."

Daryl remained silent; I had his attention.

"I told you Rose hired me to find out who killed Carl. And I'm going to. Frankly, I don't care if it turns out Rose killed him. I don't like the idea of scumbags getting away with murder."

Daryl nodded.

"There are three pieces of information critical to finding out what happened to Carl. One,"—I held up my thumb—"Carl didn't die of natural or accidental causes. In fact, there may have been more than one attempt to kill him all coincidently taking place the same night."

Dimitri could claim two EpiPen shots saved Carl's life, at least temporarily, but I wasn't buying it. Dimitri's second epinephrine shot had put Carl in serious risk of a heart attack.

I held up my index finger. "Secondly, an unauthorized person accessed your laptop and changed the trial data." I held up my hand before Daryl had time to protest. "And the fact you reported the problem tells me a lot. If anyone truly understood, they'd see you were the one totally torqued off because the data was altered. JP and Kristen were more worried about the repercussions of the news getting out, than why the data was changed in the first place.

That's what we need to figure out. Why did someone change the data? For what purpose?"

Daryl leaned forward, putting his hands on the table in front of him.

"Thirdly, someone sent threatening messages to the IT guy you hired to beef up your data security, claiming his security measures are a joke. They even threatened to expose the data breech, smearing his good name in the process."

"What the hell?"

"Exactly." I could see he hadn't been expecting this last tidbit. I didn't mention the threats Dave received involved Malcolm. Best to keep a thing or two up my sleeve.

"First, I asked myself, who would gain from Carl's death? Unfortunately, there's a long and growing list of candidates. It doesn't help me narrow anything down. That's when I started asking myself, what impact would changing the trial data make? And to whom? Especially data changes which were insignificant. They were, weren't they?"

"Yes. I only noticed because when I ran September results, I spotted a weight recorded for a participant who had dropped out of the trial a few months earlier."

"You mean dropped out of life?"

Surprise flitted across his face. A second later his shoulders relaxed, and he leaned toward me. His voice lowered.

"Yes. A woman who was part of the trial was killed in a car accident. I had to normalize my data and recalculate average weight loss for the group to make sure her withdrawal didn't skew the actual results. When I saw the weight-loss numbers recorded by her name, I checked the data stored in my pivot tables against the raw data in our database. They didn't match. I was pissed. Especially as I had been going through all these gyrations to connect and download the data to the server and back everything up manually. Preposterous in today's world. I have enough on my plate without being the company's data guy on top of it."

"You confronted Carl when you discovered someone breeched the data."

"I was upset. Carl's penny pinching drove me crazy. Ironically, there's always enough money for them to wine and dine themselves and their entourage of investors and marketers."

"How'd he take it?"

"Carl accused me of altering the data. Can you believe it? I told him he was insane."

"Was all the data changed?"

"No. As best I could tell, weights were changed for six participants. Most of the changes showed a greater loss of three or four pounds over the entire month. Two participants had data changed to show they gained weight during the month. Why would I do that?"

"You're right, those changes aren't exactly significant or make sense. Is there any relationship between these six participants?"

"None as far as I know."

"But another guy dropped out or died in one of the earlier trials, didn't he?"

"Yeah, but so what?" Daryl shrugged indifferently. "The guy was pushing five-hundred pounds, a ticking time bomb. We should have never accepted him into the trial. He stopped breathing one day on the way to work. Too bad we didn't get to him sooner."

"And the trials were six months long?"

"That's right. Participants self-report once a month and check in three months after the trial is finished to report if they've managed to keep the weight off and to submit other information like blood pressure, cholesterol levels, that sort of thing. A few pounds up or down are normal. Like I said, there's a variety of reasons for the fluctuations. It's called living. But Carl totally freaked out. He suspected everyone."

"Of what?"

Daryl leaned forward. "That righteous prick accused me of trying to cover something up. Hinted…no, warned me there better not be anything wrong with Luzit. Or what?" Daryl scoffed.

"What do you think is going on?"

"Like I told Carl, I think someone is setting me up, setting us up, messing with the data to make the data seem untrustworthy for this very reason. So we would start to doubt ourselves and delay putting our product out in the market."

"Sabotage to delay the launch?"

"Exactly. Carl didn't buy it. He kept saying, the product better not be harming anyone. I lost it. Why would I change numbers for someone who obviously was no longer in the trial and then report it?"

To make it look like you were hacked, I speculated to myself. Instead, I said, "So Carl was worried the supplement might be causing harm. That it wasn't just ineffective, two people died while taking it." That confirmed what Rose and Gina had noticed. Carl had been worried.

"Yeah. Like somehow changing a few numbers would mask that. I thought he was insane. There's absolutely no evidence of this supplement causing harm. The side effects are minimal, most people don't even exhibit any side effects." Daryl shook his head, his voice rose. "He said he wasn't prepared to go forward until he found out who was tampering with the data and why."

"You sure this woman died in an accident?"

"That's what her husband said, when he contacted me. Why would I doubt him?"

"What was JP's reaction?"

"He was more concerned with Carl's reaction than the data

breech. He could see the way the numbers were changed were insignificant and random. Why increase weight loss for a few participants and lower it for a few others? By a few measly pounds? The data change didn't amount to anything. But if this got out, it could raise questions about the reliability of our trials. He told Carl to let it go."

"Carl didn't?"

"No. After accusing me and getting nowhere, Carl turned his attention to Dimitri, and his investors."

"Dimitri? What possible benefit would Dimitri have in changing the data?"

"No benefit. That's what made it totally bizarre. Although we all know the Russians can't be trusted. They're behind half the cybercrime out there, hacking political systems, planting false reports, creating chaos and drama. They must be laughing their asses off. Not that I don't appreciate the resulting new server and proper security protocols. But Carl became paranoid. He began poking into the investors' backgrounds; making statements like 'what did we really know about where the capital was coming from?'"

"Could he have found something?"

"Wouldn't surprise me if he did. Ever wonder how a guy defects, with nothing but the clothes on his back, and ends up with millions to invest. Carl insisted on full disclosure on the source of the investment money…suspected Dimitri or one of his investors might be laundering money."

"What? Did he confront them?"

"I don't know. I don't think so. If he did, JP would have killed him on the spot. Besides, I'm sure there's no legal way to do that unless these investors have been formally charged with something. Carl began looking into the testing lab and packaging and distribution companies in Africa. Who owned them, their financial history. Dimitri provided an investor summary, but Carl wasn't satisfied. He began dragging his feet on the smallest of decisions." Daryl shook his head in disgust. "These are private companies; they don't have to make all of their data public."

"If he didn't find anything, what made him put the brakes on?"

"I don't know. He told JP they should go with an independent testing lab and a publicly traded packaging company, instead of the companies Dimitri brought forward."

"Perhaps Carl did discover something the investors and their South African interests prefer remained hidden."

"Maybe. I don't know. Knowing Carl, I suspect if he had found anything shady, he would have blown the story sky high not just quietly tried to convince JP to change suppliers. On the other hand, Carl was a bit of an old woman. Worried about everything."

"I presume his recommendation didn't go over well."

"It didn't. JP, Dimitri and Carl got into it one afternoon. JP wouldn't hear of changing suppliers. Dimitri said if his investors couldn't get a lift from their investment by utilizing their other companies, they'd have to rethink the deal. Riteweight would be cutting into what they could make on this investment, in whole."

"So, Dimitri knew about all of this?" Dimitri had told me he didn't remember anything about Carl being worried before his death, didn't know Carl had been dragging his feet on things.

I could see how Carl's behaviour might have given more than a few people reason to get him out of the way. Rose's lawyer might be interested in hearing this, if Rose ever came under more heat.

"But now someone out there knows the data was altered and is threatening to leak the information to the press from your IT guy's IP address. Either that or they're playing mind games with him."

"Does JP know?" asked Daryl. "I wonder if it's one of our competitors."

"I haven't told him. What would happen if this information reached the public?"

"Other than becoming a PR nightmare for a while, I'm not sure. Some people might put off buying the product. We'd counter the news articles and the rumours, saying the rest of the trial data was secure, the breech occurred on a standalone laptop, probably somebody's idea of a sick joke. We might even disclose the data changes to illustrate its insignificance in the larger scheme of things. Follow up with testimonials from the trial participants regarding their success. If you have forty or a hundred pounds to lose are you really going to care if you lose three pounds versus four over the course of a week with no effort? Both are great results."

"So what do you think is going on?"

"I think whoever did this is getting a kick by watching us squirm. If a competitor did it, why hasn't it been leaked to the press? What are they waiting for?" Daryl shrugged. "It doesn't make sense."

After Daryl and I parted, I ran through the various possibilities. It could be Daryl's sick way of getting revenge by making the owners of Riteweight sweat. Then why discount the possibility of competitor meddling. If he were guilty wouldn't he be embracing any hint of wrongdoing by someone else? His point about competitor sabotage was right on point. Why tamper with the data and not leak it to the press?

If something was wrong with Luzit, Carl would have been doing everyone a favour by putting the brakes on. It would also be devastating financially to the investors and JP and Carl. But if someone was trying to alert Carl to lack of product safety, why make minor changes to data on Daryl's laptop, hoping Daryl would notice it and raise it as a flag?

Whoever was involved must know the players, how they would react. Could they have known JP wouldn't risk financial ruin by catering to Carl's demands to delay. Could JP actually have been compelled to quiet Carl for good, even if not directly by his own hand? If Dimitri or one of his investors was in any way connected to the mob or other illegal activity and was concerned with what Carl found it was entirely possible steps would be taken to silence Carl.

Could Dee Dee have caught wind that Carl was threatening to delay the launch and done something stupid, something desperate to get Carl out of the way of ruining her financial security. Possibly. What if Dee Dee knew her husband was cheating on her with Kristen? Could she have accidently poisoned Carl instead of JP? Or tampered with the data on Daryl's computer knowing if word leaked out it would create a PR nightmare for her to deal with. But if I was reading Dee Dee correctly, and she knew JP and Kristen were having an affair, she'd find a way to pay them back without harming Riteweight's reputation and her future financial security.

Too bad Rose benefited in so many ways. They say some murderers are plain stupid, but the prank substituting beans took initiative and a certain vindictiveness not visible at first glance. Was it plausible to think the data breech had been another of Rose's sick pranks intended to provide her a kick out of messing with their heads, watching them turn on one another? To the point someone got killed?

FORTY

A BUZZ CUT THE air and on cue the front doors opened. Bodies poured out. I watched their eager young faces and tried to guess which of them could torment their peers. I needed to talk to Malcolm. Especially after what Dave told me.

Was Malcolm being bullied over his black attire or was it his warrior costume, his way of trying to ward off the hurt? It'd be a bitch being Dee Dee's son or daughter. Did she know Malcolm was hurting or did she write off his appearance as a childish attempt to mar her perfect family image?

I hadn't exactly been popular at school, but I hadn't been bullied. At least we didn't think of it as bullying. When someone picked a fight, we either ran or fought back. Of course, the adults had an edge back then. We were always more afraid of what they would do if they found out we'd been in a fight, than the actual fight itself. The deluge of bodies became a trickle. Ten minutes later I spotted Malcolm's friend. He came out alone. I climbed out of my truck and crossed the street.

"Excuse me. You're Malcolm's friend, aren't you?"

He stopped and pulled one of the ear buds from his ear.

"I don't know if you remember me. I met with Malcolm after school a few days ago. My name is Jorja Knight."

He backed up, looking confused. "Sorry, I gotta go."

"Do you know where Malcolm is?"

"He wasn't at school today." He turned and hustled off down the sidewalk.

Damn. I watched his stooped black frame for a minute and returned to my truck. I felt even creepier following him home.

❧

The next morning, I was parked on the Boussards' street, bright and early. I waited for an hour and a half, but Malcolm didn't show. On an off chance, I drove to his friend's house. It was a small bi-level on a quiet street filled with other 1980s bi-levels and bungalows. I had checked the city tax roster last night and discovered the Swansons lived there. Digging further, I found the boy's name listed on one of the community's former soccer teams. Eric Swanson. I rang the doorbell. I guessed right. Eric opened the door.

"Hi, Eric. We need to talk."

He glanced furtively over his shoulder.

"I know Malcolm's here. And I know someone has been cyberbullying him. His IT buddy, Dave, told me."

"So? What's it to you?" He stared at me sullenly.

"Did you know someone tried breaking into Dave's place and shot him?"

"Shit." He dropped his gaze and fidgeted with his watch strap. "Is he okay?"

"No, he's not okay. Someone tried to kill him."

"Shit," he said again and glanced over his shoulder.

"That's right, Eric. Shit. And I know Malcolm's in big doo-doo, too. The sooner we find out who's doing this the better. Don't you agree?"

"You're a private eye?"

"Yeah. I know Dave, you know, the guy who was hired by Mr. Boussard's company to provide IT services. Someone shot him and he went into hiding. But I found him. He told me Malcolm was getting threatening emails and other weird stuff was going on at the Boussards'. Now I've tracked you two down. You need to tell me what's going on. Either me or the police."

His eyes darted wildly. He wiped his palms along the sides of his jeans and shuffled.

"Man, I don't know."

"Your choice. Me or the cops. If you pick me, there's coffee or breakfast. Pick the cops and you'll be sitting in an interrogation room with your parents and possibly someone from social services."

"Okay, whatever. Hold on a sec." He backed in and closed the door.

I pulled my jacket tighter around me and surveyed the street. Two boys rode by on bicycles which angered a Bichon being walked by a man on the sidewalk. I watched it lunge its small body toward the boys, barking furiously. As they drove away, the dog spun in circles, still yapping. For a moment, I worried Eric and Malcolm had slipped out the back. I was relieved when the door opened. Malcolm came out, pulling on a black leather jacket. Eric followed.

"Hi, Malcolm. Smart choice, guys."

Malcolm shrugged indifferently.

I drove to a small restaurant in a nearby strip mall, where they served all-day breakfast. Once inside and with coffees ordered, I turned my attention to the pathetic figures sitting across from me.

"I know you're being cyberbullied, Malcolm. And more. Someone killed your father's business partner. The IT guy your father hired is in hiding because someone is out to get him. You seem like decent guys, but you're in over your heads. Who wants to tell me what's going on?" I studied one, then the other. Eric sat hunched over, his eyes on the table in front of him, his hands resting on his knees, below the table. Malcolm's shoulders sagged. He wiped his mouth with the back of his hand.

"I don't know who killed Carl. The police already asked me if I saw or knew anything. I don't."

"Okay, I believe that." He might know more than he thought. He might have inadvertently heard something. Maybe an argument between his parents or an argument between JP and Daryl or Carl. I decided to go with his personal dilemma.

"Dave told me you're being cyberbullied. Do you want to tell me about it?"

"We put up with a lot of crap at school. No one gets us," said Malcolm.

"When did it start?"

Malcolm glanced at Eric. "We've never really fit in. But a few months ago, I started to get hate mail. Real twisted shit."

"Like what?"

"I can hardly wait till you're dead. It's going to be fun watching you kill yourself. Stuff like that."

"Wow. What did you do?"

"Ignored it at first, but the messages got worse. Dozens a day, on email, Facebook. I even changed my accounts, but it didn't stop."

"Did you tell anyone?"

"Not at first. But after a while it got creepy. It was like someone was watching us or could hear what we said. The messages mentioned stuff nobody but Eric and I knew."

"That is creepy. You're sure no one was simply overhearing you?"

"No," Eric replied looking at Malcolm. "It was stuff we'd

talk about up in Malcolm's room. It's like the room's bugged. We searched the whole place but didn't find anything."

They both fell silent. I waited several minutes hoping one of them would continue. When they didn't, I plunged ahead.

"Do you want to tell me about the pictures?"

Malcolm inhaled sharply. The colour drained from his face.

"Holy shit," Eric muttered under his breath.

I watched Malcolm pull in his bottom lip. I glanced from him to Eric, suddenly aware of how young they were, children really. Malcolm turned toward me, his eyes dark and filled with fear.

"Who told you?"

"I told Eric. I tracked your IT buddy, Dave, down after someone shot him. Dave told me how he came across the pictures. I want to hear your version of the story."

Malcolm and Eric exchanged glances. Malcolm licked his lip and swiped it with his hand. "Have you ever listened to Blog TV?"

"No."

"It's a site where you can blog, you know, like a blog but with a webcam."

"Oh," I said, the twenty-year gap between us now stretching into a chasm.

"I used to blog there, under the name Darkdaze. There's this girl who followed my blog. Alana. We started chatting online." His fingers twirled the coffee cup in front of him and he stared at the small specks of cream floating on top.

"Okay."

"After a while she sent me pictures of you know…herself. She wanted pictures of me."

"I take it these were more than the regular school photo headshots."

"Yeah."

"Okay so the two of you are sending pictures back and forth showing off your body parts. I imagine there's more."

"She invited us to a party. Eric and I went."

"Where?"

"A house in Dalhousie, near the university. There must have been a hundred people there. A couple of guys brought guitars. It was cool. Everybody just hanging out." He shrugged. "You know."

I did know. Most of the attendees had probably been higher than kites. "Did you meet the girl who invited you? Alana?"

"No. The day after the party she posted on my Facebook page. She said her little sister got sick and her mom made her stay home to look after her." Malcolm and Eric exchanged glances. "The next day someone posted a picture on Facebook of Eric and me from the party."

"So?"

"Kissing." He breathed it so quietly I almost asked him to repeat it.

"Who cares? Last time I checked, people who out themselves aren't being stoned to death anymore."

"We're not gay," Eric declared defiantly. "Shit. We just felt like…you know…see what it was like…and went for it. One lousy kiss." His voice rose petulantly. "I don't even know why we did it. Malcolm's parents are already threatening to send him away to a psych clinic. If they see pictures of him kissing guys and… and then…and claiming, he's not gay, they'll think he's totally cray cray."

No wonder I empathized with Malcolm. Despite his looks, he was no different than the eighties child. Eager for independence, desperate for approval.

"We got a lot of ugly messages, on Facebook, on my blog," said Malcolm.

"What kind of messages?"

"Most just said, 'We figured you were gay' and stuff like 'Wondering when you'd out yourselves,'" said Eric.

"Some said, 'Die fag die' and 'Do the world a favour and off yourself,'" added Malcolm.

"Are you kidding?" Then I remembered the messages would be from anyone and everyone which included all the prejudiced, narrow-minded twits out there.

"One of those messages was from Alana," said Malcolm. "But she swore it wasn't her," he added hurriedly. "She said her account had been hacked."

"You believed her?"

"At first. She told me she went to St. Mary's High and her real name was Julie Dixon. She said she tried shutting down the Alana account, but someone had gone in and changed all the passwords, so she couldn't."

"Yup, that's how it works. Once someone figures out your password, they have your life."

"Eric knows a couple of guys who go to St Mary's. They said there's no one there named Julie Dixon. We searched the internet, hoping to find her."

"We did find someone named Julie Dixon," said Eric quietly and glanced over at Malcolm. Malcolm gave an almost imperceptible nod and Eric continued. "She lived in Ontario. She'd been cyberbullied and killed herself two years ago."

A cold shudder crawled up my back. "Were there any pictures of her?"

"Yeah. It's the same girl. We figured someone was posing as her and sending Malcolm photos the real Julie Dixon had sent her online stalker."

"That's totally messed up. And scary. What did you do?"

"I stopped talking to her, or whomever it was," said Malcolm.

"But they began emailing and texting all kinds of shit to our Facebook friends. They threatened to post pictures of me."

"I take it they meant the pictures of yourself you sent to this person, whom you thought was Alana?"

"Yeah."

"You didn't report this to the authorities or at least tell your parents?"

"I told the Deed I was being harassed. I wanted to move schools."

"And?"

"Silvergate Preparatory is one of her philanthropic projects. She said this was a good lesson for me. If I chose to deviate from the mainstream, I'd better be prepared for a lot of negative attention."

"Attention yes, harassment no." My heart ached. I couldn't believe Dee Dee would be so totally uncaring. Oh wait—yes, I could. "Someone took the pictures you thought you were sending privately to this Alana and started sharing them with the world."

"Yeah, well, a few of them. They said if we didn't send a video they'd post more."

I was certain they weren't asking for a video of him playing Frisbee. "Of you, Malcolm?"

"No. The both of us. They wanted Eric and me to...you know."

I didn't know but assumed we were moving beyond kissing.

"There's no way," Eric growled. "We told them to go fuck themselves. If we keep giving in, they're never going away."

"It got real creepy. It was like they could hear everything Eric and I were saying."

"When was this?"

"September. Around the time my dad told me he was beefing up security at our house, data security. 'Cause of his business."

"I figured if the place was bugged or something, they'd find it," said Eric.

"I wiped my browser history and deleted all my emails. When Dave saw that, he figured something was going on. When he gave me my laptop back I saw he'd installed tracking software. I was totally pissed," said Malcolm.

"Was this person still demanding more pictures from you?"

"Yeah. I didn't know what to do. He said he'd post all the pictures if I didn't send him a video."

Eric's jaw clenched and unclenched.

"You sent him a video," I said.

"Yeah, but just me." Malcolm wiped an arm across his eyes. Eric's face burned red as he turned away from Malcolm. "I was worried what would happen if the pictures got out while my parents were trying to get this big deal of theirs going."

"Then what?"

"I finally told Dave. Dave's a cool guy. I didn't know he was in trouble."

My mind flashed back to Dave clutching his Star Wars pyjamas with one hand as he barrelled down the alley in slippers. Cool wouldn't have been the word I'd use.

"Did Dave make any progress?"

"He didn't find anything on our laptops, like key stroke recognition software or anything that shouldn't be there. He had no idea how anyone could hear us. He even brought in equipment and swept our house for bugs but didn't find anything."

"Thorough."

"He said the girl I sent pictures to was probably this creep using her name. But we already figured as much. We shut it all down, Facebook, Instagram, email. Dave told us to wait a month and when we set up new accounts to use super strong passwords."

Malcolm squirmed and stared at the floor. Eric's fingers,

which had been tapping out a rhythm heard solely in his head, stopped.

"What?" I looked from one to the other.

"A couple of weeks in, we checked Facebook. We logged in from the public library. There were a bunch of messages, the usual. There was one from this creep, saying I'd pay big time since I hadn't done what I'd been told to do," said Malcolm.

Shivers ran down my arms. "What a nightmare."

"No shit. Then Carl got sick and died and people were running in and out of the house. A few days later, I went over to Eric's. We set up new email and Facebook accounts. We used real strong passwords." He shook his head. "At the end of the week I got another email. This one mentioned dad's partner, Carl."

"Carl? What's Carl got to do with this?"

Malcolm and Eric exchanged glances. Finally, Malcolm took a deep breath, his eyes met mine. "He knew the data was hacked."

I looked from one to the other. The silence stretched on.

"I hacked Daryl's laptop and changed the data," Malcolm stated evenly.

FORTY-ONE

"**W**HAT?" MY VOICE rose as I looked from Malcolm to Eric. "You did what?" Jumbled thoughts raced through my brain, tripping over each other. "Okay," I restated in a more normal tone. "Who's going to fill me in?"

Malcolm leaned back against the banquette, hunched his shoulders, and stuffed his hands into his front jean pockets. Head still lowered, he mumbled, "I didn't mean to hurt anyone."

My heart skipped a beat. Did I want to hear this? I didn't want to hear this.

"I was mad. Someone's ruining my life and my parents are busy with their stupid herbal supplement."

My breath caught in my throat. *No. He didn't. He couldn't have.*

His voice became stronger, defensive. "I was trying to protect them. That's why I sent the stupid video. They're the ones who made Dave install tracking software on my laptop."

"Holy Hanna," I breathed out. "You hacked Daryl's laptop and sent the video from his computer, because if you used your own laptop, your parents would know because of the tracking software. Then you wiped Daryl's activity log."

"Yeah. Daryl was over, meeting with my dad. He left his laptop in the cloak room. I figured out the password on the third try. Galen2. Galen was this dude in the first century who messed around with medicinal experimentation. My dad sometimes called Daryl, Galen."

"So, you used his computer to send the video. And what? You hacked his data as an act of revenge?"

"Not revenge." Malcolm squirmed. "I was just pissed. I only changed five or six numbers in a spreadsheet. No big deal. I didn't even think anyone would notice."

"But they did notice."

"I can't believe how ballistic Carl went over a couple of stupid numbers. It's not like it's a cure for cancer. This whole weight-loss thing is stupid, just a way for Dee Dee and my dad to get richer and buy more stuff. Like we don't have enough."

"You really need to tell your parents or the police."

"I told Dee Dee I was being bullied," replied Malcolm. "She threatened to take my computer away for a month and ground me."

"This isn't a prank Malcolm. Cyberbullying, extortion—these are punishable crimes."

Eric shot Malcolm a furtive glance, clearly uncomfortable. Malcolm shook his head. "No. I want to drop it. I shouldn't be telling you any of this."

"What aren't you telling me? They haven't stopped, have they?"

Malcolm broke down. I dug through my purse, located a tissue and held it out to him. He ignored it and used his arm to wipe the tears off his face. Eric sat mutely, clenching and unclenching his fist. After a while Malcolm spoke, his voice shaking.

"He said if we didn't send him more videos, this time with the both of us, the world would know the trial data in my dad's company was bogus."

"Wow. How does this person know the trial data was changed?"

"I don't know how. I didn't even tell Eric till the funeral."

They really had him over a barrel. Not only because of the pictures. If word got out about the hacked trial data Malcolm would have to watch the consequences to his father's company or come forward and admit he did it.

I leaned forward and slapped the table. "Someone has to put an end to this. For all we know he isn't merely using Julie Dixon's name, he may actually be the guy who pushed her to take her own life. You have to let the police know."

"No, not yet."

"Why? What are you waiting for?"

"We're going to get this asswad. We're going to catch him," said Eric.

"No, that's dangerous. Don't kid yourself, it's hard to catch guys like this. I know the guy who heads up the Special Crimes unit. They've got the manpower and technology needed. You guys are minors. No one's going to publish your names."

"The ass-wipe who's blackmailing us will."

"It's what they want…to keep you scared and thrashing on the end of the hook. Trust me, reporting this is the only way to put an end to it."

Malcolm's eyes met mine. "No, it's not."

A cold fear gripped my heart.

FORTY-TWO

I DROVE ERIC AND Malcolm back to Eric's place and urged them not to do anything stupid. Stupider. They hadn't been willing to tell me their harebrained plan as to how they were going to catch this creep, or at least I assumed it was harebrained. Truth be known, it's probably best I didn't know. Besides, they had the brilliant Dave helping them.

I needed coffee in the worst way. Now aware of what Malcolm was going through, I couldn't merrily go on to other business. A crime was being committed. And several more had been committed. I needed to do something. I evaluated a myriad of options, all of which left me wanting to eat my body weight in pastries. I needed to talk to Dave.

After securing a coffee and a muffin from McDonald's I turned the truck toward Lydia's. Malcolm's admission that he was the one who altered the trial data blew me away. It changed everything. Maybe Dave was telling the truth and the hard drive in Lydia's possession held Malcolm's data files and not proof of Riteweight's villainous ways. I had to rethink. Someone killed Carl, and someone was still gunning for Dave. Could the two be completely separate events?

Daryl insisted the deaths of two trial participants were

unrelated to the weight-loss supplements, but I only had his word for it. There was no way to get at the names of the trial participants. I bet Dave could find out who they were, but I wasn't going to ask him to peruse Riteweight's data to find out. On the other hand, there might be nothing wrong with Riteweight, its product or the suppliers and investors. Carl could have seen the data tampering as misinforming, unethical. The data breech may have inadvertently triggered Carl's paranoia about harming anyone, especially in light of what happened to his sister. A paranoia triggered by Malcolm's childish payback attempt for monitoring his computer and forcing him to use Daryl's, at least in his mind. Either way, it may have cost Carl his life.

I found myself at Lydia's apartment with no recall of driving there. I called her number. No answer. I left the truck in the drop-off zone, loped to the front door and rang Lydia's apartment. A garbled yes came through the speaker.

"Lydia. It's Jorja. I really need to talk to Dave. Is he there?"

Lydia didn't reply. I buzzed her apartment again.

"He's not here. Go away."

"Okay, okay. But I need to talk to him. Do you know where he is? It's really important."

"He just ran out to the store."

"What store?"

"Probably the Mac's on Fourteenth."

A few minutes later I pulled onto Fourteenth Street. I spotted Dave up ahead, coming out of Mac's with two huge bags, one in each arm. A small black car shot past me as I pulled over to the curb. I heard a sharp crack and my front headlight exploded. Two more pops rang out. My eyes flashed toward Dave. A stream of red exploded from his chest.

I leapt out of the truck and ran toward Dave. Every second stretched to ten. The black car careened out of sight with a squeal of rubber and a cloud of blue smoke. Dave wavered on his feet. I reached out my arm, too late. Dave crumpled to the ground. I winced as he hit the sidewalk, bounced, and lay still.

The store manager ran out, turned and ran back in, presumably to call for help. I reached Dave, fighting back the saliva building at the back of my throat and flooding my mouth.

"Dave!" I knelt at his side, shaking as my knees grew wet. I touched his shoulder. "Dave, can you hear me? Dave!" His one arm still encircled a bag of groceries. The other arm lay on the pavement in a pool of red now spreading out from his body. Cheese doodles littered the sidewalk. Dave's eyelids flickered.

"Oh god. Dave hang in there. Help's on the way."

Dave struggled to sit up. I steadied him as he sat up then staggered to his feet. Stunned, I slowly got to my feet, shocked to see him upright.

Dave lifted his hand up to his face and stared down at his red-soaked coat.

"Those bastards! That was the last damn cherry soda."

I stared at my red-stained knees. A small trickle of red emptied into the gutter.

"Cherry soda? Not blood?"

We made out the sirens at the same time. I grabbed Dave's arm and we hustled to the truck. As soon as we were in the cab, Dave ripped open his coat. "Wow, they dented my warrior knight breast plate."

I turned on the engine and pulled out.

"The bullet didn't even pierce it. That's freakin' awesome. I can get you one if you want. I've also got a chain mail hauberk and a coif. Got them from the same guy."

"Enough already. Don't you care I might be having a heart attack," I said, hand pressed over my heart. "I thought you were a goner."

"Hey, how'd you know where to find me?"

"I stopped by Lydia's."

"Damn. They must have followed you." Dave swivelled his head to look out the back window. "I can't go back to Lydia's. I'll be putting her in danger."

"Dave, this is crazy. Someone just tried to kill you. You need to report the extortion threats for sex videos to the police. Malcolm's a juvenile."

"I would if I knew who was behind the threats."

"No. That's their job, not yours."

"It must be someone acquainted with Malcolm. In most cases, it is. I'm pretty good at ferreting shit out."

"Dave. Do you even hear me?" Now I worried the bullet to the chest had done damage. Where had the third shot gone? Maybe it was lodged in his head.

"Drive me home. I need to pick up a few things and call Lydia. Tell her I'll be away for a few days."

"I'll drive you home but if you're not going to call the cops, I will. You know about Julie Dixon right? Whoever Julie was chatting with online, claimed to be a nineteen-year-old guy. The person chatting with Julie asked for a photo of her, which escalated over time to requests for more and more sexually explicit photos and videos. Just like with Malcolm. When Julie hit the limit of what she was prepared to do, the threats began. She couldn't face the social backlash she imagined she'd suffer once the photos were shared with anyone and everyone, so she committed suicide." The picture of her pretty blond hair, big blue eyes and shy smile had torn at my heart. It was hard enough to fit in without this kind of shit happening.

Dave continued to ignore me.

"I'm not telling you this for nothing. Whoever is extorting images of Malcolm may be the same guy who drove Julie Dixon to kill herself."

"I found the video Malcolm sent on a pay-for-porn site."

"What? You're sure it's him?"

"Most of the headshots were blurred. But I recognized the Doom Eternal poster against the deep-blue wall in Malcolm's room and the old car licence plates nailed to the wall below it."

"Good work. Now you can turn the information over to the Special Crimes unit," I said.

"It's on a hijacked site. The people who own the site probably don't know they've been hijacked. These guys copy the front end and set up a double site, making it look like the legit site they've copied. People directed there are given a password which lets them into the hidden part of the site, where the porn is stored."

"Well the police can get the information needed to help them track these guys down. At least they can order the hosting provider to take the site down."

"Sounds easy but it's not. The video has probably moved a dozen times by now. These guys don't take any chances. Anyone catches wind and a couple of keystrokes later, they're gone. Besides, these guys have really pissed me off. I'm taking them down if it's the last thing I do."

We stopped by Dave's place and I stood guard while Dave ran in for a change of clothes and an old laptop and some other equipment he kept there. He loaded everything into the truck and climbed in next to me.

"My buddy Akar says I can use his parents' place. They've gone back to India for a month-long visit."

"Did you call Lydia and tell her, so she doesn't go ballistic?"

"I called her. Didn't tell her where I'd be staying, so don't you tell her."

"My lips are sealed."

As I drove Dave to Akar's parents' house I urged him to contact the police.

"They want to talk to you about the other night. At least call them and let them know you're alive. All you have to say is the attempted house break-in shook you and you went to stay with your parents in Airdrie. Then you can tell them Malcolm confided in you, turn over the hard drive and let them do their job."

"I will, I will…just not today. Here it is. I'm staying in the coach house."

Akar's parents' house sat back on a secluded lot across the street from Mount Royal's Cartier Park. Most of the houses in the area dated back to early nineteen hundred, when Mount Royal gained its reputation as an exclusive neighbourhood, catering to Calgary's elite. Of course, since then, most of the homes had undergone multiple renovations.

The coach house turned out to be a small suite built over a second detached garage at the back of the lot. Although built after the original house, it was finished to match to main house's stone exterior. I waited while Dave grabbed his stuff and watched as he staggered up the tree-lined driveway. A minute later he unlatched a wrought-iron gate at the side of house and disappeared.

I needed a plan, one preferably including the police. Realizing this depressed me. This is why I couldn't pursue my infatuation with the head of Special Crimes, Inspector Luis Azagora. He needed to be above board and squeaky clean at all times. I needed to be above board as well, but sometimes I had to stay in a grey area a smidge longer than Azagora would want me to. He'd definitely see me as a liability.

If Dave didn't call the police soon, I would. I had to. I couldn't sit on this. What if something happened to Malcolm or Eric. But all I had was anecdotal stories. No proof, no emails, no hard drive. Dave could deny everything. Malcolm was adamant about not talking to the police either. Should I talk to Detective Birdie? Tell him Malcolm hacked Daryl's computer and changed the trial data? That he may have inadvertently contributed to Carl's death. Then again, maybe Carl hadn't put the brakes on because he was merely paranoid when he learned someone hacked the data. What if he started digging around in their new investors' business dealings and really did find something disturbing?

I put the truck in gear and with a heavier stomp on the gas pedal than I intended, pulled away from the curb with spinning tires and a spray of gravel.

FORTY-THREE

BIG DICK'S BAR and grille was almost full by the time I got there. A line of people waited for tables, blocking the entryway in front of me. I peered past shoulders and located Mike, half hidden behind the server taking his order. The server chatting with Mike laughed at something he said and brushed back a long curl of hair falling over her shoulder. The couple in front of me moved. I slid past and made my way to Mike's table.

"Hi, Mike. I'm so ready for a drink." I slid into a chair and the waitress flounced away. I watched her retreating back, raised my hands, palms upward. "WTF?"

Mike laughed. "Don't worry. I ordered for you."

"Oh. Thanks. For one minute there I thought I'd become invisible."

"I see you're still driving the igloo." Mike nodded at my parka as I slipped it off.

"Not for long. I'm trading it in next week. How was your day?"

"No complaints. I told you I'm visiting Julie this weekend, didn't I?"

"Yeah. When are you back?"

"Flying back Monday night, but I'm leaving again Tuesday morning. I have to head out to Vancouver. The ME out there needs help with a case. They found six unmarked graves, all within a kilometre of each other. The bodies have been there a while but still, someone is out there wondering what happened to their loved one."

"Do you think the deaths are related?"

"Too early to tell. But given their proximity to each other, probably. What about you. Kill anymore Roombas lately?"

I had told Mike about my little mishap the last time we talked. "Very funny. Hey, I managed to clear Gab's name. She even got an apology from the woman who was badmouthing her to the press *and* a big fat cheque for loss of income." I didn't mention the cheque was from my current client who was now under scrutiny for Carl's murder.

"Way to go." He saluted my success by lifting up his beer, then took a drink. I sat back as the waitress returned with a glass of Holy Grail for me and a plate of potato skins.

"Okay. What's on your mind? I know that look. Better spit it out before the game starts," said Mike.

"Am I really that transparent?"

"It's kind of endearing. Your eyes go all puppy-like."

"Puppy-like? Seriously."

"Don't get mad, you asked."

"No, I didn't. The question was rhetorical." I glared at him for a minute, until he made puppy eyes at me and we broke out laughing.

"Are you by chance familiar with the Julie Dixon case?"

"Wasn't she that young girl who killed herself? Her online boyfriend talked her into sending him sexually explicit photos and then later, when she refused to send more, threatened to release the photos he had of her to the public unless she complied with his demands?"

"Yeah. That Julie Dixon. Only, her online boyfriend wasn't

really her boyfriend, but some twisted perv. Do you know if they ever caught him?"

"I don't think so. Technology is great, but unfortunately it helps the bad guys out there carry out their shit with a certain degree of anonymity."

"Can't the police get a court order or something from the internet or hosting companies, to search for the guy like in Julie Dixon's case?"

"Sure. Keep in mind most of these guys aren't using their own legally registered IP addresses. They steal or hack into someone's computer, use it, then move on. Why? What are you working on?"

"Oh nothing." I tilted my head and batted my eyes slowly, keeping the rest of my face still.

"Ha ha. What else do you want to know?"

"What would pique the attention of CSIS? I mean, would they be the ones who would investigate...say, a Russian defector to make sure they weren't a mole, or someone here to establish a legal presence that hid illegal activity."

"Whoa. I thought you were working on clearing Gab's name when that guy dropped dead at the dinner you two catered. CSIS looks at issues of national security. They collect intelligence on things that might be a threat to us. You know, activities like terrorism, espionage, foreign interference in our political affairs. Things like that. Tell me you haven't gotten involved in anything like that."

"No, nothing like that. I assume they have a list of people that have piqued their interest though?"

"Sure. But they're not a law enforcement agency, they collect and assess information. They leave criminal investigations to the RCMP or the local and regional police agencies."

"Aww, look—those little lines between your eyes. You're worried."

Mike shook his head. "Damn straight. If you think you've stumbled onto something, let Azagora know. I know you two haven't always seen eye to eye, but he's a decent guy. Not to mention it's his job to look into shit like this."

Now I was hearing back the same advice I had dispensed to Dave. Trouble was I didn't have any reason to bring Dimitri's name up with Azagora, let alone Detective Birdie. Other than I had seen Rose meet up with Dimitri in a parking lot late one night and Dimitri had lied to me about that and about knowing Carl was digging into his and his partners' affairs. I shouldn't let Daryl's paranoid, broad-brush comments about Russians get into my head. Besides, wouldn't the police be looking into Dimitri's background and the other guests at the Boussards' dinner party?

The game came on and we watched the first two periods. By then the Flames were trailing by five points. Technically they could still win, but clearly the boys weren't on their game tonight. Mike paid the bill, despite my insistence we split it, and we packed up to leave.

There were only two couples waiting for tables by the door. Mike reached around me and pushed the door open. I stepped outside and lifted my face to the sky. The night air felt unseasonably warm and stars dotted the cloudless sky. I heard something whizz by followed by a sharp crack. Someone screamed. Mike tackled me to the ground.

FORTY-FOUR

IT WAS LATE by the time I got home. Which is why I was only just now climbing out of bed. I walked out to the living room and picked up my down-filled jacket from the arm of the couch. Down feathers continued to escape from the hole in the left sleeve as I moved it to the hall closet.

Two shots had been fired last night. The first grazed my shoulder and hit the doorframe. The second bullet hit the handle that ran horizontally across the entrance door, ricocheted and embedded itself in a nearby planter. The police arrived and took our statements, as well as that of several other witnesses, but neither Mike nor I saw the shooter.

Mike called just as I finished wolfing down a grilled cheese sandwich.

"How are you doing this morning?"

"Good. Knee is a little sore, but I'll take that over a bullet any day. Thanks for shoving me out of the way last night."

"You know, that's the second time I saved your life," said Mike.

"We're keeping score, now are we?"

Mike had wanted me to stay at his place for the night. I had countered by saying that since he was likely the target not me, I wouldn't dream of putting myself in such danger. After several minutes of jesting we had gone our separate ways, but I worried I was the intended target. My broken truck headlight went a long way to contribute to the thought.

"You heading to the airport soon?"

"Already there. Just thought I'd call to see if you were okay. And to remind you of our conversation last night. Don't mess with anything or anybody CSIS might be interested in."

"I won't."

My phone rang seconds after Mike and I disconnected. I picked up.

"Jorja. It's Rose."

She sounded winded, more so than usual. "Hi Rose. Is everything okay?"

"No. Detective Birdie is here. They want me to go downtown with them. They want to question me. I already told them everything I know." Her voice wavered. "What should I do?"

"I'm afraid you have little choice but to go with them. Have you called your lawyer?"

"I can't reach her. I left a message at her office, then called you."

"Did Detective Birdie say anything about why they want to re-question you?"

"Something about inconsistencies about the night Carl died."

"Inconsistencies?"

"I don't really understand," she whined.

"You really only have a couple options, Rose. You can go with Detective Birdie and answer their questions, or you can tell them you'll gladly answer their questions, but you'd like to talk to your lawyer before you do."

"You think I should, Jorja. Wait to talk to my lawyer?"

"I don't know, Rose. It's up to you. If you've been forthright with Detective Birdie all along, I don't think you have anything to worry about."

Rose sniffled, then blew her nose. "I think I need to talk to my lawyer."

Shit. This is what I was afraid of. "Okay. I can try reaching her as well, but if you called earlier, I'm sure she'll get the message."

"Okay. I need to go now. Detective Birdie is waiting."

After the call ended, I took several turns around the room, repeating my favourite expletives. Then I told myself to calm down. Maybe it wasn't all bad. I called Gray's office.

"Jorja. I was just about to call you."

"I presume you got Rose's message?"

"You presume correctly. I'm on my way to meet with her and Detective Birdie now. I thought I'd give you a quick call, see if you have anything new."

"Actually, I have dug up some interesting bits. I'm not sure it's going to help Rose right this minute. I'm convinced Carl was killed because he was dragging his feet on the product launch. If the launch is delayed it could have some pretty significant repercussions, financial repercussions. Not just for Rose, but the other partners as well. The timing of Carl's death is interesting too. If Carl had died after they signed their new partner agreement, JP wouldn't have inherited as large a share of the company from Carl as he did." I thought about Dimitri's story about Theagenes of Thasos. "The happy Riteweight family isn't as happy as they make out to be. There was no love lost between the Chief of Operations and the partners. I have a few leads, but it's too early to lay them on the table. I'll let you know the minute I have something concrete."

"Thanks, Jorja. Glad we got you started on the legwork early. I just hope this is a routine follow-up—but I suspect there's more. I'll let you know how it goes."

I hung up, thinking, *What leads, Jorja?* The only lead I had was that several people mentioned Carl had been digging into the new investors' business affairs. It seemed somewhat irrelevant that Malcolm messing with the trial data was the reason why. I was starting to believe Daryl's rendition of why two trial participants died and that there was nothing wrong with Luzit. That left me JP and Dee Dee and the person who was instrumental to funding its launch. *And Theagenes of Thasos.*

FORTY-FIVE

GAB AND I had agreed to meet at the Salty Dog, a neighbourhood pub roughly halfway between us. I arrived first to discover the place buzzing with talkative couples and a long table of thirty-somethings celebrating a life event. I noticed a couple preparing to leave their spot at the bar and sidled up behind them. As soon as they cleared their bill and stood to leave, I plunked myself down, setting my purse and coat on an adjacent barstool.

The bartender set a couple of drinks down in front of the couple to my left. Glancing my way, he raised an eyebrow.

"Something strong…scotch or bourbon…oh, and nothing with a man's name on the label."

Gab and my Oban Highland single malt arrived at the same time. Gab ordered a Cosmopolitan. Once her Cosmo arrived, Gab lifted her glass.

"Cheers!"

"Damn him," I responded.

"Who, the bartender?"

"No, Adan."

"Oh dear. Adan. Perhaps the universe is planning to send you someone even better."

"Always the optimist. You mean better than an exceedingly attractive, sexy man. A man who does good in the world by ministering to the unfortunate tortured souls wandering the earth. A man who…"

"I mean better for you," Gab interjected.

"Right." I took a sip of whisky, letting it slowly slide down my throat, fighting the urge to knock back the whole glass.

"Come on, Jorja. You'll find the right guy. You're smart, gorgeous, funny and kind-hearted."

"Gee, too bad you're not a guy."

"Does this mean you and Adan are just friends?"

"I don't know. I mean, I'm so annoyed. And mad—mostly at myself."

"What happened?"

"Well, we planned a picnic for today, out at Bragg Creek. You know, go for a walk, have some wine, maybe build a small cozy fire. Or at least that's what I envisioned. This morning he sent me a text and suggested we meet out there."

"Hmm."

"I got there shortly before noon. We were meeting by the Trading Post. He showed up forty minutes late."

"Forty minutes! Not cool. Did he text or call to say he was going to be late?"

"Nope. When he arrived he had three kids with him. Teenagers."

"No way."

"Yes way."

"Oh no. What did you do?"

"What could I do? I plastered a grin on my face and followed them down along the river to a picnic spot. No wine or beer though, you know, 'cause of the underage moppets."

"What did the five of you talk about? I can't even imagine."

"The kids blithered on and on and on. One of the boys kept asking if we'd see bears and if they ate people. He was thrilled when we told him bears were known to attack and kill people. That kid's going to be a problem. Then he asked if we'd see lions."

"Seriously? Lions?"

"Yeah. Most of these kids aren't our hope for a future cancer cure. Then we went for a walk. Three hours. Uphill both ways."

"At least you got in a good workout."

"By the time our little jaunt was over I was ready to go home and drink myself stupid. But no. They insisted I throw rocks into the river with them."

"You've got to be kidding." Gab snorted and picked up her glass.

"Wait, it gets better. Adan pulls out one of those collapsible fishing rods and starts teaching the kids how to fish. I guess he takes the bible literally."

A choking noise made me glance over at Gab. She spit a mouthful of Cosmo back into her glass and threw back her head laughing. I chuckled despite myself. Finally, Gab wiped tears from her eyes and managed to choke out, "I hate to ask, but how did this end?"

"The kids were actually okay. They each gave me a hug when they were leaving. Adan came over as I was getting into my truck. I expected he'd at least give me a hug or a kiss on the cheek. But no. You know what he said? He said, 'Good job. I'll call you next week.' Good job? Are you freaking kidding me? Was I on a job interview or something?"

"What the hell."

"I know."

"So, you're done?"

I sighed. "I guess so. Why am I always drawn to guys who are totally unsuitable for me?"

"You're asking me?" Gab took a sip of her drink. "What about Mike?"

"What's with you and Mike? You're always bringing up his name. You know we're just friends."

"I just think you're well suited for each other."

"Well suited huh. Maybe that's why we've become good friends."

"Oh, come on, don't tell me you don't have a thing for him. I see the way you are when you're with him—all comfortable, relaxed. You even smile more."

"Seriously, Gab. We're good friends—that's all. That's how people are around friends, happy, relaxed. See?" I gave her a big grin. "Besides, I think if I ever hinted at wanting anything different, he'd take off faster than a Peregrine Falcon."

"Ah ha—so you have thought about a different relationship with him."

"No. No, I didn't say that. He's made it clear he's not interested in any romantic relationships, ever again. You know, twice bitten—third time shy."

"That's what they all say—at first." She raised an eyebrow.

"Besides, he's not my type."

"What is your type?"

"Hmm. Tall, dark, narcissistic, full of themselves. Real assholes."

"And how's that been working out for you?"

"Touché." I touched my glass to Gab's, and we burst out laughing.

Later, Gab and I went dancing with a bunch of guys half our age. At one point in the evening I realized I could have easily given birth to one of them. Or all of them. It was a total buzzkill.

FORTY-SIX

THIS MORNING I decided to work at the office. Yesterday, I had spent the entire day at home, searching the internet for anything I could find on Dimitri Asentanko, his company Novayaera. The only thing of interest I had come across was that Novayaera had backed a couple of start-ups that had gone bust. Perhaps Dimitri's investors were putting the pressure on. Maybe Dimitri was taking steps to make sure it didn't happen this time. Dimitri wasn't returning any of my calls.

Adan had called last night to tell me he had a great time on Saturday. I was glad one of us had. He asked me if I was free on Thursday evening. Like a fool, I said I was. That's when he informed me Inner Light was having its annual potluck fundraising dinner that night and invited me to attend—with a potato salad.

I was clearly sending him the wrong message. What happened to all my girl pheromones and why wasn't he picking up? I bet they were fading, like my muscle tone and the colour of my hair. Why the hell was I letting him run the agenda?

I called Rose. Nadine answered.

"Oh, hi, Nadine. It's Jorja Knight. I was calling to find out how Rose made out. She called me when Detective Birdie showed up to question her."

"She's upstairs sleeping. She's a mess. I finally gave her a couple of my sleeping pills."

"Do you know what that was all about?"

"Oh, the damn police. We should sue for harassment. Rose and Carl worked hard to get where they are at. Now that makes them the bad guys?"

"Rose said something about them wanting to clear up some inconsistencies in her statement."

"They wanted to know why she said a bee stung Carl. How was she supposed to know if one did or didn't? An honest assumption. I mean, when someone with allergies like Carl collapses, the first thought usually isn't, oh dear, he's been poisoned. In my experience, when it comes to the police it's best to say as little as possible. Otherwise they just twist what you say and use it against you."

"Well I hope that's been cleared up now. I wanted to ask Rose about Dimitri. Did she tell you they're friends? That they've been seeing each other."

"They haven't. At least not like you make it sound. He's an investor. One Carl brought in. Of course, Rose is going to be polite to him."

"Several people told me Carl was dragging his feet on the launch, threatening to delay it. But others, like Dimitri, for example, said they weren't aware of anything of the kind."

"Well, he would know, wouldn't he? Those who aren't in the know shouldn't spread unfounded rumours, and if they do, they deserve what they get."

"Nadine, do you know anyone who was jealous of Carl? Maybe not related to his business but his status in the community? He was a philanthropist, an Order of Canada recipient, well respected. He really seemed to have his act together. Could someone be wanting the same, but falling short of the same kind of achievements?"

"Humph. It doesn't take a genius to see how badly Dee Dee craves social recognition. It's pathetic really. I don't like speaking ill of anyone, but she strikes me like the type of person who would cut down anyone, anywhere, if it meant getting ahead."

I asked Nadine to ask Rose to call me later. After the call, I paced.

I was no closer to figuring out who killed Carl than a week ago. I'd really like to find a way to eliminate at least one suspect. Although several people ultimately benefited from Carl's death, I hadn't found anything definitive. This case was driving me crazy. Maybe it was driving the police crazy too. Maybe it's why they kept circling back to Rose.

Nadine's comment about Dee Dee's aggressive status-seeking, money-hungry attitude could make her a good suspect, especially with JP's infidelity thrown in. She couldn't be happy about his philandering and wouldn't have taken well to Carl's reluctance to move forward. And she had been sitting next to Carl at dinner. Problem was, I couldn't see her rocking the boat this close to the launch. Not unless she was certain it wouldn't impact her in any negative way. I turned back to my paperwork, wrote up an invoice and sent it to Lydia.

By evening, I still hadn't heard back from Rose. Or Dimitri. The thought that Carl had been an unintended victim had crossed my mind more than once. Or that more than one person was involved in his death. Everyone had offered up a reason why someone, other than themselves, would like to see Carl dead.

Daryl told me he suspected Dimitri was up to no good but hadn't outright accused him of killing Carl. Dimitri gave Carl a second shot of epinephrine and wove me a story of envy, without explicitly naming Daryl. Rose had lied to me. In private she told me she had tampered with Gab's food to ruin the Boussards' dinner, but then had no problem lying publicly to say it was all a well-intended but horrible mistake. Dimitri lied to me about meeting up with Rose at Glenmore reservoir late one evening and denied knowing Carl was worried. Worried enough to be trying to change Riteweight's choice of testing lab. Maybe Daryl was lying when he insisted the two dead trial participants died accidently or through natural causes. Dave might be lying about the hard drive he had squirrelled away in a U of C locker. The answer to who killed Carl and why was buried under a pile of lies.

FORTY-SEVEN

MY PHONE RANG as I unlocked the office door. I stepped inside and pulled out my cell. Gina Mancini's name appeared on the screen. I hit accept.

"Gina. Hi. What's up?"

"Jorja? Hi. Hey, I thought you'd want to know. JP got a call from his wife after lunch today. Their son, Malcolm, is missing."

"Missing?"

"I don't know much more, but apparently Malcolm wasn't at school yesterday and didn't come home last night either. Dee Dee sounded pretty distraught when she called."

"He couldn't have just skipped school and spent the night hanging out at a friend's house?"

"When JP left, he said no one knew where he was, so I assume no. JP told me to cancel his meetings and then rushed off. He must be concerned. He's never rushed home like that, even when Dee Dee had her car accident last year."

Surely, they checked with Eric, which meant he didn't know where Malcolm was either. Or Eric could be covering for Malcolm. I told myself not to panic. For all I knew, Malcolm might be prone to running off. I already knew skipping school was within his repertoire. But in my heart, I knew something else was going on. Something troubling.

I thanked Gina and sat mulling my next step. I was confident the attempted break-in to Dave's place hadn't been a botched B&E and whoever had tried to get in had a specific reason. I was still conflicted as to why. Part of me favoured the idea it had something to do with Riteweight. But that was before Malcolm admitted to messing with the trial data and I found out Dave was trying to help Malcolm expose the creep who was extorting pornographic photos and videos from him.

I got up and paced. Damn Dave. He should have gone to the police with what he knew. Malcolm's parents had brushed off his mention of harassment as if it was a normal teenage ritual he was just going to have to deal with. On the other hand, Malcolm hadn't made them aware of the full extent of what was going on.

I ran through the last conversation I had with Malcolm and Eric. I had urged Malcolm to tell the authorities. Anyone. The police, his parents, a trusted teacher. But he had refused.

The room swayed and I reached out a hand to steady myself against the kitchen counter. Malcolm had told someone he trusted. He told Dave. And he told me.

I turned around, locked up and rushed back to where I parked. Half an hour later, I was standing on Eric's doorstep. I knocked rapidly on the door.

Eric answered, his eyes red and puffy.

"Hi. Eric. What's going on? I heard Malcolm's missing."

He stepped aside, and I entered the small, blue-tiled foyer, the mirrored coat-closet doors less than an arm's length away.

"I heard Malcolm wasn't at school today, that he didn't come home last night. Do you know where he is?"

Eric shook his head.

"When did you last see him?"

"After you dropped us off the other day, we played video games until around four. Then he left. Said he was going home. We texted on the weekend and on Monday. I didn't see him Monday, I was out all day on a field trip. He wasn't at school yesterday."

"He didn't say anything about not going to school?"

"No."

"Has he ever taken off before?"

"No."

"Have his parents called the police?"

"I dunno. His mom called this morning to see if he was here."

"This morning? You weren't in school this morning either?"

"No. I…ah…I don't feel well."

"Come on, Eric." I caught and held his eyes. "What aren't you telling me?"

His head jerked and eyes shifted to gaze at something behind my right ear.

"Nothing. Honest. I told you, I don't know where he is."

"You're his friend, Eric. Malcolm's in trouble. He needs help." A chilling thought occurred to me. "Was Malcolm planning to meet the guy who's been blackmailing him?"

Tremors shook Eric's body. He rushed past me out the front door. A moment later he was emptying the contents of his stomach on the Magic Carpet Spireas in his mother's flowerbeds. I waited until I heard dry heaves and stepped outside.

"Eric, even if he swore you to secrecy, there comes a point when you have to use your own judgment. Whatever he had planned may have gone wrong. He might at this very minute be praying you're worried enough to ignore his request for silence."

"I have to leave my mom a note."

Eric went back inside. I ambled back to the truck and climbed in to wait. Mostly I craved distance from the Spireas. Maybe he was telling me the truth, maybe he did have a stomach bug.

Five minutes later Eric came out, climbed into the truck cab and wiped his nose with the inside corner of his jacket. He stared at me with moist eyes. "Honest, I don't know where he is."

"Is there a chance he went to meet these people?"

Eric shrugged. "Maybe. There was another email on the weekend. They threatened to spill the beans to the press."

"What beans? That he was sending pornographic material to his supposed girlfriend?"

"No, the email said when word got out people in the weight-loss trial died, he and his family could kiss their cushy life goodbye."

I sat back, stunned. "Where was he meeting them?" I needed to believe we weren't too late.

"I don't know." He gripped his head in his hands. "Honest. I don't know if he went to meet someone. I don't know who this person is. I don't know where he is. Why don't they leave us alone?"

Part of me was tempted to drive Eric straight to police headquarters. The other part reminded me the last time I had presented them with half-baked theories and unsubstantiated accusations, it hadn't gone so well. I revved up the truck.

"Let's go talk to someone who knows what's going on."

FORTY-EIGHT

VIOLATING MOST OF the posted speed limits, I drove to Akar's parents' house. I parked and Eric and I made our way up the tree-lined driveway, past the double attached garage and through a wrought-iron gate at the side of the house. When we reached the staircase leading to the coach house, I stopped.

"Wait here," I whispered. "When I signal, call Dave."

I crept up the stairs. At the top, I placed my ear against the door and waved at Eric. He pulled out his cell. A few seconds later, I heard a phone ring inside, followed by several sharp barks. I waved at Eric to come on up and knocked on the door.

"He's not answering his phone," said Eric.

"He's in there all right." I knocked louder. The barking inside became frenzied.

"Come on, Dave. Open up. It's me and Eric. It's urgent."

A second later the door opened a crack, the safety chain still slid in place.

"Dave. Thank god you're here. Malcolm's missing."

Dave closed the door. We heard the chain being slid from its latch, and the door opened. Dave peered through the crack, then opened it wider. "Hurry up. Did anyone see you?"

The drapes were drawn across all the windows. Dave rushed over to one, peered in all directions and turned back.

"Cujo, be quiet," Dave admonished the little brown-eared, white Bichon Shih Tzu jumping in circles at our feet.

"Cute dog. Is that blood?" I pointed at a red streak that ran down its chest.

"No, ketchup. Don't let his size fool you. He can put way almost as many fries as I can. Why are you here?"

"Malcolm's missing. He wasn't at school yesterday or today and no one's heard from him."

"What do you want me to do about it?"

I looked at Dave. He didn't seem to be as bothered about Malcolm's disappearance as I thought he'd be.

"Eric says he got another threatening email. We need you to hack into his email and see if there's anything more."

"That's illegal."

I glared at him. "Seriously? So is resisting, interfering and not cooperating with a police investigation."

"Okay already. Watch your shoes," Dave admonished, as he led the way to a marble-topped table with Lucite chairs. "Akar said he'll have my balls if I don't leave the place as clean as I found it."

I took a second to look around. The coach house was probably all of six hundred square feet, but each square foot must have cost a thousand dollars. Several empty Doritos bags and a pizza box lay on the couch. I congratulated myself on being childless.

Dave sat down in front of his laptop. Luckily, Eric remembered Malcolm was going to pick a revenge-themed password. Half an hour later Ani4aNi! got us in. Eric and I huddled over Dave's shoulder.

"Let's see if there's anything on his Facebook page."

Eric logged into Facebook and connected to Malcolm's page.

"Whoa, what's all this shit?"

I peered over Eric's shoulder. There were dozens of posts. My breath caught at the third one from the top. A post from Malcolm. *Glad CJ is dead. Sweet karma.*

There were the usual responses, *Who's CJ?* and *Why are you glad he's dead?* The reply read, *Old fart, dragging down my family.*

"There's no way Malcolm wrote that," said Eric.

Several more people weighed in. We scrolled through the comments.

Old people should off themselves.

How'd he die?

He was full of toxins

Old people are toxic

Old people are bat-shit crazy

You're toxic. You should die

"Look at this," I said pointing to the last post. "There are forty-six likes. You've got to be kidding. Who are these people?"

"Someone's hacked our new accounts. Oh shit. Look, there's one from me. I've never seen this shit before," screeched Eric.

We read the post from Eric's new account. *Who do we knock off next? Ask and you shall receive.*

Dave opened the deleted-messages folder. Luckily, the auto purge of the trash bin hadn't yet occurred.

The first message read, *Your family is going down. Tomorrow's news—Riteweight CFO dead after discovering trial data coverup on multiple deaths.* The next email was pretty much as Eric said. They demanded Malcolm send a video with explicit instructions on what the video should show, or the newspapers would be contacted.

"Damn it. I know I'm getting close. I just need a few more days," said Dave as he tore at his hair.

"For what?"

"I'm going to get this guy, I'm closing in. I'm going to make this scumbag pay."

"Dave, I'm serious. Malcolm is missing. What if he's been kidnapped? God knows what they're doing to him." I was afraid for Malcolm. I could no longer hide what I knew from the police.

"Look, I'm in this too. If he sends out the news about the hacked data from my computer, no one is going to want me touching their computer systems for a very long time."

"I can't believe I'm hearing this. Malcolm's life is in danger and you're worried about your reputation?"

"Not just me. Malcolm's folks could be ruined. Don't forget, this is why Malcolm went along with these guys, to protect his parents, their business. I'm so close to finding this guy I can taste it. I just need twenty-four more hours. Forty-eight tops."

"What happens in twenty-four hours?"

"I think I know how this creep is doing it. I think he's using a surveillance van to bug the Boussards' house."

"Cool. Like in the movies?" Eric asked.

"No. Like the cops have. If the cops have them it's a cinch the bad guys do too. Today you can outfit a vehicle with enough shit to listen in on what's happening in your neighbours' houses or even a competitor's office across the street from you. The whole world of espionage is now available to anyone who's interested."

"Why is someone listening in on the Boussards? Is it to gather data on Riteweight or are they hoping to hear something they can use to put pressure on Malcolm?" At the speed at which Dave was spitting things out, I was having a hard time processing. "How sure are you about this surveillance van?"

"Pretty sure. Either that or the aliens have infiltrated. Like in the Village of the Damned." Dave looked up, eyes glistening.

I shrugged, shaking my head.

"You know…where all the children in the village could read minds and control people." Dave's speech quickened. "They could get them to do anything. I mean anything. Even kill themselves."

"I saw that one," said Eric. "The special effects were sic."

"I'm going with the surveillance van idea. Are you saying you think this guy has been listening in to the Boussard household hoping to pick up something he can use to blackmail Malcolm into sending more photos and videos? I'm not buying. That's a lot of effort for some illicit photos."

"There's the psychological aspect too. This guy is getting off on watching people squirm. All I know is we have a reprieve. Maybe Malcolm found a way to buy me some time."

"A reprieve? What are you talking about? You think Malcolm is hiding somewhere?"

"Look." Dave pulled up the email Malcolm was sent. "It says if he doesn't cooperate the news will be released tomorrow. Look at the date. Tomorrow is today. There's nothing on the news. Malcolm knows I'm getting close. He must have negotiated something with the creep."

Eric remained mute, frozen at Dave's left shoulder.

"Or he's dead," I said. "Dave, I can't keep this quiet anymore. I have to go to the police."

"No. Don't—not yet. I know I can figure out who's behind the threats. It must be someone acquainted with Malcolm. In most cases, it is. I'm so close."

"This is crazy. What are you two not telling me?" I looked from Dave to Eric. Eric looked away.

I couldn't let go of the idea that Dave knew a lot more than he was telling me.

I turned to Eric. "I need a minute with Dave. I'll meet you back at the truck." I tossed him my truck keys and waited until he was outside.

"Look, Dave, I'm not going to argue with you about this. Let's say someone was listening in on the Boussards. Specifically, to listen in on Malcolm and Eric. They find out the trial data was hacked. Now they not only have photos and videos of Malcolm they can threaten to expose if he fails to send more, they suddenly have a way to up the ante by threatening to ruin his parents. How lucky is that?"

"Half of what happens out there is pure luck. Look, I'm not going to pretend I know what's going on at Riteweight, and Carl's death and all. All I know is Malcolm is being cyberbullied and exploited. When I tried to help him, I got shot. And someone's tried to kill me twice since then. The trial data was tampered with and this creep knows about it and wants me to be the fall guy when it's leaked."

I expelled a huge breath and rubbed my temples. "Okay, Dave. Here's the thing. Despite all the fancy surveillance equipment you claim they're using, they don't seem to know that Malcolm is the one who hacked Daryl's computer. He is the one who changed the trial results."

"Whoa." Dave ran a hand through his tangled hair. "Why would you think that?"

"Because he told me himself."

"Whoa. No way. So, the product's okay? There were no deaths?"

"No. I didn't say that. But the trial-data tampering—that's on Malcolm. He messed with the data when he used Daryl's computer to send the first video. He didn't use his own computer because of the tracker you installed."

"Oh man. So, he messed with the data to get back at me. At them?"

"Sounds like it."

"Suddenly, I'm feeling better about this. But someone is still threatening Malcolm and extorting sexually explicit material from him."

"I'm not feeling better about this at all, Dave. The data breech may have triggered Carl's paranoia about harming anyone, especially in light of what happened to his sister. He started to drag his heels on the launch, started to question the investors' integrity. Maybe he found something, maybe not. Either way, it may have cost Carl his life. The best way to stop whoever is doing this to Malcolm is to expose what he's doing. You've been working on this for weeks. Now Malcolm is missing. I can't go along with this, Dave."

"You have to trust me. Malcolm is going to be okay. Just give me twenty-four hours."

"And what if Malcolm isn't okay. Why should I trust you?"

Dave closed his eyes, sighed. "You think after all this, I'd let something happen to Malcolm? We've almost got this guy. I don't want him to slip through the cracks so another kid like Malcolm falls victim to him. Or another Julie Dixon."

"I can't promise you twenty-four hours. I need a couple hours to think about it. That's what I'm willing to give you—a couple hours."

I turned, yanked the door open and stepped out. I gulped in mouthfuls of cool air as I hustled back to the street but couldn't make the tightness in my chest go away. I reached the truck and climbed in. My fingers reached for the keys, dangling in the ignition, and I zapped back to the present. No Eric.

Heart pounding, I climbed out of the truck and looked around. That's when I saw the small scrap of paper under the windshield wiper. I pulled the paper out, a piece torn from a paper bag. I could barely make out the scrawl, left by an obviously dull pencil. *I'm walking home. MB ok.* Had Eric heard from Malcolm? Why were Eric and Dave insisting Malcolm was okay? Was this part of some hairbrained scheme they had cooked up? Or were they so hell-bent on catching this guy they were willing to risk Malcolm's wellbeing in the process?

I tried sorting out all the bits swirling in my head as I drove to Pump Hill. The Boussards' place was locked up tighter than a drum. Several vehicles were parked on the street but none of them appeared of particular interest nor looked familiar. No sign of the police, or anything else that would indicate something was amiss. I called the Boussards, but the line was busy. Ignoring the recorded suggestion to leave a message, I hung up. I would check with Eric or the Boussards in the morning. If Malcolm was still missing, I'd contact Detective Birdie and share what I knew.

FORTY-NINE

THE BLACK PANTS fit me like a glove. The green, gold and cream speckled blouse brought out the golden flecks in my eyes, and my hair glistened. The cowl neck of my blouse barely skimmed cleavage but fell away at the back. I turned sideways and peered over my shoulder. The back was low enough I had to forego wearing a bra. Another five years and I doubt I'd be able to pull it off. *Screw five years.*

I made up a smoky eye, applied my shiniest rose lipstick and sprayed, scrunched and twisted handfuls of hair into gentle layers and wisps. Standing back, I liked what I saw, but could hardly enjoy the moment. Yesterday's news about Malcolm weighed heavily on me. My views on whether I should contact Detective Birdie about what I knew had flip-flopped the whole day. Surely the Boussards would have filed a missing person report. Malcolm was underage. Why was there no amber alert? I checked the newsfeed on my phone hourly. There was nothing about Malcolm's disappearance in the news.

By dinner time I still hadn't contacted the police. What would I share with them? They must know he was missing by now. Surely his parents would mention he was being cyberbullied. They might not know someone was blackmailing him though.

If I contacted the police would I mention the bits about Malcolm hacking the trial data, dead trial participants, Carl's investigations into Dimitri's partners? Would I tell Detective Birdie Rose admitted to me, and only me, her ridiculous prank with the underprepared beans was an act of vengeance as to how she was being treated by the Boussards and others present at dinner. Including her husband. Maybe she did kill him with cyanide and the bean prank was to throw the cops off. And when I caught on, she played it one step further by making it out to be an immature, silly prank? If so, it would be kind of brilliant. I shook my head. Was I prepared to share information with the police that would make them deepen their suspicions that Rose poisoned Carl, without any proof? The whole thing was one convoluted mess making it hard not to pull out one piece of information without unravelling the next. Why was I letting this go on? Who did I think I was protecting? Or was I putting my reputation ahead of what I knew was the right thing to do?

I called the Boussards' number. This time I left a message saying I had heard Malcolm was missing and to please let me know if there was anything I could do to help. I called Dave. No answer. I called Gina. She hadn't heard anything either, except that JP called in this morning and said he was taking a few personal days.

I pulled on my three-inch heeled, olive-green, open-toed booties, strode into the kitchen and emptied four containers of KFC potato salad into a clear plastic bowl and saran wrapped the top. Grabbing my purse and a sweater I headed downstairs.

On the way downtown, I listened to my Tony Robbins CD, hoping his upbeat messages would drive my worry over Malcolm out of my head. My own words to Eric repeated in my head. What if this was some scheme cooked up by Dave and the boys. A scheme that was going horribly wrong.

I found myself downtown without remembering the drive. I parked and climbed out, leaving my stretched-out cable-knit sweater in the truck.

The air was bitingly cold. I hurried past a smattering of couples on the sidewalk and the usual array of homeless huddled in doorways, leaving a trail of white gauzy breath behind. Someone whistled, but it was no one I wanted to encourage. Inner Light was buzzing tonight. I opened the door, stepped into the welcomed warmth, and followed the signs downstairs.

The folding wall between the two main meeting rooms had been pulled open and the room was festooned with posters, streamers and balloons. A guy wearing a bib apron relieved me of the potato salad and ushered me in.

The place was packed, most people wearing casual business attire. I stopped to chit chat with a couple of women I recognized and slowly made my way over to one of the tables displaying items for the evening's silent auction. A warm hand on my bare back froze me in my tracks and my knees weakened. I turned and stared into Adan's deep-blue eyes.

"You made it. Aren't you dressed all fancy?"

Fancy? You made it. Seriously? That's all you got? I laughed. "I guess I'm a tad overdressed for the event. But I'm meeting someone later and won't have time to go home and change."

He dropped his hand and gazed around the room. "Quite the turnout, isn't it?"

"It sure is."

"I'm glad you came. Help yourself to food."

I caught his eye and held his gaze. "I'm glad I came too. I'll let you get back to mingling with your guests." I turned and walked away.

I *was* glad I came. It was worth the flash of clarity. As hot as Adan was, and as attracted to him as I was, logic told me it wasn't going to work. A pang of sadness caught at my throat. Adan needed a cheerful, granola-eating, wholesome, kind and nurturing woman who would throw herself into his life's work. I didn't fit the bill. Except for the granola eating.

Making my way across the room to the buffet table, I spotted Azagora and froze. He was talking to a tall guy in his twenties, with tattoos running down his neck and arms. The guy fidgeted, shifting from one foot to the other. I didn't blame him. My path and Inspector Azagora's path had crossed several times. As head of Calgary's Special Crimes unit Azagora didn't exactly exude warmth. But there was no denying I had a mind-blowing crush on him, despite the fact I perceived him to be an arrogant ass. For one brief minute, I considered spilling my guts to him. Just unload the whole, Carl, Rose, Dimitri, Dave, Malcolm fiasco at his feet. Then what?

The guy talking to Azagora shuffled away. I didn't need Azagora to solve my problems, chastise me for messing with police business or pat me on the head for bringing something to his attention. I could, however, use a few nights of riotous sex.

Why did I find myself attracted to someone so blatantly arrogant? The answers came quickly. It might be his smouldering brown eyes or the way his hand shot through his closely shaven hair whenever he was frustrated or concerned. Or the way his muscular back curved into his hips, begging for a hand to be laid there. Azagora turned and caught my eye as this last notion ran through my head. My face grew hot. I watched the confusion in his eyes melt away as he made his way over.

"Jorja. Jorja Knight, isn't it?" His eyes were dark pools. A tiny muscle twitched in his strong chiselled cheek. His aftershave was subtle, warm, woodsy with a touch of spice.

"Inspector Azagora. Long time no see."

"Please, call me Luis. I never pegged you for a supporter of the work Inner Light does."

I threw back my head and laughed as if he had said something totally hilarious. I spotted Adan standing in the distance looking our way. Recovering, I caught his eyes and smiled.

"Sorry, I was just thinking the same thing about you."

His eyes darkened, and he smiled back. "You still running your PI business?"

His body warmth radiated along my bared arms and I desperately tried to ignore his closeness. I glanced heavenward and begged the universe to help me from sounding like a complete lunatic.

"Yes I am. I assume you're still working to keep our streets safe?"

He smiled, but his eyes remained dark, serious. I saw something in them I wanted. I saw something in them he needed. He stepped toward me, put his hand on my waist and leaned in. I glanced at his strong forearm and followed it up to the curve in his shoulder. I held my breath, his breath warm along my cheek.

"You probably have plans for tonight, but if you don't, I'd love to buy you a drink."

My breathing was shallow, and I tried to keep my voice even, light. "Well, Luis, unfortunately I do have plans tonight. Can I take a rain check?" My eyes met his.

He ducked his head and smiled. His dark, close-shaven head now inches from mine. "You bet. I believe I have your card. I'll give you a call."

I felt his hand pull ever so slightly at my waist. He leaned forward and brushed my cheek with his lips.

"Then, I'll talk to you soon," I replied.

We stepped back, his hand found mine, and gave it a squeeze before I turned away. I moved toward the doorway, fighting the urge to look over my shoulder. I stopped to say goodbye to a woman I had chatted with earlier. Chancing a quick glance over my shoulder, I was pleased to find Luis still staring at me. I gave him a finger wave and made my way out the door. Holy Hanna, what just happened?

A few minutes later I found myself in my truck. A quick glance at the clock on the dash told me it was after nine o'clock. Gab should have finished her couples' cooking class by now. I turned on the engine, pulled out my phone and hit her number.

"Hey, Gab. You'll never guess what happened."

"You won tonight's Lotto 649?"

"No. Remember Azagora? Inspector Azagora. He just hit on me."

"Eww, what a creep."

"He asked me out, but I told him I was busy tonight."

"Good for you. The nerve of him coming on to you after the unprofessional way he treated you."

Suddenly I could see Gab and I weren't on the same page. She didn't know the full depth of the fantasies I harboured about Azagora. Why would she. The few times his and my path crossed he had been a total cold-hearted arrogant prick. That's the Azagora Gab would know about. But there was no denying the chemistry between us, and now I knew he sensed it as well. Sure, I was drawn to Adan. But all Adan was putting out were friend vibes.

"He's not that bad. He's just doing his job."

"Are we talking about the same guy?"

I laughed. "Yeah. Inspector hot-ass...agora."

Gab laughed. "Yeah, well, make sure you don't get burned."

After we disconnected, I sat in the truck, replaying the encounter in my mind. Once Azagora engaged with me I lost all consideration of Adan, even though I was certain he had continued staring our way. Perhaps he also had a moment of clarity. I pulled on my sweater, shivering but not from the cold. Before I could put the truck into gear my phone vibrated on the seat beside me. I reached over and picked it up, expecting it to be Gab.

"Hey."

"Hello? This is Malcolm. Malcolm Boussard."

FIFTY

MALCOLM RATTLED OFF an address, warned me to not call police and hung up. I was relieved to hear his voice but worried. Where was he calling from? The twenty-second phone call seemed strained, unnatural. I pulled over and checked google map one more time. I wasn't familiar with this part of town. I put the phone down and pulled back out onto Barlow. I should have called the Boussards if not the police. Malcolm sounded scared. Why had he called me? And why did he want me to meet him way out here?

I turned right on Fifty-Second Street which ran north to south, along Calgary's east edge. I peered through the dark, trying to make out the street signs. Finally, I spotted the turnoff for Mahogany Boulevard. The houses here were narrow two-storey structures with postage-stamp front lawns, crammed together. Malcolm said to drive until the pavement ended, continue down a gravel road and take the first exit on my right.

I slowed and peered at the street sign. Marquis Crescent. Most of the houses on this end of Mahogany Boulevard backed out onto bald-ass prairie or were still under construction. I was definitely on the edge of civilization. Was that really Malcolm on the phone? Now I wasn't even sure I'd recognize his voice if I did hear it. Was I walking into a trap?

A block further in, the pavement ended. I checked my rear-view mirror for reassuring signs of traffic, but there were none. I slowed as my truck bumped along the pitted gravel lane until I came to a cul-de-sac on my right. I stopped.

Foundations, already poured for several new homes, stood like ghostly remnants of an abandoned civilization. Disposal bins dotted the streetscape. I checked to make sure my doors were locked and rolled down my window an inch. *This is stupid.* I glanced at my beaded evening bag lying on the passenger seat. I was prepared for a fundraiser not a fight.

I turned in, rounded the cul-de-sac and parked. The voice on the phone could have been anyone's. Or maybe it was Malcolm and he had a gun to his head. I had asked if he was all right, but he just rattled off an address and instructions to here. I scanned the area looking for signs of life.

My heart caught in my throat. I leaned forward. My eyes peered through the darkness and revealed a pile of cement bags lying next to a bin, not a body. I let out a breath then froze.

Someone was out there.

A dark figure made its way past dirt piles surrounding a foundation. It hesitated and turned toward the truck. I held my breath as the figure approached.

It stopped, twenty or so feet from the truck. Why was someone out here this time of night? Why was I?

I rolled down my window and stuck my head out. "Malcolm? Is that you?" I yelled out over the sound of my engine.

The figure started up again and moved toward the truck. I cursed and reached over to unlock the door. Malcolm climbed in.

"Malcolm. Are you all right?"

"Yeah." Bits of dried grass stuck to his hair; his jacket sleeve was ripped.

"Shit, everyone's worried sick. What are you doing out here?" I put the truck in gear and rolled forward.

"I don't know. I lent this woman my cell phone and someone grabbed me. They took me somewhere, a warehouse or something." His eyes searched the dark frantically as I sped up and exited out of the cul-de-sac. He peered over his shoulder as we hit the pavement. "Where are we?"

He wasn't making much sense. "We're on the southeastern edge of the city. What's this about a woman and your cell phone? Who brought you out here?"

"I don't know. I stopped to help a woman with car trouble. On my way to school. While she was using my phone to call for help someone grabbed me. I thought they were going to kill me." He snuffled and wiped his arm across his face.

"You were kidnapped?"

"Yeah."

I checked the rear-view mirror, afraid we were being followed. "My phone's in my purse. Call the police."

"No. Just take me home."

"Malcolm, I'm not joking. These guys may still be in the area. The cops will have a better chance of finding them if we call now."

"No. That's not part of the deal."

"What deal?"

"They said they'd let me go but I couldn't go to the cops. If I did, they'd hurt someone in my family."

"What did they want?"

"I don't know. After they dumped me in a field, they asked me for a name of someone, an adult, to come get me. They said not my parents. I gave them your name. They held up a phone to my ear. I was to say my name, to take the first righthand dirt road at the end of Mahogany Boulevard and tell whoever answered to come alone and not call the police."

"Did you give them my number?" I glanced in the rear-view mirror and pressed down the accelerator, eager to get back onto Fifty-Second. I glanced over at Malcolm.

"No. Just your name. I don't know your number. I'm not sure how they got it. After a few minutes, they told me what to say. After the call, one of them cut my hands loose. Said to count to a thousand before I moved. Then I could get up and find my way to the street. I was to tell you to take me home. They said if I called the cops, or you did, someone in my family would suffer the consequences."

I swallowed. "Did they hurt you?"

Malcolm shook his head. We didn't speak the rest of the way home. Malcolm sat shivering, his hands between his knees. He occasionally brought one out to wipe tears off his face. My brain madly churned through all the possible reasons his kidnappers called me, rejecting one right after the other.

I turned the corner onto Pump Hill Drive and took the first left. The Boussards' driveway gates were closed. I pulled up to the curb, killed the engine and climbed out.

"Hands in the air. Hands on your head. Don't move."

I froze, hands in the air. Lights blinded me. Someone pushed me into the side of truck.

"Turn around. Hands on the roof. Spread 'em."

I could see Malcolm on the other side of the truck, three guys in flak jackets surrounding him. He glanced back.

"Leave her alone. She didn't do anything."

I saw him being hustled through the gates as a pair of hands patted me down. Cold steel encircled my wrists.

FIFTY-ONE

I GLANCED AT THE wall clock. Three a.m. We'd been at this for hours. Detective Kroch's jacket was off, one shirt sleeve rolled up, the other one lagging. One shirt end had come untucked from his tan pants, his jowls more prominent than when I met him, five hours ago.

Detective Kroch wanted to know how I knew Malcolm and the Boussards. I told him I had helped Gab cater the Boussard dinner, the night Carl Johnson died. That I was working for Rose Johnson to help find who poisoned Carl and that I had first seen Malcolm at the Boussards' and later spoke to him in case he might have seen or heard something that could help with my investigation. I was now going through my story for the third time.

"No. I had no idea Malcolm had been kidnapped, until I picked him up. That's when he told me he'd been abducted on his way to school. All I knew up to that point was that he was missing."

"And how'd you know he was missing?"

"Mr. Boussard's executive assistant, Gina Mancini, called to tell me, the day before yesterday."

"Why would she do that?"

"She knows I've been looking into Mr. Boussard's partner's death. She knows Rose Johnson hired me to do so."

"So, she called you out of the blue to share this news with you."

"Yes."

"Why did she think you'd be interested in this latest development?"

"Don't know. Malcolm's a nice kid. Maybe she thought I could help. You'd have to ask her."

"Were you concerned?"

"Not at first. For all I knew he skipped school. But as the day wore on, it bothered me."

"Why?"

"It's a lot of misfortune to befall the Boussards in a short period of time. Mr. Boussard's partner is killed, then his son goes missing?"

"You thought there was a connection?"

"No. But I'll admit, I couldn't help but wonder if there could be." I was sure Malcolm was going through his story as I went through mine. Would he tell the police about the cyberbullying, the blackmail and extortion? Would he have gone to extremes to keep it a secret, only to be spilling his guts now? I could only hope his story of what transpired in the last few days lined up with the little information I had about what went down.

"So, what did you do about it?"

"Well, later that day, I called the Boussards. There was no answer. I contacted Malcolm's friend, Eric Swanson. I met Eric the day I went to talk to Malcolm, to find out if he knew or heard anything the night Carl Johnson was poisoned that might be of help. I'm sure Detective Birdie, who is investigating Carl Johnson's death, interviewed Malcolm as well, since he was home the night Carl was poisoned. Eric confirmed what Gina told me. He didn't know where Malcolm was, only heard Malcolm was missing when Mrs. Boussard called him to see if he knew where he was."

"Then what?"

"The next day I kept looking for news on Malcolm. I called Gina but she hadn't heard anything more. I called the Boussards again. The call went to voice mail. That time, I left a message saying I heard Malcolm was missing and offered my help."

"Like what?"

"I don't know. I just wanted to reach out to let them know I was willing to help any way I could."

"And help you did. You delivered Malcolm to his home last night. Why don't you tell me again how it is you were the one the kidnappers called."

"Look. I told you. When I picked Malcolm up, he said the kidnappers asked him for a name, someone who could be called to pick him up. Not his parents. I don't know why Malcolm gave him my name, I've only talked to him once or twice. But he did. He said the kidnappers held a phone to his head and told him what to say, and to say only what they instructed him to say when the phone was answered."

"So again, Ms. Knight, how would the kidnappers know you, know what phone number to call? Why not call his parents?"

I had my suspicions but that would open this whole can of worms into something that would have far-reaching repercussions without any proof whatsoever.

"I told you, I don't know. Maybe, the kidnappers were afraid the police were watching or working with the Boussards yet wanted Malcolm returned safely. Malcolm told me on the ride home that they asked him for an adult contact name other than his parents. It's not hard to find my phone number on the internet once you have my name. It's the same number I list for my business."

"And you can't think of any other reason they involved you?"

Omitting information was the same as lying. I could lose my licence. I could be charged with an obstruction of justice. But it was too late now. Besides, I really didn't know if the kidnapping was in any way related to whoever was blackmailing Malcolm.

They eventually let me go home.

This morning I was ticked off, worried shitless about the gaps of information in my statement to the police, and truck-less.

Dave and Eric had both insisted Malcolm would be fine. Dave wanted twenty-four to forty-eight hours to wrap up whatever he was doing. Malcolm was returned within that window. What was I to think?

I slid open the closet door and pulled out my jacket. I rummaged around until I found an old roll of duct tape and slapped a piece over the hole in the arm. Further rummaging yielded a pair of thin wool gloves. I pulled on both and continued taking a mental inventory of all the lies I had been told these last few weeks as I made my way to the bus stop.

I told Detective Kroch I'd just left the Inner Light fundraiser, when they asked where I'd been when I got the call. I gave them Adan's name, but didn't mention Azagora. Thankfully, I hadn't run into him at headquarters last night, but he'd probably hear about my visit today. I was sure Detective Kroch would be following up with Detective Birdie to see how or if their two cases were connected. This worried me the most. I knew there was a connection and I had failed to disclose it. This is why Azagora and I would never work out. As head of Special Crimes, Azagora couldn't afford a relationship with someone who was constantly being hauled in for questioning by members of his department.

An hour and two bus rides later, I was at JumpIn Jalopies, my go-to car rental place. I pulled open the glass door and stepped inside, glad to be out of the wind. Liberating a slightly used Kleenex from my jacket pocket I dabbed my nose with one corner and made my way to the rental counter. Neil stood behind the counter, helping another customer. Neil was my favourite rental guy, always polite, always cheerful. His boss was the antithesis of nice guy. I surveyed the service area, fearing he would materialize to help me. The guy at the counter moved on and I stepped forward.

"Neil. How are you?"

"Lookie here! If it isn't Calgary's sharpest PI. We haven't seen you in a while."

"The truck's been good. A tad cold now with winter approaching."

"I see. You need something a little more winter worthy."

"Yes. Except it'll be a few days before I can bring the truck back."

Neil cocked his head to one side and peered at me through the swatch of dirty-blond hair falling across his face. His eyes flit to the duct tape on my sleeve.

"Police impound lot or auto body shop?"

"Police impound lot. Oh. And the left headlight is broken."

Neil peered up at me through the swatch of hair that hung over one eye. "Okie dokie. Let's pull up your file."

After a few minutes of frantic typing, Neil turned and chortled happily. "I have just the vehicle for you."

"Awesome."

With the paperwork finished, Neil looked up. "They're bringing it out from around back." He tilted his head toward his shoulder. "Now don't go getting yourself killed."

"Thanks, Neil. You're a godsend as usual. You have yourself a great day."

I made my way to the glass entry doors and stepped outside. A soft-top green Jeep Wrangler rolled to a stop in front of the door.

A guy in a red jumpsuit climbed out and held the door open for me as I slid inside. At least the driver door opened.

I located and tested the window wipers and lights and adjusted the mirrors. Everything worked as it should. I glanced down at the stick shift. I hadn't driven a manual in decades, but it was like riding a bike, wasn't it? I released the hand emergency brake, depressed the clutch, put it into gear and lurched forward. I lurched my way to Macleod Trail, until ancient memory kicked in and I got the hang of it. At least with all the shifting, my mind didn't have time to wander. A gentle warmth filled the cab. *The heater works!* The radio spewed some static and cut in and out a few times but if that was the extent of the Jeep's issues, Neil had done well.

My thoughts turned back to Malcolm. Had he been kidnapped by whoever was extorting illicit photos and videos from him? Why wouldn't they have just blackmailed the Boussards? Demand hush money for their silence on the trial data tampering and the promise they wouldn't release the photos and videos they had of Malcolm. Kidnapping is a risky move. I hoped like hell this wasn't part of Dave's brilliant scheme to flush out Malcolm's tormenters. If it had been, I didn't see how it helped. I considered the possibility that Malcolm's kidnapping was a separate event. The Boussards had been in the press a lot lately. Maybe whoever snatched Malcolm didn't realize that, until Luzit came on stream, the Boussards were a tad cash strapped.

By the time I arrived home, I was certain all of this was connected. I sure as hell hoped I hadn't just become an accessory to kidnapping.

FIFTY-TWO

THE NEXT MORNING, I slept in, then tried reaching Dave with no success. His forty-eight hours had come and gone. I wondered if Malcolm said anything to the police about the blackmail and extortion threats he'd been receiving. Now I wondered why I hadn't. That, in and of itself, gave me concern.

I called Eric's house, but no one answered. I told myself to stay out of it. The less I knew about the kidnapping and whatever Dave, Malcolm and Eric were up to, the better. But now I was lying to myself. By early afternoon, unable to contain myself any longer, I got into my Jeep and headed to Rose's.

I had the manual shift under control, until the idea of having to parallel park in front of Rose's place came up. I drove past her house, turned into a strip mall, parked, then walked the two blocks back.

Rose answered the door, hair freshly permed into tight dinky sausages, the ammonia odour still prevalent. She wore a black sweater with three pumpkins across the chest.

"Nice sweater," I said.

"Isn't it fun? It's my Halloween sweater."

This is why people Malcolm's age reasoned old people needed

to die. And Rose wasn't even old, at least not in my books. I followed her out to the kitchen.

"Would you like tea, I just made some. Oolong."

"Thank you, no, I'm good."

Rose carried her tea over to the table and we sat.

"Did you hear what happened to the Boussards' son?" she asked.

Her question caught me off guard. "I did. Quite the ordeal it must have been for him. Glad he's okay."

"Okay? The police picked Malcolm up at his house this morning. They took him away in handcuffs. I'm still in shock." She laid a hand on her chest. "Why would he want to hurt Carl? Carl never did anything to him."

I sat back abruptly. I couldn't have been more surprised if she had thrown her tea in my face. Was she saying Malcolm killed Carl or that he hurt him by tampering with the data?

"Hurt Carl? What do you mean? Malcolm was kidnapped on Tuesday. Someone held him against his will until the night before last."

"Kidnapped? Detective Birdie didn't say anything about that when he came to see me this morning. He couldn't say much, of course, but he did tell me there've been some developments. He said they were questioning someone about Carl's death."

"That could be anyone. If Detective Birdie didn't say much, how'd you hear about Malcolm?"

"One of my book club members lives down the street from the Boussards. She saw the police taking Malcolm away in handcuffs."

"In handcuffs? That can't be. He's a victim not a suspect. The police can't possibly think Malcolm had something to do with Carl's death," I said more firmly than my churning gut said. But if they wanted to question him about the kidnapping, they wouldn't have taken him away in handcuffs. I felt sick.

The back door opened, and Nadine came in, cheeks red from the cold. She stepped out of her garden clogs and shed a navy wool jacket.

"Oh. I didn't know you were coming. I was just sorting through some of the things I keep in the shed out back." Her smile didn't quite convey warmth. She glanced from Rose to me. "Did Rose tell you? I guess my sister won't need your help anymore now they've caught Carl's killer."

"Rose just told me they picked up Malcolm Boussard for questioning. Doesn't mean he's guilty of anything. Let alone Carl's murder."

Nadine strode to the cupboard and brought out a mug. "Is that tea, Rose?"

"Yes, oolong," she said, waving at the tea pot. "Help yourself, I just made it."

"It doesn't take a genius to see the boy's strange," said Nadine. "All dressed in black. Even his eyes."

Rose protested feebly, "I wanted Carl's killer caught, but Malcolm's just a child. His life is going to be ruined forever."

"Why on earth would you think he killed Carl? Did he even know Carl?" A thought floated through my consciousness. What if Carl was the one behind the porn site? I dismissed it. No way. Not righteous Carl. Rose prattled on.

"Of course, he knew who Carl was. We didn't socialize much with the Boussards, but Carl often went over to JP's on business."

"He must be mentally ill. Or on drugs." Nadine smiled smugly as she flit around the kitchen, adding first sugar then milk to her tea.

"Now why would you think that?" Her glib attitude annoyed me almost as much as her accusations. I was seeing a side of her I didn't like.

"It's shocking how many of these kids get into these dark cults and such. I suppose because they feel unwanted. There was a case like this in Lethbridge a few years back. The boy killed his whole family in some sort of cult ritual. He was only fourteen."

"I remember it too. But that kid was on drugs and in trouble with the law since he was ten. He also robbed his family and stole money and their car after killing them. Whereas, what? Malcolm cleverly poisons Carl somehow, and the next day just goes back to school? What for? Why?"

"I'm sure they'll discover all is not what it seems. I've seen some of his drawings, all creepy and dark. Dee Dee must be having a coronary. More tea, Rose?"

"Really?" Why was I listening to this drivel? "And here I was thinking maybe Carl found out something about Dimitri or his investor syndicate. And that someone killed him for it or at least for stalling the launch."

Rose came out of her tepid trance. "That's silly. Dimitri would never hurt anyone. I'm sure his investors are all above board." She looked to Nadine for support.

Nadine looked over her shoulder at Rose, sucked in her cheeks and pursed her lips. With a slight shake of her head, she turned to face me, cup in hand.

"I'm sure it will eventually come out, so you might as well hear it now. Seems the police are interested in the cyanide they found at the Boussards'." Nadine dropped the bombshell smoothly.

I stared at her dumbly. A wave of heat flashed over me. I lifted a hand to my forehead. It didn't feel feverish. "What cyanide?" I choked out.

Nadine was giddy with excitement. The smugness flitting around her lips reminded me of Rose's face as I cleared plates that night, right before Carl collapsed.

"It was only a matter of time before they found out Malcolm

and his friend had access to cyanide. His friend's dad makes or used to make jewellery."

"Eric? So? I still don't get it."

"Oh, I thought you'd know. Cyanide is used in the gold-plating process. Anyway,"—she brushed back a strand of hair—"it was at Carl's funeral I first noticed Malcolm's cross. It was quite striking. Made of Lucite or another clear material like it and had these beautiful gold threads embedded inside. He was standing all by himself looking awkward. I went over and introduced myself. After all, I didn't know many people there either. I asked if the threads were gold. He told me they were gold plated. We got talking. He told me his friend learned how to plate gold from his dad."

"I'm sure Detective Birdie was grateful for the tip."

"Somebody had to say something to them. I'm not sure how these brainless twits ever solve anything on their own otherwise." Nadine's chest puffed slightly. Rose appeared apologetic, but she always did.

I stared at Nadine, then at Rose. Rose sat docilely, sipping her tea, the cup nestled in both hands, seemingly oblivious to what was being said. My eyes turned back to Nadine. She had such poise, such grace. But now I could see her other swanlike qualities. When threatened, swans bite and attack, they'll even try to drown you if you give them half a chance.

"I came by to give Rose an update on my progress, but I can see you don't need one now." I turned back to Rose. "Or do you?"

Nadine replied, "We're both grateful for your efforts but I don't see any need for you to continue. The police have picked up the guilty party. It's ludicrous to think my sister could have done anything to harm Carl in the first place. Rose, what do you say?"

Rose's eyes told me she was in the place she always went to when faced with a decision. After a few minutes, she glanced up, seeming surprised to see she still had a guest. "Oh...no. I suppose not. I'm sad for Malcolm but the police will take care of this now."

I quietly sucked in a deep breath and rose to my feet. "I'll finish up my report and send it to your lawyer, Ms. Gray, along with my invoice. It was a pleasure to meet you, Rose. I'm sorry it was under these circumstances. You too, Nadine."

Nadine smiled broadly. "I'll see you out."

I followed Nadine calmly to the front door while fighting the urge to tackle her to the ground and land a few kidney punches before running off. But the Dobermans materialized, making it easier for me to slide quietly out the door. A moment of panic jolted me as I stared at the empty curb in front of me. Then I remembered I'd left the Jeep in a strip mall and turned in that direction.

I had been so empathetic toward Malcolm being bullied I hadn't even considered putting him on my suspect list. Who puts children on a list of suspected murderers? The knot in my stomach grew heavy. Big mistake. Everybody needs to be on the suspect list until there's enough evidence to take them off.

Was Malcolm capable of murder? He was willing to be publicly humiliated and sexually exploited in order to protect his family. I reached the Jeep and touched the hood to steady myself. The ground titled under my feet and I found it hard to swallow. I took a sharp breath. Could Malcolm have killed Carl when he realized Carl was going to delay the product launch? A delay that could cause financial ruin for his parents and others? A delay he inadvertently triggered by messing with Daryl's data in a fit of childish anger.

FIFTY-THREE

I STOPPED BY AKAR'S parents' place, but Dave wasn't there. The dog wasn't either. I called Dave's parents', but Dave's mother insisted he wasn't there. Lydia didn't know where he was either. I suspected she was telling the truth. Dave didn't have a history of staying put.

Nadine had more than hinted that Malcolm had access to cyanide through Eric's father. I always knew Eric was in this as deep as Malcolm, but it was going to be hard to get access to him. I phoned Eric's house. A woman answered.

"May I please speak to Eric?"

"Who is this?"

"My name is Jorja Knight. I'm a private investigator. I'm the one who located the Boussards' son a few days ago and returned him to his family. I'd like to ask Eric a few questions."

"Eric's not talkin' to reporters or any investigators other than the police."

"I spoke to Eric and Malcolm at the Boussards', several days ago. I have a quick follow-up question."

"I said no, and I mean no." The phone went dead in my ear.

I returned home, feeling like the whipped dog I was. I threw in a load of laundry and tried to stop the mental abuse I heaped on myself. I tried shaking off thoughts about Carl and Malcolm, but couldn't let it go, even though I'd clearly been let go from the case. I told myself none of this was my problem. I had done what I had been hired to do. I helped Gab clear her name. I had found Dave. More than once. Police attention had shifted off Rose and Nadine was delighted with the new development. The police obviously had something on Malcolm that connected him to Carl's death.

I paced the living room. Maybe I was ahead of the police, not lagging. If I was right about being a step ahead of the police, it meant they'd be looking hard for a motive too. It was only a matter of time before they learned the trial data had been tampered with, if they didn't already. Malcolm might break under the pressure and confess to changing the trial data, which would give him the motive the police were looking for. The earlier knot in my throat was now replaced by a gnawing unease.

I couldn't believe how easily Rose and Nadine accepted the idea Malcolm was guilty. I sent Eric an email, hoping he would reply. I stared at the screen. My heart ached for Malcolm. His world was truly fucked up. My gut told me the killer was still out there. I couldn't just sit here and let Malcolm be victimized again.

If Malcolm had slipped cyanide into the food, he risked killing his own parents, which kind of defeated the whole idea of killing Carl to protect them.

And what I knew, and Malcolm knew, that the extortionist didn't seem to know, was that Malcolm had tampered with the data. That was now my sticking point.

An hour later, I was walking up the front sidewalk of a narrow two-storey. Like all the other houses in the neighbourhood, it was clad in pale vinyl siding and stood ten feet from the road. None had an attached garage. The white pages told me a Robert Swanson lived here. Eric's parents had divorced years ago. I wasn't sure if this Robert Swanson was Eric's dad, but the Auburn Crest Way address demanded my attention. Auburn Crest Way lay less than half a kilometre, as the crow flies, from where I had picked Malcolm up, the night he was released. The two locations were separated by an empty field, a few construction sites, and Fifty-Second Street.

I stepped over a tricycle and made my way up the two front steps and onto the front veranda. I rang the doorbell and a minute later a woman arrived at the door, a howling two-year-old straddling her hip. As soon as she opened the door the darling Lilliputian turned his face away and ramped up his howl. Interestingly, he shed no tears. A little girl ran up asking repeatedly, "Who is it, Mom, who is it?"

"I see you have your hands full." I smiled. "My name is Jorja Knight and I'm a private investigator. I'm looking for Eric Swanson's father, Robert Swanson."

"Oh no. What's Eric done this time?"

The little girl pounded the side of her mother's leg with her fist.

"Who, Mom? What's who done?"

"Eric's not in any trouble. His friend, Malcolm, was abducted but has been returned safely. I'm trying to track down where Eric and Malcolm were in the hours leading up to his kidnapping in hopes of finding out who did it."

"Mommy, I need juice now!"

"Bob went out on an emergency call, but he should be home any minute now. Oh, there he is." Relief flooded her voice. She backed inside and disappeared down the hall, both kids' voices loud and demanding. I turned to see a tired-looking man in his forties get out of a van and make his way up the walk. He wore a black ball cap, black polo shirt and grey cotton drill pants. As he closed the distance between us, I could see *Plumb Bob* lettered on his shirt above a logo of a smiling man holding a plunger.

"Are you Robert Swanson?"

"That's right, but most people call me Bob."

"Jorja Knight." I held out my hand. "I'm a private investigator. I'm not sure if you know but a friend of your son's was kidnapped. He's been found okay. I'm the one who picked him up when he was released. I'd like to ask you a few questions, if you don't mind."

"You don't think Eric had anything to do with it, do you?"

"No, nothing like that. I'm trying to reconstruct Eric and his friend's movements prior to the kidnapping. It might provide a clue as to who the perpetrators are, or at least lead to someone who might know."

"Come in then." He pulled open the door and I stepped inside. The wailing noises grew louder, the boy and girl now howling in unison. "Want a beer?"

"No thanks, I'm fine."

"Have a seat." He pointed at the brown couch immediately to the left. It was covered with a multicoloured striped afghan. I sat on the edge avoiding something I told myself was probably mashed banana.

"You said a friend of Eric's was kidnapped?"

"Yes. I don't know if you know him. Malcolm Boussard?"

"Oh, Malcolm. Yeah. Eric's mentioned him, but we've never met. They go to the same school."

"Yes." I surveyed the threadbare surroundings. He must have noticed me inspecting his living room.

"Eric's mother and I split up when he was five. I pay a little child support but it's never enough. She's on welfare. I have a hard-enough time supporting my family let alone her and Eric. Eric's a smart kid. He got a bursary or grant or something to attend Silvergate."

I nodded. "When did you last see Eric?"

"Let's see. It'll be a couple weeks now. That's right, second week of October. It was Lucy's fourth birthday."

That made it four or five weeks ago, but time flies when you're having fun.

"Does he visit often?"

"Used to. Now that he's older, he's busy with his friends and all."

"I understand you do or used to make jewellery."

"I did, not much anymore."

"And Eric? Is he into making jewellery?"

"Naw. Eric seemed interested when he was eight or nine. We made a few pieces. But he lost interest."

"Gold pieces?"

He laughed. "Copper mostly. It's malleable and cheap. I did plate gold jewellery at one time, but gold got expensive and I ran out of time."

"Would you ever go back to it?"

"Probably not. I had a bunch of equipment stored in the garage out back. But someone broke in and stole most of what was there along with some tools. They took an extra shop vac I kept back there, but left the rock saw," he said, shaking his head.

"When did this happen?"

"Oh, mid-October, I'd say. I don't go back there much. I park out front. Might have even happened a week before I noticed. Someone broke the window in the side door. Jerk cut himself on the glass. Serves him right."

"Did you report it?"

"Had to, for the insurance. Cops said it happens all the time. Nothing's going to stop it. Even though the cops found a bit of blood on the glass, the chance of matching it up with someone is zero to nil. The whole world's going to hell in a hand basket."

"Your jewellery-making equipment was stolen? Including chemicals?"

"Yup, the whole shebang. Except for a small rock saw I had

back there. Don't know why they left it. The chemicals were old, not worth much. I don't even remember what all was back there anymore. Well except for the spare tools I use for my plumbing business."

"Are chemicals like cyanide used to make jewellery?"

"If you're talking about plating gold, you need an alkali-cyanide-based wash. That's what contains the gold. At the right acidity and temperature, the gold ions bond with the metal you're plating. The process for plating silver's the same, except you need to use alkali-silver cyanide."

"Where did you get your chemicals?"

"I used to be able to buy them from a rock and mineral shop in Kensington. Same place I got my gemstones and semiprecious stones. Later, they stopped stocking it. Luckily, you can order it online."

"Anyone can order it online?"

"You have to register, give them your name, address, credit card information. It's considered a hazardous good, so they make you go through the whole rig-a-ma-role to get it."

"Has Eric shown any interest in jewellery or the plating process recently?" I didn't like that the theft occurred roughly the same time his son had visited.

"Naw. You know kids. He played around with it, 'cause I was doing it. I gave it up a few years after Eric's mom and I separated, and Eric lost interest."

"Have you ever seen this guy around here?" I pulled out a picture of Malcolm I had downloaded from Facebook. He pulled it closer and studied it for a minute.

"I figured my kid dressed like a weirdo. This his friend?"

I nodded. "Yes. That's Malcolm."

"Nope. I can't believe they put up with this crap at his fancy school. I suppose everyone's worried they'll damage their precious little psyches. My old man used to beat me when I did something wrong and I turned out all right."

An involuntary shudder ran through me.

"Daddy! Daddy!" The little girl ran into the room, this time a small blanket billowing out behind her, two corners tied around her neck. She launched herself into the air and landed on his lap knees first. Air exploded from him as he lurched forward.

I stood up. "I can see someone else wants your attention. Please, don't get up. I'll let myself out. Thanks again for your time."

I was barely at the door when he bellowed, "How many times do I have to tell you not to jump on me like that?"

"But I was Wonder Woman," the little girl shouted back, dissolving into tears.

I stepped out into the cool air and closed the door. Now muffled, I could still hear Bob inside. "And for once, stop your goddamn crying."

Yup. He turned out all right. A stellar dad. Probably a loving husband too.

I walked down the sidewalk and pulled myself up into the Jeep. I made my way over to Fifty-Second Street and found the cul-de-sac where I had picked Malcolm up. I parked and slid out.

Most of the houses here were also less than ten feet from the road but in this neighbourhood front-drive garages were prevalent and the houses bigger than the one the Swansons lived in. I made my way cautiously, in the dark, back to the entrance of the cul-de-sac and continued down to the end of the deserted street. There were no streetlights here. An empty field backed the development to the south.

I peered into the blackness and made my way over to a large sign of sorts. Using my phone for light I studied the sign. The area behind the houses was slated for Phase 3 development. It showed dozens of building lots laid out, all perfectly narrow at front, widening slightly toward the back. Two of the lots had sold stickers plastered across them. I located where I was standing on the map. I peered into the dark, taking a few steps forward. Here the plant material had been scraped off, bare dirt exposed, ready for excavation. I made my way back down the side street and around the corner to the front street.

I had never liked coincidences but over time I had grown to view coincidences differently. When we focus on our surroundings, our brains pay more attention. What we notice was always there, but unless we are open to seeing, it remains invisible to us. So, in a way, we can say the universe sends us messages, because the messages are always there. Whether we receive them or not is up to us. Paying attention meant you had to live in the moment, and I wasn't terribly good at living in the moment. But I was paying attention now.

Malcolm had been released in a field five minutes from his best friend's dad's place. I'm sure tons of random people were familiar with the area, but Malcolm's best friend, Eric, was too. It meant something. Not to mention Eric's dad had a cyanide-based solution stolen, right around the time Malcolm's father's business partner died from a lethal dose of cyanide. I still didn't know what was going on, but I was certain Eric wasn't merely a loyal friend standing innocently by his friend's side. Whatever was going on, Eric and Malcolm were in it up to their armpits.

I needed to revamp my thinking. Riteweight's data had been tampered with by an angry, hurting teenager. Everything might have been fine had Carl not taken this to heart and insisted on delays, more testing, questioning the partners, even risking his own financial wellbeing. Someone killed him for it. I needed to believe Malcolm was telling the truth now, but the queasiness in my gut wouldn't subside. He had helped me clear Gab's name and now stood at the top of my suspect list. Malcolm's life was far from idyllic. He was being tortured at every turn. Kids had killed for far less. The possibility Malcolm was one of those kids shook me to my core.

FIFTY-FOUR

I FELT A STAB of unease as I made my way to the Boussards'. A dark-blue Dodge Charger was parked across from the house with two men inside, probably undercover police. I pulled up next to the curb and made my way up the driveway to the front door. The wind was cold, the sky dark grey, threatening snow. I pressed the bell and waited.

Last night it had been on the news. Police were questioning a person of interest in the Carl Johnson homicide. Names were not being released. It had to be Malcolm.

A person of interest wasn't always the suspect, sometimes it was someone who witnessed or had information relevant to the crime. I hoped it was the case here. And maybe the nosey gossip who reported Malcolm being led away in handcuffs embellished the story to make it more dramatic than it actually was.

As the chimes inside faded, I pressed the bell again. Jeannine answered.

"Hi, Jeannine. I heard about Malcolm. I'm here to see JP or Dee Dee. I believe I can help."

"Come in. Dee Dee's upstairs, she's not seeing anyone. If you wait here, I'll see if Mr. Boussard will see you."

I waited in the foyer while Jeannine went to do her thing. The house was deadly quiet, a sharp contrast to the night of the party. The enormity of the place would make it easy to avoid spending time with the other inhabitants. For a teenager, I imagined it could be both welcoming and lonely.

Jeannine returned. "Please, come this way."

I followed her through the massive reception room and to the den. JP was on the phone, but glanced up when we entered, nodded at Jeannine and waved me to one of the chairs in front of his desk. I sat and waited. JP listened intently, nodding and occasionally grunting. After another minute, he thanked whomever he was talking to and disconnected. He studied a space behind my left ear, his expression blank.

"Thank you for seeing me, Mr. Boussard."

He ran his hand through his hair, and slowly re-engaged. "Please, it's JP. And I should be the one thanking you for bringing Malcolm home the other night." He faced me squarely. "I need a drink. Can I convince you to join me?"

"Under the circumstances, I'm willing to break protocol." I nodded.

"Scotch?"

"Perfect."

JP walked over to a mahogany credenza, opened one of the three decanters and poured two glasses. "Salute," he said, handing me a glass. I held up the glass, inhaling its woodsy aroma. I swirled the glass and took a sip. The golden liquid slid down my throat, like warm caramel. For one brief second, I forgot why I was here.

JP sat back down.

"I don't believe your son had anything to do with Carl's death."

"I appreciate you saying so, but the police obviously presume otherwise."

"Have they said anything to you?"

"They showed up yesterday with a search warrant. They took

his laptop, books, CDs, movies, and a bunch of stuff from the upstairs washroom. They checked the garage, the potting shed. They even hauled away stuff from out there."

"Why? I don't get it."

"They think he knows something about Carl's death, more than he's saying. They haven't formally charged him with anything. Our lawyer says they can hold him for twenty-four hours without laying charges. He's down there with Malcolm now."

"Have you talked to Malcolm?"

"I spoke with him last night."

"What did he say?"

"He says he didn't kill Carl or know anything about who did."

"Do you know he's being cyberbullied?"

"He mentioned it." He shrugged. "Life's tough. You can't let other people's opinions of you get you down."

"These weren't opinions, Mr. Boussard...JP." My hand tightened around my glass. Afraid it would shatter, I set it on the desk. "Malcolm is a victim of harassment, extortion, sexual luring."

He gave a quick bark of laughter, then stiffened. "Wait. What are you saying? Sexual luring. What the hell do you mean?"

"Someone was blackmailing your son into sending sexually explicit photos and videos of himself. Several of those have ended up on a pornography site."

JP let out a groan. "No. No that can't be." He shook his head and leaned over, head in his hands, elbows on the table. I watched his fists clutch two handfuls of hair. After a minute, he looked up, his eyes hollow, his face ashen.

"He's a victim, JP. He did what he did to try and protect himself and his family. He may have made a few stupid decisions along the way, but he's no murderer."

"What do you mean? How's he protecting the family? By making and sharing naked pictures of himself?"

I told him how Malcolm had been duped into thinking he was communicating online with a potential girlfriend, how they had exchanged photos of themselves and how the person behind the scam threatened to make the photos public unless videos and more sexually explicit material was provided. Malcolm complied in the hopes of avoiding public scandal until his parents' company successfully launched their new product. JP sat shell shocked.

"I had no idea."

"There's more."

"Do I want to hear this?" he said, getting up to pour himself another drink. He shuffled over to the credenza, picked up the decanter and waved it my way. I shook my head.

"You have to hear this. The person or persons who are doing this were or maybe still are spying on your home. They may have audio surveillance equipment, powerful enough to hear conversations being held in your house."

"Jeezus. Espionage?"

"I can't prove this isn't related to your company's dealings, but I don't believe it is. Unfortunately, they seem to have overheard that someone tampered with your company's trial data. They used that information, threatened to go to the press with it unless your son sent them additional photos."

"Son of a bitch." JP paced like a trapped animal realizing its escape route had been cut off. He lifted his glass, drained it and sat back down. The colour slowly returned to his face.

"What makes you think it's not corporate espionage?"

I took a deep breath. "Because whoever's been blackmailing Malcolm over the tampered trial data wanted sexually illicit photos." I swallowed hard and took a deep breath. "And they didn't know Malcolm was the one who changed the data."

JP sank back in his chair. He no longer resembled the robust, assured man who greeted me earlier. His face was grey and tired, his shoulders stooped. I wondered if Gab would find him so attractive now.

"I don't understand. Why in hell would he do that?"

Half an hour later he was versed in what I understood of the situation, or at least most of it.

"Unfortunately, I only have Malcolm's word that this happened as I've described, but he can deny it just as easily. But I do know someone who can confirm what I've told you."

"I still don't understand why the police imagine he had anything to do with Carl's death?" JP mused out loud, then bolted upright. "God no! No." He shook his head, his agonized eyes met mine. "You don't suppose he killed Carl because Carl was threatening to delay the product launch until we ran another trial? Because of the tampered data. The data he changed. Oh god," he moaned as he sank back. No semblance of the arrogant, overconfident businessman remained. I pushed off the empathy creeping in.

"Stop acting like your son's guilty. He says he didn't do it." I couldn't be too harsh. After all, the same thought had occurred to me earlier.

"Can you help prove it? That he didn't have anything to do with it?"

"I'm trying."

"I'll pay you whatever you want."

"I don't want your money. I want to help prove your son is innocent. I have an idea, but also a few glaring gaps. Right now, I could use some answers from you."

"What do you need?"

"Your son went missing for fifty-four hours. Why wasn't an amber alert or any notification to the public issued?"

"We received a phone call demanding money for his return."

"When? What did they say?"

"My wife got the call. A man said they had our son. He wanted twenty-five thousand dollars in cash for his safe return. He told my wife she had twenty-four hours to get the money together. She was to tell no one, especially the police. At first, she thought it might be a hoax, so she called the school. They said Malcolm hadn't shown up that day or the day before. Someone claiming to be me left a message on the school's phone system to say Malcolm wouldn't be in, he wasn't feeling well."

"Sounds well planned out."

"My wife phoned me in a panic. She told me Malcolm hadn't shown up at school and about the call. She didn't know what to do." JP rubbed his forehead with both hands. "By the time I got home, my wife contacted a few of Malcolm's friends. No one had seen him or had any idea where he could be. We began figuring out how we could get the money. We don't have that kind of cash lying around."

I eyed the pewter-embossed crystal decanters on the mahogany credenza and the hundreds of leather-bound books lining the shelves behind JP. I peered at JP's wrist, not wanting to be too obvious, but I was certain I could see the distinctive crown logo of Rolex peeking out from below his black micro-checked Armani shirtsleeve.

"Dee Dee called her parents and told them what happened. Her father said they'd give us the money but only if we called the police."

"Did you?"

"Yes. Dee Dee was furious and bereft at the same time. She said if Malcolm died it'd be my fault." He rubbed his eyes with the palm of his hands. "It's always my fault."

A vision of him walking down the street with his hand on Kristen Lee's lower back wiped away any empathy bubbling up.

"What did the police do?"

"They sent over a couple of plain-clothed detectives and rigged up the phones. We waited for a call. The kidnappers contacted us the next day. They insisted Dee Dee be the one to drop the money."

"Oh dear," I said, before realizing I voiced it out loud.

"I offered to go in her place, but she wouldn't have it."

"What did the detectives say?"

"They weren't happy but what choice did we have? They put a wire on my wife and a GPS tracker on the car. We put the money in a women's sports bag like instructed and Dee Dee left with it shortly before the drop."

"Where was the drop?"

"They told her to go to Chinook mall and wait for instructions. They'd contact her on her cell."

"Nice move on their part, Chinook's always busy."

"Once there, she got a call telling her to go inside through Chapters. From there she was to go upstairs to the movie theatres."

"Were the detectives following her all this time?"

"One of them was. They had a couple of other guys listening through the wire. Once she was upstairs, the kidnappers called and told her to buy a ticket, go into movie theatre number four, and wait for further instructions. She did. Later, I found out the detective following her went in shortly afterwards and sat five or six rows behind her, across the aisle."

"Was the place full?"

"About half full. They made her sit through most of the movie. It was nerve-racking. We didn't know what was going on or if they had spotted the detective. Ten minutes before the end of the movie, my wife got a text message telling her to get up and take the bag into the women's washroom."

"Clever. Not many people are going to be leaving right at the climax of the movie."

"Exactly. The detective couldn't get up and follow her without giving himself away. By then, the cops had another undercover detective, a woman, waiting in the lobby. She saw Dee Dee come out of the theatre and go into the washroom. Unfortunately, some teenage flick in the adjacent theatre let out minutes earlier and the whole place was jammed with teenage girls. They could hardly make out anything through Dee Dee's wire. Dee Dee was told to wait for the third stall to become available. They lost audio."

He spoke confidently, now back in control, telling his story.

"Once she got into the stall, she got another text telling her to slide her bag to the stall on her right. She was told to take off the wire, drop it into the toilet and wait. After a few minutes the bag was slid back, and she got a text telling her to leave immediately and turn the bag in to one of the staff in the lobby saying she found it in the washroom. Then get in her car and go home."

I had to admire the complexity of the move. "Did she look in the bag?"

"No. She said it weighed roughly the same. She was in complete shock."

"What did they do?"

"Detective Kroch told me they didn't know what to do at first. They were worried someone had spotted them and was using this whole charade to check out if the police were involved."

"Clever. I can see the dilemma. They'd have had no idea if the money was still in the bag."

"Right. Dee Dee walked up to one of the theatre staff, a woman who was making sure exiting customers were moving along in an orderly fashion, turned over the bag saying she found it in the washroom, and left. She, in turn, turned over the bag to her manager. The detectives were scrambling to find out who the manager was and a number to call. They also had someone keeping an eye on the washroom to see if anyone came out with a duplicate bag."

"I have to admit, the whole set up is impressive."

"Dee Dee got home a while later. She was a mess. I was a mess. There had been no other communication. We were afraid we'd never see Malcolm again. Detective Kroch warned us about the risks of cooperating with kidnappers. They don't always return their victims once the ransom is paid."

I nodded. My friend Mike had a lot of his own police stories confirming what JP and Dee Dee had been told.

"One of the detectives came back to the house a couple of hours later. A few others were parked down the street. They were trying to figure out what happened. There was no word from the kidnappers. The sports bag Dee Dee handed over to the usher at the theatre contained cut-up paper. They were still trying to figure out what happened, they had no idea if the girl or the manager of the theatre were part of this. There was nothing in the washroom. Clearly the money had been taken out of the bag and carried out by someone. We were starting to panic." JP's voice wavered; a small tremor ran across his chin. "We thought we lost him."

"Then I showed up with Malcolm."

"Yes, then you showed up with Malcolm." His voice broke and he held up a fist to his mouth. "Sorry," he choked out. "When they walked in the door with Malcolm, I saw him differently. He wasn't a screwed-up, annoying kid. He was a young man, who had been put through hell. And I haven't done right by him." JP brought his fist up to his lips again and I waited while he composed himself.

"What did Malcolm say happened?"

"Malcolm says he left for school as usual, the day he was abducted. It's a five-block walk to the bus stop. A couple of blocks from the bus stop he saw a broken-down car. The hood was up and a woman, whom Malcolm assumed was the driver, was pacing nearby. As Malcolm got closer, she ran up to him and asked to borrow his cell phone, saying she didn't have hers with her and her car had died. He handed her his cell phone assuming she'd call for help and walked over to the car thinking he'd have a quick look in case it was something simple. He felt something come down over his mouth. He couldn't breathe. He vaguely remembers a man getting out of the back seat, and he and the woman pushed him inside. The next thing he remembers is waking gagged, blindfolded, with his hands tied behind him."

JP's hands were now fists lying on his desk, the knuckles white. He slowly pushed himself upright, his eyes moist, and walked to the window behind me. He leaned one hand on the window frame and swiped his eyes quickly with the other. Without turning to look at me he continued.

"He figured he'd be tortured, killed or both. He had no idea who his kidnappers were or why he'd been taken." JP turned and walked back to the desk. "There were two of them, a man and a woman. He said they didn't talk much. He was tied up, gagged, his head kept covered by a burlap sack. He figured he was in a warehouse somewhere—the floor was concrete. They left him tied up, lying on a mattress of sorts. One of them, the man, returned later and took off the hood but left him blindfolded. He gave him food and water and let him relieve himself. Then he put the hood back on, tied his hands back up and left."

"And he still didn't know what they wanted?"

"No. He said he asked but was told to shut up. He had no idea how long he was there, but we know it was nearly two days. Eventually someone came, hauled him outside and shoved him onto the floor of a truck or van and drove off. He was blindfolded the entire time. He couldn't tell if it was the same man or if the woman was with him. He figured they drove for a good twenty minutes or longer. There were a lot of turns and after some time the ground or road became bumpy. The man asked him for a name, someone who could come to pick him up. Not his mother or me. He gave him your name. He figured being a PI, you'd know how to handle yourself. After they stopped, they told him what to say and a phone was held up to his head. I guess they called you. After a while, someone cut through the rope around his wrists part way and pushed him out of the truck. The man told him to count to a thousand, remove his blindfold and the bindings. When he was free, to make his way to the houses in front of him. A truck would be waiting to take him home."

"That's pretty much where I came in. I guess while he was tied up in the warehouse was when you and your wife were contacted for the ransom."

"Yes."

"When I got the call, I picked him up at the location he gave and drove him home. The police were waiting and took me downtown. Malcolm tells them what happened. I tell them my side of the story. Thirty-six hours later they take Malcolm in for questioning regarding Carl's death. Why? And what happened to the ransom money?"

"I don't know. Malcolm told them his side of things, exactly as I told you. The night he got back they took samples from under his fingernails, his hair. They bagged up the clothes he had been wearing. I presumed it was to see if there were traces of anything that might lead them to where he had been kept, or the vehicle. Malcolm didn't want to go to the hospital. He insisted they hadn't harmed him in any way. He had a couple of scrapes and a bruise on his cheek, but otherwise was fine. He slept until noon the following day."

"The police let me go home around three in the morning. They checked my cell phone log and retained my truck. Malcolm told me pretty much the same thing he told you and the police. Did the police tell you anything else about the ransom, after Malcolm was returned?"

"The sports bag contained bundles of cut-up newspaper. They questioned the manager and the girl at the theatre, but they're convinced they weren't part of it."

"So, the kidnappers did get the money."

"Looks like it. The following afternoon the police were back, asking Malcolm more questions. They insinuated Malcolm was part of the kidnapping scheme. My wife was upset. I demanded to know what was going on."

"Whoa. What gave them that idea?" Uneasiness engulfed me, as the same idea percolated in my mind. I remembered the determination on Dave's face when he announced they were going to catch this guy. Trap him. And Malcolm's renditions of his kidnapping, to me then his father and the police, sounded so similar, I wondered if they were rehearsed. But why only ask for twenty-five thousand dollars? It wasn't exactly a huge amount. On the other hand, it was if you were a druggie, or unemployed...or a teenager. I suspected the police thought so too.

"I don't know. I told them to leave. The next time they asked to talk to my son it would be with our lawyer present."

"What did Malcolm say?"

"Malcolm said he had no idea what they were talking about. He was upset. The following day they arrived with a search warrant. I called our lawyer, but we had no choice but to let them in."

"Were they still theorizing he was involved in orchestrating his own kidnapping?"

"I assumed so. They took our computers, his laptop, my wife's iPad. They asked to see our phones and checked through them. They were in his room, the pantry, kitchen—although I don't know why. They had a pretty thorough look through the place a week or so after Carl died. Then they went outside, there were five of them out there."

"What were they doing?"

"They checked the potting shed out back, walked around the yard, poked into flower beds, checked out the garage. They bagged up stuff all along the way. I don't even know what all they hauled away."

Something had interested them. I wondered if they were looking for recently disturbed earth where the money could be buried?

"They came back a while later and requested Malcolm accompany them downtown for questioning. We called our lawyer. He came and went to the police station with him. When they left, we still assumed it was regarding the kidnapping. Later, our lawyer called and said they were questioning him about Carl's death."

"Perhaps they found the same connection I did, the hacked data, the cyberthreats and extortion. Or Malcolm told them."

"Whatever's going on, they're not saying."

"So now what?"

"He's got the best lawyer I could find."

"You don't believe he had anything to do with Carl's death, do you?"

He paused just long enough for me to mentally call him a bastard. "He's a good kid. Sensitive. I've never seen him be mean to an animal or another child. I can't see him taking another person's life."

Then again, JP couldn't see him being bullied either, expected Malcolm should suck it up. He didn't see him going out on a limb to keep his father's company out of the tabloids. He couldn't see his son was hurting. Hurting bad.

"I don't believe your son killed Carl. If I were you, I'd practice denying his involvement as vehemently as possible."

"Right."

"The police aren't going to let me visit or talk to Malcolm at this point. Or tell me anything. I'd like to talk to Malcolm's lawyer."

"I'll see what I can do. I was talking to him when you arrived.

He doesn't think they have enough evidence to charge Malcolm. He expects they'll release him later today."

"Even better."

JP said he'd give me a heads-up if he heard anything else. I left JP's even more certain Malcolm's kidnapping was part of Dave's harebrained scheme to expose or capture Malcolm's extortionist. And I was starting to form a very different idea about who killed Carl.

FIFTY-FIVE

I WAS BEGINNING TO think the man and woman who snatched Malcolm were Dave and Lydia. That they had faked Malcolm's kidnapping. Is that why I had been called to pick Malcolm up after the ransom was paid? They didn't want the Boussards to pick up their son, on the off chance they had called police. So they called me, my cell, and put me in the middle of their stupid scheme. A scheme which Malcolm might end up paying for.

Dave blatantly admitted he was on a mission to bring down whoever was cyberbullying and extorting pics from Malcolm. Revenge for being bullied himself, angry because someone was taunting him, threatening to ruin his reputation. Malcolm was probably unravelling at the police station this very minute. Then I'd be back on the hot seat for not being completely open about what was going down.

The drapes were pulled at Akar's parents' house, the driveway gates closed, no sign of vehicles parked in front or on the driveway. I circled the block and made a wider loop. I didn't spot anything unusual. Leaving my Jeep parked on a side street, I jogged back.

I continued up the sidewalk, past the house and around to

the back. The coach house was dark. I stopped and listened; all was quiet. I unlatched the gate and made my way across the lawn. My heels sunk into the grass and I switched to tippy toes. Making my way up the stairs I reached the door and tapped three times. I counted to ten and tapped again. I put my ear to the door. Nothing.

"Dave, open up," I said rapping loudly on the door. I repeated my demands to no avail. I climbed down the stairs and back across the lawn. A large cranberry bush inhabited the space between the house and the gate, half of its reddish leaves still intact. I tucked myself into the gap between it and the house and waited.

It was darker back here, the house blocking the light from the overcast sky. My feet were freezing. I tucked my hands into my jacket pockets and pulled the collar up against my ears, hoping I wouldn't have to wait long.

Shortly before five o'clock, Eric came down the street. He glanced over his shoulder several times as he approached the house. When he was several feet from the gate, he pulled out his cell phone, stopped and typed something into it. He shot one last glance over his shoulder and walked up to the gate. I stepped out when I heard the gate latch lift. Eric screamed.

I pulled open the gate and hissed, "Stop screaming like a little girl and get in here."

"Nuts. It's you."

"Yes, it's me. Although when I finish with you, you'll wish it wasn't me."

The gate clicked behind us and we made our way along the cobblestone sidewalk. I followed Eric up the coach house stairs. Eric knocked once, waited a few seconds and knocked again. The door opened a crack and I pushed Eric inside. Dave's jubilant face fell when he spotted me.

"Oh shit."

"Yes, Dave, shit. And your buddy Malcolm is in the biggest shit pile of all."

"No, he's not. He's going to be fine."

Eric's eyes bulged open. "It worked?"

"It worked." Dave grinned as he punched a fist into the air. "We got 'em."

"Got who...? Whom?"

I ogled the room. Akar would be horrified. The table we sat at a few days earlier was covered in Styrofoam takeout boxes, sticky globs of food, pizza boxes and litre-sized Slurpee containers. I stepped forward and my foot crunched a Doritos chip. The wall around the light switch contained several orange handprints. I discovered the source a minute later. Several half-eaten bags of cheese puffs lay on the sofa along with a laptop and the TV remote control. The Bichon Shih Tzu sat on the couch, the fur around its mouth a shocking orange. The open bags of cheese puffs no longer interested him.

"I called my friend on the way over here. Inspector Azagora. He heads up the Special Crimes unit. I told him if I didn't call back in an hour to send his guys over to this address." I inspected my wristwatch. "You have twenty-three minutes to tell me what I need to hear." I hadn't called Azagora but depending on what I learned in the next ten minutes, I might have to.

"Okay, okay. I sent in the video half an hour ago. The cops will have it now. Here, I'll show you."

Eric and I followed him to the couch. Dave pushed aside a bag of cheese puffs, sat down and pulled up his laptop. Eric plopped down on his right. The dog sat on Dave's left, and growled as I approached. His teeth were stained orange. I walked around to the back of the couch and peered over Dave's shoulder. The Shih Tzu barred his teeth at me, lay down and continued to growl.

Dave pulled out a memory stick and stuck it into the side of his laptop.

"I encrypted it and routed it through several sites. Here. Look at this," he exclaimed gleefully.

I watched the video come to life. It showed a C-Train platform. I couldn't tell which one, but it was an older station, probably the southeast line, one of the first to be built. A few people arrived. A train rolled in and stopped. Passengers disembarked onto the platform and the ones waiting on the platform grabbed their vacated spots on the train. Most of the arrivals made their way down the platform and into the station through the metal doors. A heavier-set man remained on the platform while most of the disembarking passengers went inside. He wore jeans, a black hoodie under a leather jacket with the hood pulled up over a black ball cap and gloves.

The train pulled away. I watched the man make his way down the platform and over to one of the trash bins. The hoodie obscured most of his face. He paced back and forth in front of the trash bin, stopped, and peered inside. Looking around, he wandered down the platform to the second trash bin. Now positioned at the second bin, he checked up and down the platform. A few people remained by the station door, waiting for a connecting train. A moment later he reached into the bin, rummaged around and pulled out a white plastic bag. He turned to exit the platform at the end opposite the station.

The video showed a white guy with scruffy beard, around five foot seven and weighing two hundred or so pounds. He wore his black ball cap pulled low on his forehead, his hoodie over it. He turned; a logo clear on the left sleeve of his jacket.

"It's the wizard!" Eric yelled out.

"Hey…is that the ransom money?" I asked.

Dave nodded. "This is where he wanted the money dropped off."

"You know this guy?"

"His real name is Verne Wizel. Known to his online friends as the wizard."

"He owns Death and Daggers," Eric chimed in.

"Which is?"

"A gaming and video store over on Seventeenth Avenue. Near Fourteenth Street. They carry new and used games, videos, comics, figures."

"Let me guess. He's the creep who's been extorting pics from Malcolm."

"Yup. I sent the cops this video, a link to his store's webpage and another link to the pay-for-porn site on which I found one of Malcolm's videos. The pictures of him on his store website will help solidify he and the guy on the platform are one and the same."

"He always struck me as creepy," announced Eric. "The way he licks his lips when he talks to you."

Everybody always found creeps creepy, after the fact.

"It's the perfect set up, isn't it?" I said, looking at Dave with newfound admiration.

"Yeah, took me a minute or two. But I found him. He has access to these kids' email, their credit card numbers, and addresses. On top of it he's a gamer, he's played half the guys who come into his store online. He knows people's account names."

"Malcolm is probably one of several he's hitting up."

"I bet half the photos on the porn site I found are from his victims," said Dave.

"He befriends them online posing as an interested girl or boy friend, talks them into something relatively innocent and it escalates from there."

"Seems he's supplementing his income with a sprinkling of porn on the side, which doesn't cost him anything to acquire. Except a bit of his time."

"What a douche," said Eric.

"This time he was offered cash instead of a video," I said, my admiration growing. "Quite the scheme."

"What scheme?" Dave plastered a look of innocence on his face.

"Right. Pure speculation on my part."

"Mine too," echoed Eric, snickering.

"I don't want to know any more." I glanced at my watch. God knows what was happening at the police station. I needed to trust however they set up the fake kidnapping, it was solid enough to not fall apart under questioning. And it probably would be if they kept to the same story. It was kind of brilliant. How else would a sixteen-year-old get together enough money to offer his extortionist instead of a video? And I could see how it would appeal to this scumbag, Wizel. He'd get his money upfront, cash, and no need to wait for someone to purchase porn off his site. Too bad what they had done was illegal.

"Well maybe you've solved one problem. If Malcolm sticks to his story and doesn't break, they may not be able to prove he was part of this crafty, devious, *illegal* scheme. Hopefully, they'll find enough to send this Wizel guy away for good. There's still one little problem though."

"What problem?" Dave and Eric asked in unison.

"You don't know? They're questioning Malcolm in relation to Carl Johnson's death."

"There's no way they can pin that on Malcolm," said Eric.

I stared at Eric, and held my breath, my mind frozen.

"I didn't mean it like that. How can they pin that on him when he didn't do it?"

"Nice rebound, Eric, but the police obviously have something on him. They came to his house with a warrant, took his laptop, papers, books, stuff from his bathroom, the tool shed outside."

I heard Dave's fingers tapping on the keyboard. "I don't like this. I hope they don't…"

"So?" said Eric.

"Eric. This isn't a stupid game. Did you know your dad's garage was broken into a few weeks ago? That someone took all the chemicals he had, the ones he used to make gold-plated jewellery?"

"No." Eric looked puzzled.

"When was the last time you were at your dad's?"

"On Lucy's birthday. Oct. 4th. Why? What's that got to do with anything?"

"Your dad didn't mention his garage being broken into?"

"No. I'm sure if it had been, I would have heard all about it. He thinks every little thing that goes wrong is someone sticking it to him."

I tried to mentally reconstruct the timeline of events in my head, but it was too much to handle.

"Rose's sister, Nadine, said something about cyanide, when she told me about Malcolm being taken away in handcuffs."

"Oh shit," Dave cursed.

"What?" Eric and I said in unison.

Dave angled the computer screen toward us.

"We watched Detective Birdie exit through a wrought-iron gate, a uniformed officer followed carrying a black sack and a green plaid backpack.

"Where is this from?" I glared at Dave.

"It's Malcolm's backyard."

"Hey, that's my backpack," yelled Eric, pointing at the screen. "How'd you get this?"

Dave ignored Eric and looked at me smugly. "Two can play the game. When I figured someone was listening in on the Boussards, I set up a video cam, hoping to see the van or whatever they were using to listen in to Malcolm and Eric. For a second there, I was worried the cops might have found it."

"I don't even want to be standing here, letting alone hearing this."

"Funny," said Dave. "Yet you have no issues entering someone's home and discharging a firearm."

"It was a BB gun."

"Why do they have my backpack?" screeched Eric again.

Dave and I stopped throwing verbal jabs and turned to face Eric. The implications of what he was saying sank in. The room fell silent. The Shih Tzu whimpered.

"Why do they, Eric?" I said.

"I don't know. Shit. It's my old backpack from junior high."

"When did you last see it?"

"I...I'm not sure. The last time I saw it, it was at my dad's place. It was hanging on a hook in the garage."

Dave, Eric and I looked at each other silently as Eric's words sank in.

FIFTY-SIX

I THRASHED, TOSSED AND turned all night, revisiting each and every detail swirling in my head. Malcolm's slight frame and dark tortured eyes reappeared each time I drifted off. I worried my own role would have implications, should Dave, Eric and Malcolm be caught in their kidnapping scheme. I went over everything in my mind, first paranoid I'd be implicated in something illegal, then exercising my natural desire to obsess. As daylight crept into the room, I got up, more exhausted than I'd been six hours earlier.

JP had called me after I got home last night to let me know Malcolm had been released. Malcolm had answered their questions and held steadfast in the details of his kidnapping. He swore he had nothing to do with Carl's death and wouldn't change his story to the day he died. They had finally let him go home, but he wasn't exactly out of the woods yet. Malcolm's lawyer told JP they didn't have enough conclusive evidence to charge him at this point but were working on it.

I got up, showered and dressed, and stopped at the chart paper taped to the wall in the short hallway leading to the kitchen. I had spent hours last night churning through every bit of information

I had and madly scribbled the timeline of events as best as I could reconstruct them. I stared at my masterpiece.

A quick call to Eric's dad told me the garage was broken into about two weeks after Carl died. The gold-plating chemicals stolen weren't the likely source of cyanide used to kill Carl. Of course, he only knew the date he reported the break-in—not the actual date of the break-in itself. Eric's dad admitted the window might have been broken days or even weeks before he noticed. It left me worried. Could Eric and Malcolm have broken in and taken the chemicals and later, someone noticed the broken window and helped themselves to the rest of the stuff? But murder?

Dimitri had opened my eyes to the possibility that Carl's death had been an act of revenge. Or it might just be a clever way to deflect my interest in him or his business dealings. Unfortunately, my investigation into his offshore business dealings was severely restricted, in terms of data access. There was only so much data private companies needed to make available to the public.

In my mind, there were two possibilities. I started to pace. Last night's turmoil and hours spent sorting through the mish mash of information I had collected made me certain I had Carl's murderer in view. Trouble was I had no proof.

I stood back, thinking hard. Nadine had been downright gleeful to hear police hauled Malcolm away for questioning. As I had gotten to know Nadine a bit better over the last weeks, I could see she was more than a little overbearing. She clearly bossed her little sister. Of course, Rose seemed to invite it. First, she let her husband run the agenda, and now Nadine was going to take his place.

I desperately tried to recall the conversation we had the morning she told me Malcolm had been picked up by police. I was certain she said the police had found cyanide at the Boussards'. I was also certain she had tipped them off.

I called JP. The call went straight to voice mail. I left him a message asking him to call me as soon as he got a chance.

I circled my living room for the umpteenth time. Slightly dizzy from my circuit, I grabbed the lone apple out of the wire fruit bowl on my kitchen counter, poured several cups of cheerios into a baggy and jammed both into my purse. I retrieved my Walther BB gun from the drawer in my nightstand and paused, hefting it in my hand. I stared at the clip still lying in the drawer. I stuffed the gun into my purse, grabbed my coat and headed downstairs.

Once downstairs, I checked the Jeep tires and the gas level in preparation for my drive south. I knew Nadine lived in Lethbridge before she moved into her sister's house. A quick google search told me Nadine had been married twice, widowed both times. Her first husband died three years after she married him, in a diving accident while on holiday in Mexico. Apparently, he had surfaced too quickly. They tried to get him into a hyperbaric chamber but there was nothing local. By the time they drove him to Veracruz it was too late.

Nadine's second husband had been a professor at the University of Lethbridge. His obituary didn't say much, other than he had died unexpectedly with his loving wife of twenty-five years at his side. They had one daughter. Rose had mentioned Nadine's daughter was living in Australia. The obituary mentioned that Nadine's husband, Henry Roblau, was also survived by his mother, an aunt and two cousins. I'm not sure what I expected to find, but Nadine seemed to be more concerned about the state and direction of Riteweight than her sister.

The day was cool and clear, and once I was beyond the city limits, the gently winding highway stretching south from Calgary to Lethbridge held hardly any traffic. The surrounding fields lay brown, dusty, and ready for winter. Skiffs of snow lay in the ditches. On rare occasions, I spotted a farmer rushing to get the last of his fields prepared before the snow, his equipment churning up clouds of dust. Round bales of hay dotted the undulating fields like giant curlers on mother earth's head.

Just past the town of Cayley, a red light lit up on my dash, warning me to pull over. I cursed, slowed and made my way over to the shoulder. I got out and looked at all four tires. They seemed fine. I checked the oil. The radiator wasn't steaming. I looked at the silent fields around me. No way was I going to call a garage to have someone come out to check a red light. I restarted the engine; the warning message was gone.

Within thirty minutes the oil light came on. *Seriously?* I pulled over, popped the hood and checked the oil. It was down a bit but not enough to worry about. Forty minutes further on, I reached the northern edge of Lethbridge. The gas gauge still read full. How could that be?

I pulled into a Shell station and added sixty-four dollars of fuel. Now I knew what was wrong with the rental. I congratulated myself on catching the defective gauges in town rather than when the tank ran empty on the highway. I used the washroom and checked google maps.

The address for Nadine's mother-in-law lay east of the university. I turned onto University Drive and after a few kilometres, east on Whoop-Up Drive. Five minutes later I was on Eighteenth Street. The trees lining the street were tall, now bare, their branches reaching into the pale-blue emptiness above. An occasional spruce tree stood green and dark against yellowing lawn. Most of the houses were typical of those built in the fifties and sixties.

I had no trouble finding the address I was looking for and was soon parked in front of a tiny white-clad bungalow. I made my way up the sidewalk and opened the gate on a small white picket fence. The grass could use a trim, but the place was well kept, despite starting to show its age.

I rang the doorbell and waited. When no one answered, I pressed the doorbell a second time. I could hear the chimes fading away inside. A scuffling noise told me a safety chain was being released and the interior door opened. A small thin woman, with short grey hair and blue watery eyes, peered at me through the screen door.

"Hello. Mrs. Roblau?"

"Yes?" she answered through the still closed screen door.

"My name is Jorja Knight." I pulled a card out of my wallet. "I'm a private investigator. I'd like to ask you some questions regarding your daughter-in-law, Nadine Roblau."

The deeply veined hand on the screen door handle turned and the door opened a crack. She took my card and studied it. She looked me over. "Got any other ID?"

I dug out my PI licence which had my picture on it and my driver's licence and handed her both through the crack. I tried not to smile while she alternately studied me and the photo on my ID, so my appearance would match the photo, which resembled that of a crack whore in prison. For life.

Satisfied, she opened the door another inch, handed my licences back and invited me in. Three feet of white linoleum demarcated the entryway and separated it from the brown carpeted living room. She waved me toward a loveseat covered in a tan fuzzy fabric with large brown flowers. Mrs. Roblau perched on a small stiff-looking wooden-armed chair.

"She's my *former* daughter-in-law, you know. My son died."

"Yes. I'm sorry to hear your son passed away."

"Ummff. Passed away."

"He died a relatively young man."

"They say he died of ace-fix-ee-ation."

"You don't believe it?" My spidey senses were now on full alert.

"No."

"Would you mind telling me what happened?"

"Nadine called me that afternoon. Said Henry was having trouble breathing. She took him to the hospital around midnight. A few hours later he was dead."

"Did he have breathing problems or the flu or something?"

"He had a touch of asthma. Other than that, he was fit as a fiddle."

"What did the doctors say?"

"They found a tear in his lung, from coughing."

"I'm sorry. It must be hard on you. Have you stayed in touch with Nadine?"

"No. I never cared for that woman. I kept a civil tongue in my head for Henry's sake and Amanda. That's my granddaughter, you know."

"Do you mind my asking why you and Nadine didn't get along?"

"She thought she was better than us. Putting on airs. Henry worked hard. Real hard. All she did was spend his money."

"She didn't work?"

"No. At first she had her hands full lookin' after Amanda. But once Amanda was in school, she ran around telling everybody she was an on-tray-pre-neur."

"She had her own business?"

"She made necklaces, bracelets, gaudy stuff. Never made any money at it. Whatever she made didn't come close to covering her costs. It didn't stop her from running her mouth how great a businesswoman she was. An asset to the community."

"She made jewellery?" *Well, well.* "She never mentioned that. Do you know if she continued making jewellery after your son died?"

"Don't know. I suspect no more or no less so than when he was alive."

"But they stayed together all those years. I read in the obituary they were married over twenty-five years."

"Don't mean they got along."

"There was trouble between them?"

"Henry bent over backwards to please that woman. In the end, nothing he did appeased her."

"Why? What happened?"

"Henry got an offer to do research at a university in Spain. Nadine wanted him to take it. Henry declined. Nadine was furious."

"Do you know why he declined?"

"He was comfortable here. His friends and family are here."

"When did he get the offer?"

"'Bout a year before he died."

"Do you think Nadine would have left him if he had lived?"

"She threatened to. But she wouldn't have unless someone better came along. Better meanin' richer. After that, she spent a ton of money renovating that house of theirs. Henry told me he'd be paying it off till he was old and grey. Guess she figured out how to pay it off herself."

"How's that?"

"She got five hundred thousand dollars from the insurance company. And not a penny went to Amanda. Henry must be turning in his grave."

"I guess you probably know Nadine is in Calgary now. Living with her sister."

"No, I didn't know."

"Yes. Her sister's husband died a few weeks ago. Nadine has put her house here up for sale. She's planning to live with her sister."

Mrs. Roblau pursed her lips, her eyes narrowed. She lifted a bony hand to her chest and pointed her other one toward me.

"You mark my words. She had a hand in Henry's death. Now her old boyfriend, big-shot brother in-law is dead too? Ha! You watch your back, girlie."

"Wait. What do you mean old boyfriend?"

"Oh, you didn't know?" She cackled, gleefully. "Nadine and Carl were an item, back in the day. He dumped her for her little sister. Ha! That must have made thanksgiving dinner fun."

"Carl dated Nadine and dumped her for Rose?"

"That's right. Nadine claimed Carl married Rose out of pity. Felt sorry for her or was wanting a wife who could look after his mother and his crippled sister. A nursemaid, not a partner."

"Wow. I didn't know that." I wondered what else I didn't know. "How did Nadine meet your son?"

"She knew Henry from high school. As soon as she got her ass dumped by Carl, she was back here, digging her claws into my boy."

"Wasn't she married to someone who died in a scuba diving accident?"

"Makes me wonder sometimes if it were an accident. No, this was after. She was a widow less than a year before she latched on to Carl. That lasted maybe a year. After that she went after Henry. I warned him she was no good." She sighed. "After a while I learned to keep my yap shut. She twisted everything I said to try and turn Henry against me, so I learnt to smile and keep my opinions to myself, especially once I saw how smitten Henry was with her, god rest his soul."

"I hope she brought your son some happiness. She doesn't seem to have much luck when it comes to men or marriage."

"Luck is what you make of it. Nadine's done well for herself. Her first husband left her some insurance and Henry set her up nicely. Most folks would be happy with half of what she's got."

I left Mrs. Roblau's a lot smarter than when I arrived. Eric and Malcolm weren't the only ones who knew about jewellery and gold plating. I didn't believe everything Mrs. Roblau told me. She seemed somewhat paranoid and living alone she had plenty of time in which to tell herself the same stories until they became truth in her mind. But she confirmed my view of Nadine. The woman was smart and driven. I could see her wanting a piece of Riteweight. Now I understood her possessive attitude when it came to Rose and Riteweight. She could have been Rose, sitting on a potential goldmine. Maybe she was still going after what had slipped through her fingers all those years ago.

I noticed I had a call from JP. I called back hoping he hadn't gone off to another meeting or some such thing. He answered on the fourth ring.

"JP. It's Jorja. Thanks for trying to get back to me earlier. I won't keep you, but I need an answer to one quick question."

"Shoot."

"When the police arrived at your house with a warrant, did they say what they were looking for? I mean, specifically?"

"No. They just said they had a warrant to search the premises, and that it was in relation to Carl's death."

"I see, so no specific mention of cyanide?"

"No. Is that what they were looking for?"

"I don't know at this point. I'll let you know the minute I come up with anything useful."

After the call, I drove to the library and searched back issues of the Lethbridge Herald. I found a couple of interviews with Henry. He and his grad students had been studying the ratio of water to non-water molecules in the biological system in the hopes of figuring out what went wrong when the system failed. I also read a few articles written by his peers on his passing. There was no hint of foul play. He had died from complications of pneumonia. So much for that.

I searched for anything on Nadine. Mrs. Roblau said Nadine liked to think of herself as a successful entrepreneur. I quickly found several interviews and articles. Several dated back to when her daughter was a teenager, and swimming competitively. In one interview she talked about what it took to be the mother of a child with aspirations to reach the Olympics. Now that I knew Nadine, I wondered who had the aspiration, daughter or mother?

Then an article popped up from this year's sports week in Lethbridge, with pictures from various events that were held across the city to support youth sports. One in particular caught my eye. Nadine standing with Dimitri close at her side. The caption identified them, by initial and last name only, as members of the business community who gave generously to support youth programing.

FIFTY-SEVEN

NADINE'S HOUSE WAS a well-built but understated brick two-storey. It stood on a large lot, in a fabulously old neighbourhood near Henderson Lake. Double garage, brick front, nicely treed. The real-estate agent pulled up behind me as I was parking. I got out of my Jeep and walked to the back of my car.

"Hi. I'm Jorja. Are you Wendy?" I had found Nadine's house listing on the city's real-estate website and arranged to see it.

"Yes, I am. Hope you haven't been waiting long. Well let's go inside, shall we. It's a stunning property."

The entry way was open to the second-floor ceiling. Wendy gave me a flyer with the house specs. The house was described as a twenty-eight hundred square foot, fully renovated beauty built for family living or entertaining. The family room was centred on a cozy fireplace. It and a spacious dining room, library, and gourmet kitchen made up most of the main level. The house had been fully renovated five years earlier and had a new roof and new windows. Listed at just over half a million, it would easily be worth double that in Calgary. Wendy invited me to have a look around and said she'd wait for me in the kitchen.

I made my way up the staircase to the second floor. I peered into one bedroom made up in purple and continued down the hall to the bathroom. I opened the medicine cabinet and the vanity drawer. Everything had been cleaned out. Continuing down the hall I entered the master bedroom. I checked out the dresser and walk-in closet. The king bed remained, as well as two side tables and a small loveseat under the window. I checked the bathroom, but found it sparkling clean and devoid of personal belongings.

I descended the staircase to the main level, taking time to poke my head into a laundry room and half bath, before continuing down to the walk-out basement. The entertainment area held a leather sectional and a pool table. A bar ran along the far wall. Behind it, shelves held various glasses, but the liquor had been removed. The walk-out patio doors led to a spacious garden with a small building at the back.

I returned upstairs and made my way through the dining room into the kitchen. Wendy sat in one of the stools at the large white marble-topped island. The kitchen cupboards behind her were white, topped with black granite. The stainless-steel Subzero fridge, Miele dishwasher, and Thermador induction oven gleamed.

"Does the furniture belong to the owners, or is the house being staged?"

"No. The owner left the furniture behind. It gives buyers a good sense of the space. She'd be willing to sell it if it interests you."

"What's the little building out back?"

"It's a workshop. I guess it could be used as a potting shed or even extra storage."

"Can I have a look?"

"Sure. I'll get the key."

A few minutes later I followed her across a bricked patio and down brick pavers forming a path across the lawn to the workshop. She unlocked the door and held it open for me.

The opposite side of the shed held an entire row of windows.

Sunlight poured into the space; dust columns dangled in the air. A poured-concrete work shelf ran across three walls. A large island, with dozens of small drawers stood in the middle. I ran my hand over the smooth-surfaced top, also made of concrete. "Nice."

"It is, isn't it?"

I opened a few drawers, noting they were empty. "I love all these tiny drawers. You said it was used as a workshop?"

"The owner used to make and sell her own line of jewellery."

I nodded and continued around the island. On the other side, I opened a couple of doors and bent to peer into the space. Several mortar and pestles remained on the shelf and behind them a smattering of jars, bottles, a battery and various clamps and cables.

"Lots of great space. This is wonderful."

She locked up behind us and we made our way back inside.

"How do you like the place?"

"I love the brick, and the walk-out basement. The yard is beautiful, and I adore the workshop out back. It may be a bit big for me and my fiancé. At this stage in my life I don't imagine there are going to be any little feet running around. Not human ones at any rate."

"You know what they say. You can never have too much space. It's always more problematic the other way around. The house just went on the market last week and I've already had quite a few inquiries. If you're interested, keep it in mind. I'm sure it'll go quickly. It's well priced for the area."

I thanked her and pulled away from the house hoping all her other showings hadn't been lookie-loos like me. I stopped at the Starbucks and bought a Thai chicken wrap and coffee. Making my way to the back of the café I selected a small table, sat and ate the wrap, while booting up my laptop. After I finished eating, I called Rose.

"Rose, it's Jorja. Sorry to bother you."

"Oh, Jorja. No bother. I was sitting here wondering what to make for dinner. I had a meeting today with JP and the lawyers. You know…about the company."

"Are you considering stepping in as a working partner?"

"No, I don't think so. It's a lot of work. I might take Nadine's advice."

"What is she advising?"

"Since the company's value is low at this point, I could sell Nadine a portion of my shares and let her have my proxy vote. Nadine's always had a head for business."

Nadine's mother-in-law had not underestimated her daughter-in-law. "Can you do that?"

"I suppose. Dan Hyde said he'd go through the partner contract and have an answer for me tomorrow. It's only ten percent."

"Well, good luck. I have a quick question for you. Is Nadine still making and selling jewellery?"

"Oh no, she's given that up. She auctioned off her jewellery and got rid of most of the supplies and equipment even before Henry died."

"Do you know why?"

"No. I remember they were contemplating moving to Europe, you know, for Henry's job. Maybe that had something to do with it."

"She didn't bring any of her jewellery-making supplies or equipment to your house with her, did she?"

"No, no. She's been purging her house in Lethbridge for months, getting the house ready to sell. She's moved the few items she's keeping here. But no jewellery supplies. I told you, it's been years since she made jewellery."

"Another question. The morning I came by, Nadine said the detectives who picked Malcolm up for questioning found cyanide at the Boussards'. Do you remember?"

"Oh. I don't remember that."

"Hmm. Do you remember Detective Birdie stopping by that same morning? Did he say anything about cyanide being found at the Boussards'?"

"I do remember his visit. No, he said there had been some developments in the case, but he never mentioned cyanide. Why?"

"Nothing really, just trying to tighten up my final notes on the case. By the way, is Nadine much of a gardener?"

"Nadine? No. I'm the gardener in the family. She and Henry hired, you know, a service, to look after their yard."

"But she is a big supporter of youth sports."

"Well, yes. Amanda used to swim competitively. She was quite good. But it's a big commitment and as she got older, she wanted to experience other things. The pool was pretty much eating up all her time."

"I see. Nice of Nadine to still support local youth sports though. I see she even managed to get Dimitri to contribute to the cause."

"What do you mean?"

"Oh. I thought you would have known since you and Dimitri are such good friends. I saw a photo of Nadine and Dimitri at some fundraising event in Lethbridge this past spring."

"No." Rose's voice cracked. "You must be mistaken."

"I can send you a copy of the photo if you like." My offer was met with silence. I thanked her for her time, disconnected and emailed a copy of the photo I had snapped with my iPhone. Nadine was wasting no time, making her move to get in on a piece of Riteweight. And perhaps making a move on Dimitri as well.

My phone pinged. It was Eric replying to my earlier email, confirming what his dad told me. His dad no longer made jewellery, and Eric only messed around with it as a child, helping his dad. I asked him if he had been there when Nadine quizzed

Malcolm at Carl's funeral about the Lucite cross with the gold threads embedded inside. Eric replied that he hadn't attended Carl's funeral, so I sent Malcolm a text.

Malcolm replied almost immediately. Nadine did ask him about it at the funeral. She had wanted to know if he had made it himself. He told her Eric's dad had made it for his mom. Several years after their divorce, she came across it and earmarked it for a garage sale, as it wasn't worth very much. Malcolm had taken a liking to it and she had given it to him.

I sent Malcolm another text, asking if Nadine had ever made inquiries about Eric's dad. He replied she had asked for Eric's dad's name, saying she might recognize it as she herself used to make jewellery. Malcolm had told her, but she said she didn't recognize the name.

Sitting back, I contemplated this last bit of news. Nadine had told the police Malcolm and Eric had access to cyanide, and immediately afterwards homicide showed a lot of interest in Malcolm. Nadine knew Eric's dad had made jewellery at one time. But apparently, she only found out about it after Carl's death. She couldn't have broken into Eric's dad's garage and used the cyanide solution found there to kill Carl, if she didn't know he had chemicals stored there. And if Eric's dad's vague recollections were right, the break-in happened after Carl's death as well. Was I barking up the wrong tree? I had one last way to find out.

FIFTY-EIGHT

EAVING THE JEEP down the street, I tucked my flashlight into my running belt and my BB pistol into the back of my pants. I followed the sidewalk up the front of Nadine's house, and around to the back. The gate squealed as I lifted the latch and pushed it open. The backyard was pitch black, the large trees circling the backyard filtered out the moonlight. I made my way across the yard.

Reaching the door to the workshop I glanced back. The house to the right remained dark. I could make out lights in the back of the house to the left of Nadine's, but the trees provided decent coverage, even though most of the branches were bare. If someone spotted a movement in Nadine's yard, they'd likely chalk it up to imagination. I pulled on latex gloves, took a huge breath, pulled out my lock pick and began to work. Thirty seconds later I was in.

The place was warm, having trapped the heat from the day's sun. I slid my feet forward, until my outstretched hand touched the centre island. Using the island as my marker I made my way behind it. I needed a closer look at the jars and equipment I had seen earlier. Crouching, I pulled out my slim flashlight and turned it on. I pulled open the cupboard door in front of me. It was empty.

The lights blazed on and I instinctively reached up, shielding my eyes from the glare.

"What are you doing here?"

I straightened to face Nadine. Nadine with a freakishly long black gun in her hand. Her face was pale and moist, her breathing laboured. Her hands trembled, and I realized the gun she held was an ordinary gun with a freakishly long silencer.

"Hi, Nadine. I'm sure you already know the answer."

"You're right. Wendy called me. She told me someone was interested in the house. You should have given her a fake name."

"I would have, but then I couldn't have counted on you coming down here."

I saw the confusion on her face. I plowed forward. "Yes, Nadine, you've done exactly what we envisioned you'd do."

She glanced furtively over her right shoulder. "You don't know squat."

"I know you came here this afternoon and removed the evidence."

"You can't prove anything. I still own this property. I have a right to come and go as I please." She lifted a hand to her throat. "No one will blame me when they find out I came out here to pick up a few items. A woman all alone. I'll tell them how frightened I was when confronted by an intruder. I'll act horrified at having shot you. I'll swear off guns forever."

"The video will show otherwise."

"What video? You're bluffing." Her eyes ricocheted around the room, the pupils large and black, sweat visible on her upper lip.

"Like I'm going to tell you where the video feed is located," I said sarcastically.

She didn't look good. I watched her fingers curl around the neck of her sweater.

"Your move, Nadine."

A microsecond later a searing heat flooded my shoulder. *The bitch called my bluff.*

My hand flew back, and my fingers curled around the handle of my Walther Compact. I pulled my right hand out from behind me and looked down at it. It shakily held the smallest gun on earth. An empty, impotent little gun.

My eyes met Nadine's horrified ones. Why was she horrified? She pulled the trigger. Maybe it was the sight of my blood.

I glanced down at the red stain spreading over my left shoulder. Nadine's gun pointed downward and slipped from her hand.

Nadine's eyes bulged. Her hands clawed at her throat.

I stared down at my gun again, realizing it couldn't have fired. Nadine fell to her knees, both hands now at her throat.

Froth foamed at the corners of her mouth. A strangled gurgle emerged from blue lips seconds before the sickening sound her face made as she hit the floor.

I reached out and groped for the edge of the island and sensed myself slipping downward. Rose's face swam before me, a half-smile on her lips.

FIFTY-NINE

DAVE'S PUFFY FACE floated into view. His lips moved. A white Bichon with orange teeth appeared, its teeth bared, growling. I closed my eyes, willing the image away.

"Jorja. Jorja. Can you hear me?" A woman's voice persistently tried to break through. I squinted against the bright lights and felt arms behind me as I struggled to sit. "It's okay, take your time. You passed out for a minute. You're okay."

Passed out? *No bloody way.*

Sitting upright, I gazed around. I was still in Nadine's workshop. Dave crouched on the floor beside me, the Bichon cradled in his arms. I waved my hand at the cheesy garlic odour wafting toward me. "Dude."

"Jorja! You're alive. Welcome back."

"What are you doing here? What's going on?" My eyes searched behind Dave. No Nadine. No Rose. I inspected my shirt.

"A flesh wound," the woman said, noticing my gaze. My eyes flit back to the EMS logo on her shirt. "We've stopped the bleeding and applied a dressing. It might leave a small scar, but you don't even need stitches."

I nodded, relieved to find myself in good hands. The last

few minutes replayed in my mind's eye. "Where's Nadine? What happened to her?"

"The ambulance is taking her to the hospital. We're not sure what her condition is."

I slowly got to my feet, leaning heavily on the island's massive solidness for support. I waited while the room stopped turning and tilted back to its normal position. Two uniformed officers stood outside talking to someone who resembled Eric. I noted Dave's worried face. "Eric?" I croaked.

"Yeah. Me and Eric followed Nadine down here to Lethbridge this afternoon."

I nodded numbly but it didn't make any sense. Nor did I have the strength to correct his grammar.

The hours blurred. I don't remember how Dave and I got to the local police station. Maybe Dave drove us there. After giving my statement, I was told I could go. I found Dave and the Bichon waiting for me in the lobby. Eric was still talking to the police. I lowered myself onto the scarred wooden bench next to Dave. The Bichon snapped at me.

"What are you guys doing here? I mean, I'm glad you showed up, but how'd you know to find me?"

"The day after we sent in...you know," he tilted his head toward me, winked creepily and whispered, "the wizard file, we went back to you-know-where." He nodded at the dog. "We spent a couple of hours straightening the place up. While we were there, Eric got a call from his dad wanting to know what was going on. He said some PI had been around asking a lot of questions and seemed interested to hear about the garage break-in a month or so back. His dad said if he had anything to do with the break-in, he'd better come clean. Eric was steamed at the suggestion. It did seem odd though, that you'd be interested in a hokey dime-store break-in at Eric's father's place."

Then Eric got my email asking if he recalled a conversation with Rose's sister Nadine, about the gold-thread-filled cross Malcolm had worn to Carl's funeral. He hadn't. So, he texted Malcolm and asked him the same question. He got back a positive reply.

"I asked Eric about what supplies his dad would have had stashed away in the garage. When I heard that some sort of cyanide wash was used in the process, I reminded Eric that Carl died from cyanide poisoning. One idea led to another and here we are."

"Wait a minute. Back up. How'd you know I was here?"

"We didn't. When Malcolm told us Nadine noticed his gold-filled cross and seemed overly interested in the fact Eric's dad made it, we made the connection. We drove over to Nadine's, well actually, Rose's place. We thought we might be able to find some way to get Malcolm off the hook."

"You know you're going to have to go back to your regular life one of these days," I said.

"I don't know. I kind of dig this investigation type of stuff." Dave belched. "Sorry. Where was I? Oh yeah. We were sitting outside Rose's place, trying to decide what we should do, when Nadine tore out of the house, jumped into her car and roared off. She looked pissed. We decided to see what the big hoopla was all about."

"So, you followed her all the way to Lethbridge?"

Dave laughed somewhat sheepishly. "It's a nice day. Beats cleaning up Akar's parents' place. They won't be home until Saturday, anyways."

"While you were roaring down here, I must have been at the

library, poking through old newspaper articles, trying to find out what happened to Nadine's husband."

"You should have googled."

"Thanks, Dave, I'll remember that for next time."

"When we got to the house, we had no idea who it belonged to. Nadine broke the speed limit all the way down, so we thought it a bit odd she ended up at an empty house."

"You saw her go to the little workshop in the backyard? But when did you call the police, or ambulance?"

"No that was later. After we got to the house, we were just sitting there, when Nadine came around from the back of the house lugging a box. She put it into the back of her car and took off. We followed her to a fire station. She carried the box inside. After she left, we went in and asked if a woman had just brought something in for disposal. When we were told yes, we asked if we could see what was brought in."

"And they said yes?"

"Sure, why not? It's not a police station, it's a place for hazardous goods recycling. Anyway, this nice lady takes us back to their storage room. Eric immediately recognized the containers from his father's garage. One of the bottles still held a sticker of a white-faced grim reaper, that Eric had applied himself as a ten-year-old. We asked them to call the police."

Of course, unbeknownst to them, I had already seen the brown bottles on one of the shelves, along with various trays, clamps and cables and had been planning my return visit. Shortly after dark, I returned to Nadine's workshop hoping to confirm what I had seen earlier and perhaps get some information off the containers that would indicate they came from Eric's dad's stolen supply. By that time, Nadine's realtor had made her aware I had been to the house. She anticipated my return to the workshop and had lain in wait. Luckily for me, Eric and Dave related what they knew to the police and they had all shown up at Nadine's place shortly after I did.

"What the hell happened to Nadine? One minute she's trying to kill me and the next she's turning blue and foaming at the mouth."

"No idea. When we arrived, we were told to stay in our car while the cops went out back. A while later we heard sirens. An ambulance arrived and another police car. We were worried you might have been hurt. After they went into the backyard, we followed. EMS already had Nadine on the stretcher. They left with her, seconds before you came around."

"Just for the record, I didn't pass out. I just didn't want to take any chances and thought it best to lie down…you know, in case I got light-headed from all the blood loss."

"I know. Like the time I got shot outside the Mac store."

My respect for Dave grew a little more.

"Well I'm sure glad you followed up on your hunch. You may have saved my life."

"Just returning the favour, sister."

SIXTY

THE DETAILS TRICKLED out over the following weeks. Nadine survived and was charged with the murder of Carl Johnson. Once the news was official, I arranged to meet with Rose.

Today she stood straighter, spoke stronger when she opened the door. "Jorja, please come in."

"Thanks for seeing me. How are you doing, Rose?"

"Not too bad. I mean, I still have weepy days, but other days I go hours without thinking about Carl. It seems like it all happened a while ago."

I nodded. I remembered the painful months following my parents' deaths. But the pain eventually lessened, thanks to mind-numbing physical and emotional exhaustion. I had slept for days.

"Well, you're looking better."

"Thank you, Jorja." I followed her into the sitting room we had first sat in days after Carl's death. The brocade couch was gone, now replaced with a modern but comfortable tweed sofa. Rose watched me taking in the change.

"I hated that brocade couch. But Carl's mother bought it for us when we built the house. I didn't have the guts to get rid of it even after she died. But now..." she trailed off.

I ran my hand along the tweed fabric. "This piece is definitely more you. You know, Rose, there comes a time in life when you have to focus on doing what's right for you, and the hell with everyone else."

For a second, I worried this might send her into another crying jag, but she smiled at me through watery eyes. "Thank you, Jorja. I'm seeing Dimitri." She rushed on as if she waited a second it would remain a secret forever. "Just casually. We're taking our time. It's important to be friends first. He's helping me with Riteweight, you know."

"How's it going?"

"Everything is on track. We had a shareholder meeting the other day. I didn't know the data had been tampered with. JP told us everything. He was rather nice. He said he blamed himself, that his son was driven to go to such extremes."

"You believe in the product?"

"I went back on it a couple of weeks ago. I watch what I eat and go for daily walks. I've already lost eight pounds."

"Good for you." It's always best to believe in your own product.

"Have you talked to your sister?"

Rose's face crumpled. I waited while she fought to regain control.

"Yes, a few days ago. You heard she's been charged with Carl's death."

"Yes. Has she admitted to killing Carl?"

"No. I asked her straight out if she did it. She said her lawyer advised her not to discuss anything related to the charge." She shook her head. "I don't know. If it was me and I was innocent but had been charged with someone's death I'd be yelling my innocence, no matter what my lawyer said. I didn't know this, but she told me she promised our mother on her death bed that she'd look after me." Rose sniffled, looking at me. "I'm sure Mother meant well, but what a horrible burden to put on Nadine. It's not right. No one should be responsible for anyone else's wellbeing. At least anyone able bodied."

Great. Another way to lay a guilt trip on Rose. "Well, you'll never know. I mean you only have Nadine's word your mother asked her to look after you. You'll have to decide for yourself if what Nadine says can be believed."

Rose eyed me thoughtfully and nodded. "Dimitri said when she asked him if he'd be willing to make a donation to the Lethbridge sports youth charity event, he was glad to. She invited him to the donors' dinner. He said she clung to him all night. He didn't want to say anything to me or Carl. It was awkward."

"I didn't know she dated Carl, before the two of you got together."

"They weren't together very long. Nadine was already dating someone else, when Carl asked me out. When she found out Carl and I were dating it caused a rift between us. We didn't talk to each other for several years. Dimitri says Nadine is one of these people who always wants what she can't have."

"She's Theagenes," I muttered.

"Sorry, I didn't catch that."

"A few weeks ago, Dimitri told me an old fable, about a man named Theagenes of Thasos, whose jealousy of someone eventually led to his own death. At the time I thought he might be trying to tell me Daryl killed Carl out of jealousy, but now I see how Nadine's jealousy of you, your life with Carl, led to her decision to kill Carl."

"How strange. I was the one who always felt jealous of Nadine. She's the pretty one, so smart and confident. She has a daughter, had a wonderful husband, belonged on a board, did charity work. Now I'm starting to realize some of it was self-serving."

"The prosecutor obviously has enough evidence to have

charged her with Carl's death. Do you have any idea how she got poisoned the night she attempted to shoot me?"

"Carl had a lot of issues with his stomach. He used to buy these soft-chew antacids. They came in a box of sixty, six individually wrapped in each of ten packs. He'd always take one or two before meals, another one before bed. The night of the dinner, Carl meant to take them when we got there. But his phone rang, and he handed me one of the packs and I put it in my purse. There were only three soft chews left. As we sat down for dinner, he asked for one. You know what happened next. The police of course came to our house later and searched through the medicine cabinets and such and took a bunch of it away to test. They didn't find anything. Of course, I made no connection to the soft chews, he took them all the time."

"Of course not, why would you."

"A few weeks ago, I bought a new box of antacids, the same kind Carl used. I guess out of habit. I took a few. A few days later I was cleaning out my purse when I found the other ones, so I just added them back to the new box. I remember the day Nadine went down to Lethbridge. She wasn't feeling well. She went upstairs and got the soft chews. She asked me how old they were. I told her I had bought them the week before. Which was true," she added hurriedly, "since the police pretty much cleaned everything out of the medicine cabinet shortly after Carl died. But I forgot I had added the leftover ones Carl had handed me. She must have taken one she tampered with and at some point, ate it. When the EMS arrived, one of them smelled almonds on her breath."

"She's lucky. Less than thirty percent of the population can detect the almond smell typical in cyanide poisonings."

"After they found out Nadine had been poisoned, they focused right back here. I mean of course they would. They went through the medicine cabinets again including the soft chews. They found one contained cyanide. There were no other reports of any problems with product tampering, so they began with who had access to the soft chews. It was pretty much limited to Carl, Nadine and me. The police took me downtown for more questioning. It was awful."

Ironic that she killed Carl and inadvertently poisoned herself not realizing Rose had added back the tampered product. "Do you know cyanide has a marker in it which can tie it to its source?"

"Really? I didn't know that."

"It's why I went back to Nadine's house once I saw the bottles and equipment left behind in her workshop. I was hoping to get my hands on them, but she beat me to the punch. The police must have tested all three sources of cyanide. The traces found in her workshop, the soft chew and powder they found at the Boussards'."

"Powder? At the Boussards'?" Nadine's brow furrowed.

"Remember they picked young Malcolm up for questioning?"

"Yes. I remember feeling just horrible thinking he might be to blame."

"They found traces of cyanide in the Boussards' potting shed. In an old backpack. Someone called them with an anonymous tip. Of course, Nadine pretty much copped to it the day I came to see you and she informed us the police had taken Malcolm in for questioning."

"She did? I don't remember."

"She said the cops were never good at figuring out anything on their own. Up until then, I never suspected Nadine had anything to do with Carl's death. But she was downright ecstatic when Malcolm was taken in for questioning."

"I remember. I thought it was heartless of her."

"What Nadine didn't know was that Malcolm was being

bullied. He was convinced someone was listening in on his conversations in the house. His IT friend suspected it might be a van or truck rigged up with surveillance equipment. Malcolm and his IT buddy set up video cameras around the place, in addition to the one the Boussards had as part of their security system. Nadine avoided the Boussards' security camera but the one the boys installed picked up Nadine making her way to the potting shed, through the Boussards' backyard late one night, several weeks after Carl's death."

"Oh Nadine!" Rose's mouth trembled. "Why on earth…?" I waited a moment while Rose processed this information. "So, she planned all of this. And then she deliberately tried to frame the Boussards' son!"

"It's looking that way."

I didn't want to tell Rose that when her kidney bean prank had been exposed, Nadine had started to worry about the attention being focused on Rose. She subsequently discovered that Eric's dad had once made gold-plated jewellery and being familiar with the process herself, decided to throw suspicion on Malcolm. Not that she had anything against Malcolm, she just didn't want the attention to be focused on her or Rose.

Even with all the bad news of late, the emotional frailty Rose displayed in the weeks after Carl's death was ebbing. Rose pulled her shoulders back and gazed at me squarely.

"I love my sister, but whatever she did, she did for herself. I refuse to be her excuse any longer."

"You are a wise woman, Rose. I hope you can live your life the way you want, the way you deserve."

I left Rose's feeling lighter, happier than I'd felt in weeks. Until this moment I hadn't realized the emotional angst I'd been suppressing. Wanting to help Rose prove her innocence yet afraid I'd end up proving Malcolm did it, wanting to spill my guts to

Azagora about Malcolm's cyberbully yet worried about my own knowledge of the situation and the optics of not reporting it earlier. I did it. I helped find Carl's killer. The only thing that marred the victory was the knowledge I had danced across the line once or twice.

SIXTY-ONE

I PULLED OVER TO the curb a block from Doodlebug's, got out my cell phone and initiated a parking session. I'd agreed to keep the Jeep for three months and now had pencil and paper tucked under the visor where I diligently recorded mileage driven between each fill-up. The Ford F-150 had been returned to JumpIn Jalopies, no worse for wear.

A few minutes later, I pulled open Doodlebug's beaten and scarred wooden door and let my eyes adjust. Dave and Lydia were already in a booth near the back.

"Hey, you two."

"Great to see you," said Dave. Lydia gnawed on a French fry.

"I see you're out of hiding."

"Yeah, I've got my life back. Did you hear they arrested the wizard?"

"I did. I hear he's not challenging the child porn and extortion charges. But he's adamantly refusing to admit to the kidnapping charges, even though the ransom money was found at his place."

Dave snickered. "They found it stashed under his bed, taped to the underside of the box springs. They also uncovered a white Mike Myers meets Phantom of the Opera mask in his closet. Sounds a lot like the one that guy who pointed a gun at us at

Lydia's apartment was wearing. He's having trouble explaining why his van is filled with surveillance equipment including recordings of Malcolm and Eric discussing my discovery of Malcolm's video on a porn site and how they were going to refuse to send more."

"So how is he explaining the ransom money?" I said.

"He insists he found the bag of cash in a trash bin at a C-Train station—by chance."

"Oh yeah? And some innocent bystander just happens to videotape him finding it, and then sends the video anonymously to the police." I remembered Dave showing me and Eric the video of the whole thing going down.

"That's exactly what happened." Dave looked at me wide eyed. "I just wanted to get a few shots of him, in case he turned out to be the guy who was extorting illicit photos from kids. So, one day I waited for him at the store, and when he left, I followed him to the train station. How was I to know he'd find money in that trash can. Pure luck I caught it on video."

"Keep saying it, Dave. You might even convince yourself."

Lydia snickered and poked Dave in the ribs. Dave looked over at her and grinned. Lydia reached up and nuzzled his neck. "You always were lucky, my little lucky boo."

"Wanna hear something even better?" said Dave.

"There's better?" I said.

"They matched one of the bullets they retrieved from the door jamb of my apartment to a gun found at the wizard's apartment. Of course, he claims he had no idea the gun was there, that someone must have planted it there to frame him."

"The jury is going to have a hay day with this. Especially if Malcolm sticks to his story that a couple snatched him off the street and nothing comes up to contradict it. Like video from a street cam or something."

"I'm pretty sure the video cameras in the area were experiencing technical difficulties that morning."

I looked from Dave to Lydia. "How convenient."

"Yeah, that was freakish. Go figure. And I heard they couldn't trace the number to your cell phone because the kidnappers used one of those cheap prepaid throw-away phones."

Loud gurgling noises erupted from Lydia as she slurped up the last millimetres of her drink with a straw. Dave leaned over and kissed her on the cheek, which she immediately wiped off.

Lydia emitted a final loud slurp. I studied her. Was she the one in the women's washroom at the theatre? The one who emptied the money Dee Dee carried to make the exchange with the kidnappers. Dave grinned. Neither of us spoke for a few minutes while I digested all of this. They had taken a big risk. They broke the law.

"I can't believe you two pulled this off."

"Pulled what off?"

"Right." I decided we best drop it before someone openly admitted to doing something they shouldn't admit to.

"What's happening on your other case?" said Dave.

"They've charged Nadine with Carl's murder. And attempted murder of yours truly."

"The cops must be confident the cyanide that killed Carl came from Eric's dad's garage."

"The traces of cyanide found in Nadine's workshop, the supplies she turned in to the fire station and the powder found in the backpack she planted at Malcolm's house all matched. Interestingly, it didn't match the cyanide they recovered from the tampered soft chew that she used to poison Carl. The chemical attribution signature was different."

Lydia looked confused. "What does that mean? She didn't do it?"

"I hear they've tied the cyanide she used to kill Carl to the supply the University of Lethbridge purchased for their chemistry lab."

"No way."

"Yeah. I'm curious as to whether she stole it from her husband's lab or bribed someone to steal it for her. Even though her husband died two years ago, she kept in touch with some of his coworkers at the University. I also heard the police are investigating her husband's death. Maybe she had nothing to do with it, but on the other hand, it left her with half a million dollars of insurance, and the house."

"So, she broke into Eric's dad's place and stole his supplies all to frame Malcolm after she killed Carl."

"Yes. The police were showing too much interest in Rose and she wanted to throw suspicion elsewhere. They're positive she was the one who broke into Eric's dad's garage. She has a scar on her wrist from where she cut herself when she broke the garage door window. I actually noticed it shortly after Rose hired me to clear her name. The police may even have confirmed a match of Nadine's blood type to blood found on the garage door window. Nadine told me she cut herself gardening. Rose recently told me Nadine would rather contract the plague than garden. The cops also located the shop vac she stole from Eric's dad. She actually sold it on Kijiji."

"You're kidding?"

"Nope. Some people just can't pass up the opportunity to make a buck."

❧

It was a few minutes shy of nine o'clock by the time I got back to my condo. I was still grappling with the near certainty that Lydia was the one who took possession of the ransom money. She and Dave were quite the pair. At least they had lied, schemed and extorted for the good guys.

I poured myself a scotch, turned on the TV and muttered, "Here's to another Friday night." I flipped through the TV guide. A hundred and two channels and nothing of interest. How was that possible? I had a lot on my mind but didn't want to deal with any of it.

Inspector Luis Azagora and I had gone out to dinner once since the fundraiser at Inner Light. We discussed how bad an idea it would be for the two of us to get involved. Even though we didn't work together, it might get awkward since our professional lives were bound to intersect every so often. And not in a good way. The way he had slipped my blouse off my shoulder and kissed the now healed scar left by Nadine's grazing bullet softened the message. Adan on the other hand had sent me a text from a wilderness hike he was on with members of a teen group home saying he would thank the good lord for sparing my life.

The real trouble was I had nothing on my slate. I'd found Dave. Dave in turn found the scumbag who was tormenting Malcolm and Eric. Nadine had been charged with Carl's death. Rose was going to be all right. Gab's roster of paying clients was building. I had no open cases. I'd sent out all my invoices, and once I collected, I'd be able to cover next month's bills.

It wasn't the lack of potential clients that weighed on me. It was the boredom that came with not having any. I'd survived several attempts on my life the last year or two and I found myself craving the adrenaline. I turned off the TV, grabbed my scotch and headed for the washroom.

I stood in the shower a long time, shaved my legs, plucked several stray eyebrow hairs and stared at the woman in the mirror. *Who the hell are you?* I padded out of the bathroom with my remaining scotch and into my bedroom. Pulling out my warm flannel pyjama pants, I topped them with a white T-shirt and crawled under the quilt. I turned off the light and lay there, watching shadows flicker across the wall as the moon hid and emerged repeatedly from behind the clouds.

The moment when Rose had declared she was no longer going to harbour any guilt about Carl's death or her sister's actions came back to me. I had struggled to free myself from the same affliction for years, even with the help of a psychologist. Nothing worked. And then one day, it all clicked into place. I was in no way responsible for my father's actions. Actions that resulted in him killing my mother and then himself. I always thought the moment I released myself from my inner torture would be more uplifting. No angels sang, nor did I hear trumpets. But it did restore confidence in who I was as a person.

I had two interesting men flitting around the edges of my life and I didn't know what to do with either of them. Or did I? Adan was a stand-up guy. Anyone could tell he wasn't a player. He was working to make a difference in the lives of those around him. Troubled lives. He'd be a good friend. I didn't know what his needs were but over the last few months I realized whatever they were, they weren't in alignment with mine.

Then there was Azagora. A smile crossed my lips and I shivered involuntarily. I knew what he wanted from me and me from him. But beyond the physical attraction I wasn't sure. He would be a hard man to figure out, let alone get to know. I didn't know all that much about him. I knew he was born in Puerto Rico. That he came to Canada to live with an aunt when he was a young boy. There was something dangerous about him, yet his job title screamed trust.

The blue numbers on my clock radio flickered and I turned my head. Ten-thirty. I closed my eyes, but sleep was a million miles away. I contemplated getting up and having another drink but given my mood it would likely lead to another, and another. Followed by the inevitable headache in the morning. My cell phone vibrated on the bed side table. I reached over and picked it up. My heart fluttered as I stared at the screen. Azagora. I took a deep breath and answered.

"I want to see you," he said. "Are you doing anything?"

"You mean now?"

"Yes."

"I was contemplating turning in."

"You kidding? It's early. Any chance I can convince you to postpone and meet me for a drink?"

Twenty minutes later I was on my way to the Kensington Pub. I knew I was asking for trouble, but there was something intriguing about Azagora. And I was dying to figure out what.

ACKNOWLEDGEMENTS

The prolific British author, G.B. Stern, once said, 'silent gratitude isn't of much use to anyone.' I couldn't agree more!

I want to express my deep gratitude to all those who have been so generous with their time in helping me get Knight Trials out into the world. Thank you to all those who read my book, provided edits, offered helpful comments, wrote reviews, and cheered me on. Special thanks to Kelsey Marklund, Sue Matsalla, Brenda Lissel, for going the extra mile to help me get the word out. I also want to thank and acknowledge all the interviewers, bloggers, podcasters and booksellers, who are working hard to support indie authors like myself, and especially Brian Richmond and Joanna Vandervlugt, who were kind enough to feature my work.

I want to express my deep gratitude to my talented editors, Adrienne Kerr and Taija Morgan, you are a dream to work with.

Writing is a solitary endeavour and one I enjoy immensely, but every once in a while, it's important to come up for fresh air. I'm so blessed to have the most amazing friends who have helped me in so many ways. Thank you for dragging me out of the house to walk, even in the dead of winter, for sharing your own lives, interests, opinions and experiences with me, for the many laughs we've had along the way, and for being my constant reminder that happiness and joy are found in the smallest of things. Thank you.

As always, love and thanks to my beautiful and talented family, Leanne, Paige, Tyler, Sean, Katherine, Malcolm, and Kevin, for inspiring me and cheering me on.

Last but not least, a huge thank you to my readers. Thank you for reaching out to me on social media, joining my Readers Bulletin, and for all the messages you send me via my website, email, and Facebook, telling me you love my books and are eagerly awaiting more. Your kind words and positive feedback fuels my muse and brightens my day. Happy reading my friends!

Read an excerpt from the next
JORJA KNIGHT MYSTERY

THREE DOG KNIGHT

Available Summer 2021

ONE

THE COLLECTIVE INGENUITY of humans is awe inspiring, so I shouldn't have been surprised when I discovered that someone in our increasingly complex, technology-driven world had found yet another way to kill people.

But right now, I was trying to figure out which way to insert my passport into the automated border control system at Calgary's new arrival eGate. The woman, peering over my shoulder, jostled me for a third time. I pulled out my passport and retrieved the machine printout. The comparison photo on the cheap paper confirmed it. I looked like a crack-whore on her way to prison.

I sailed through several gates and barriers, pleased at the efficiency of the system yet perturbed that the scanners all accepted the photo as a good enough likeness of me to allow me to pass. The last set of doors slid open with a hiss and I stumbled onto the concourse. I didn't bother to scan the sleepy-eyed bystanders waiting for loved ones and headed for the escalator.

The whole place was chillingly hushed, the shops all closed for the night. I shifted my carry-on higher onto my shoulder, stepped past the few bystanders at the arrival gate, and headed for the escalator.

Reaching the end of the corridor, I stepped onto the escalator and rested my bag on the handrail. I glanced at my watch and groaned. I was meeting Laura Bradford in less than five hours. She hadn't told me why she needed a private investigator when she called to set up the meeting, just that she might. I stepped off the escalator, turned right and entered the frigid connector between the airport terminal and the parkade.

I glanced out through the glass walls of the connector as another plane landed silently on the runway. I shivered and turned the corner. A jumble of rubbish lay against one wall. I shook my head to clear the brain fog that had formed from too many hours of droning engines and mindless chitchat of my unduly social seatmate. *Of course, it's not rubbish.* I could now make out muddied sneakers sticking out from underneath a ratty blanket, a newspaper lay spread over the face. I tightened my grip on the carry-on, pushed back a strand of dark hair, and hurried past.

The elevator at the end of the corridor seemed to take forever. A noise made me glance over my shoulder, but there was nothing there, nothing other than the human bundle. Anxious to get into my car and start the heater I stepped into the elevator as soon as the doors hissed opened. I paced the elevator as it whisked me up three flights. The doors opened and I stepped into the dim light of the parkade.

The buzz of an occasional florescent light broke the eerie quiet of the parkade. My footsteps echoed on the frosty pavement. The air was colder here, biting through my jacket. A bank of lights in the next aisle flickered and went out. *Just the storm, nothing more,* I reminded myself. The pilot had mentioned an Alberta clipper was moving in, bringing a fresh dump of snow. I pulled up my jacket collar and tucked in my chin.

I stopped, suddenly alert, all my senses in overdrive. Were those footsteps behind me? I glanced over my shoulder at the ghostly rows of vehicles and held my breath. Nothing.

Stepping forward, I heard it again. Or was it my imagination? I veered left and reaching the open parkade wall, peered at the lit corridor below. The human bundle was gone.

I took a deep breath and rushed along the middle of the aisle, my ears straining for sounds other than the empty echo of my own feet. I picked up my pace.

The footsteps resumed.

Slinging my purse up higher on my arm I unzipped the top, my previous exhaustion gone. My fingers closed in on the cold metal of my car keys.

The steps behind me quickened.

My eyes swept from side to side, searching for another human. Behind me, the footsteps grew faster—louder. My feet pounded on the pavement, my breathing ragged, loud in my ears.

Section H, Section H. There it is. I grabbed at the car door. My carry-on slid down my arm as I inserted the key, my eyes scanning the cars around me. The footsteps had stopped.

I wrenched the car door open, threw in my carry-on, and jumped in.

Locking the door behind me I whipped my head around, expecting to see a grotesque face, half man—half bird, with red eyes, curved beak, and clawed hands.

My hand shook as I turned the key in the ignition. Certain some evil apocalyptic creature lurked nearby, ready to pounce and drag me from the car, I shoved the gear shift into reverse. My eye caught a piece of paper jammed under the windshield wipers. It would have to wait.

Backing out, I lay rubber and reached the exit ramp, my sense of dread still on high. *Faster, faster,* my brain urged as my car entered the darkened tunnel. My eyes jumped back and forth from the rear-view mirror to the beams of light cutting the darkness in front of me.

Tires squealing, I rounded each spiralling curve down the concrete ramp to the main level. My car shot out of the tunnel and into the frost-laden night.

Nothing appeared in the rear-view mirror. Several cars stood idling at the exit gate ahead of me. Breathing a sigh of relief, I headed to an empty payment lane.

I pulled up to the payment machine and got out of the car, inserted a credit card, and snatched the paper from under the windshield wiper. I looked back at the ramp as another vehicle emerged. Its headlights caught the snowflakes floating silently to the ground. I slowed down my breathing, told myself I wasn't in danger. The machine spit out my card and while waiting for it to do its thing I unfolded the paper.

I staggered back, cursing.

Each heartbeat pulsed wildly in my neck. The machine spit out a receipt and flashed green.

Feeling lightheaded, I grabbed the receipt, threw the paper onto the passenger seat, climbed in and rolled forward as a truck pulled up behind me. I swallowed hard as my eyes flitted back to the paper, unable to get a full breath.

Staring back at me, centered in a crudely drawn black heart, was a newspaper photo of my dead parents.

TWO

UNBUTTONING MY COAT, I breathed in the warm coffee aroma intermingled with cinnamon and vanilla. A coffee bar on the left and the dozen or so small tables and chairs to the right made the place feel cozy. A wall of windows at the far end overlooked the lake, the snow reflecting a mesmerizing display of sparkling crystals in the morning sun.

I had dozed fitfully for a few hours last night, more perturbed by the note left on my windshield than I cared to admit. This year marked the twenty-year anniversary of my parents' deaths. It was only recently that I managed to separate the memory from the emotion that threatened to overwhelm whenever it came to mind. But someone didn't want me to forget. Someone had dug up the story and left a copy of a twenty-year-old newspaper photo on my car windshield for me to find.

I selected two easy chairs by the windows, overlooking the lake and the spruce-lined patio below. A waitress brought coffee, dropped off breakfast menus and pointed out the coffee refill station. I took a few sips, the hot liquid sliding down my throat and easing the tension in my shoulders.

My eyes drank in the scenery. The warmth of the room, and happy murmurings swirling around me, slowly displaced the unease from last night. Still revelling in the comforting surroundings, I noticed a woman at the door. Her eyes searched the room uncertainly. At her second pass of the room, I raised my hand, and she headed my way. She was near my age, late thirties or perhaps a few years older. I stood.

"Are you Laura Bradford?"

"I am. You must be Jorja Knight. Sorry to keep you waiting. My daughter has taken to dawdling in the morning, delaying her inevitable departure to school."

"Not to worry. I've been quite content to sit here and admire the view."

She slipped off her coat and looked out at the lake blankly. "I suppose it is pretty. I never seem to have time to notice."

"You live in the neighbourhood?"

"Yes, on the other side of the lake. My daughter's school is quite close to here, on Fairmount Drive."

The waitress arrived, refilled my coffee and returned a few minutes later with a cranberry scone and green tea for Laura. Laura took a few breaths. Her hand shook as she reached for her tea. "I've never talked to a private investigator."

"No need to feel nervous. It's just a job like any other. All I do is run around asking questions, hoping to sort out fact from fiction."

She gave me a weak smile. "Do you remember hearing about a murder in Calgary a few months ago? A man named Stephen Wallis?" Her chin quivered as she reached for a napkin.

"Stephen Wallis. Wasn't he found shot in his home?" I leaned forward. "Now I remember. It was on the news when it first happened, and for weeks afterwards. He was shot by an invisible assailant and even though the home security cameras captured the whole thing from a bunch of angles they never provided an image of the killer. The press started to call him the Houdini killer. But there hasn't been much on the news since."

"No, there hasn't. The police told me they don't have much to go on." Laura looked out at the lake for a moment, then turned back to me, her eyes filled with tears. "Stephen was my brother."

"I'm so sorry to hear that." I couldn't think of anything else to say. I picked up my coffee and stared at the happy faces around us, oblivious to the conversation happening at our table.

Laura took a sip of tea and dabbed at the corner of her eyes. "My brother was a brilliant man. Even when we were kids, I knew he'd go far. He was so smart…and funny. He never let his success change him. He was just the same kind, dependable Stephen he always was. And now he's gone."

"I'm so sorry. This can't be easy for you."

"No. Sorry. I get so emotional just thinking about him. And the thought that whoever killed him might get away, makes it that much worse."

"No need to apologize, take your time," I said.

Laura nodded gratefully. She took a sip of tea and stared vacantly at the lake.

I wondered if she noticed the ice crystals sparkling like fairy dust in the air or whether all she saw was vast cold ice.

She gave her shoulders a shake and turned back to me. "Not the best way to start. I guess I should tell you what I know. I last saw Stephen on Christmas Day. He left around ten o'clock that night. He had to catch a red eye to Vancouver, to meet with a potential investor the next day." She paused, choking on the last few words. "Sorry. That's the last time I saw him alive."

A peculiar tingling sensation rippled through me. Followed by guilt. How could I let my own excitement about the case, over-shadow this woman's hurt? I forced myself to sit back.

"Tell me more about Stephen. What did he do?"

"He owned a company called Xcelerate. They help entrepreneurs get set up." She smiled shakily. "You know, provide them a space to work, put together business plans, help raise money, that kind of stuff."

"Oh, a business incubator," I said.

"That's right. Stephen called his entrepreneurs game changers. One of his start-ups created edible wrappers for ice cream bars. They sold the rights to Brun-cow last summer and it's going to be used for several of their products."

"That's amazing," I said. My brain was already whirling, getting ahead of itself.

Laura squared her shoulders. "Stephen planned to be back from Vancouver on the 29th. The police confirmed he did catch a flight back that evening. The next day, he dropped by the lab. A couple of his guys were there working, they're always working. They said Stephen left mid-afternoon, said he was bagged and was going to spend a quiet night at home."

I nodded. Homicide would have confirmed his movements.

"His friend Brad had a New Year's party the next night, but Stephen never showed."

"He said he'd attend?"

Laura shrugged. "Stephen hadn't been dating anyone for a while. Brad figured he didn't want to come alone. Nobody saw him at the office or lab the next day, but it was a holiday, so no one expected him to drop by." Laura pulled down the sleeves of her sweater until only her fingertips were showing, then continued. "His driver showed up at his house the following day to take him to a meeting. Stephen didn't answer the door or his phone. The driver called the office and the lab. No one had heard from him. The police were called. They found Stephen in the den. He'd been shot." Laura's chest rose and fell rapidly, her breathing shallow. Her hand shook as she raised her tea to her lips and took a shaky sip. She put her cup down and drew in a long slow breath, expelling it through pursed lips.

"It's slowly coming back to me," I said. "The place was highly wired and secured."

"That's right. The police found no sign of break-in or forced entry. The deadbolts were engaged from the inside, the windows closed. Nothing was taken or out of place."

"The police called for witnesses or anyone who might have been in the neighbourhood at the time. Has no one come forward?"

"They interviewed a number of people. No one remembers seeing or hearing anything out of the ordinary. Stephen had security cameras inside and out. None of them show anyone entering or leaving his house. I've hardly had a full night's sleep since it happened. It's been hard on our mom. I already see the toll it's taking on her."

"So where is the investigation now?"

"Detective McGuire is in charge of the case. They're no closer to figuring out what happened than they were on January 2nd," she said, shaking her head. "Now they're shifting some of their resources to more current cases."

I nodded. "They'll keep at it, but no telling if it'll get solved next month or years from now." I didn't know what she was going through, nobody really could. But having dealt with my own parents' unexpected deaths, I could empathise. The finality of death was overwhelming, hopes and dreams irretrievably broken.

Laura looked at me through tear-rimmed eyes, her mascara in need of repair but her voice defiant. "My mother doesn't have years and years. My kids adored their Uncle Stephen. I can't sleep, I can't eat or focus. I figure the only way I can get my life back is to find the person who did this. I know it's only been a little over two months, but I need answers. Besides, there's one person the police haven't considered carefully enough."

"Oh? Who would that be?"

"Chloe, our darling half-sister."

FREE NOVELLA—KNIGHT SHIFT

Join my Readers Bulletin and let me send you a **free** digital copy of **Knight Shift**, the prequel to the Jorja Knight Series, along with occasional updates on new releases, **giveaways,** and other news!

To get your **free** copy of Knight Shift just go to
www.alicebienia.com

ABOUT THE AUTHOR

Alice Bienia is a Canadian Crime Writer and author of the Jorja Knight mystery series. Her debut novel, Knight Blind, was a 2016 Unhanged Arthur Ellis Award finalist. She is a member of Sisters in Crime, Crime Writers of Canada, and the Writers' Guild of Alberta.

With a Bachelor of Science degree in geology, Alice spent her early career conducting field exploration programs in remote regions of Canada, where she honed her passion for reading, storytelling, coffee, and adventure. After riding the energy industry rollercoaster for thirty years, Alice has finally found a way to put her inherent introversion to use and now writes full time.

When not plotting a murder, Alice amuses herself watching foreign flicks and exploring Calgary's urban parks and pathways. Visit her at www.alicebienia.com